THE
WOMAN
IN THE
WATER

THE
WOMAN
IN THE
WATER

KELLY HEARD

bookouture

Published by Bookouture in 2021

An imprint of Storyfire Ltd.
Carmelite House
50 Victoria Embankment
London EC4Y 0DZ
www.bookouture.com

ISBN: 978-1-80019-674-2
eBook ISBN: 978-1-80019-673-5

For Lillian, with love.
I hope you would have liked this one.

CHAPTER ONE

Now

A fisherman found my sister's body in the swamp, washed up over the giant root of a cypress tree, only two miles from the house where we grew up. It was the day after Thanksgiving. Her legs were tangled in a fishing net, and, somehow, an arm of moss had wrapped itself around her head, giving rise to half a dozen nicknames when the story hit the local news: *The Reverie Girls Claim Another. Swamp Babe.* One of the more salacious headlines read: *Murdered Mermaid.* Though, from the beginning, everyone seemed to agree, her death was an accident.

The day before I heard the news, on my evening run along the beach, I stepped on a piece of glass, and, when I picked up my foot, wincing, I saw that the glass was the same green as my sister's eyes, a wisp of blood spreading across its surface. I had to pick fragments out of my foot, and as I did, I couldn't shake the feeling I was pulling Holly away, that she was leaving me somehow. Returning to my apartment, I continued with my standard routine and went to bed early.

But I slept poorly, waking every hour or so, to a ghostly voice calling my name, one that sounded as if it was just beyond the window, rather than years and miles away. Just like the one I had heard on that long-ago night at the deserted fairground, a whistling singsong, curling through the dark like vines. We all should have known better than to be out there, James, Holly, Cody and me. Page hadn't wanted to be there in the first place. All my life, everybody's parents had warned us of the Reverie Girls, lonely ghosts of drowned girls in the swamp, jealous of the living. I thought that was all they were: fireside stories, meant to keep children from wandering.

But it was no human voice that called to me that night—no human hand that tugged on my own, down into dark water that looked bottomless. What I didn't know then was that it was also a warning, signaling the end of that dream I was living in. The next few months would see every last person I trusted give up on me: my parents; the boy I loved; even my own sister. But those breaking points were moments of truth, not anomalies. Nobody ever turned on me who hadn't already seen me as deceitful, unbalanced, a cautionary tale for other people's children: in other words, a teenage girl from the wrong part of town.

Like solving both sides of an equation—simplifying, combining like terms, isolating the variable—what it came down to was this: my heart got it wrong. So wrong I almost chased it to the bottom of the lake. From that understanding, I was free to make good, sensible choices, for the rest of my life.

I woke at three in the morning, my heart beating a steady, echoing rhythm that let me know I'd be awake for the day. I hurried to the shower, standing under the scalding hot stream, washing away the memory of swamp water and mud. The beaches here are bright, the water sparkling. Even when things are washed up, they wash up clean. That's how I think of myself, now: a piece of beach glass, or a smooth piece of driftwood, in the form of a woman. That's what rests beneath my ribs.

So, despite my sense that Holly was in trouble, I didn't call her. I moved forward, as I always have done, a well-established habit. Working as a nurse, especially in pediatrics, I'm used to long days and hard work. People say nursing saps you like it's a bad thing, but that's what I was looking for. When I leave for the day, I don't have much left for myself—of energy, of empathy, of feeling in general—and I don't want much, either. After a few years working in the States, I applied to a travel nursing agency offering temporary placements, often no more than a few months at a time. There's always work, but no promise as to where. Which suits me perfectly well. My last placement, in San Antonio, went through last spring, which was coincidentally when my last relationship ended. Derek Hannon, a soldier from Montana, who fell in love with me, another small-town stranger far from home. Maybe I thought I could extinguish it, this old strangeness that still calls to me. For better or for worse, tie an anchor to it. Derek was steady. Handsome. Even-tempered. I couldn't be my whole self with him—I'd put it at around half. But the part of me left behind wasn't the smooth part. It wasn't the good part. I could not find one reason not to marry Derek. I thought I loved him, too—I did, really, until he proposed, and I knew I had to end it.

I wanted to say yes. Or, maybe, I wanted to want to say yes. I'd even practiced writing my first name next to his last name: *Felicity Hannon*. But they had never looked like one whole, just two pieces next to each other. I called the agency and told them I needed a new assignment, and wound up here, in the Virgin Islands.

Despite my foreboding dreams, I was feeling better by the time I went home to begin my evening chores. Cleaning, dinner, perhaps a walk on the beach, and then bedtime.

And then the phone rang.

"I'm trying to reach Felicity Wheeler." A man's voice, asking for me by name, in a southern accent.

"This is Felicity."

"I'm Rob Dawson, Brightwater PD. This is—"

"Dawson, is that really you?" Smiling, I walked toward the kitchen, opened the freezer and filled an etched glass with ice. "It's a nice surprise to hear from you. But how did you get my phone number?"

"I got your phone number from your mother."

"Oh." I was a bit surprised to hear that my mother had my phone number, as we spoke so rarely. "How are you? It's only been thirteen years." Rob Dawson, who had been called by his last name for as long as I could remember, was one of the rare people who had never, in my life, given me reason to worry about anything. He did not drink, never flirted, and rarely even made jokes. And, though he was a bit dull, if I could have chosen anyone to be my big brother, it would have been him.

"Yes, Rob Dawson, from Brightwater."

"Did you say PD, as in police department?" With my phone tucked between my ear and shoulder, I measured and poured one half-shot of rum over the ice in my glass, topped it with sparkling water, then reached for the bowl of limes.

"Yes." Dawson was on the wrestling team, and had a strong jaw, dull eyes. He went to public school, not the academy Holly and I attended, but we knew him the way you always know your neighbors in a small town. I remember him always showing up where Holly was, wistfulness so out of character on his straight-forward features. I figured he'd always be in love with her. Holly let Dawson take her to one party, but she must have lost interest quickly, because she was married to Silas McDaniel before the end of that year. She was never interested in safe choices.

"It somehow doesn't surprise me that you're a cop now." It was a mechanical series of motions, making my seven PM drink. Slice a lime, squeeze it over the drink, nestle the slice onto the rim of the glass. "It just seems like a good fit for you."

"Well, thank you. Felicity, did you hear what I said when you answered the phone?"

"No," I answered, tasting the lime juice on my fingertip. I carried my glass into the living room and took a seat on the chaise, facing the window.

"But you did hear that I said I'm calling for work, Felicity," he pointed out. "You said being a cop was a natural fit for me." Something unpleasant flickered across my mind as I sipped my drink, crossing my knees and leaning into the cushion. Maybe there was something I didn't like about Dawson. Maybe he always did this, pointing out any tiny, harmless inconsistency. A natural fit, indeed.

"Um."

"Are you sitting down?"

"Yes," I sighed, as if brushing off an overprotective older sibling. "Why?"

It clicked, then, and suddenly I felt trapped, as if the bars of some cage had clasped into place and I was on the wrong side of them. That wrong feeling in my stomach all day. The bad dreams I'd had, the certainty Holly needed me somehow. And a voice, whispering through the dark, from hundreds of miles away.

"Felicity, your sister Holly's—"

"No." My voice came out petulant, shaky. "That's not possible."

I had been so certain that she needed to talk to me. Shock, mingled with guilt, set my limbs tingling with dread.

"Your sister Holly has passed away."

I could hear my ragged gasp echoing on the line.

"Felicity. There's more."

I tried to put the words together, *Holly*, and *passed away*, and the combination kicked up a confusion in my mind that almost knocked me to the floor. "But I need to talk to her. I knew something was wrong."

"I'm so sorry," he repeated. "And I'm sorry to have to bring up travel plans, but—"

"I'm not coming back," I answered mechanically. "Holly knew that."

"Everyone does," he allowed, "but Holly's will establishes you as the emergency guardian for the girls."

"Me? But why?" I hadn't even thought of Tess and Frankie. "Are they okay?" My voice skipped up several notes. "Dawson, what—what happened? To Holly?"

"She drowned," he said. "If it's any comfort, and this isn't official yet, we're all but certain it was accidental. And the girls are safe."

"Why me?"

"Felicity, if you can't manage it, the courts will appoint someone."

"I'll come." Standing up, I take the lime from my drink and chew on it, only barely aware of its bright, bitter flavor, realize I'm crying. "Is my mother okay?"

"Um. Well, she—"

"Why isn't she calling me? Why you, instead of her?"

An uneasy pause followed. "I have no doubt she'll be glad to see you."

"Then why'd I have to hear this from you, instead of her?"

"I—" Dawson cleared his throat. "She's been refusing to speak to anyone since she identified the body."

"Oh."

"If you'd like, I can meet you at the airport, talk you through picking up the girls." As if he already knew I didn't have any family willing to meet me.

"Thank you," I murmured, forcing a sense of control over my voice. "That would help, Dawson. I'll be on the first flight tomorrow morning. I'll let you know the details when I get my ticket."

When the line goes silent, the words crystallize. It's real.

I let the phone drop, feeling a distinct sense of weight above me, something heavy, dangling only by a thread. In an effort to shake off the dread materializing around me, I toss back the rest of my drink and stand up straight, sweeping my hair into a ponytail. I've devoted enough effort to my peace of mind that standing guard around it is a reflex. But now, I sense all the things that follow me, these unwanted companions. *Cold night air on scraped knees. Swamp water on Holly's jeans.* This isn't what I do: I can't afford to. *The smell of whiskey, sharp enough to make you forget things you shouldn't. Holly's eyes in the dark, bright with hurt, calling me a liar.*

Holly and I were always mistaken for twins, though she was a year older. Only people who paid attention would notice that she was stronger than I ever was, that she was our voice and I was our conscience. The same things have always befallen Holly and me, one way or another. I was pregnant; she was a mother within a year. And today, I dreamed of drowning and woke up to learn that Holly was dead. A wave of foreboding shocks me and I nudge it back.

Numb, my mind wandering, I begin to make travel arrangements, but I'm lost in my mind, tripping through the empty fairground from that long-ago night. I move on autopilot to pour a second drink before sitting down at my computer to book a flight.

Morning finds me a shaky mess. I'm a lightweight, and a second drink in addition to my standard one is enough to throw me off. I call the hospital to double-check they got my message. I've saved up all my time off, just like I do with my paychecks. I'm at the airport before I'm fully awake, thankful I'm feeling rotten enough to keep the larger swamp of grief and shock at bay for now. My hangover's just clearing as the sun rises over the Caribbean Sea, leaving me blinking. The clouds gleam like mother-of-pearl, and I pull down the shade on my window. The man in the seat next to mine grumbles quietly, and I nod an apology, but I can't manage words. I see the little boy at his side gazing longingly at the closed window.

"Sorry," I say, giving in. "Would you like to switch seats so you can look out the window? It's a nice view, isn't it?"

The boy smiles and we shuffle to trade seats. As he slouches into the window seat, he gives me a shy nod: *Yes, it's a nice view.*

I'd guess the boy and his father are on their way home from a vacation. As the morning passes, they trade observations: *The sea is so blue. Almost green. And it shines in the light, like jewels, much brighter than at home.* What they don't know is that all water, no matter where, is really the same. Water hides, and it takes, and what you're lucky enough to get back is irreparably changed. Even from this height, even far from home, I cannot imagine a body of water without seeing a cold, pale hand breaking the surface. Whether seeking help or to pull me down, the only thing certain is that it reaches for my grasp. It took hold of me once and has never really let me go.

CHAPTER TWO

Before

It was a little over a month ago, the last time Holly and I spoke. I woke up to three missed calls, the phone buzzing on the nightstand, and, trying to check the number, accidentally answered it. She was musical, as she always was after a few drinks.

"Hey, Holly," I murmured, head still on my pillow. "So late."

"I always forget you work mornings." Her cheery lilt fades. "And the time difference. It's one hour later there than it is here, I know." I was wrong. She wasn't drunk at all.

"That's okay," I said. "What's up?"

"Lissie, you know, Tess started her period. Twelve years old—can you believe it?"

"Hardly." *Time slips away a bit like a wave*, I thought, still half sleeping. One moment can rise tall enough to knock you flat, then slip out of your arms, years washing away into the distance.

"I've been thinking. I can't stop thinking about it."

"About what?" I asked, groggy.

"I didn't realize how young teenagers are. Now Tess is almost the same age you and I were when you left home."

"Ah. Right." My mind slipped into something like work mode. Polite, surface level. "Well, there's really no need to—"

"She's a child," Holly continued. "Like you were, back then. I'm so sorry. I wish I'd done more for you." I sat up in bed, rubbing my eyes.

"Enough, Holly." The polite note in my voice bordered on warning, but my sister either failed to notice or pressed on regardless.

"I always kind of knew something bad happened to you. You never told me, but I should have seen it. I just didn't want to look."

Just like that, I was back there again, in our shared bedroom on the night before I left. *He would never even look sideways at you. You were just my stupid baby sister, tagging along, like always.* I stood before her silent with shock: had she felt this way all along? I thought we were best friends. Then, I realized, it was only one more thing I'd been wrong about.

Now, I tried to imagine her saying these different words instead: *I always kind of knew something bad happened to you.* In that alternate reality, her rage would have melted into understanding, and her arms would have folded around me, restoring the seamless closeness we once shared. In that version of events, maybe I didn't creep out before dawn, suitcase in hand, and book a bus ticket for the furthest destination I could afford.

But that wasn't what happened.

When I answered her, my voice was icy. "What exactly would you like me to say?"

"I'm sorry. No, no—that's not what I want you to say. I mean, I'm the one who's sorry."

"At least you're being honest for once, right?" Angry, suddenly wide awake, I heard the twang surface in my voice. The same way it used to at our private Catholic school, announcing that I was from the muddy side of the lake, that my family never should have been able to afford the tuition. "Why now? After all this time?"

"Tess," Holly whispered. "She's so much like we were. She's old enough to get herself in trouble, but she's still a child."

"Well, I hope you feel better now you've told me." I paced in front of the open window. "That's what you're after, right? You want me to tell you it's okay?"

"No." Holly's voice softened, and when she paused I could picture her pressing a hand to her eyes. "There's something else I need to tell you. That I haven't been able to, for all this time."

"Save it, okay?" I felt myself regaining the impersonal territory where I was comfortable. "I don't want to process anything else tonight."

"I tried to tell you then, but I wasn't brave enough." Holly went right on, as if she hadn't heard me. "Especially with everything else you were going through. You wanted that baby."

"I didn't," I spit, "and you're crossing a line." The baby was one thing I couldn't talk about, not even to Holly. My own Reverie Girl, as much a phantom, to me at least, as the rumored ghosts lurking in that tangled swamp. Between my own insides and the murky land where I grew up, it's hard to say which is the more haunted.

"You think I would have been happy, stuck in a dead-end town, with that man's baby?"

"Oh, stuck like me?"

"I gave up everything for you." My voice was blank, as if I was reading a grocery list, holding those recollections safely at bay. "Don't talk to me like I left you in the dust. You—" I have to pause, rubbing a hand at my temple. "You don't know what it was like."

"What if I did know?" The quiet exhale that followed her words felt like a knife in my ribs. "If I can fix it, will you come home?"

"Holly, if you had any idea what you're talking about, you wouldn't say that." Where was this tenderness when I had needed it so badly, and why was she showing it now, when it could serve only as a reminder of what we'd lost? "You can't fix it. Nobody can fix it." I felt my chest soften as she cried quietly. I told her I loved her, but if there was any love in my voice, it was distant. I told her I wasn't ready to talk about it. That I might not ever be.

Now, I know, that will always be the last time we spoke.

CHAPTER THREE

Now

When the flight attendant passes by, I reluctantly order a cup of coffee, which I hope will clear my head before landing. As we approach the Atlantic Coast, the ground beneath looks gray, almost as gray as the water. From the air, home is a spongy-looking expanse of deep, lush green and brown, veins of water creeping through it here and there. The lake is clear and beautiful toward the west, while the east side blurs land and water in an expanse of swampland that stretches on for miles near Virginia's southern border. It was back in the 1950s that a businessman from New York built a fairground, which he called The Reverie, right where the water meets the land. The population was booming, and it was meant to bring tourists and locals alike, linked to the town over the water by a long, scenic boardwalk. Just a week after it opened, the disappearances started, his own daughter the first among them.

By the time the fall came around and five girls had disappeared there, it was closed and deserted. A few years later, a worse-than-usual hurricane disturbed the water level, moving so that the fairground was firmly located within the swamp, vines and murk overtaking the curvature of its structures, the boardwalk half submerged. In the heart of the fairground, where the ground was driest, the old dance hall still stood, fragile as a gingerbread house.

But to those of us too young to remember the disappearances, it was just The Reverie, the best spot for parties or late-night walks. Could there have been anything more American than growing up by an abandoned fairground? I remember, like I'm thumbing through old photographs, James Finley and me, the quarterback and the cheerleader, stealing out for a quiet, close walk down the boardwalk after a football game. To everybody else, he was Fin or Finley, but I only ever called him James. From the first time we locked eyes, I felt something solemn between us, and calling him by his first name felt both formal and intimate. It was a small-town fairy tale, right up until the day it wasn't. Just because something feels brighter, sweeter than reality, that doesn't mean it's real. Looking back on it all, I feel a pang of sympathy for the naive, optimistic man who built the fairground, as if daring the lowlands and their storms to do their worst. Which, in time, they inevitably did.

I hear an announcement over the PA system: "Ladies and gentlemen, we're now fifteen minutes from arrival. The weather today is sunny and clear, but we're expecting storms later. Hope you packed umbrellas!"

As the pleasant voice asks me to buckle my seatbelt, I realize that I haven't packed an umbrella. I don't think I even own one. The plane begins its descent, my ears popping with the change in pressure. It gives a feeling of being underwater, one I can't shake, as if even to look at the place I once called home distorts my reality, as if I'm knowingly walking into a carnival mirror.

CHAPTER FOUR

Now

In the airport, I stand uselessly at the arrivals gate, dialing Dawson over and over, the call failing to go through each time. I begin to walk, wandering from one terminal to the next, until I find him sitting outside a coffee shop.

"Afternoon, Felicity."

"Hi, Dawson." I hurry over to greet him, switching my carry-on bag to my other shoulder.

"It's all right," he answers, extending one foot to push out a chair for me on the other side of the table. "It's good to see you. I'm sorry it has to be for this reason."

"You, too." When he reaches out to grasp my hand, I realize my fingers are freezing, his warm. "Sorry I'm late. I tried to call you."

"Do you have US coverage on that thing?"

"I don't know, so probably not." I drop into the seat, holding my bag in my lap.

"I'd update it," he suggests, something fatherly in his tone. "Long as you have reception, you'll be able to make emergency calls, so no worries there. But you'll want to be able to reach people while you're here."

"Thanks."

"You're welcome. You want a coffee?"

"No, thanks." Since I've last seen him, Dawson has aged into himself, that heavy jawline a little more natural in his mid-thirties than it was at eighteen. I'm not sure why he offered to meet me—not even really sure whether he's here as a police officer or as my friend. Dawson has always been the type of person to jump in and help. Maybe I should just be grateful he's here.

"How are you holding up?"

"I'm all right," I answer crisply. "Thanks. Sorry about last night, I—"

"No," he insists. "No apologies. So, about Tess and Frankie—"

"They're all right?"

"Yes," he answers. "With a relative. Wendy Wheeler."

"Wendy?" I remember cousin Wendy as a standoffish woman several years older than me, someone I saw only at family get-togethers, who was always brimming over with cautionary tales. "Why not at home with their father?"

"You didn't talk to Holly much, did you?" Dawson realizes. Admonished, I shake my chin. "Holly and the girls had been living at your mother's house, since she and her husband separated—"

"When did that happen?"

He raises an eyebrow before answering me. "Silas is an alcoholic—don't know if you knew that already. And your mother hasn't taken the news well—not that I blame her. So, they've been with Wendy for the last few days. Honestly, at first glance, there's no clear-cut guardian for them. But you're the emergency guardian, which means Holly trusted you to figure something out. And to take care of them until you do."

I wonder if Holly would have told me about Silas, if I hadn't shut her down when she called last month. "I think I am going to get a coffee, on second thought."

He nods and I turn quickly on my heel, walk up to the counter and order a coffee, black. I'll be jittery later—I usually drink tea, and only one cup—but that isn't really at the top of my list of concerns. I return to the table, holding the paper cup between my hands.

"Do you need directions to Wendy Wheeler's house?" he asks.

"I think I remember how to get there."

"What else, then?" He looks at me with something like concern. I could have sworn that, in my memory, his eyes were blue, though now they are a puzzling tone of gray. "Car rentals are that way—"

"I hope you know that I appreciate this." I sip my coffee. I know what Dawson must see when he looks at me; I know well enough what people said behind my back, and even if Dawson wasn't saying it, he surely heard it. The private school homecoming queen, turned pregnant dropout. The daughter who skipped town rather than face the rumors. "But I want to be clear: the past is in the past. If I couldn't handle this, I wouldn't be here."

"Holly would have wanted me to look out for you."

I nod, staring down at my coffee cup. "I need you to tell me what happened to her."

"The details are unpleasant, Felicity."

I level my eyes at him. "I said I can handle it."

He sighs and pulls his chair a bit closer.

"She attended a Thanksgiving party at Cotton Blossom—that's the diner where she worked."

"I remember." It's the only diner in town, or it used to be.

"So, that's the last time she was seen. And then, nothing. Your mother got in touch with us when she wasn't at home by the next afternoon. We found her body—I mean," he pauses, squeezes his nearly empty paper coffee cup in his fist, "we found her the following evening."

"Are you quite sure it was her?"

Dawson nods. "Your mother confirmed it."

I bite down on my lip, pondering this sense that it must be a mistake; this cannot be true.

"She could have been wrong."

"She wasn't wrong. I'm sorry, Felicity." He shakes his head, answering my refusals patiently. "Your mother hasn't spoken with anyone since she left the coroner's office that day. Now that you're in town, I hope you can check on her."

I see that warning look of pity in his eyes, straighten up and tie my hair back into a ponytail. "I want to see pictures."

"No. You do not." Dawson's shaking his head, but I suspect now he's talking to me as a friend, not a police officer. "Forensics estimates that she died that first night," he says. "Two days in the water, Felicity." Another moment passes, and though I'm doing my best to remain calm, I know I have to see proof if Dawson wants me to believe Holly is dead. Finally, he reaches under his chair and produces a tan briefcase, shuffles through it and removes a folder, which he hands to me with some hesitation.

The way he warned me about seeing these images, I half expected to see something monstrous, disturbing. But the truth is so much worse. It's not a nightmare, but my sister. I can't help tracing over her limbs, wishing I could feel some warmth there. Holly was all long legs and weightless blonde waves, a mermaid's golden hair. I used to think she was what I'd look like if I were beautiful. But she had something else, too, something that lit her up from the inside, that made her special. Even now, the difference between us strikes me. I was just the stupid baby sister, tagging along.

And there are those long legs, bare, tangled in fishing line, and I observe that the curve of her body over that root does look, a bit, like a mermaid's tail. Face forward, her arms hanging down in an almost graceful gesture. A tangle of seaweed or moss around her hair.

Nodding, biting my lip, I look up as Dawson reaches for the folder, pull it back toward me.

"How did she die?"

"She drowned. No signs of assault. No real injuries, other than a couple of scratches, and a mark on her head. All signs point to her having slipped into the water. That place is disorienting enough without bad weather."

"Did she leave the party with her purse?" I ask, staring at this photo as if I can disprove it, logic it right out of existence.

"Nobody's seen it. If it went in the water, or made its way into the lake in the storm, there's no telling." Nodding dismissively, I turn the first picture aside to find a close-up image of Holly's wrist, marred with a small line.

"Which hand is this?"

"Why?"

"It's her left hand," I whisper, tracing the image as if I could hold her hand. "Where's her charm bracelet?" My mother gave one first to Holly, then to me when we turned seventeen. My own bracelet was long since misplaced. Dawson props his elbow on the table, looks at his watch. "She always wore her charm bracelet."

"If she was wearing it that night, likely it could have snagged on a branch. Or slipped off. Anything, really." Dawson watches me carefully. "You know that swamp, Felicity. It's dangerous enough in good weather. That night, there was a storm. Late-season hurricane." I'm holding the pictures, struggling to look away from them, when Dawson holds his hand out.

"I do need those back, if you don't mind."

"Of course." With an energy that seems to shock him, I return his photographs, push my chair back, and stand up.

"Let's keep moving, then. Where did you say the car rental is?"

He nods, quickly gathering his things from the tabletop. "This way." I follow him past the terminals, to wait in line at a rental office. Dawson's watching me cautiously, waiting for me to burst into tears. But I stand patiently, listening to the tick of the clock on the wall. I tell myself that if I can only make it to pick up the girls, I'll be all right. When it's my turn, I'm grateful for the distraction provided by the paperwork I need to complete for the rental. Finally, the clerk hands me a key and directs me to a nondescript green sedan, with a warning: "Drive carefully if you're near the swamp. The storm hit bad out there last week." I thank him, wait for him to walk away, then turn back to Dawson.

"Where was she, exactly?"

"Beg your pardon?"

"You mentioned the swamp. I have to ask."

"No, you don't." He looks back at me, mouth pursed with regret. In reverse, they're the same words we spoke to each other, that one night he found me walking by the roadside and drove me home. My disheveled cheerleader's uniform. The jacket around my shoulders that wasn't mine. *I have to ask*, he'd said. *No*, I answered, *you don't*. Of course, he must have found out something about what happened. Everybody did, eventually, find something out.

"Where exactly was she?"

"You know the fairground, right?" I nod yes. "Just past the far edge of the old Ferris wheel."

"No. That can't be right." Reaching to put the key in the car door, I miss, dragging it across the green paint with a jagged, tinny screech.

"No?"

"She would never go there."

"You mean alone?" he offers. "She'd had a few drinks, Felicity, and a rough year, by any measure. She might not have been—"

"She wouldn't have gone to that spot in a crowd, in broad daylight, on the nicest day of the year. Let alone in a hurricane."

"A lot of time has passed," he answers softly.

"Excuse me." I drop my bag onto the passenger seat and turn abruptly back toward the building. "Just going to find a restroom before I start driving."

I push through the doors and rush through the rental office, back into the airport. I'll be damned if Dawson sees me cry again. Holly wouldn't even speak of Page, wouldn't even mention the swamp, let alone go near it. Dabbing at my eyes and nose with a tissue, I check in the mirror to make sure I don't have makeup running down my cheeks. Somehow, I'm certain Holly would never go there again. If I'm wrong about that, then my sister and I had grown further apart than even I thought possible. But what if I'm right?

When I walk back to the car, Dawson gives me a handwritten note with directions to Wendy's house, handing it over with a lingering touch and a glance that makes me certain he knows I've been crying.

"I'll check in," he says. "Call if you need anything. And remember, you don't have to do this—"

"Yes, I do."

"You can walk away if you want to."

"I'm sure I'll run into you, Dawson. Have a nice day."

As I drive away, I catch sight of an airplane ascending from the corner of my eye, give it a longing nod. I wonder if Dawson knows how wrong he is, when he says that I could leave now if I wanted. It wouldn't be the first time that he has overlooked a little of the truth, as a form of kindness, as a means to make the unbearable make sense.

CHAPTER FIVE

Now

Wendy Wheeler, eight years my senior, lives in a pert, white-painted suburban house, about a half hour outside of the city. It's a maze of crisscrossed bridges and highways to get there, and this area confused me even driving on a good day, back when I was familiar with it. I'm in the car for more than an hour, turning back and checking street names, before I finally find it, park on the street, and approach to knock at the door.

"Oh, Felicity." She's well maintained, seems certain of the correctness of whatever posture she affects, pulls me into a too-fragrant hug. "It's so terrible. I'm just heartbroken for you."

"Hi, Wendy," I murmur, drawing a breath of unperfumed air over her shoulder.

"How did it happen? We're all so shocked." Something like worry lengthens the lines of her face. Like me, Wendy has the classic Wheeler cheekbones, the strong brow. She eyes me, though, like I'm a zoo exhibit.

"I couldn't tell you about her life. Holly didn't fill me in on much," I answer, feeling ashamed as I look at her spotless couches, the pillows arranged just so. "We spoke last month, but it was brief." I was hoping to patch things up. To be closer again. I'd wanted to do that for years. Why did I wait? I almost speak these words aloud to Wendy before I recognize her expression, the unmistakable sparkling eyes of someone always on the lookout for weakness.

"That so?" Wendy clicks her tongue. "I remember you two being so close. Ah, well—sisters always love each other, even if you don't talk often."

"Yes."

"Well, she left Silas a few months back, and I don't know whether it was because of his drinking, or if her leaving him kicked off this binge he's on, but he can't be there for them." I sense she is enjoying this, imparting this sort of knowledge, but there's something about her tone I distinctly dislike. "Holly and the girls were staying with your mother. But she's in no shape to care for children, Felicity—the way she's taken this news, she needs caring for herself."

"I don't doubt it." I don't doubt it, but I can't be the person to do it.

"Poor thing," she says. I suddenly feel like she knows about my headache. "Here, sit down. I haven't seen you since that picnic your mom had, what was it, thirteen years ago?"

"Yes, that sounds right."

"Who was that boy, at the picnic with you?" This is the Wendy I remember, with her preternatural homing instinct for whatever topic you'd most like to avoid.

"Like you said, it's been years. Honestly, that could have been anybody."

"I remember he was a football player." Wendy's eyebrows lift gently, as if she wants to help jog my memory. "Tall, nice-looking. *Beautiful* eyes."

Trying not to roll my own eyes, I mumble a response. "I suppose it could have been James Finley."

"You two looked really in love."

"Young love's about as real as the tooth fairy." What James and I had was like a meteor that put all the stars around it to shame, a short-lived blaze that had left my heart a cratered and foreign place. My first week rehearsing with the cheer squad, we were warming up while the football team was practicing across the field. My first glimpse of him was just broad shoulders, a tousle of dark, almost black hair that gleamed under the lights. But when he turned and saw me, we locked eyes and smiled. Half a second later, the football hit his chest and he blinked at me like he'd just woken up. I shook a pom-pom and grinned. We hadn't spoken a word to each other, but I swear my heart flipped over inside my chest. Even from this distance, I can admit that nothing since has ever felt that real. James wasn't a great quarterback. The coach said he had the size, the strength for it, but not the temperament. *You're not playing chess here, Fin*, the coach had yelled. James stood up, brushed himself off, and turned that warm smile back my way. I thought everyone was wrong, that he had a depth that made brute strength unnecessary. Turned out he wasn't much for fighting for anything.

"I met my husband when we were seventeen. I know it looked like it happened fast, but when you actually fall in love, you know it's real. We were married with kids within a couple years." For some reason this spurs my temper. I've been in love. I've been pregnant. I haven't been married, though Derek proposed. I wonder what it would feel like, to have your life all in one place, all those milestones linking you to a single person.

"Oh." I look down at my sandals. "Sorry. I mean—not that you found the one for you early on. Sorry for—"

"Anyway," Wendy cuts me off. "Well, these two—" Her eyes begin to water, and she takes a tissue from the box on the table. "I'm worried for them. What a horrible, frightening thing." Her tears could be contagious. I bite down on my lip and force myself not to think of Holly, not yet. "And nobody to care for them."

"I'm here," I offer. Wendy responds with a manufactured smile that lets me know she's got about as much faith in me as I do.

"They need stability. Right now, of course, but they have needed it for some time. Tess has run away from home more than once. Holly let them run wild, and their father…" She shakes her head. "Felicity, you left your family for a reason. You know children need someone dependable, a predictable life. The quiet runs thick out there on the swamp. You know what I mean."

"Oh, I do?" I turn to the doorway at the side of the room. "Where are they?"

"And I'm concerned about what their home life was like," Wendy continues. "I believe Holly was unfaithful to Silas. Holly had things she couldn't explain sometimes, nice things—I wouldn't be surprised if those girls aren't his children."

"Enough, Wendy."

"Whoever their father is must have been—you know—well-off," she finishes, as if I hadn't interrupted her.

"Holly didn't waste time on gossip, and I don't either," I snap, cutting her off. I don't appreciate the fixation with the past, with parents and secrets and children, any more than I imagine Holly did. I don't know why I defend my family like this. Except that Wendy seems to be talking trash about me, too. "Whatever else is true, I'm here now. And I may not know why, but it was her wish for me to be here."

"Not yours, you mean?"

It's then I see the girl watching me, slouched against the doorframe in the next room. There's a flicker of motion beside her, a tiny version of the older sister. I cross the room to speak to them and Tess's chin juts out, an arm sweeping out like a narrow branch to push her sister behind her.

"Hi, Tess." She only stares back at me. I look down at the littler one. "Hi, Frankie. I'm your—" I'm fumbling already, the older girl's snapping green eyes calling me to account. She's looking at me like I'm a stranger.

Because I am.

"I'm your aunt."

She gives a brief nod of her chin, and her meaning is flawlessly clear: she already knows this.

"Where will you take them?" Wendy asks. "You live overseas—do you have a place to stay here?"

No. Nowhere. No plan. I got here as fast as I could. None of these answers seem sufficient. Wendy said they were staying with my mother. I take a gentle glance at Tess and decide to take a risk.

"Yes," I answer, watching Tess as I speak. "We're going to stay at my mother's house in Brightwater." As an afterthought, I find myself hoping my mother will let me in the door, after thirteen years without so much as a visit.

Tess's mouth drops open, eyebrows lifting in what I hope is a sign of relief, then, just as quickly, her expression snaps back into blankness. She drops to her knees, whispering with Frankie, then the two of them walk past us, up the staircase.

"I've tried to draw them out," Wendy offers. No statement follows to soften this one. Just an admission of failure. As I'm beginning to wonder if I'm going to have to follow and look for them, I hear footsteps on the stairs. Holly's girls appear as if marching into battle, green eyes sharp as that glass I pulled out of my foot just two days ago, suitcases in hand. They look so much like Holly. I recognize myself in them and remember that I look like Holly, too.

Tess looks at me, then nods at the door.

"Goodbye, girls." Wendy bends to offer a hug, but Tess shakes her head.

"Bye, Aunt Wendy." Wendy moves to place a kiss on Frankie's head, murmuring a goodbye. Frankie turns and hurls herself against Tess with a fearful cry.

"I told you," Tess snaps, eyes sparking. "Don't touch her."

They're not overly gentle with each other: they're closer than that. I recognize it, remember it. The year Holly and I started being gentle with each other, afraid of the effect our words might take, we had grown apart, even if we didn't realize it at the time.

Wendy nods, jumps back, and looks at me regretfully. "Frankie will only speak to Tess, and they don't want to be touched." Wendy looks so hurt that it makes me angry, not for her, but for the children, who shouldn't be asked, on top of everything else, to worry about hurting Aunt Wendy's feelings.

"This is fresh," I remind her. "There's no wrong way to act when something like this happens. You shouldn't take it personally."

"Yes, but still, I just—"

"But still nothing. They're not your emotional support children." I've worked with enough children in the hospital to recognize the shock that comes before grief, the still surface concealing depths of turmoil. When Wendy opens her mouth again, I toss myself at her, arms out, and silence her with a big, sudden, if genuine, hug. "Happy holidays, Wendy."

Tess taps her toe against the polished wood floor and, finally, speaks to me.

"Let's go."

I tell Wendy goodbye, lead the girls outside to the rental car, unlock the trunk and pack their suitcases in, open the passenger door for Tess, then reconsider.

"I'm not sure where you'd prefer to sit, but take your pick."

"We'll sit together." She opens the back door and helps Frankie in, nimble hands buckling her sister's seatbelt, then climbs into the seat next to her.

I pause by the open door, feeling I need to say something. "I'm glad to see both of you," I begin. "I'm so sorry it has to be like this. But—"

"Listen." Tess stretches her long legs out of the seat, the heels of her shoes braced on the curb. "You said you'd take us to Grandma's house. Can we just go?"

I nod, imagining what the last few days have looked like for them. Frankie leans close to Tess, their blonde hair exactly the same shade. I drop into the seat, start the engine, and pull out onto the road.

We drive in silence for a few minutes, until Wendy's suburban neighborhood is behind us. Sitting at a stoplight, Tess catches me looking at her in the rearview. Her mouth sharpens. She sizes you up as certainly as her mother did, I can see that. I was the one who always got people wrong.

"Can I say something to you both?" I ask. They raise their eyes to mine, which I take as permission to continue. I hesitate. Children have an uncanny ability to detect a lie, I know this. So I don't bother with any vast professions of love or declarations of safety. I take a breath and speak. "I'll level with you. This is terrible. But we all loved your mom. And I'm—I'll do anything to help you, and take care of you, whatever that turns out to be." I lean closer, hoping they can feel that I mean it. "I promise you that I'm on your side."

I don't expect an answer. I watch them for just long enough to know that they've heard me. And then, a couple more turns, and we're off, heading south and east toward the coast.

"Just because you're family doesn't mean we're going to be friends," Tess says, her voice flat.

"That's okay too," I answer.

I remember how it feels to be young with nobody on your side. Tess doesn't know it, but that's something we have in common. Even if they weren't my blood, that would be all it took.

"Do you even know how to get there?" she asks.

"Yes," I answer. "Of course I remember."

CHAPTER SIX

Now

Another hour down the road and the highway's narrowed to two opposing lanes. The trees and plants take on that gray-green look that I know so well, and the smell of marsh water comes in through the car vents. Like incense that's gone sour.

The roadside is dotted with tiny, ramshackle roadside houses, and occasionally livestock. We pass a feed-and-seed shop with a faded hand-painted sign, at the edge of an expanse of marshy field. My heart leaps. This bare delight at the place I grew up was here before any of the things that sent me running away from it, and it seems it's here still. In the summer, these lowland fields explode with flowers, wild daffodils and chicory and—my favorite—swamp rose mallow, looming white blossoms with magenta at the heart of the petals. Now, late fall, only a few scattered, faded blossoms remain amid the jumbled greenery, but it whispers with familiarity just the same. Every few minutes, I hazard a question, but receive only Tess's non-answers: Tess and Frankie aren't hungry. They don't want to listen to music. They don't want to stop and stretch their legs.

We haven't been on the road more than a couple hours when I hear a chattering, then a groaning cough from within the car. It jerks a bit, then follows with a roaring hack. The engine shakes, the wheel tugging wildly side to side in my hands.

"What the…" My hands turn to stone on the steering wheel, my eyes scanning the dash for anything amiss. Plenty of gasoline, the temperature seems fine—nothing wrong, so far as I know how to read. But then it happens again.

"What in the f—"

"Tess, how do you know that word?" I gasp, speaking loudly over the noise.

"I'm twelve years old!" she shouts back, as if she was just saving this admonition for the right moment. I notice that Frankie's absolutely silent. They're both watching me, for how I respond to this.

"You're right," I answer, trying to talk over the jarring noise of the car, my own clamoring heartbeat. "You're not a child, Tess. I know."

I pull off the road and try to act as if I know what to do. I pop the hood open, after fumbling for the release latch. I stare at the tangle of metal and wires as if it could tell me anything. Nothing seems to be smoking, or obviously on fire. Thoughtlessly, I brush a hand over its interior, pull back with a yelp as my fingers land on something hot. I brush my hand on my dress, leaving a dark smudge. I return to the driver's seat and look into the back seat to face them.

"Tess, there used to be a service station where route twelve crosses Morgan's Creek Road. Do you know if it's still there?"

"Yes," she says. "The one by the Presbyterian church?"

"That's the one," I say. "That's our next stop. Frankie?" I say her name and the big green eyes rise to mine, though the chin stays tucked. "Don't worry, okay? Everything is fine."

I think.

"We're going to drive to the station. It can't be more than fifteen minutes. We're completely safe." When they nod their assent, I start the engine again, wincing. The sound isn't quite as bad now, though I wonder if I'm just acclimated to it.

"It sounds like the car ate something bad," Frankie says. She's speaking to Tess, not to me, but for the first time I hear her clear, bell-like little voice. "Like a sour tummy."

"Well, that's the important thing about an upset tummy—it doesn't last forever," Tess answers. As I continue driving, my heart's beating wildly somewhere between my throat and my eyeballs, I'm so afraid we're going to break down. I watch the heat gauge closely, though it stays where it should. The check engine light blinks on, but, I think, it's a few minutes too late.

"The Presbyterian church is up ahead past that barn," Tess says. "It's across from the pond. The station should be just past that."

"Thank you." She's the type of kid who keeps her eyes open, observing smartly what's around her. Not the kind I was—dreamy, always turning inward. The odd thing is, I find I haven't forgotten anything. I try not to show the relief on my face when I see the familiar repair shop, slow down and pull over.

"It sounds better," Tess says. "You could just keep driving."

"I'd rather be sure." When I answer her, she rolls her eyes again.

Bradley Potter's service station, with its dusty green-and-yellow sign, hasn't changed a bit. Everything is the same: the cracked parking lot. The row of three gasoline pumps, practically analog, they're so ancient. We walk inside and I face the counter, a yellowed boundary between the customer and the rows on rows of cigarettes and chewing tobacco behind it.

"Can I help you?" Mr. Potter hasn't aged a day in thirteen years, though he never looked young, his narrow, weathered face peering up over the register. I approach the counter and set down the key for the rental car as Frankie sidles up to eye the candy shelf.

"Pick out anything you'd like," I whisper, then turn to address the man. He's a bit of a legend because his store was the only one that didn't always check ID, and so one of the places local kids would come for alcohol. "Is there someone here who could take a look at my car?" The man gives me a curt nod.

"That'd be me. What seems to be the issue?"

"It's a rental," I answer. "I just picked it up this morning. It started making a—a noise."

"Can you tell me anything else about it?" he asks. Frankie sidles up and drops a gathered handful of candy bars onto the counter.

"It has a sour tummy," she answers. Mr. Potter raises his eyes to me and I shrug my shoulders.

"I'm afraid that's the extent of my expertise."

Mr. Potter rings up Frankie's candy and Tess's Coke, then takes my car key and heads out through the side door. As he starts the car, I hear the spluttering noise, just a shadow of the grinding, chewing sound it was making half an hour ago. He pulls it into the garage and I peer through the interior window, watch as he opens the hood and inspects it.

The waiting area is a row of dingy metal folding chairs facing a small television set. The reception is poor, but I can make out the static-waved figures of a talk show host and a guest seated in a chair. The girls seem content to snack and watch. When Mr. Potter returns, he looks skeptical, one elbow angled, hand in his back pocket.

"I checked everything. Doesn't seem to be anything the matter with it, ma'am."

Tess lifts an eyebrow, looks at me as if to say, *I told you so.*

"I heard a little cough when we started her up, but…"

"If you say so," I answer. That's the trouble with places like this. I have no idea, and I sense I'm bordering on rudeness by even hinting that I might not trust his answer. "It sounded terrible. It really did." He looks at the smudge on my dress.

"I don't know what to tell you, ma'am. Anyway, no charge."

"Oh, I—" This, also, I dislike. I don't want to owe anyone.

"You bought half my stock in candy," he says, smiling at Frankie, then offers her another lollipop. "Didn't have to do any work on your vehicle. Call it even."

"Thank you," I manage.

"Could have been anything, a temporary noise like that," he adds. "Could have been something stuck in the tire." I want to tell him that it wasn't coming from the tire, but I can see he wouldn't take my opinion seriously.

"Hope she doesn't give you any more trouble," he says, nodding again as we make our way toward the door.

"Sorry, Tess," I manage. There's a damp chill on the breeze and I cross my arms. I should have worn something better suited for the weather here, but of course I don't own anything that fits that bill. "I guess I should have listened to you."

"Yeah," Tess says, with a flippant wag of her head. "Maybe next time." She sits down and helps Frankie buckle her seatbelt. I look down the road, which has led us almost to Brightwater. It's only three more turns, one more bridge, and then the swamp road that takes us to my family's house. Off the side of the road, a yard or two back in the brambles, I can see a large, dilapidated wooden sign in once-cheery 1950s pastels, advertising The Reverie, a painting of a Ferris wheel and a larger-than-life ice cream cone. Sometime in the 1970s, Hurricane Isidor, I think, paid a visit and the Ferris wheel toppled over, and now rests where it fell, one half rising above the murky water at a shallow angle. I'm in no hurry to get closer to it, any of it.

"Since we're here, we might as well put some gas in the car."

"It's half full," Tess observes. She does not miss a thing.

"I'd rather do it now," I say. "I don't like to let things run low. Don't like to leave things to chance." Maybe she can tell this is the truth, because she shrugs instead of arguing with me. I drive a few yards to the gas pump, hop out, and close the door behind me. As soon as I step out of the car, I'm standing in a puddle, slick with silt. Mud and oil-tinged water run over my toes. I wiggle my toes, trying to shake it off, only succeeding in splashing it on the hem of my dress. The card reader doesn't work on the first try, or the second. The keypad is faded to illegibility. Finally, the screen reads: *Error. Please See Cashier.*

I could just keep driving and hope we make it. After all, it is half full. Glancing back toward the door, where I so recently made a fool of myself, I see a row of newspapers that I'd missed. *Swamp Mermaid: Local Bartender Found Drowned.* I realize, with a jolt, that there's every chance the girls had to walk past a headline or a photograph featuring their dead mother. As I'm trying to decide what to do next, I'm smacked with a grainy, black-and-white photograph of a stretcher being loaded into an ambulance, beneath the headline *Decades Later, Reverie Girls Claim Another.*

"Thanks a lot," I hiss, slapping the screen with resentment I didn't know was there. I walk back to the newsstand, pick up a copy. *Local woman found dead after two days missing. In a shock to the small town of Brightwater, the body of Holly McDaniel was discovered on November 27. The fisherman who found her thought at first he'd seen a mermaid. Holly, who had lived her entire life in Brightwater, was a former student of the exclusive St. Benedict Academy...*

Across the parking lot, a car door closes. Footsteps pick up, then slow. I take the whole stack of newspapers in my hands, cast a guilty glance to either side, and carry them to the trash can at the side of the gas pump. I attempt to drop the entire stack in, but the lid is too small, and it's already nearly full. I'm clutching the papers to my chest, cramming them in one at a time, when I hear the voice ringing from my left.

"Excuse me, but what do you think you're doing?"

I sense a figure approaching and assume it's someone who works here. Mindful that the girls are on the other side of the tinted glass, my first answer is a hiss, almost a rainstorm of quiet curses. "Frankly, these shouldn't have been here in the first place. It's more gossip than news." I stuff another newspaper into the trash. "Didn't anyone care that she has friends, family who live around here, who might not care to see this?"

"I ought to call the police."

"Go ahead. They know me." I'm fighting with the remainder of the newspapers, trying to trash four at one go, the only thing on my mind being that the children shouldn't see them. The amusement in his voice confuses me. "Holly's my sister. And for your information—"

"Come on, ladybug. It's me." When he begins to laugh, I recognize his voice immediately. He's right next to me, just as he's remained in my thoughts all these years: blond hair, glinting blue eyes, straight nose. You could call him handsome, which people always have, but the truth is that his appearance is perfectly generic, not a feature out of measure or a single hair out of place, never a movement offbeat. "It's so good to see you."

"Cody!" A flutter of bewildering memories crosses my mind, leaving a momentary sensation of shock, as if an unseen flock of birds has just taken to the air. I reach out a hand, unthinking, just to see if he's real, a gesture he apparently interprets as a hug. When his arms wrap lightly around my back, I find my voice again. "Has anyone ever told you you're not as funny as you think you are?"

"All my life, Felicity." Cody, being the principal's son, was all the more popular for his class clown act. Scanning the newspaper in my hand, his smile fades. "I'm so sorry to hear the news." When he reaches for another hug, something in my chest shifts, as if I want to guard this grief, not ready yet to look at it head-on.

"Thanks." My arms fold up over my chest as if I'm braced for a crash landing, my cheek against the warm, scratchy wool of his coat. Cody played soccer in school, and still has the lithe limbs and effortless bearing he always did.

"How are you?"

"I'm here." One of my shoulders twitches up in a meaningless shrug. He looks toward the car, and I stifle an impulse to stand in front of the window, to block the girls from sight.

"Something wrong with your card?" He points at the card reader. "I'm going inside. Want me to tell them to fill it up? It's on me."

"No, thanks," I answer. "It's the card reader. There's nothing wrong with my credit card."

"I don't mind." Once again, his face softens into that careful smile, one eyebrow just raised, as if he knows I want to run from here, as if he understands. "Wait here." He opens the door of the gas station and I see him lean over toward the counter. "Thirty bucks on three." Watching him walk back to my side, my feet fidget inside my sandals, half sunk in a mud puddle that's collected between cracks in the paving. When he takes a step closer, the toes of his boots near mine, I'm inching away, before I realize that he's reaching for the gas pump.

"I've got it." I put my shoulder in his way, reach for the gas pump. Cody leans back against the rental car as if enjoying a pause in conversation. The collar of my coat is too tight, suddenly, and I'm reaching for my neck with both hands to loosen it when I realize with a dash of confusion that I'm not wearing a coat.

"You've barely aged a day, you know."

"Same to you, Cody." Once I've said it, though, I realize that Cody has changed. He's grown up, his sharp blue eyes balanced with broader shoulders, the once-pale blond of his hair now a sandy wave. As for me, I think I might have been pretty once, in a straightforward, milkmaid sort of way, with yellow hair and pink cheeks. I was a cheerleader back then. The cheer squad at St. Benedict's was small-town famous, with our red-and-black outfits. Everyone called us the ladybugs. At away games, the opposing school would yell that old song, dozens of youthful voices turning into a cloud of mist on a chilly night: *Ladybug, ladybug, fly away home.*

"You're wrong, though," I murmur, looking down. "I've got little lines around my eyes."

"Nope," he announces. "You definitely have a portrait aging in an attic somewhere, collecting all your secret sins."

"If you say so." I can't help it: with this one, he finally wins a laugh. "And how are you?"

"I just got into town a couple days ago myself," he says. "Home for the holidays, as usual. It was hard to get a day away from work, though." I glaze over while he goes into some detail, and I gather something about finance, an office in a corner suite. Cody never needed luck. I hear the gas pump click as the handle pops up, letting me know the tank's full. Maybe thirty seconds have passed, but I jump as if it's been hours, as if I've just woken up.

"Stop." It sounds more abrupt than I'd intended. Cody pauses mid-word, looking at me with a blank confusion that leaves me stammering. "Sorry to interrupt you, but I really need to be going."

"Oh, of course. What am I thinking? Well, let me know if you need anything while you're around. Okay?"

"Thanks." My eyes tick between his boots and my exposed, muddy toes. "Sorry—I'm not really myself today."

"Nonsense," he answers. "You're still Felicity. We're friends, remember?"

"Sure." Apparently, no matter what. "Bye, Cody."

I listen to his footsteps and force a breath in that's more of a hiccup. Then, one more breath, this one better than the last, but still not good enough. When I breathe in and prepare to open the car door, I'm standing here looking right at Holly, and for a moment I think I must be in a dream where I'm a child again, because she's younger, too, and she's fixing me with that terrible, sad stare that says she knows I'm holding something back, but she's afraid to ask what. Holly reaches out to touch me. Her hand is cold on my wrist.

"What are you doing?"

The rain is blowing onto my hair and my face and I blink, the mirage lifting as quickly as it descended. Tess has gotten out of the car and she's standing in front of me.

"Sorry." I summon a smile. "Just lost in thought. Let's get going."

I slide into the driver's seat and turn up the heat on my toes.

"Okay, Tess, Frankie," I say, trying to rally. "Let's go home."

Frankie looks to Tess as if to ask her to confirm this information, while Tess is studying me in the rearview. I stare straight ahead, squeezing the steering wheel.

"What's wrong?" Her eyes are sharp, like a hunter. Like she knows she's seeing something I don't want her to see, and seizing onto it all the more for that.

"Nothing. I'm fine."

She glares back, and we both know I'm lying.

CHAPTER SEVEN

Now

I start the engine and pull onto the road. Evening is falling, and dusk here is all cast with shades of green and murkiness. Soon, a fog hangs in the air, clinging to the car like dust. We pass farms, great patchwork chunks of land, where they grow soybeans and cotton during the warm weather. They're a sight in the springtime, the cotton blossoms opening like tiny, buttery full moons, blushing to pink in just a day or two, the fields dotted with white and pink. I had forgotten until just now that those fields are the namesake for the diner where Holly worked. The Cotton Blossom. A few flecks of cotton puffs linger at the roadside, but this time of year, the plants are long past blossoming. At the border of the pastures, tall, swaying pines rise.

As we pass over a bridge, the pine forest gives way to looming dark cypress trees, inhabitants of the swampland. Their buttress roots stand taller than I am, extending from the water. Here and there, the cypress knees extend above the surface, outgrowths from the submerged roots that reach upwards. It isn't deep, in most spots, but the water is dark even in daytime, stained with the tannins of decaying leaves and wood. Sometimes, in sunlight, it has the look of over-steeped tea; other times, on a cloudy day, the water looks dark as night. I've always thought the name of our town, Brightwater, must have been intended as a joke. For those who aren't careful, it isn't difficult to fall in, into water deeper and trickier than you expected, or find yourself outnumbered amid the swarm of life that thrives in the swamp. The snakes and gleaming frogs; the innumerable insects and birds of all sizes; the open mouths of ghosts calling you down, just out of sight.

As I drive past the last cluster of pine trees, which seem to protect the house both from outside noise and sights, and over the tiny bridge that separates us from the mainland, it leaps into view as if to block my path. Seated on a bluff that reaches out into the water, the house is nearly a hundred years old, and looks more like it belongs somewhere in New England with all its bay windows. A house designed to breathe the air around it. Hardly practical for a place like this, prone to storms and floods.

A rooster crows, somewhere nearby, shockingly loud as it announces an arrival. Following the rooster, the chickens cluster around the car. Mom always called the chickens her alarm system. Glen, my father, had never permitted them. Two weeks after my mother finally put her foot down in an argument with him, he decided he had been miserable with us all along and needed to leave. I was seventeen, newly pregnant. My mother was too kind to admit it, but I've always known that my refusal to name the baby's father was part of why Glen left. And he didn't just leave: he moved across the country, and started a new family inside of a year. Mom bought four chickens that day, and from the looks of it, the flock has continued to grow. I crack the door open, then, hearing the din of their crowing, quickly pull it closed again. The rooster sounds more like he wants to chase us away than welcome us. Tess is unbuckling her seatbelt before I've even put the car in park.

"Pop the trunk," she says. "So I can get our bags."

"I, um—"

"What?" She opens the door, swings a leg out, and pauses. "You scared?"

"Why don't you go ahead?" I offer. "I'll bring your bags in."

With light footsteps, they hurry ahead of me, making a beeline for the door, stopping to greet the chickens that follow them up the steps. As I step to the ground and begin collecting suitcases from the trunk, bracing myself for the mud that squelches around my toes and heels, a couple of hens trot behind me, following me back up to the porch.

"Haven't you got anything better to do?" I mutter, cursing myself for not thinking to bring any more practical footwear. One of the hens pecks at my ankle. "Go on," I say, swaying my foot to shoo her away without kicking her. "Go lay an egg!"

The front door swings open when I turn the handle, and I remember my mother's perpetual habit of leaving it unlocked, hear a long-ago memory of my father's voice asking, *Who left the damn door open again?* The front corridor is dimly lit, the stairs to my right leading up into darkness. I put an arm out, give Tess a quick look, asking her to wait, walking ahead of them. The hallway dark. Living room, empty, the familiar shapes of the sofas huddled in the gloom. I'm not sure why, but even from here, in the dark, I've a sense that nothing about the house has changed.

At the end of the corridor, the space widens into the kitchen, occupying most of the first floor, frayed screen doors that open onto the screened porch. The lights are on, but the room is still, the open cabinet doors and cluttered countertops giving an impression of a freeze-frame. Only ashes and remnants of a charred log remain in the fireplace.

And then I see her, asleep, I think, in her seat in the corner by the table, behind a small mountain of knitting. Her dark, wiry hair hangs around the knitting needles as she huddles, but her hands don't move.

"Felicity."

I drop my bag, hands leaping up in shock.

"Mom."

She's not asleep. Just sitting there, holding her knitting, as if she wanted to catch me out at something. Her expression shifts, and I see what Dawson and Wendy made reference to. Her thoughts are faraway, unanchored. I feel my feet crossing the room, pause in front of the table.

"I came as quickly as I could." In response, my mother nods, her lips a firmly set line. Tess ducks under my arm and walks through the doorway, Frankie clinging to the pocket of her blue jeans. When my mother sees them, she rises to her feet, and the chairs and clutter that blocked her from my view seem to melt out of her way.

"Oh, thank goodness," she says, regarding Tess and Frankie with a warm smile that renders a hug unnecessary. "I know Aunt Wendy cares for you, but sometimes it's just nice to be somewhere you know, right?" She's a steady tick of motion, stepping halfway out the side door to fetch a piece of firewood, tucking it into the hearth with a light touch.

Resembling feral creatures that have suddenly been tamed, the girls sit on their knees on the worn tiles of the floor, while my mother strikes a long match and lights the kindling. "You sit by the fire," she says, "and I'm going to make you some dinner, and when it's ready I'll put on a movie for you. Your room is just as you left it." Frankie's smile glimmers up at her. The sharp tension of Tess's shoulders seems to soften. I'm sitting uselessly at the table, stunned into perfect silence. Where did this mother come from? She makes them grilled cheese sandwiches and cups of tomato soup, and I walk silently behind her as she shepherds them into the living room, tucks blankets over their laps, turns on the television. I wouldn't say the children look happy, but there's an at-ease satisfaction, their features lax, as they blankly watch the screen. When she sits down to watch with them, I turn and walk back into the kitchen, resuming my seat at the table.

It's nearly seven. I should be at home, finishing dinner, cleaning my dishes—I never leave dishes in the sink—getting ready to prepare my drink. It's been twenty-four hours since Dawson called me. My mother walks in and sits across the table from me, resumes her knitting.

"I know you didn't want to come back."

Whether it's an accusation or a roundabout thank you, she's correct.

"I would have done anything for Holly."

"That so?" My mother's eyebrow rises just a touch. "All you would have had to do was show up, and everything would have been fine. Just like it was."

"That isn't true." My hands flutter nervously, and I cross my arms.

"It is true, and you know it is."

Let her think what she wants. Convincing her otherwise would mean opening a series of overdue conversations, ones that I'm content to keep shelved for the rest of time.

"The police said something strange about Holly."

She lifts her eyes to stare at me.

"I mean, where they found her. She wouldn't have gone out there, don't you think?"

"I think you didn't know her anymore." Once again, she says the same words: "All you had to do was show up."

I have nothing to say in this moment that might fill its ringing emptiness. Holly was the one who could conjure a laugh out of silence, whose easy chatter could warm a room. As I sit in a chair at the kitchen table, the grandfather clock chimes from the hallway, sounding either eight or nine times, though it seems instead to be announcing that I'm too late.

"Is it all right if I stay here with them until I figure out what's going on?"

"What do you mean, what's going on?" she asks. "Holly left you custody of her daughters. Now you're home."

"That's not true." My voice cuts sharp. "And, more importantly, the girls don't know me. They don't want to live with me."

"Not in Saint Thomas, they don't." Her laugh is unkind. Her laugh has always left me with a sense that she thinks she's caught me in a pretense, that she wants to see me dismantled. "They want to live in their home, with their family."

"Of course they do," I say, my temper growing. "I know that. I work with children."

"You work with children," she echoes. "What do you know about family?"

"Enough. I know enough." My fingertips tap in a soft sequence on the tabletop. "So, Holly wrote my name in her will, and here I am. It feels like she didn't give me a choice."

My mother shrugs her shoulders. "You have the choice to decline custody and let the courts sort it out. Of course I'd take them. Holly knew that. And that Silas would help, if he could get into shape. But that's not what you want, either, is it?"

Damnit. She's right.

"Where do the children sleep here?"

"The blue room."

"Oh." It comforts me, unexpectedly, to think of the girls asleep in the bedroom with its twin beds that Holly and I used to share. Down the hall from there, my parents' bedroom, now only my mother's.

"The pink room is mostly storage now, but the bed is still there. Why don't you sleep there?"

"Thanks." I take another look at my mother's face and feel something twist in my chest, hurriedly stand up. "I'm going to—"

"Need a hand with something?"

"No. I'm going to take my bag upstairs."

In the living room, I pick up Tess and Frankie's empty plates. "What else can I get for you? Anything for dessert?"

"Grandma will get it," Tess retorts.

"I'll take your things up," I offer, practically begging for some way I can feel helpful. She nods without taking her eyes off the screen.

"Frankie," Tess says softly, bending close to her, "you look tired. I'll help you get ready for bed if you want." Frankie shakes her head mutely, refusing bedtime. I know too well how laying alone in a bed leaves you with just your thoughts.

The stairs creak gently as I walk up, the smooth wood of the banister seeming to rise to meet my hand. I drop my bag off in the guest room across the hall with its pale pink walls and return to the blue room, which, aside from a half-full laundry hamper and a cracked windowpane, is almost exactly as I remember it. I hold my breath and step through the doorway. As I place Tess and Frankie's bags on the bed, I stare around my old room, noticing with some surprise that it's hardly changed. Holly's posters, my photo of James pinned to the wall by my bed, my cheer uniform folded neatly on the top of the bookshelf. Holly had grinned at me when I made squad. She said ladybugs marry well. Got invited to the best parties. When I walked around campus in the uniform, people would whistle or call, "Hey, ladybug."

At the corner of the room, opposite the large bay window, the door opens to a bathroom, and I check that everything is in working order. I exhale sharply. It's then I hear the little footsteps on the stairs.

Frankie stands in the doorway yawning, her hands hanging at her sides.

"Hi, Frankie. You must be sleepy."

She watches me with unconcealed curiosity.

"Do you want me to help you get ready for bed?"

I don't even hear her feet against the floor, but she draws a step closer, still watching.

And though she doesn't speak, she leads me through her bedtime routine: turning expectantly for me to undo the button at the back of her neck, then extending her arms up for me to help her with the nightgown. Next, Frankie walks into the bathroom, handing me a hairbrush and elastic, then sitting at the foot of one of the twin beds, her back turned to me. After a moment passes, she looks back with an inquiring glance. Sitting behind her, I begin to brush her hair. It's fine and wispy, prone to tangles, though I know well enough how to brush it gently, as it's so similar to my own. I move to an armchair by the bay window, standing by as she brushes her teeth. When Frankie clambers onto one of the beds, pushing the quilt back with her toes, I move closer. "Do you want a story?" She shakes her head. "A song?" Again, no. "I meant what I said earlier, Frankie. I'm going to make sure that everything is okay." I should know what to say here. I've talked children through situations that make no sense many times before, but never children I was related to. "Do you have any questions, or anything you want to talk about?" With some finality, Frankie shakes her head once again, and points to the light on the table that sits between the beds.

"Okay. So, lights out." I click the light off, leaving a band of yellow light coming in the door from the hallway. "Grandma said I could sleep in the pink room. Call if you need me—I'll wake up right away."

I have a feeling I won't be sleeping much, but she doesn't need to know that.

CHAPTER EIGHT

Now

With Frankie in bed, I tiptoe back down the stairs, into the living room. The movie has ended; my mother is knitting, now in an armchair, while Tess dozes on the couch. She opens her eyes immediately when I sit at the far corner of the couch, near her feet. Everything in me wants to ask her if there's anything I can do for her. But, exhausted, I remind myself that she's twelve, that it's my job to know what to do.

"Maybe you'd like to come to bed soon," I say, holding a gentle eye contact with her. "Would you like anything else to eat before you go to sleep?"

"No," she says, then, sullenly, adds, "thanks. I'm not tired enough to come to bed yet. I will in a little bit." I nod and look over to my mother.

"What can I help you with?"

"Oh, nothing. I need to go round up the chickens before I go to bed. There's things that need doing," she continues, the needles clicking together, "even now, you know." Her voice dwindles and I sense her fragility.

"Yes, Mom. And I'll help you, if you just tell me what I can do." Maybe Dawson was right: she does need caring for. "You don't even need to tell me, okay? I'll clean up the kitchen before I go upstairs, and—"

She drops the knitting in her lap, glaring at me. "I'd like to keep my hands busy."

"Yes, of course."

She recedes, with a bustle and a bit of a resentful look, and I remember her insistence on keeping busy. I've heard people use the word *willowy* to describe her, but they're not quite right. Her expression, with her high forehead and our family's cheekbones, is unyielding. I think her beauty resembles more an oak, something firmer than willow.

"You could have visited."

"I've been busy."

"For thirteen years?"

"I called you to check in." I say this, and though it's technically true, I know it's a lie in spirit. I called to let her know I was still living, to assuage my guilt.

"Yeah," she says, gruffly. "Suppose you did. Goodnight, Felicity."

As I retreat up the stairs and into the cluttered guest room, I reflect that I'd like something to keep busy with, too. My mother needs a foil, not someone who takes things on the same way she does. Maybe that was why she tolerated Glen, despite his sour temper and tendency to yell at the television. He drew her out, into the world, in a way that Derek, a soft-tempered man the perfect opposite of my father, had done for me. The same way Holly did for both of us. For a moment, I consider calling Derek, craving his steadiness and warmth, before I realize how unfair it would be. Pacing around the pink room, I hum to keep from crying, then unzip my bag.

I take everything out of my carry-on, fold my clothes into the tall, narrow dresser. I take a shower, though I've never liked the smell of the tap water here, as if it came right out of the swamp. Which, probably, it does. Back when I was in school, I was always afraid I smelled like mud—I was fooling myself, to think I could ever really fit in. Holly and I were always the girls on scholarship.

Even when my school uniform was clean, there was never a damn day there wasn't mud on my shoes.

The clock in the downstairs entryway has chimed eleven before I hear Tess's footsteps up the stairs. With her in bed, I feel a gentle tick of relief, realize I'm tired, and begin to get ready for sleep. With the light off, the room is full of shapes, the stacks of boxes and stored furniture taking on odd forms, casting shadows that appear to waver. I'm reaching to turn back the covers when I hear the door creak behind me, and turn with a jolt. At first, I don't see anything, just the gap in the open door.

"Who's there?"

"I have a question."

Frankie stands barely taller than the level of the doorknob, and I draw closer, dropping to my knees so that I'm eye level.

"What is it?"

"Will you stay with us?"

"Yes, Frankie," I whisper. "I'm right here."

"No, I mean in the blue room. Tonight. I can't sleep."

"I would love to."

I follow her across the hallway and into the blue room, note Tess's sleeping form in the bed opposite the door. "You know, I'm happy to be here with you," I say, standing by as she climbs into the bed. "I'm so sad that your mom is gone. But I'm glad to be here with you."

"Me, too," she answers, watching me with a guarded eye. "Why is Mom gone?"

"Truthfully, I don't know." It never does any good to smooth over the worst of things. "I don't know, Frankie, but I'm so sad that she is."

"Are you sure?" Her little chin tilts back as she looks up at me from the pillow.

"Sure of what?"

"Are you sure she isn't coming back?"

"Yes, Frankie." It hurts, but lies in a moment like this hurt worse. I lightly sweep wisps of blonde from her forehead, tug the blanket up to her shoulders. "I'm sure of it."

"Tess doesn't like you."

"That's okay," I answer. "I'll be right there, in the chair. Okay?"

She nods and turns away, and I tuck the covers around her shoulders.

Settling into the recliner by the window, I swivel just a bit so it faces into the room. I can see Frankie's eyes on mine, then she blinks once, twice, and slips into sleep.

This armchair has never been comfortable, scratchy upholstery thinly layered over springs, so when I find myself yawning, my eyelids heavy, I know I must be several degrees beyond tired. I'm half asleep when a soft noise startles me. I think at first that it's a gasp, or a gust of air through an open window. Then, I see Tess sit up, the bed sheets rustling, move her legs to the floor. She crosses the room and reaches into the closet, to a hook on the back of the door, nearly obscured in shadow. When the door creaks, she starts visibly, one thin shoulder lifting in surprise at the unwelcome noise.

"Tess?"

"What are you doing in here?" Her voice is sharp, louder than I expected, and Frankie sits up in bed with a whine.

"I asked her to come in." Frankie's eyes water and in the low light, I see her small fists clenched tight on the blanket. "I couldn't sleep."

"Ugh." Tess turns from the closet, visibly forcing calm. "It's all right, Frankie. You can go back to sleep." She turns to me. "You can go."

"No," Frankie insists. "I want her to stay."

"Would you like to sleep in the pink room, with her?" Tess asks, still hovering by the closet. I begin to focus on her movements, sensing something guarded about her stance.

"No." Frankie's voice squeezes out in a whisper. "I want to stay here. And I want her to stay here."

Rising from the chair, I sweep a gentle hand across Frankie's forehead, then turn to Tess. "I'm sorry to have surprised you. When Frankie asked me to come in, I didn't want to wake you." I tilt my head and hazard another step closer. She cradles something in her arms, seems to be trying to fold herself in against it. "What's that, Tess?"

"It's—" Her eyes rise to meet mine, and I see her face settle, as if she knows she can't hide this, but refuses as well to discuss it.

"It's a purse, looks like?"

Tess nods.

"Your mom's?"

Again, a quiet nod. It takes an effort not to wrap her in a hug, to shield her from all these ugly questions.

"Hey, come here for a second, would you?" I gesture softly toward the door, then turn to Frankie. "Be right back, okay?"

Tess reluctantly follows me into the light. She holds the purse out as if she's not supposed to have it, but I don't reach for it, and it drops to the floor between us. I sit down with a sigh, and Tess does the same, her thin hands carefully opening the zipper, coming up with a handful of objects: a lipstick, Holly's ID, a car key.

"She always said she needed to be more organized," she whispers, then, with a furious look, upends the purse and gives it a shake, loose coins and cards clattering to the floorboards. I nod my head again, watch gently as Tess blinks, eyelashes wet.

"Tess, did your mom come home from the Thanksgiving party that night?"

"I don't know. I was asleep." Tess begins to collect Holly's belongings, one by one, and replace them in the bag, and I pick up coins and keys, handing them to her one at a time. She runs nimble fingers over each item, as if she could breathe her mother in.

"You knew where her purse was, though, right?"

Tess's eyes jolt to meet mine. "That's where she always puts it."

"Of course." I start to hand her a red-and-white-striped peppermint and she snatches it, the wrapper crinkling in her fingers, then leans over and sweeps everything toward herself, stuffing the items back into the purse.

"I meant what I said to you earlier. You can talk to me about anything. I'm on your side."

"And I meant what I said." Tess clutches the purse to her chest. "We're not going to be friends."

"That's okay. Listen, if you'd like your privacy, maybe you'd prefer to sleep in the pink room? Frankie asked me to stay with her, so I'd rather not leave her alone."

"It's my room, too." Her mouth sharpens into a scowl. "I guess I don't mind if you stay."

With this uneasy truce, we return to the bedroom. Tess places the purse on the bedside table before climbing back into bed while I settle into the armchair again.

And, though I feel the weight of exhaustion in my limbs, I can't sleep. Dawson didn't know where Holly went that night. Dawson didn't know that she came home, left her purse. And somehow, by that morning, she was gone. Drowned in the one place I know she would never go.

From the corner of my eye, I see a flicker of light from the window, and my attention is called to a half-circle grove of cypress trees a few yards off the shore. I stand up in the dark, trip over something, and grab the windowsill for balance.

Like a tall, skinny phantom with a spiderweb of stilts, the trees stand almost as if in conversation. I wonder, suddenly, the clock creeping toward three in the morning, was this what it was like, the place where they found my sister? In the cypress trees, beyond the old Ferris wheel? I hold back tears, watching her girls sleeping peacefully. I hear her voice again, now, as if she's right here: *We need to talk. You know we do.*

CHAPTER NINE
Before

Holly had always liked Cody Redford. Since junior year, he had been dating Page Winslow, who I knew from cheer squad. Page was regal, tall and dark-haired, and rarely laughed. It was an odd match, for her to be dating the boy who could make anything funny. I suspected Cody was drawn to her precisely because she didn't fawn over him. At a party, the August before senior year, Page screamed at Cody and threw her Diet Coke at him. People were a little afraid to talk to Page, leery as high schoolers are when it comes to scandal. But Holly, who was always braver than the rest of us, saw their breakup as an opportunity. *Tell James to tell Cody to hang out with us*, she begged. Enough times that I finally agreed.

Labor Day weekend, the last Saturday before our last year of high school, Holly and I had planned a quiet night out, and James had promised to get Cody to come along. Brightwater offered nowhere to party, not that I partied anyway, so we'd planned to meet for ice cream. I was nervous around Cody—too handsome, too funny, he seemed to glimmer like a mirage, with an energy that made me recede into myself, while Holly appeared to enjoy it. I thought he liked her, too, until he showed up at the ice cream shop with Page, turning a double date into an awkward group of five.

James and I retreated to a corner of the table, and my sundae dripped as I watched Holly. "He didn't mean anything by it," James said quietly. "I'm sure he just misunderstood." I nodded and agreed. Holly chattered brightly and joked with Page and Cody both, though I knew she'd taken Page's appearance here as some kind of challenge. Page followed me when I went to the bathroom, stopped me nervously by the sink. "Was this meant to be a date?" she asked. "He didn't tell me. I'm so embarrassed." I assured her not to worry, and we returned to the table. When my ice cream had melted, James and I stood up to leave, and I thought Holly would come along, as she had driven with us.

"Where are you two going?"

"Nowhere," I answered. "Probably out for a walk, then I'll go home."

"I have to be home early," Page added, turning a nervous glance to Cody.

"Oh, well, I wouldn't want to get anyone in trouble," Holly said, too kindly, her eyes sparkling. "I'm going to take one of Dad's boats out. To the fairground."

"Really?" Cody's eyes lit up. "I've never been."

"It's not safe," Page added.

"It's perfectly safe," Holly said. James nudged my foot with his under the table.

"Isn't it dangerous? Frightening?"

"It's beautiful," Holly answered. "And peaceful. You can take a boat to the old dock and then walk right in. So long as you watch your feet."

"What about the ghosts?" Page asked. "The Reverie Girls?"

I couldn't help but jump in. Out of all the silly things people said, this was one of the easiest to correct. "Page, there are no ghosts out there. I promise."

"If you're too scared," Holly said, speaking in a tone that was a little too sweet, "I don't blame you." She finished her ice cream and helped herself to a taste of Cody's. "What about you? Scared?"

He watched her with a carefree smile before answering: "No."
Holly turned her daring green stare toward Page for one wordless
moment, then broke into laughter. I don't think anyone but me
saw the look that passed between them.

"If nobody's scared," she said, "then we should all go."

I didn't like it any more than James did. I think we only went
along because we were worried about the other three. But once
we were there, in the comfortable, musical evening, we drifted
off on our own, first walking down the boardwalk, which was
still mostly sturdy, if coated with moss in spots, then across the
marshy ground to the old dancing hall. Inside the fading clapboard
building, vines and bird nests curled around the remnants of what
was once probably a beautiful room, a wide-open first floor, and
a balcony at the level of the second floor, wrapping around the
length of the wall. There was a piano, coated in dust, and a cracked
chandelier. I laid a fingertip on one of the piano keys, middle C,
and the whole instrument seemed to shuffle and cough a distorted
note back at us. Laughing, I sat down on the bench.

"Look what I found," James said, calling from one of the darker
corners of the room. He returned holding something between his
hands, approaching where I sat at the piano. He showed it to me, a
ladies' saddle shoe, the black-and-white leather coated in dust. I held
up my left foot and kicked off my sandal, waiting for him to slip it
over my toes, as if I were a princess who'd left it behind. A spider
skittered out of the shoe and ran across my foot. I kicked it free and
jumped to my feet, leaping into his arms. The space around us didn't
echo. It seemed instead to absorb our laughter, as if we were sealed
off in our own world. We walked quietly and solemnly around the
room, slow-danced to imaginary music, and it felt almost as though
the piano could have played a tune on its own. My cheek was nestled
against James's when I heard someone call my name, a sound distorted
as if through mist, or walls, or time itself. I stood upright.

"Did you hear that?"

"No," he answered. "Hear what?"

I waited for another several seconds, then eased back into his arms, into the promising warmth of shared daydreams. We told ourselves the same charmed stories we always did: our plans to go to school together, to move back here after finishing our degrees. We wanted to marry after college, and have three children. We had a long list of places we wanted to visit, but we knew we were already home.

Only a few minutes had passed when, with a sudden clatter of footsteps, Holly burst in through the doorway. The dance hall seemed to shudder around her, that quiet moment glimmering like a mirage before it vanished, and before I knew it Holly's hand was on my shoulder, pulling me away from James.

"What is it?"

"You have to come." She didn't need to tug me along, but she did anyway, moving with an urgency I didn't understand.

"What's wrong?"

Holly was never lost for words. When she didn't answer, I knew better than to ask again, following her with silent, tripping steps over the marshy ground to the boardwalk. There, she picked up pace, and I had to run to keep up. I nearly slipped when Holly took a sharp right turn off the path, dark water splashing around her ankles, and made her way to the Ferris wheel, which looked like an abandoned spinning top. Here she steadied her pace, moving heel to toe along rusted metal that groaned when I jumped up to follow her, my breath quickening.

As we crept along, the murky ground gave way to water. We weren't more than two or three yards above it, but my palms began to sweat. Finally, Holly stopped, and in the silence I could hear her ragged breaths. Cody sat hunched over where two metal beams met.

"I can't get to her." Confusion made his voice childlike. "Holly, she's—"

"*No*. She's here. It's not too late—we have to get her out." Holly turned back, our eyes locking as she knelt over the edge, preparing to jump. Beginning to understand, I looked down at the water, back to her, and nodded. I didn't realize I had jumped until I was already underwater.

Beneath the surface, the water was cold and—I felt it immediately—hungry. Sensing my sister's warmth behind me, I pushed in the other direction, both hands reaching forward, forcing my eyes open as if I could have seen anything in the dark. When my hand closed around a tree's root, I clung to it like a rope, pulling my body downward, waving my arms about blindly. Before long, I had to surface for air, rising back up with a kick. With water dripping from my ears, the sound of Holly's voice was distorted, but I heard that she was arguing with Cody. I heard his voice pleading with her to be careful. I couldn't make out Holly's response, but her tone, and volume, signified a refusal. When she disappeared beneath the surface once again, I took a deep breath and did the same.

It had taken Holly and me three minutes, at least, to walk from the dance hall out here. Which meant six minutes since Holly left. If Page had been underwater for at least six minutes, then… Suddenly, grasping for warmth in the murky water, it occurred to me to be afraid. That this could be a hopeless endeavor. But then my hands met something solid. I felt fabric and skin, and, as my lungs burned for air, wrapped an arm around a limb—a leg, I thought—and pulled.

Halfway to the surface, she slipped from my arm, and, still kicking my feet, I bobbed upward. I shouted—something—and took a desperate breath before going under again. The dizzying rush of oxygen buzzed in my throat, and, disoriented, I took in a gulp of water. But I couldn't lose a moment. I felt arms near mine, motion in the water. Page—no, Holly, her hand holding mine—no, I couldn't tell. I was pulled nearer, relief flooding my mind, despite the painful cough caught in my lungs. And then the grasp tightened, a cold two-armed embrace, pulling me harder. Downward.

Surfacing wasn't a conscious decision. I was breathing air again, kicking to stay afloat, one hand clinging to a weight that wanted to pull me down. Blinking water from my eyes, I saw my sister come into focus, only her face above the water.

"Let go," I managed. "She's too heavy."

"No. We can't leave her."

I looked up to realize that Cody was shouting frantically to us. I reached for Holly, for Page, unsure whose limbs were whose. My legs burned, and though I drew deep breaths, they didn't seem to be working.

When James pulled me out of the water, I could see fear on him, eyes wide, jaw tensed. Holly tried to push James and Cody both away, tried to go back in. I had to say it out loud for her to be still: "We can't save her now."

Cody called the police. As we waited for their arrival, I thought I heard him crying. Holly was silent, limbs rigid, and I could feel how badly she wanted not to give up, to tell the water to give our friend back. James wouldn't let go of me, his hand tracing my damp hair, my shaking shoulders. "I saw the three of you in the water," he said. "I couldn't tell which was who. I was so scared." He hugged me close. Sweet-natured, with a natural inclination to good manners, part of James's charm was that he carried himself the way those from money often do: he took it for granted that people would give him the benefit of the doubt, that they would assume he had pure intentions. In that way, Cody and James were the same, close friends as they were.

"Why was Page in the water to begin with?" I asked. Even on a perfect summer night like this one, it was hardly the place for a swim.

"We were playing truth or dare." Holly wept into her hands as she spoke. "I dared her to jump in, and she did. I didn't know she couldn't swim. I tried to get her out."

"I know you did." I leaned away from James to grasp her hands. "It wasn't your fault."

The eerie voice echoed in my ears, the memory of hearing my name called. When I saw the flashlights and heard the police calling for us, the relief I should have felt turned to guilt. My parents' warnings about the swamp, about the young women lost out here, had been wasted on me. But that was before I felt the weight of that dark water, felt how it wanted to take and keep us; would have kept all three of us girls if it could. I didn't tell James, but in that moment, I couldn't have told Holly from Page from myself. I couldn't have told him that there was a part of me, despite the air in my lungs, that still didn't know which one of us girls was lost, or whether any of us came out of the water in one piece.

CHAPTER TEN
Now

With Tess and Frankie in their beds, I try to make myself comfortable in the armchair. When the sound of their breathing is even and smooth, their limbs slack with sleep, exhaustion settles heavy around me. Outside in the mist, the mud across the drive shows a set of tracks, almost like a faded set of footprints. Without thinking, I walk down the creaking stairs, outside into the mud and place my feet over the blurred footprints. I look up toward the bay window. The window that gives a view of the recliner, just where I would be sleeping.

A cold touch brushes my hand and I whirl around to see my sister, her green eyes luminescent in the gray, moonlit night.

"Holly!" My voice twists in my throat, tears springing to my eyes instantly. Just as in my daydream earlier, her hand finds my wrist, a cold and tightening grasp. She digs her heels into the damp soil and pulls backward, trying to bring me toward her. I follow Holly for a few steps, her walking backward, the two of us face to face, until my heel slips and I realize we're at the edge of the water.

"No—stop." I wrap my hands around hers, rubbing to try to warm them.

Holly answers with a reproachful, injured look, one that warns of things unsaid. She tilts her chin out toward the swamp, then, slowly, back to me. Then, she repeats the motions. As if to say, *You, there*.

"Then tell me." When she tries to pull away, as if the shadowed swampland holds its own gravity over her, I hold onto her wrist. "Something's off—I can feel it. Tell me, please."

I realize I'm not awake, that this is impossible. A sudden breeze rushes around us, the kind that threatens a storm. Holly leans her face closer to mine, her wide eyes desperate.

"You told me you knew something bad had happened, Holly. Why didn't you talk to me then?"

But when I look at her again, I'm not standing in front of Holly but Page Winslow, her dark, wet hair clinging to her face. And again, I hear that voice calling me, the Reverie Girls, and it occurs to me that even all these years later, they have not forgotten my name. But I can't get my legs to move.

It's a nightmare. I toss my head side to side, pinching my arm, trying to wake up.

I'm supposed to be in the armchair in the blue room. Before I fell asleep, I curled my knees up under a knit blanket.

My mother's rooster is screeching, a loud, ungodly noise that makes me clench my jaw. I open my eyes, and I'm standing knee-deep in the water at the edge of the yard, curls of translucent algae clinging to my legs. Again, the rooster calls. Staggering backward into the yard, away from the familiar pull of the water, I stumble unevenly across the grass. At the sound of tires in the dirt drive behind me, I snap to, suddenly wide awake. I throw my arms out as if reaching for solidity, slip and catch myself on my hands, and then jump out of the drive, just in time to hear brakes.

It's a mail truck. The mailman hops out, chipper and in uniform.

"Ma'am, are you all right?"

"No," I answer, wrapping my arms around my body. "I mean, yes. I think so."

"Can I call anyone for you?"

"I'm Lucinda's daughter," I answer. "I—I'm visiting from out of town."

He nods, unconvinced. "I always thought this place looked haunted."

For some reason, this is the word that calls me into being fully awake. If there are ghosts here, I don't want to be counted among them.

I run back inside, my feet leaving muddy prints on the wooden stairs.

By the time the children are up, I've been awake for hours. We walk downstairs to find the house silent, along with a note from my mother, informing us that she's left for work. Tess and Frankie walk outside to greet the chickens, leaving me to cook alone. I watch them from the screened-in porch for a few moments. From across the yard, the rooster spies me and crows, as if an announcement of my presence here, my unfamiliarity, isn't the last thing on earth I want. I walk back inside, clattering around in the oversized kitchen as I try to remember where anything is. My mother's kitchen is spacious but disorganized, pots and pans hanging mismatched and doubled on the hooks above the big fireplace, food jumbled in the refrigerator. Mom has a way of conjuring up a perfect meal out of this chaotic room. It left me with a lasting impression that anyone who had a real talent for cooking didn't need organization. My kitchen in the apartment in Saint Thomas is always spotless. Throwing my hands up at the inscrutable jumble, I walk back outside.

"What can I get you for breakfast?" I call. "Anything you like to eat?"

"Grandma usually makes eggs and bacon," Tess says.

"And grits," Frankie adds.

"We could go out for breakfast," Tess suggests.

"Oh, I know," Frankie murmurs, tugging on Tess's hand. "We can go see Grandma at work, at the school. Please? It's so fun there."

"Fun?" I suppose it could be, for them, all those labyrinthine corridors, the shadows punctuated with a statue here and there. The spacious, portrait-lined halls. I could happily spend the rest of my life without seeing that place. "I'm afraid not, Frankie—but I'll do my best to make you breakfast here."

"Do you know how to cook?" Tess is scrutinizing me. My stomach growls, reminding me I skipped dinner yesterday. I turn to walk back inside and they climb the porch steps, following me in.

"I can manage eggs and bacon," I tell her. "I'll try my best with the grits. You want to watch TV while I get started? Maybe—" Wincing, I open the refrigerator. There's something so uncomfortable about using somebody else's kitchen. I think longingly of fresh air, fruit and hot tea. I continue to speak as I look in the fridge. "Milk? Juice? There's orange juice."

Tess nods; Frankie doesn't answer. I scramble, looking for cups or glasses. Tess smirks and, suddenly, I'm frustrated. I realize she knows where everything is. Challenged, unwilling to let up, I keep looking, opening every cabinet until I've found them. Hands shaking, I triumphantly pour two glasses of orange juice. "Here you go," I say. "I'll get breakfast together for you, and then—"

They're already walking off down the hallway. Big house like this, it's a good thing it's so old, because you can hear every creak, know exactly where a footfall lands—if you know the place. And I hear their footsteps, announcing to me that they're heading down the hallway toward the family room, where, I'm willing to bet, the exact same L-shaped corduroy sofa, threadbare cushions in spots, fills a small room, huddled around the television set. But then I hear a different noise, this one a footfall from upstairs. I look out the window: no cars here. My mother has left for the day. My childhood home is the last place I ought to feel this jumpy, but, for some reason, something chills my blood ice-cold. I hear it again and, this time, I know for certain. Someone else is in the house.

"Hey, you two?" My voice rises, suddenly thin and almost sharp. I check myself, softening: "Can you come back in here?" A moment passes. "Now, please?"

They walk back into the kitchen, eyes all questions. "You didn't do anything wrong," I say, hushing my voice. "Someone's in the house."

CHAPTER ELEVEN

Now

"Who is it?" Frankie asks. I raise my eyebrows and direct my voice to Tess.

"Does anyone else live here?" I ask. She shakes her head. We stand still as statues and I listen again. Footsteps, from the second floor, upstairs corner bedroom. My eyebrows rise at the same moment as Tess's, and I think we're thinking the same thing.

"That's the blue room," she says.

"What's going on?" Frankie asks. I give her shoulders a quick squeeze, trying to pretend I'm not scared.

"Someone's in our room," Tess repeats, her voice rising, with something like anger, or excitement, I'm not sure what. Suddenly, she shoots down the hallway, toward the stairs.

"Frankie." I drop to my knees and give her a quick, gentle squeeze, then lead her toward the closet in the back of the kitchen. "Can you please stay right in here and wait for me? Pretend we're playing a game? I'll be right back to get you, okay?"

"Stay in here?"

"Yes," I order. "Please. I'll be right back. I promise."

Once the door closes behind her, I take off after Tess.

"Tess!" My voice is louder than I expected, a staccato echo in these familiar, close walls. Despite the years that have passed, I make it down the hallway, turn a sharp corner holding the banister, and run up the stairs just like I used to, and pull again on the banister as I turn right and run down the hall toward the corner bedroom. I hear low voices in the bedroom, and in this moment I couldn't say whether they're ghosts or real.

"Tess," I repeat, reaching the doorway. "Are you okay?"

Tess stands near the writing desk in the corner. A man is seated in the chair, his back to me. They seem to be in some kind of conversation. Tess looks up at me and nods, but I'm already approaching, wedging my body between hers and the stranger.

"Who are you?" I demand. "What are you doing here?"

He's a heap of slumped shoulders, a wrinkled flannel, sad but sour brown eyes over a gritty expanse of stubble. I've seen him in photos. In Holly's wedding pictures, Silas looked a little like a backwoods 1980s rock star, long hair and muscle-bound arms, cutoff sleeves. Now he looks puffy, wrinkled. I almost didn't recognize him.

"I'm Silas," he says. "And I'm assuming you're Lissie."

"My name's Felicity." Felicity is a name I've always liked: four tidy beats, neither too sharp nor too soft, each consonant neatly rounded by a vowel. Lissie sounds like a little girl's name, someone easily swayed. He's tall, broad, easily twice my weight. When he speaks, the smell of whiskey hits me in the face, and something sets me on edge, arms crossed, hands curled into fists. "You didn't answer my other question. What are you doing here?"

"This was Holly's room." He hangs his head, and his eyes begin to water. I'm torn between empathy and annoyance. "I miss her. It still doesn't feel real. I guess I wanted to feel near her."

"Yeah, well, this was my room, too."

"Thing about Grandma's house," Tess says, grudgingly making excuses for him, "people who know her, they just kind of come over. She never locks the door. She wouldn't have thought anything of it if Silas came by."

"Dad," he corrects her, giving her a terribly needy stare.

"Dad," Tess says with a diffident shrug.

"Well, I still don't like it," I say. "I can't have people just showing up. Especially people I don't know."

"You don't know us, but we know who you are," Silas answers, his voice wavering just a bit. There's something I don't like about a man who's crying but also angry. Something that frightens me just a little. "You forgot about your family. It hurt Holly. She never gave up on you."

Tess glances sidelong at me, then away. It's apparent that she's heard these words before. Nonetheless, for her father to show up unexpected, worse, intoxicated, at ten in the morning—that I can't allow, no matter what they may consider normal.

"She's right. I deserted everyone." I hold my hands out as if presenting the world's biggest failure. Silas looks up at me again, huddled over his elbows, and I see resentment lurking there. "But I'm here because Holly asked me to be here." I answer evenly, neither aggressive nor backing down. Silas exhales and watches me, then glances around the bedroom again, clearly trying not to cry.

"Let's get you back outside." Just when Silas looks up at me hopefully, I'm finishing my sentence: "So you can get going. Are you—driving?" I ask. Silas shakes his head no, and gestures out the window at a little canoe that's tied up to the rickety dock.

"Of course," I sigh, looking at him with reproach, trying not to spell out too much in front of his daughter. "Well—not like that's much safer. But okay. You'll come back and visit, this evening, maybe. First, get some rest." He wipes his nose on his sleeve and nods toward an old photograph of Holly, pinned to the wall above the desk.

"She was proud of you." I hear Silas's voice interrupting my daydream.

"Why?" I scoff, an involuntary show of bad temper, the kind of thoughts I usually try to hide.

"She said you were tough," Silas answers. "That you had a heart that could see you through anything, as long as you would listen to it."

"She did see the best in people." I don't say it, but I'm afraid it's obvious that Holly was wrong about me.

In answer, Silas openly begins to cry. "All right." With both hands, I grab the chair and pull in a futile attempt to scoot it back from the desk. It doesn't even budge. "Come on, Silas. On your feet. Downstairs." Despite the firmness of my voice, I can't help it: I jump back a little when he rises to his feet, hold my breath rather than inhale his whiskey-laced body odor again.

The room still seems filled with the magic whispers of teenage girls, of secrets both shared and unspoken. I lead him down the hallway, down the stairs, leaving that haunted space behind us as if walking forward in time. Tess is lingering behind us. I stand a little closer to him, so hopefully she can't hear us. "You're their father, Silas, and I want you to be here, supporting them. But do not show up here drunk at ten in the morning. Your daughters shouldn't have to see that."

"My daughters," he repeats. "Where's Frankie?"

"I sent her to hide when I heard footsteps upstairs." It's probably clear enough that he's frightened me, but that doesn't mean I'm going to admit it.

"Hey," Tess says, suddenly sounding sorry. "Silas, we're making breakfast. Why don't you stay and have some coffee, at least?"

"Oh, well, I really couldn't…" He looks at me, waiting for my permission.

"It's no trouble." I try to conceal my frown.

"You wanna go get Frankie?" Tess asks. "I'll go in the kitchen and pull out the food and the frying pan."

"Would you really?" My face must show my relief; she gives me a hint of a smile.

I hurry to the hallway closet, where Frankie's peering out of the barely cracked door, waiting for me with a luminous, expectant stare. "So? Is she here?"

"Is who here?"

"Tess said somebody was upstairs," Frankie repeats, smiling. "Is Mom back?"

"Oh, Frankie." I bend down and swoop Frankie into a hug, rocking her just a little. "No, honey. Your Mom isn't coming back. I'm so sorry." She swivels her head around to face me, her smile receding, face slack.

"Am I in trouble, Aunt Lissie?"

I realize this must be how Holly and the family have referred to me: Aunt Lissie. Out of Frankie's mouth, it has a small-town ring to it, but a sweet one.

"No, Frankie. You're not in trouble at all. Listen, I have a surprise. Your dad's here to see you."

When she grins in response, I think I'm seeing her for the first time. She's all eyes and cheeks and that glowing blonde hair. "Daddy?" she yells, running past me and around the corner, not knowing where he is, only trusting he'll hear her voice and find her.

Silas greets Frankie, who seems overjoyed to see him, giving her a long, tight hug. I see her relief in his arms. I struggle through making breakfast until Tess offers to help. We serve the food and I reluctantly agree to eat a little. As the girls eat, I stare at Silas, not sure whether his tears are genuine, or exactly what they're for. He needed to feel near her, he says. That's why he came here. Sure, if I wasn't worried for our safety, it's innocent enough, but since when is it okay to walk into someone else's house just because you need to feel something? I'm relieved when he drains the last of his coffee with a sigh and rises from his seat without needing any prompting. He gives me a nod, as if acknowledging the uneasy silence here, and heads down the hall toward the front door.

"Felicity," he says, rubbing his eyes. "I'm sorry."

"It's—" *All right* was going to be next, but then I realize it really isn't. I rise from the table to follow him, choosing my words as I catch up. "I know I'm a stranger, but please let me know what I can do to help you."

"You?" He laughs, reaches to brace a flippant hand on the doorframe, misses it by about a foot. "If you could do anything to help your family, you'd have been here years ago."

"Regardless, please don't show up here like that again." I push the door open, ready to send him on his way, and then pause.

"Silas, the police said Holly went to a party the night she died. The Thanksgiving party at the diner."

"Did they?"

"Were you there?"

His eyes jump to mine, and I wonder if he's more sober than he's letting on. Tess is coming toward us in the corridor.

"Silas," I repeat, lowering my voice. "Were you there?"

"You want to do this now?" He nods at Tess, then turns his chin toward me.

"I—" I turn back to Tess, then Silas. He's so tall that he blocks the doorway. "I don't know."

Silas gives a warm, knowing laugh, as if I know the answer but I'm playing coy. "Another time, then."

The overly friendly, shrewd tone of his voice makes me distinctly uncomfortable. He calls goodbye to Tess and then walks with a rambling, uneven gait to the dock. I hear the water whisper around the canoe, and then he's gone.

I turn back to Tess, trying not to let her see the pity in my eyes.

"He gets paid every other Thursday," Tess says. "Plan on him being drunk until Monday or Tuesday. He'll come around and visit again after that, all cleaned up." Her eyes look blank. "One of us ought to go see him on Thursday. If he's going to get really sick or get himself into trouble, that's when it will happen."

"I suppose I might have overreacted. Sorry."

But Tess only shrugs her shoulders, as if to concede a small chance that I might have been in the right.

CHAPTER TWELVE
Before

From the street, St. Benedict's appeared as just a steeply pitched roof, guarding the spire that rose from the chapel. Behind a wrought-iron fence, over the gently crested hill, it yielded a quiet wealth of enchanting details. Holly and I had always loved the statue of the school's namesake, standing in the courtyard below the crossed gables of the main hall. The first day of school saw it humming with activity, the warm chatter of voices, the undercurrent of whispers, accounts of the accident mutating and spreading. *They were playing truth or dare. Someone said Holly dared Page to jump. Holly thought Cody was her date, until he showed up with Page. Of course she didn't want her there.*

I was no stranger to feeling like an outsider here, and following the shock of Page's death, the multiplying rumors seemed small and distant. At first. By lunchtime, my neck hurt from ducking my chin and pretending not to hear. Fourth period was art history, and, when the teacher paused to click to a new slide, I overheard a classmate, whispering to a friend from the desk behind mine. *I heard she pushed her. Sure, maybe it was an accident. But that doesn't mean nobody was to blame.*

In a streamlined motion, I rose from my desk, murmured an *excuse me*, and hurried out the door, a bewildered sob sticking in my throat. But instead of heading for the bathrooms, I crept down the corridor and through the exterior door. A chill passed over me, and I felt again the weight of the water that night. Holly had not spoken to me of it, and I understood nothing of what had happened, except that Page had died. Except that I was stuck in that moment where my own body and voice were indistinguishable from the others, alive or dead.

In the courtyard, I heard footsteps, and ducked into an alcove behind a stone bench; seniors were given a certain amount of leeway, but it would not extend to sneaking outside during class. When I thought the steps had passed, I walked into the chapel through a side door. From inside, the sunlight illuminated the rose window's colors with a glow that felt almost brazen. I sank to a seat in a shadowed pew, the multicolored light falling over my knees like a blanket, and folded my hands over my eyes. The flutelike whisper of that voice rang in my ears again, musical as it was insistent. I tried to calm myself by running my hands over my arms, tapping my knees. When I heard footsteps drawing near, I knew it must have looked as though I was in prayer, my lips moving, hands tracing the lines of my ribs, trying to find proof that this body belonged only to me, finding none.

"Hey, Felicity."

"James?"

He sat an arm's length away from me, and a searching look bounced between us, each unable to look at the other, an invisible fear crowding the space between us.

"I saw you pass by in the hall."

I nodded my understanding.

"I guess—maybe you wanted to be alone. Sorry." Again, he paused, all but pleading with me to speak to him. "Are you—"

"Oh, I—I'm all right." I rubbed my hands along my arms to warm them, but my fingers were just as cold. James's eyes, deep brown, widened with what I recognized as hurt. He knew I had lied to him. I closed my eyes against my tears and turned my chin away. I didn't know how to tell him the truth, which was that my sister had barely spoken to me since that night. That I was afraid of what she might say if she did. Could those rumors be true? We had always talked late into the night after bedtime, but since Page, she slept facing the wall, her back to me, a chill of reproach deepening the distance between our beds.

When I felt James's hand on mine, I seized it, still facing away, holding tight until it warmed my own. He inched closer, laid an arm around my shoulders.

"Tell me how to help." His lips moved close against my temple, and I let myself lean into him. "I don't know what to do, Felicity."

"I wish I knew." The response came out sharper than I meant it, and I pressed closer to him in apology.

"I love you." He spoke as if it were an offering, as if it were the wrong currency but all he had to offer. "For whatever it's worth, Lissie. All my heart."

"I love you," I answered, my courage warming. "Everything will be okay."

"They'll be looking for you."

"You're right." Still holding his hand, I got to my feet, wiping my eyes. "I need to go back to class. I guess you do, too."

We crossed the courtyard together, then parted ways, back to our respective classrooms. If only I could have read my sister's thoughts, I was certain I could fix the distance between us. After returning to my seat, I tuned out the art history lecture, putting together everything I could remember from that night. I had spoken of it with James more times than I could count. He didn't know any more than I did—he'd been at my side that entire time. I resolved to find a moment to talk with Cody Redford, who must have seen whatever passed between Page and my sister. But Holly was the only one, I knew, who could have told me what I'd done wrong. We had never had to guess at the other's thoughts, any more than we would have considered hiding anything. But now, where I had used to look at her and see everything I knew and loved reflected back, I found instead a condensed, threatening silence.

CHAPTER THIRTEEN

Now

On the second night, I'm exhausted enough to sleep clear through, despite the rooster and the lumpy armchair. My mother wakes early and prepares breakfast, and she is already dressed for work by the time I walk downstairs with the girls. Tess prepares a plate for herself and one for Frankie: oatmeal with butter and raspberries for Frankie, along with a glass of chocolate milk. For herself, she takes only a bowl of raspberries, then announces that they'll eat their breakfast on the porch, leaving me with nothing to buffer the silence between me and my mother.

"Did you sleep well?"

"Well enough." I wince as the rooster shrieks outside. "I slept through that, apparently. That rooster is dreadful. I thought they only crowed at sunrise."

"That's Elvis." Her eyes find mine immediately. "And he's letting me know there's someone new here."

"Elvis?" I can't help but smile, trying not to laugh. "Well, he's no Elvis Presley, but he is very loud."

"No need for an alarm clock, with him around." She glares at me across her coffee cup. "Or an alarm system, for that matter."

"That reminds me," I interrupt. "Silas came by yesterday. Not in great shape. Were you expecting him?"

"It's Silas," she scoffs. "He's fine."

"Is he, though?" I ask. I remember the bulk of his form, the glimmer of fear I felt when I smelled the whiskey on his breath.

"Of course he is," my mother says. "Silas is a big puppy dog. A big, broken, drunk puppy dog."

"He seemed off."

"Everybody seems off to you," she scoffs. "He's the girls' father. So, he's flawed—a flawed father is better than none."

"Speak for yourself." My mother has always put her trust in men who didn't deserve it, has always expected me to trust them with her, regardless of the cost. Maybe that hasn't changed.

"Silas is nothing like your father, Felicity." Her mouth twitches, and one eyebrow lifts. "Plenty of children grow up longing for a father. Normal children would have been happy with him. Holly was."

"I guess you're right," I agree, picking at my memories of him as if they could reveal something new. Showing up was the start and end of what we were allowed to expect from Glen.

"I put my foot down with him," she insists. "I took your side."

"You took Holly's side." *Too late for it to mean a thing to me*, is what I don't say. "There's something else I wanted to ask you about. The police officer said they never found her purse."

"Oh?"

"It was in the closet."

My mother shrugs. "Maybe she went to the party without it."

"I'm wondering if she may have come back home that night."

My mother lifts her big, sharp eyes, the green gaze cutting right through me. "I don't think so. I was asleep."

"I can't stop wondering," I admit. "I can't imagine Holly would have gone to the fairground, for any reason. They found her near where…"

"Don't say it." My mother's voice lowers to a hiss. "You should know how painful it is for me to have to hear about that night."

"For you," I answer drily. "Of course."

"You and Holly should have never taken your friends out there. Your father and I always told you to stay away from the fairground."

"That was years ago, and it's over. I need to know what happened to Holly. Why was she out there?"

"You had all these years to patch things up. Where were you then?" My mother rises from her seat and puts the coffee cup, half full, in the sink. "I'm going to work. I'll be back this evening."

"All right," I nod. "Have a good day."

Once she has left, the kitchen feels both too large and too close, crowded with memories, and I'm anxious for fresh air. Walking outside to join the girls on the porch, I sit in a rocker. "How does a change of scenery sound?"

"Yes, please," Tess mumbles.

"I was thinking we could go out for lunch. I'd like to see the diner where your mom worked."

"Oh, Frankie loves going there." Tess smiles, the corners of her eyes tilting up prettily, before she remembers that she doesn't like me. "I mean—yes, that would be fine."

"Perfect. We'll leave in ten minutes, if that sounds okay to you."

I turn back inside, pour water over the fire to extinguish it, and go to collect my purse and car keys. My mother is too lost in her grief to be of any help. And Silas may not want to tell me anything about the night Holly died. But I'm going to find someone who can. Besides, this house feels like it breathes memories in and out, old conversations and whispers teeming around me. And I don't think I could stand to be here for another minute.

Outside, a gentle rain has picked up. I'm guarding my eyes with a hand as we walk to the rental car, but the girls seem almost not to notice it. Unbeckoned, an image of my sister's body in the water flashes across my mind, and I imagine my hair turning slick and green, as I gratefully open the car door and duck out of the rain.

"Scared of rain?" Tess mutters. "You're not going to last long around here."

"I'm from here," I remind her. "I lived here longer than you have. I just—don't like it." As I turn the keys, I hold my breath, remembering the prior engine malfunction, but it starts without a hitch.

We drive down the narrow, tree-sheltered road that leads back into the middle of tiny Brightwater, holly and pine trees crowding the road with their fragrant and shining greenery, turn right on a bridge over the creek. After parking, we hurry to the door in the chilly rain, ducking under the red-and-white-striped awning. The door of the red-brick building jingles shut behind us. A boy who looks high school age comes to take our order, and he greets Tess quietly after introducing himself as our server.

After the girls have ordered their food, I excuse myself, asking Tess for directions to the restroom. It's on the other side of the restaurant, and as I walk through the dining area, I try to picture Holly here. At work, walking between the booths, with a smile that made everyone feel special. The restrooms are down a small corridor just past the bar. I try to picture her as she was that last night, and draw a blank. I don't even know what drink she would have ordered.

The hallway that leads to the bathroom feels claustrophobic, low ceilings hung with holiday decorations. Had my sister stood at this same sink, glared into this same mirror? But it shouldn't hurt like this, to see the plain truth of how little I knew about her. Page's death, and those dreadful weeks that followed, put a daunting distance between us.

At the corner of the corridor, I pause before returning to the table, pretending to glance at the television above the bar. Nearly every seat at the bar is full. And, save for one woman who broods over a cup of coffee, the small crowd seems so at ease that I almost feel I've walked into someone's living room. Could any of them have known Holly? When a commercial ends, one man nudges another's arm with his elbow, lifts a finger to point to the screen. I soon gather why, seeing the banner of the local news station beneath a photograph of Holly. In the snapshot, she turns a brilliant, candid smile to the camera, and one of the men watching whistles.

"Excuse me. Would you mind turning it down?" My voice is lost in a chorus of subdued exclamations, friends shushing each other to gesture at the television. Though I try to catch the bartender's eye, she is also trained on the news.

"Turn it off." I take a step closer, casting a frantic glance toward the table where Tess and Frankie are seated. Where they ought to be, only now I don't see them. Years have passed since I felt this sting so clearly, the sensation of speaking and being unheard that spurs my pulse.

"In a sad conclusion to an event that's shocked the small town of Brightwater, Holly McDaniel's death was ruled accidental."

Before the news announcer says another word, I've walked behind the bar, located the black cord running along the wall below the television, and pulled it from the outlet in a tightly curled fist. The bartender turns abruptly toward me.

"I asked you to turn it off." I take a few quick breaths, press my lips together between my teeth. I did not want this audience: all these faces now turned my way, curious more than annoyed. And, beyond the row of bar stools, eyes wide with shock, is Tess, holding her sister's hand. I offer the electrical cord to the bartender as if returning a stolen object. "Nobody was listening to me." I draw myself up, raise my chin, and cross the room to put my arm around Tess.

"We were coming to check on you." For the first time, she doesn't shrug away from my touch.

"I'm so sorry. Let's get out of here."

But now, all those faces have turned, their gazes following me across the room. "I thought that was Holly at first," one of the men says.

"Her sister," the bartender answers in a lowered voice.

"The cheerleader? No way," he answers with a tipsy smile, his eyes following me. "They could almost be twins." I wonder now if he was the one who whistled at her photograph. My hand tightens on Tess's shoulder.

"Would you be quiet already, Chris?" The woman with the coffee raises her voice, close to tears. "You are disgusting, you know that?" She swings her feet to the floor, then closes the space between us. Just when I think she's heading out the door, she drops to her knees and wraps Frankie in a hug.

"I am so happy to see you girls." She stands up and gives Tess a meaningful pat on the shoulder. When she looks to me, I see that she's struggling not to cry.

"Why don't you come sit down with us?" She nods and I steer her back toward our booth, where I offer her a napkin. She blots at her eyes while Frankie scoots close to her on the bench, leaning quietly against her arm. Gathering that she was a friend of Holly's, I decide to give her a few minutes to collect herself, turning protectively away from the rest of the crowd. When the bartender approaches to place the woman's coffee on our table, I'm half afraid she's going to ask me to leave.

"I'm so sorry." She pauses, clears her throat. "I guess you must be Felicity."

"Yes."

"If I'd had any idea Holly's children were here, I—"

"I'm not a child," Tess adds.

"I would have never had the news on if I did. And I'm sorry about Chris. He's a creep, but he doesn't mean any harm."

You never know that for sure, though. Not until it's too late. Absorbing my glare, the bartender gives an empathetic nod, as if to agree with me. "Anyway, we didn't mean to ignore you. Everyone here loves Holly."

"Thanks."

"Your food's on the house." She pats the table with some finality, then turns and walks back to the bar. Across the table, the other woman is looking mournfully into her coffee.

"I'm Kendall." After drying her eyes once more, she reaches across the table to shake my hand. "I've known Holly for a long time. Knew. We worked together—here, actually—back when I was in grad school."

"Kendall was our first babysitter," Tess offers. Kendall nods.

"It's good to meet you." I can't help but feel a pang of jealousy, greeting a stranger who probably knew my sister better than I did. Frankie offers Kendall a share of her apple pie, and while they talk quietly, Tess and I exchange a wary look. I can feel her sizing me up, and imagine the picture she's painting, based on what we've seen of each other. My lack of preparation for the weather here, showing up in sandals. *But I left in a rush*. Making a fool of myself at the gas station. *But I was so worried the car was unsafe*. Storming behind a restaurant bar to unplug a television. *But I couldn't bear for them to see their mother on the news*. It isn't Tess's job to know or care why her estranged aunt acts so oddly, even if it's because I care so much for her, in a way I don't even understand. Tess kicks my foot softly under the table. I gasp and look up to see her smiling.

"You're not so bad, Aunt Lissie."

"Thanks."

It's only after we've finished eating, as Kendall is walking us to the car, that I remember what I heard the newscaster say. Holly's death, ruled accidental.

Kendall hugs each of the girls as they get into the car, promising to see them soon, as the doors close. She smooths her dark hair and gives me an apologetic look.

"It's so nice to meet you. Holly talked about you often."

"Thanks."

"I promise you, I'm not usually at bars midday. I guess I wanted to be somewhere that reminds me of her. I kept thinking I'd see her walk around the corner."

"You don't work here anymore, though." Before Kendall can trail off again, I tilt my head, leaning against the car as we talk. "Right?"

"Right."

"So, you wouldn't have been at any staff parties, or anything like that. Right?"

"The Thanksgiving party. Yeah, of course I was. Those things were basically open-door, if you knew anyone who worked there." Kendall looks back toward the restaurant, her voice growing wobbly again, as if she's left something inside.

"So you were there?" Resisting the urge to snap my fingers to keep her attention, I find a packet of tissues in my purse and offer it to her. She nods her head, then straightens her jacket as she steps back from me.

"Yes. I should go."

"Please, wait." I catch her hand and hold it gently, then lower my voice. "You know, don't you?"

"The news report, just now—they said it was an accident." She still won't meet my eyes. "I suppose I should be relieved."

"You know that something's wrong."

"It's only a feeling." Her whisper is haggard, and she pulls her hand loose, crossing her arms. "When Holly left the party, she had plans to meet someone."

"Who?"

Kendall wipes her eyes again, then her hands flutter open, no answer. "When Holly didn't want to talk about something, there was no point persisting. But I know that she was going to talk with someone else that night. The way she spoke about it, I assumed someone was meeting her at your mother's house."

"Who else knew about that? Was her ex there?"

"Yes, but they argued and he left early," she answers, eyes glassy with tears. "They seemed really upset. She stormed off—he tried to hold onto her wrist, and she pushed him away."

"He held onto her wrist?" The photograph of Holly flashes across my mind: the mark on her wrist, beneath where that bracelet had rested. "But then he left? Who was she meaning to talk to later?"

"I couldn't say if it was him she meant to speak to." She takes her phone from her purse and checks the time. "I did tell the police about all of this. I should really be getting back to work."

"I understand. Just one more thing—do you have any pictures of her, from that night?"

Kendall sniffles and nods, swiping through her photos until she lands on one of Holly. In the photo, Holly doesn't look like she's about to die. She's smiling her brilliant smile, laughing at the camera as if to say, *Put that down*. And, just as I knew I would, I see the same purse hanging from her shoulder that I found in the closet, the silver charm bracelet around her wrist.

"When somebody dies, they always say 'she lit up a room,' or whatever. But Holly really did." Kendall withdraws her phone and wipes at her eyes. "I really do need to go now. I'm so sorry for your loss."

"Thank you."

I open the car door and sit down, apologizing to the girls for keeping them waiting. As we head toward home, the words from the news broadcast linger in my thoughts. But I know that my sister left that party and went back home. And that she argued with Silas that night. Could they have arranged to meet, to resolve the argument? And why didn't Silas want me to know he was there?

The more I hear, the less likely an accident sounds. I picture Holly as she was in my dream, the one that had me sleepwalking into the water. How she looked out toward the swamp, almost like she wanted to show me something, to pull me out there with her. As if she didn't care that it frightens me. As if she wouldn't know, every bit as well as I do, the cold hunger that waits beneath its surface.

CHAPTER FOURTEEN
Now

All the drive home, Tess is quiet. Her eyes are round with worry, lips pursed, and I can sense a difference from her usual, too-cool silence. In the rearview mirror, I catch her eye for a brief moment then look back to the road. She knows I'm here, for whatever it may be worth. No sense asking her what the matter is.

"It's Thursday." When she finally speaks, she seems to expect I should know what this means. "Will you go over and see Silas later?" I can see how difficult it is for her to ask this, to ask anything of me.

"Oh—right. Yes, I'm sure I can do that."

"Frankie should stay here." She looks at her younger sister as if gauging how much she can say without frightening her. "I could, if you want, just—"

"No worries, Tess." Despite my very real worries, I nod and smile. "I'll go after my mom gets home from work, and you can stay at the house with her and Frankie."

She watches, as if waiting for me to add a condition or take it back, then gives a single nod and falls back into quiet.

"Are you talking about Dad?" Frankie asks.

"Yes, Frankie." I steer carefully around a wide puddle on the road. She leans over and whispers to Tess for a moment, who gives her a reassuring look and addresses me again.

"Grandma promised to get a Christmas tree next Friday."

"Mom said Dad could come over to decorate the tree with us," Frankie adds. "You'll let him, won't you?"

"It's not up to me," I answer. "Your dad can come if you want him to."

"It is, though," Tess observes. "You're our legal guardian. Doesn't that mean you could say no, if you wanted to?"

"I promise, I will not go against your wishes."

Tess isn't convinced. "That's a pretty big promise."

"Your dad will be there to decorate a tree with us next week, even if I have to go and fetch him myself." And not least because I intend to make him tell me exactly what happened the night of that party.

As we drive across the bridge, the house coming into view, I sense something different. Tess, too, is craning her neck, looking out the window.

"Where are the chickens?"

"Who knows," I murmur, relieved as I step out of the car with nobody clucking and pecking around my ankles. As we're walking toward the house, I see them, the flock clustered around the edge of the yard, where the pine trees grow closer together. Their clucks are murmurs, and something gives me the impression they're alarmed.

"Go on inside, okay? I'll catch up." When they've walked in the door, I hurry over. The chickens don't scatter as they usually do, a few of them turning to me almost expectantly. Something's quieter than it ought to be. It's then I see the rooster on the ground in the middle of the huddle. Instantly, my eyes begin to water, as they always do upon seeing a dead animal of any kind. I bend to pick him up, trying not to focus on the warm dampness on my hands. Elvis might have had natural predators around here: foxes, dogs, even hawks. But his body is surprisingly intact. The sound of my car could have scared off whatever animal killed him. It makes enough sense.

Except for this, the thin elastic around his limp neck. And attached to it, the small embossed gift tag. *To: F.W.*, printed in block letters.

To F.W. *Felicity Wheeler*. The *from* field is every bit as blank as my mind, except for the impulse to get inside and lock the door. I tug on the elastic until it snaps loose amid a flurry of tiny feathers.

I'm walking numbly toward the back porch, rooster in hands, when I hear my mother's car on the drive. She hits the brakes in the driveway right in front of me.

"What happened?" She leaves her car idling and walks out to meet me. "Is he hurt?"

I stretch my arms out and offer her the bird. "I'm sorry. I found him this way."

"You what?" She looks at me and back to the rooster, then snatches him away. Inspecting the body, she clicks her tongue. "Poor thing," she whispers, voice strained, hands gentle.

"I'm really sorry, Mom."

"Why?" She lifts her eyes from the animal to look at me. "Did you—"

"I found him like this." I can smell the swamp, hear its whisper. Whatever, whoever killed the rooster could easily be watching, listening to us right now.

"A fox, maybe?"

"No." I reach into my pocket and feel feathers under my hand, lift my eyes to my mother's numbly. "Somebody did this."

"Somebody," Mom echoes, eyes narrowing. "Did he get under your car, or something?"

"No!" She trusts me less than she would trust a perfect stranger. Her arms fold around the animal as she turns away from me. "Somebody—I found—" Grasping for the gift tag, I pull at the lining of my coat pocket until it turns inside out, coins and receipts scattering in the breeze. Sinking to the ground, I part the scraggly grass until I see the damp ground beneath it, but find nothing. My mother is watching me with growing suspicion.

"You said you didn't like him."

"I didn't say that," I answer, trying to keep my tone even, though the implication offends me. "Somebody did this—on purpose."

"You said he was dreadful."

"I only said he was loud! I'm so sorry he's dead."

"He isn't!" My mother's eyes light up with a purely irrational glow.

"Mom."

"He's alive." She hurls this announcement at me, daring me to disagree with her, then, with the bird in her arms, she turns away from me and stalks across the yard. As her footfalls land on the steps, across the porch, and in through the door, I look outward, to the trees and their shadows, wondering if anyone is looking back.

My gut reaction is to let her go, as I always have when her emotions are this high. Glen would have gone after her, calmed her down somehow. But she and I don't have that effect on each other. With swift, even steps, I walk over to my mother's station wagon and turn off the engine, then close the door.

Tess and Frankie are seated on the porch swing, side by side. My body itches to run back into the yard, dig through the grass and moss, even the thickets at the boundary, until I find that note. Or, better, whoever put it there. But their expressions are so tranquil, so accepting. For two children to see a dead animal, practically a pet; then to see an outburst like this from one of the adults meant to look after them, ought to prompt shock, or at least dismay. Unless they're accustomed to adults whose moods are unpredictable, to avoiding their bad temper.

"I'm really sorry you two had to see that." I sink into a wicker chair across from them and draw a breath. "She's upset, not only about Elvis. And I'm so sorry you had to hear me raise my voice."

Their eyes flutter up toward me, then away, Frankie staring at her hands, Tess looking right through me.

"None of it is your fault. None of these problems should be your problems." I grasp at several thoughts, not one of them coherent, my hands moving meaninglessly in small gestures. "And, Tess, I haven't forgotten about going to see your dad." Tess's mouth scrunches into a half-scowl. "Would you two like to look at my photos from Saint Thomas?" Frankie nods her head, and, encouraged, I continue. "It's very pretty. I have the pictures on my iPad. Would you like to come upstairs with me?"

She trots after me as I move toward the door, and I notice with a faint glow of relief that Tess gets up to follow her.

Tess and Frankie curl together in the recliner and I unlock the iPad for them. They scroll through my photos, talking quietly to each other about the beaches, the architecture, the beautiful, swaying palm trees. Once they've settled in, I begin to feel I should check on my mother.

I had forgotten how brightly the daylight streams in on the second floor, with windows along the hallway and in all the bedrooms. When the windows are open, it feels more like being in a treehouse than indoors. But as I reach the end of the hallway, I see that my mother's room is darker, the curtains pulled shut. I knock at the door, then peer in.

"Hi, Mom."

She gives no sign of having heard me, and I see she's huddled over the rooster's body, tears on her cheeks, face frozen in a twisted attempt not to weep. I approach to sit next to her, but when she startles and draws back, I sink to the floor and sit cross-legged instead, chin propped in my hands.

"You can cry. I don't mind." She huffs a sigh in response, and I let myself absorb her anger, pretending I'm at work, dealing with someone else's impossible situation. "We don't have to talk about any of the rest of it. I'd rather we didn't, really." She lifts one hand to her mouth and covers a sob. "Whatever you're feeling, it is normal." When she finally looks at me, I sense betrayal in her expression, though I'm afraid I might be projecting it. These are words I've spoken to strangers, no less applicable here. "I should know the right thing to say, I know that. I'm not what you want." That's always been true. Suddenly, I'm veering hard back toward impersonal. "But I am here to help, for whatever that's worth."

"They said I didn't have to identify her in person, but I had to do it."

"I understand."

"It wasn't like I thought it would be," she says, stroking the rooster's mussed feathers. "They told me to expect her to look different, that she'd been in the water for some time. So I went in expecting something hard to recognize. My God, Felicity. Then I was just looking right at her."

"I only saw a photograph," I tell her. "But it made me feel the same. I can't imagine—"

"Whatever you think of your dad, it would have been easier if he were there." She sniffs loudly and leans her chin back, blinking. "Give me a few minutes to calm down, and I'll come back downstairs."

"You don't have to calm down." I know this needs to be said to grieving people, but part of me hopes very much that I find a reason to walk out soon.

"I want to have a regular evening, as much as we can." She turns her eyes down to the rooster in her arms. "He's dead, isn't he?"

"Yes," I answer gratefully. "If you like, I'll help you bury him. It might not be a terrible thing for the children."

"You're good with them."

I catch her eye briefly and look away. She can't expect me to thank her, to take this as some kind of earned praise. When I was a pregnant teenager, digging for something hopeful in an unbearable situation, she was the first to let me know she didn't have any faith in me.

"We'll bury him, then. I'll get an old sheet from the dresser in the pink room." I quickly stand and walk to the door, then turn back over my shoulder. "I want to hear you say you know I didn't hurt your rooster. Even if I had hit him by accident, I wouldn't have lied about it."

Her focus solidifies as she watches me from her seat on the bed. "I know you didn't. But don't pretend you don't have a knack for holding back part of the truth."

"I didn't." My hand tightens on the doorframe. "That's all I want you to say. I can't stay here if you think I'm a—"

"Of course, Felicity." She answers me with a dry, removed chill that's somehow dismissive and accusatory both.

"I'll get you a sheet for Elvis."

I walk back into the guest room where my few belongings are unpacked, then open the dresser, trying to remember where I saw the extra linens yesterday evening. The top drawer is full of papers and old books, one of which catches my eye. A yearbook, from our last year in school. There are a couple pictures of me, from football games, mostly, and one from school spirit day. I flip to the extracurriculars section. By the time this yearbook would have been delivered, I was long gone, living in Chicago by that point. I remember placing an order for one, early that fall. That's why I've never seen this picture, of me and James, lingering at the edge of the field after a game. I remember the way he used to tilt his head when he was about to kiss me, smiling that special, only-for-me smile, like he thought he was the luckiest person alive. Like he thought I was special. I close the book and stuff it back into the drawer, fumbling through the other drawers until I come across an old bed sheet, faded white cotton with a yellow floral print.

When I return to my mother's bedroom, she's adjusting her hair, looking into the mirror.

"I'll be coming downstairs in a moment. I'm going to make a roast for dinner."

"Thanks." Wincing, I pick up the rooster's body and wrap it in the sheet. "I need to go somewhere, if you don't mind. Will you keep an eye on Tess and Frankie for me?"

"Yes," she says. "Where are you going? Visiting old friends?"

"No," I answer, stifling an impulse to laugh sharply. "I don't have any friends here anymore."

Maybe I never did.

CHAPTER FIFTEEN

Now

After years without practice, I expect the canoe to be tricky, but I find I haven't forgotten how to balance my weight as I step in, how to hold the paddle in my hands. Leaving our yard, the boat slushing through the thick water and grasses, I skirt around the edge of the lake, where it's a bit easier to navigate, then to the canal. The houses are small here, built to withstand flood after flood, some just painted cinderblock, some adorned with a screened porch. One of these houses belongs to Silas, but I don't know which. Farm fields to the west side of the water are low, tender, their grass bright, soft green despite the season, verdant with frequent flooding. Outside one house, a radio playing country music disturbs the stillness, the quiet rush of water noises around me.

I tie up at a tree and splash through the last eighteen inches or so of water. My feet slosh through the shallows and I press forward, slapping the marsh grasses and cattails out of my way as I step onto the shore. Walking down the strip of land that borders the backyards of these houses, I try to guess which house might be his. Before I can choose one, I hear Silas calling me.

"Can I help you?" His voice beckons to me from two houses down. I nod and hurry over to him.

"I came to talk with you about the other morning." I see his house isn't one of the concrete boxes, but an almost sweet-looking

little house, seafoam-colored shutters against siding that was probably once white, now stained with moss and age that's got it close
to the same shade of green. Of course, I realize: this was Holly's
house, too. This was Tess and Frankie's home. Until something
came between them, and it wasn't.

"Who are you?"

"Silas, we met already. I'm Holly's sister."

"Oh," he says, scratching the stubble on his chin. "Oh, sure.
Lissie?"

"Felicity."

"Okay," he says, nodding, taking a little too long to absorb this
information. "Is everybody okay?"

"You tell me." Against my will, an inkling of empathy draws
me to notice the sadness in his eyes. "Tess wanted me to check
on you, after how you showed up the other day."

"I'm struggling," he answers plainly. "It isn't something I hide."

"I trust you're all right now?" His complexion seems normal.
Hair's clean enough. His clothes look reasonably kempt, and he's
not noticeably drunk, although that doesn't mean much.

"The hell's that supposed to mean—am I all right? My wife
just died."

"Well, pardon me for intruding, but Tess wanted me to make
sure you're not dead or in jail, and I'm not exactly thrilled to be
here, either."

"Huh." He reaches an arm behind his shoulder, scratches the
nape of his neck, as if he's sizing me up. "You want to come inside
and talk?"

"Okay," I answer, halfway between curiosity and politeness,
though I make little effort to be friendly. The screen door opens
into a mud room, then a carpeted, wood-paneled family room.
I follow him into the kitchen—patterned linoleum and aged
cabinets—and sit across from him at the table. When Silas leans
his elbows on the tabletop, it looks like doll furniture.

"I can tell you're here on a mission," he says. "What is it?"

"I told you," I answer. "I came to check on you."

"I hate that Tess is the one worrying about me."

"Me too. They need you," I remind him, considering he seems to have forgotten. "Whatever you're going through, this is worse for them than it is for you, and they're my concern now as well. So…" When I speak, the words seem to knock the breath out of him, and he looks up at me from beneath that heavy brow, his eyes teeming with feeling.

"So?"

"So how do I get you help? If I find you some resources, will you—"

"I'm trying." His voice is low with resentment.

"I know. And you're the only person those girls can call a parent." He's nodding, messing with his hair. "It's not enough for a father to just be around. If that's the best you can do, you might as well quit trying. They need your support, Silas."

"Do you think I don't know that?" His fist hits the table and I see he's trying to scare me off. As if he's desperate to get me to stop talking.

"Okay." I look off to the side, taking a survey of the kitchen counters. A negotiating softness creeps into my voice. "I'm here to help. That's all."

"So why'd you come?"

"What?"

"You can go back and tell Tess I'm still breathing. Could have done that ten minutes ago. Why are you here?"

"I told you, it wasn't even my idea." I cross my arms and focus on the little window above the sink. "Tess asked me to check in—"

"Tell me why you're here, Felicity Wheeler." He unwinds the syllables of my name with a lazy precision, something too close for comfort about the sound of it.

"I don't—"

"You don't know?" Silas scoots his chair back and stretches his legs, long enough to block the door back into the entryway. His question hangs between us until, with a flinch, I realize he's right.

"You were at the party."

"Go on." He lowers his chin and watches me intently.

"You were there, and you fought with Holly, and you left early." I begin to stammer, sensing he already knows what I'm about to say, unable to stop myself asking.

"You came here to ask me, with that prissy stare, where I was the night my wife died." Eyes watering again, his voice goes thick and tense, the noise of an animal who's grabbed something and doesn't want to let go. "Like it's any of your business. I came back here, fell asleep on the couch. Woke up wondering where Holly was, why she didn't come back to me yet. Like I always do."

Maybe he's already talked with the police. Maybe they have reason to know that what he's told me is true, that he came home and stayed at home. Or maybe not. But something convinces me to drop the subject for now.

"You haven't talked with anyone about losing her, have you?"

He doesn't answer me.

"It's good to, you know, process your emotions. But I'm not the person you need here."

"You're not kidding." He laughs unkindly and sprawls forward in his chair. Without meaning to I scoot my chair back from the table a bit. "Processing emotions? You know, I can tell when people don't have a damn clue what they're talking about."

"What do you mean?"

"You're so uptight, you look like you haven't processed an emotion in over a decade."

Sucking in a quick breath, I find I'm standing up, shuffling toward the door. He shakes his head and sits up straighter, a conciliatory gesture, but I'm already moving.

"I don't like the way you talk to me, Silas."

"Felicity! Take a breath, come on." He lets out a great thunder-clap of a laugh, as if we're friends. I wish I could hit him, imagine throwing my small, sharp fist against his big chest. "Did I scare you somehow?"

"No." As if it's something to laugh about, as if a woman needs a reason to be scared in the house of a man she doesn't know, someone who slams tabletops to make a point and smells of liquor.

"You know, there's something not right about you." I recoil as he speaks.

"I need to get going."

"Oh, yeah. You definitely know it." He's using a friendly tone, as if he's joking. I'm hurrying toward the door before it occurs to me to say goodbye.

"My mother's getting her Christmas tree next Friday. Frankie asked if you'd come by."

Silas doesn't answer. Standing in the entryway, the kitchen is just out of sight, and I have to take a step closer to lean my head around the doorway. With a faint ticking noise, I feel a soft breath from the empty space behind me, a shout frozen in my throat, recoiling from the smell of whiskey that lingers in the room. And then I see him, still sitting at the table there.

"Did you hear me?"

"Yes," he says. "Thanks. I'll be there."

"Take care," I tell him. "Please. They need you."

"Take care yourself." He lifts a hand to wave goodbye. "You look like you've seen a ghost."

CHAPTER SIXTEEN

Now

Through another sleepless night, I pace around the house, afraid to go to sleep and wake up somewhere strange. The sound of Silas's laugh echoes in my ears, fueling an argument between my thoughts and gut instinct. He didn't act as though he had anything to hide—did he? But his voice, his look—there *is* something wrong about him. A flicker of motion catches my eye, and I pause in the downstairs hallway to slide open a window, lean out into the cold, fragrant breeze.

I don't trust him.

Then again, that doesn't mean much. Whatever mechanism people have that balances instinct with thought and context—mine's calibrated all wrong.

Before sunrise, I go outside to collect eggs from the chickens, taking the basket my mother keeps by the door. By the time anyone else is awake, I've started a fire in the hearth and prepared a full breakfast. When my mother sits down at the table, she takes one knowing look at me before her eyes soften with sadness.

"I know how you feel, Felicity."

"I'm fine."

She shakes her head gently. "I'm the same way, remember? I understand."

We are *not* the same. She's emotional and unpredictable. I'm the practical one here.

"I'm not going to tell you to try to rest," she continues. "Goodness knows, trying to wish that feeling away won't help you. Why don't you go out for a drive?"

"I don't know."

"That antique store you and Holly used to like is still open. There's a new café next door to it. A change of scenery might give you a little comfort."

With the rest of the house still quiet, I realize that my options are staying here with her, continuing to avoid conversation, or following her suggestion.

"I think I will go out. Thanks."

The car starts smoothly, though as I drive toward town, I can't shake the fear that it is only waiting to break down at the worst possible moment. With a touch of amusement, I realize that my mother was right: to see different sights, breathe different air, it's a relief I didn't know I was craving.

The oppressive haze of guilt, of exhaustion, of the paths my thoughts have trodden these last several days, seems to thin, and by the time I park the car outside the antique shop, I'm feeling almost human. In the adjoining building, a converted warehouse, is the new café my mother recommended; the facade of the antique shop, though, is welcomingly unchanged.

As the doorbell jingles behind me, I call a greeting to the clerk, who doesn't seem to take much notice. I soon lose myself in the aisles of shelves, laden with beautiful trinkets and decor, each item carrying a secret history. A stained-glass lampshade in an exaggerated, art deco style in the shape of a peacock sits next to a stack of lifestyle magazines dating from the 1960s, the fanned covers showing women with haunting, darkly made-up eyes and shift dresses.

A stuffed rabbit with glass eyes perches on a shelf next to a carved ivory and wood pipe, still stained with old ash. It's soothing, always has been, to imagine where all these items came from, whose hands may have touched them. After admiring an old dollhouse, I spend several minutes in front of the bookcase. These days, books are available to many people easily, and that's, I think, what matters, but it doesn't change the fact that the books of my grandparents' generation are more beautiful than any printed today. And the fragrance of them—almost like vanilla. I run a finger along the spine of an old edition of *Doctor Zhivago*, open it to find an inscription on the inside cover. *To my dearest Olga, on our second anniversary. Yours, Ed.* It's dated September 29, 1952. It's impossible not to wonder who would give this as an anniversary present; if there's any story that promises only ruin to people who fall in love, this is the one.

With the book resting in my hands, I turn and walk toward the checkout counter, wondering whatever happened to Ed and Olga. I pay for the book, still caught up in the feeling that I'm in a carnival of other people's memories. But I have to stop once again, on my way out, to admire the jewelry counter. I don't wear jewelry, but I love the bold yet delicate shapes of the mid-century pendants and earrings.

"Oh," I whisper, entirely without meaning to, leaning close to the glass case to admire a pair of ruby earrings set in filigreed silver.

"Need anything else?" the woman at the counter asks.

"No, thank you. I don't wear jewelry, but these are just lovely. Oh, and there's a—" My voice stops working, suddenly. The cashier walks over, reaches into the glass case, her hand hovering over the earrings. "These ones?"

"No." I point a finger and trace just to the right of the rubies.

"You look so familiar, for some reason."

"Couldn't say why. I don't live around here," I tell her, pointing into the case again. "That one. Could I see it?"

A silver bracelet. It's out of place here, neither vintage nor finely made. Just an ordinary charm bracelet.

"This one? Are you sure?"

I nod my head. "It's just like my sister's."

She drops it into my hand, and that's when I see the charm with our initials.

Just like my sister's? It is my sister's.

"How long has this been here?" I lean closer, then step back and look anxiously at the aisles around us. "Where did it come from?"

"Can I see?" When she reaches for the bracelet, my hand instinctively tightens on it, before I relinquish my grip. "It doesn't have a tag—but, you see, sometimes the tags slip off." She nods down at the jewelry case, and I see she's right: there are at least half a dozen loose inventory tags.

"This shouldn't be here."

"What do you mean?"

"It belongs to my sister."

"Yesterday was very busy," she answers, eyeing me doubtfully. "Anyone could have dropped it in the shop, and I might have placed it in there by accident. But I must admit that the inventory can get a little disorganized."

My impatience tempers as I hold the bracelet in my hands, tracing the engraved charms with my fingertip. This is Holly's bracelet. I'd recognize it anywhere—wouldn't I?

"That's it." The shop assistant takes a step back with a satisfied smile. "I've seen you on the news. That's why you look so familiar."

"You've seen my sister on the news, because she died two weeks ago. This bracelet has been missing since that night."

"I'm so sorry." Her voice drops to a whisper. "I really wish that I could tell you more."

I look at the bracelet in my hand, close my fingers around it. "How much?"

"Take it."

Still staring down at the silver links in my palm, I walk unevenly out the door.

If someone hurt Holly, why not just let the bracelet disappear into the water? Or hide it somewhere? Why leave it in a display case?

Unless someone was meant to find it.

At a stop sign, I dial Dawson's phone number. If he brushed off my worries before, surely he'll listen now. But the call won't connect, the phone service unreliable as always out here. Reminding myself to call him later, I drop the phone on the seat and continue forward.

CHAPTER SEVENTEEN
Now

Later in the afternoon, we hold a meager funeral for Elvis. He's too big for a shoebox, so we bury him wrapped in the flowered sheet, the soil soft underneath him. More rain fell overnight, and the ground is scattered with damp leaves, but I pace back and forth, beginning to wonder if I imagined that gift tag, tied to the rooster's dead body.

I watch the girls carefully as my mother places him in the ground, invites them each in turn to speak, to drop a handful of soil over the tiny grave.

"You always knew when somebody was coming," Tess says, unusually solemn. "And you always let us know about it." And did he sound his screeching alarm, right before someone walked up to this very yard we're standing in now and broke his neck—or did they?

Frankie tells Elvis that he was a very pretty bird, then turns her eyes to Tess as if to question that she's said the right thing. I'm shocked when my mother looks to me, clears her throat.

"Um. Elvis. We didn't know each other long, but thank you," I manage, "for the warm welcome." Tears rise up in my throat again as I try to imagine what I would truly say to Elvis, if I could. All he wanted was to peck around the yard and raise hell whenever he heard someone coming. All he wanted was to look out for us, and the last thing he heard me say was, *Be quiet.* Resolutely, I purse my lips until the threat of tears subsides. The version of me that permits myself these feelings would weep endlessly.

And if Elvis was killed, on purpose, by somebody who left him with my initials written on a gift tag, then how will I know if they come again?

Maybe practicing rituals of loss isn't a bad thing here. They're all eyes, even Tess. Maybe death is less of a horror when we can admit it's not a stranger. After the rooster is buried, the girls scamper away and begin to kick a soccer ball back and forth. Of the two of us, I think, my mother is more uneasy in silence. She always speaks first.

"Why were you so sure somebody killed him?"

"I thought I saw something on him, but when I went back to look for it, it was gone."

"I see." Her response is a frown of concern, a familiar expression that feels like a threat. Sometimes, when people say they're worried about you, what they really mean is: *You're wrong about things. I don't believe you.*

"Holly's bracelet was at the antique store."

"Felicity, be careful. You feel things so deeply—sometimes you get lost in that."

As if I don't pull myself back from that edge several times a day. When I glare, my mother gives me a maddeningly knowing look.

"You don't believe me?" I take the bracelet from my pocket and hold it out in my palm.

"That could be yours, you know. Yours looked just the same." She barely even glances at it, her expression unchanging.

"It isn't mine. I lost mine years ago."

In response, she sighs sharply, as if I have wounded her again. "You never liked that bracelet as much as Holly did."

"I'm trying to tell you something, Mom. I wish you'd listen." But she is measuring me against an idealized version of myself, so focused on my failure to be the daughter she wanted that she cannot hear or see me, even standing this close. I shake my head and stare out at the water, unwilling to jump into another round of having my senses, memories, feelings, marched out and interrogated, as if they have anything to do with her. I had seen the gift tag so clearly. Held it in my hand.

Like anyone else, my imagination grows louder, darker, when I haven't slept. I have the common sense to know when to dismiss what my eyes tell me: an imagined slip of paper, a pale hand beneath the water. *Right?*

"Is it all right if I take the canoe out?"

"Yes. Why?"

"Just want to clear my head."

She's still nodding as I walk down the dock and ease into the boat. Maybe my imagination does push its boundaries, try to create something more real. But why does that only happen here, and nowhere else on earth I've ever been?

CHAPTER EIGHTEEN
Before

The days and weeks passed quickly, with no regard at all for my inability to make peace with what had happened to Page Winslow. Or to this new version of Holly, who spoke largely in furious, silent stares. I didn't need to ask her out loud to tell me about that night, about what I wasn't there to see. There was no doubt in my mind that she knew I wondered, that she read my awkward silence, my fear of the answer, for precisely what it was. Though, to my relief, the suspicious whispers and stares over Page's death subsided, as gossip always finds a new target.

On an October morning, I brushed past Holly in the hallway as she left the bathroom, headed back toward our bedroom.

"Hey."

"What?" I swiveled to face her, certain I'd misheard. "Did you say something?"

"Yes." She gave me a reckoning sort of stare, looking closely at my eyes, her gaze skimming over my body. "We always get our period at the same time."

"So?"

"So, we haven't had to buy tampons since September."

I had shrugged it off. We were out of sync in a dozen other ways, and this one seemed only another symptom of the distance growing between us. But then, later that day, as I tried to hide the fact that my cheer outfit no longer fit properly, I realized it could also be another kind of symptom.

On a day when my mother was working late, I drove to the next town over and bought a pregnancy test. I couldn't risk using it at home, inviting disaster by trying to hide it in the trash. I carried it to school, hidden in my backpack, the second Friday of that November, which I recall because it was the last football game of the season. My plan was to use the test and then hide it in the trash in the locker room, before the game. I wasn't surprised when it was positive. A sense of dread rushed on me, paralyzing. I felt suddenly light, knocked sideways. I took a quick account of everything that would break under this weight. I skipped over one particular question, never even asking myself if I wanted to have a baby. Instead, my thoughts had leapt immediately to a kind of preparation, as I considered what it would mean to tell my parents, to tell James. Of what it would mean for my college plans. In a rush, I left the locker room to catch up to the rest of the girls.

And, in what might have been the first truly unexpected turn of events that night, our team won. It wouldn't be long before my mother was there to pick me up, and I hoped she was alone, so that I would have a chance to talk with her before facing my father and sister. On my way back to the locker room to collect my backpack, I had to cut through the courtyard, through a crowd of students. I ducked my head, made for the side of the crowd. There was no hope of talking to anyone alone here. I caught James's eye—it was easy, because he was taller than almost everyone else, and started to wave a hasty goodnight. He didn't smile back, instead lifting his eyes to mine with a worried half-frown. The sound of voices around me dropped to a hush, though I heard a few whispers: *Oh, look, there she is. That's her.* One of the cheerleaders took my arm and pulled me aside. "I'm so sorry," she said. "I only meant to pick up your backpack to bring to you. It just fell out."

"Oh." For a moment, I stood stupidly, arms crossed, looking around at the kids I'd gone to school with for the last four years, as well as a few from the opposing team's school, all listening with unmasked curiosity. Without another thought I dodged through the crowd to James. He drew me close to him and looked around with an unassailable glare.

"Anyone care to say that to my face?" he called, his tone half joking, half warning. With a few uneasy laughs, everyone fell silent. "Ignore it," he said. "Idiots. It's someone's dumb idea of a joke."

"Come on—I need to talk with you." When I reached for his hand, he drew back as if he thought I'd hit him. "Don't listen to them." I was certain that we were above this, the stupid way that children joked with each other, misunderstood each other. "Look at me, please."

I began to hear whispers around us, like pebbles hitting me in the back, and wished I had snuck away quietly when I had the chance.

"You know she's on scholarship? Her mother's the lunch lady."

"Oh, he does *not* look happy."

"James, please, let's go. I want to talk to you." I raised my eyes to his, too shocked to move.

"So it's not yours, James?" A small group of his friends had gathered around him.

"Not a chance," another girl answered. "They were waiting for each other. At least, that was what she told him." I could see that he was swayed, the shock of what he'd heard next to the embarrassment of a spectacle pulling him further from me. To my left, I heard someone laughing: *Immaculate conception, then? Yeah, right.*

"James, please." I tried to hold his gaze, as if I could pretend it was just us.

"Is it true?" Voice jumping up a note in shock, his eyes swept around the courtyard, landed back on me, as if he had sought an answer and failed to find one. He leaned closer. "Felicity, were you hurt? What happened?"

Again, I couldn't answer, lowered my eyes to the ground. "I need to talk to you," I repeated. "Not here. Alone. Please. I can—" I saw the spark in his eyes before he spoke, saw that he was hurt before he was angry.

"You can explain that you slept with someone, but not with me?"

"James, please."

"Can you tell me it's not true?"

I couldn't tell him that. Nor could I add anything else.

"Felicity, how could you?"

My eyes closed in a long blink against a swarm of responses, each one more impossible to say aloud than the one before it.

"Ladybug," I heard a whisper. "More like bedbug." Then, from further back, a huddle of kids from the other team picked up the familiar singsong: *Bedbug, bedbug, fly away home*, in a tone that was almost soft, as if it wasn't meant to be overheard.

"Say something." My ears were ringing with shock, so that I could barely hear the words I whispered to him. "Say something, *please*."

He only stared, keeping back from me as if something about me were contagious. I knew him better than this. I knew he was kinder than this, than watching me stand here with my eyes burning as everyone tossed insults at me. But maybe that moment changed both of us: my readiness to expect the best, his impulse to trust. He could have made it stop. He could have agreed to talk to me alone, even if only as an excuse for us to walk away from the crowd.

"Let's get out of here, Fin. Don't let anyone make you say something you'll regret." Cody appeared at his side, stepping in between us. He was James's friend before he was my friend—I knew this—but it hurt nonetheless. James's gaze tracked toward Cody, then back to me. "Ladybugs will break your heart if you let them. And let me tell you, they know money when they see it."

James gave me a final, pained look, and then turned away toward Cody. "Yes," he answered. "I guess you're right."

"Come on, man. Let's go."

Cody blinked and nodded at me as they turned away. In his way, this was the greatest kindness he could offer. And, for the first and maybe only time in my life, I was grateful for his ceaseless stream of ready jokes, for the distraction it provided. But it was the last thing I needed to shove me into a gasping, breathless shock, standing with my arms crossed and chin down, hoping by some miracle to be transported or vanished. I waited until James was out of sight, still hoping he might turn back. "You know Fin's a catch," someone said. "What a whore. Sad, really, but I don't think girls like her know any better."

When I saw my mother's car on the far end of the parking lot in the pickup circle, I stood up as straight as I could, pulled my hair back into a ponytail, and walked away all the straighter, calmer, for the mean whispers I heard behind me. I sat down in the car with a sigh of relief.

"You don't have your bag." As my mother spoke, the shape of her eyes changed, and I could see that she knew something was wrong.

"No," I said, tears in my eyes. "I'm not going back."

"Don't be silly," she said. "Go on—it won't take long."

"I will not."

It was the first of many moments when I decided it wasn't worth going back to get something, fled a scene empty-handed. There was no point in trying to hide it from my mother. I saw her first reaction when I told her the news. Before anything else, she wanted to help me. But she wouldn't spare another word until we got home, where she summoned Glen from his seat on the couch to follow us into the kitchen. He pretended he'd misheard me, so I had to repeat, *I'm pregnant* three times. He thundered a series of one-word questions—*when, who,* and so on—until finally he figured out that I wasn't going to answer, his massive hands squeezed into reddish fists. I waited for my mother to interrupt his tirade. When she wanted to calm him, she used a special tone, clear and soft as spring water. But she said nothing, and my silence only seemed to further irritate him.

Holly had crept into the doorway, where she stood in the shadows, looking at me from behind their backs. It was as if she was looking at a mirror, her eyes so unquestioning.

Look at me when I'm talking to you, Glen said. *Do you know how ashamed your mother will be, when she has to go to work? Do you know how hard she worked for you to have access to a good school?*

Even if I could have told my parents, I wouldn't have. All my life, I had overheard Glen's jeers at the television, the particular bile he reserved for any woman news reporter. He dismissed women with short hair or shoulder pads for appearing less feminine, then turned the same animosity toward any women on the television who, by his measure, were too exposed, "dressed like whores." Logic suggested that any woman with a microphone constituted a personal attack. Once or twice, Glen had railed about what he would do to any boy who hurt me or Holly, but I sensed he had been picturing a man with a knife in the bushes. If I told him the truth, I knew what he would ask: *But are you sure? Why were you there in the first place?* Most of all, *What were you wearing?*

"Felicity, what are you going to tell James?" my mother asked.

"It isn't James's baby."

"Tell the truth," she demanded. Her eyes watered, and she glared straight at me, as if she wanted me to see her cry, a gesture that felt inexplicably violent.

"I am."

"You are not. You're trying to protect him."

Her mind was made up, and arguing my point further would have, by some irrational magic, pushed her further into her belief that she was right. Instead, I wondered, my thoughts a dull hum, why she had always trusted me less than Holly. Was it because I tended to be quiet, where my sister was more open, more giving of her thoughts? Suddenly, it was plain that Holly had always been more lovable. Staring past my mother and Glen, I raised an eyebrow, held my breath as Holly met my eyes. She shrugged, turning away to study the floor, as if to say, *What do you want from me?*

My features smoothed into a removed, mild frown. It was plain enough that I was the only one of them who had any control over my emotions. Except for Holly. From the shadowed doorway, she studied me silently.

If James had listened, he would have understood. I made a show of going to bed early, changing into my nightgown and pretending to sleep for a few hours. Under a bright half-moon, jacket and rain boots over my nightgown, I paddled the canoe silently out from the dock, away from the tangle of trees, across the shining, still surface of the lake. The Finley house was all birchwood and windows, a series of steps leading from the dock up toward a patio. I bent to the ground and scooped up a handful of tiny pebbles, damp and moss-tangled, and tossed one at the right-hand window on the third floor. My aim was always dreadful; it dropped against the otherwise spotless patio with a muffled click. But the light was on in James's room. Squinting in the dark, I could see that the window was cracked.

"James?" My voice was scratchy with crying, my breath blossoming out around me in the chilly fog. I chose the smallest pebble in my hand, pulled my right arm back to try my aim again.

"Felicity, stop." James's mother was on the patio, a pashmina around her shoulders over a dressing gown that moved in the wind. She was so beautiful, with short, dark hair framing her luminous eyes, wreathed with laugh lines. She had always been kinder to me than I expected. Now, she walked down those steps, to where I was standing in the mud, and stood barely an arm's length from me.

"I need to talk to him."

She shook her head sadly. "You need to go home." Her voice was kind but unyielding, just the kind of tone you'd expect a protective mother to take. "He told me what happened."

"But I—"

"Felicity, maybe you don't understand. I'm trying to raise a family here. My children—" She trailed off, and I saw for the first time a depth of suspicion behind the kindness in her face. She glanced down at my body, and I remembered I was wearing my nightgown. For an adult to leave the house in their nightclothes means something other than when a girl does so by accident.

"I understand." I crossed my arms tightly against the cold and turned to leave. "Goodnight."

She watched as I left, giving me a sense she thought I'd try to sneak in and steal the silverware. I held myself up straight, stepped into the canoe as if I were weightless, and closed my hands on the oar. It was only as I was pushing off from the dock that I saw James, silhouetted against the window, so quiet I hadn't even known he was there. His silence felt like a meteor hitting the ground, what had once lit up my sky now fragments sunk deep in my mind.

I couldn't bear to go home yet, steering across the lake, into the dark of the swamp. Cypress and ash limbs seemed to drape close around the canoe in the dark. Still, each branch, each curtain of vines somehow yielded to let me through, inviting me deeper into their midst. When I passed under the rusted beams of the Ferris wheel, I willed my breath silent, praying that the voice that summoned me once would do so again, my lips shaping the form of the word *please*.

The answer, though silent, came sharp and cold. The numb persistence I'd clung to, that had kept me afloat for weeks, disappeared into sadness. What was left that I could count on? How had I been so wrong about everything? At the edge of the canoe, the water lapped dark and thickly, and, whether imagined or not,

I glimpsed a pale form just inches beneath the surface, that could as easily have been a branch as it could an arm or an ankle. I saw a body beneath the water with waving, open arms, as if welcoming me down, to where my loneliness could be gone forever.

A jolt of fear woke me from my stupor. My mournful reflection stared back at me, ghostlike. The water was hungry. People always said that girls disappeared out here. I didn't need to wonder why, or how. I turned and headed home as quickly as I could, through foliage that seemed now reluctant to let me through, to let me back into the open air.

CHAPTER NINETEEN
Now

I use the oar to nudge past the tangles and plants of the swamp, find my way out to the canal. Before I know it, I'm heading to the old fairground, tugged forward by memory, or curiosity, bending toward it as if I have no choice. I could say that I need to see it, to lay eyes again on the place that has haunted me, that came so close to claiming me for its own not once, but twice. But the truth is that I need it to prove something to me. The darkness of the forest, which seemed so conscious, so ravenous, had made me believe, once, that I'd seen impossible things. Now, with my daydreams and anxieties blurring into my waking life, the place calls me to confront it once again. I'll walk right through the heart of it, in the light of day, and I'll know, for certain, that it's nothing but mud and water. That whatever I saw and felt here were only products of a traumatized imagination. Sometimes, under immense stress, people can glimpse something that isn't entirely real. Like a holiday gift tag on a dead rooster.

I tie the canoe up and take my chances on the boardwalk, which used to offer a beautiful, peaceful walk, so long as you minded your step. This, too, is even less steady than it used to be, and I walk heel to toe along its right side, the left edge sagging toward the water, rising and falling with my steps as though I'm walking over its ribs, its lungs. But I'm not scared. Even though

I have to say the words aloud: "There's nothing to be frightened of." Navigating on foot was a bad idea. I turn to go back to the boat, but up ahead, something flickers in the fog. I lean forward, squinting, and keep walking.

The boardwalk trails through the swamp, past beautiful buttress roots and under vines, over patches of marshy ground and water that, impossibly, seems to glimmer. The sky is clouded, fog thick in the air, so it's as if some light has become trapped beneath the filmy surface. I blink again, take several more steps, the wood planks here just inches above the water, which looks deeper than I remembered.

Again, ahead I see a flicker of light, or movement. It reminds me of the pale yellow-gold of Holly's hair. And I'm transported back to my dream, to the sadness in Holly's eyes, her confounding silence. All these years, she had told me, she knew something wrong had happened. That it wasn't just kids messing around. I want to reach back into that mist and grab her, hold on, whatever it takes to make it possible. Anything so that I could ask her: *Why didn't you talk to me? Where were you when I needed you, when everyone else turned on me? I gave up everything to protect you from being blamed for Page's death, upended my entire life, and you wouldn't even talk to me.* Up ahead, a shuffle of movement snaps me out of my thoughts, something stirring in the trees or the water, and I quicken my pace.

I keep walking until I see the Ferris wheel, resting at a shallow angle in the water. It's coated with vines, trees growing through its spokes. As I approach, I hear the scatter of animals as they sense an intruder, and imagine the shelter these rickety structures must offer now to birds and other forest animals, though it's hardly inviting for people. I lean a little bit over the handrail, looking across the dark water beyond, to the rather leaning structure of the dance hall, and suddenly the entire section of the boardwalk tips precariously forward.

And there, in the water, I see a flicker of butter-hued light, twisting away into the dark.

But it's only a glimmer of light, my own reflection, lingering over the surface of the water. Again, I force myself to speak the reassurance out loud: "It's only your reflection." *As if I'm already down there, looking up at a different version of myself.*

For a moment I flail, and I can almost taste the water in my mouth. I run back off and get away as fast as I can, shivering. It felt for all the world like something wanted to pull me down. But then, it does that sometimes. I hurry back to the canoe, rubbing my arms against the damp chill in the air. My last visit here before I left town, I was alone, late at night, bare-armed in my nightgown. The water had seemed to invite me, to whisper of comfort. I was so frightened, or so tempted, that I never came back. Never until just now, to find it whispering the very same song.

My intention is to get away as fast as I can, but I forgot you can't go fast, not in this water, navigating a path for the little canoe between trees, the half-islands that rise out of the water here and there, the remnants of the fair. Trees and vines whisper, and the grasses brushing together seem to be saying, "Reverie, reverie," until my heart's racing and I wish I'd just stayed at the house. I wasn't ready for this, to feel so near my sister, and I'm suddenly powerless against this sorrow, pause with tears in my eyes. Holly always knew what to do. She was the one of us who was brave. Who did she expect me to ask for help now, without her here?

As I paddle back to the house, I'm eye level with tall grasses that grow in clumps where the mud is high, then, a few minutes later, ducking under a tall cypress root, brushing cobwebs from my face. I startle a heron on the water, but it doesn't fly off, only looks at me with annoyance. The wind blows over me warm, like rain's coming. I reach the dock at the edge of the yard in mist so thick that I don't at first see Tess where she sits hunched at its edge, dangling bare feet into the water.

"Tess, look out!" My gut reaction is fear—not just that her feet will be cold, but of this image that steals across my mind, of a hand reaching from beneath the water to grab at her ankle, pulling her down.

"For what?" She turns her face up and I try to readjust.

"Nothing, just—aren't you cold?" She stares back, chewing on her lower lip. "What are you doing out here?"

"You left." She cowers away from me when I sit beside her. "Why did you leave?"

"I just went out for some air."

"You argued with Grandma, and then you left." She's furious, hands gripping the planks tightly.

"But I only—" I stop, realizing this isn't a question of logic. "Tess, you were afraid I wasn't going to come back."

"I wasn't." Tess answers without looking at me, and her voice grows thick. "I don't even like you." Her shoulders tremble and I imagine the feeling of breath held in small lungs.

"You barely know me, so I'm not asking you to trust me." I lower my voice, not demanding she answer, though I know she's listening, has been this whole time. "But if you give me a chance to earn your trust, I am not going to let you down."

"What does that even mean?"

"I'll always come back, okay? No matter what else happens, if you need me, I'm going to be here." I lean over to hug her.

"That's what Mom said, too. How long is it going to take for you to go off into the swamp and never come back?"

Tess leans into my arms, crying softly, and I rest my chin on her hair and look out into the distance. To go off into the swamp and never come back. It sounds almost like she's talking about her mother leaving—though, in fairness, she could be making reference to any time Holly promised to come back.

"When did she say that?"

"Uh." She ducks her head to wipe her eyes on her sleeve. "I don't know. You know? Whenever she went somewhere, she was always going to come back." When the cooler evening breeze picks up, I inadvertently scoot closer, my hand pressing over Tess's.

"Your hand is freezing," she says, wiggling her hand away from mine. "Is that your only sweater?"

"Yes."

"Mom wouldn't mind if you wore some of her clothes," Tess says. "Just while you're here."

"What about you?"

She turns to me with a soft curve in her brow. "Mom wouldn't want you to be cold."

As we sit huddled together against the breeze, my chest fills with a sense of relief. There is an explanation for every earthly occurrence. For each trick of the light, for each troubled mind that misinterprets a play of light on water.

"Oh, I almost forgot." Tess shifts to reach into her pocket. Her thin arm darts out and places something on my knee. "I found it in the yard."

"What?"

"It was over there, near the driveway."

To: F.W.

On the rain-warped card, the block letters remain, so tidy that they look as though they were printed with a stencil.

"Oh no, Tess." My hand lands on her shoulder as I begin to stand up, tugging her to her feet. When the card flutters from my knee, I scramble to pick it up. "Thank you. Come on—let's get back inside." Each shadow, each hollow becomes a menace, each falling leaf sounding more like the noises that I followed into the swamp.

"Is everything okay?" When Tess lingers on the dock, my hand tightens instinctively on hers, keeping her moving at my side. I pull her several steps, until we're nearly at the door, before I find my voice, managing to speak over the hammering in my chest.

"I don't know." I cast another look over her shoulder, then pull her inside. "But I'm afraid not."

That night, after my mother and the girls are asleep, I walk the house, checking each door and window to make sure they are locked. I place the water-stained gift tag in a drawer, next to Holly's bracelet. *I didn't imagine that gift tag. Somebody killed Elvis and left him for me to find.* I repeat the lap, looking out into the dark from each windowpane. My mother doesn't believe me, but I know Holly didn't walk out into that swamp by herself. More disturbingly, how did her bracelet turn up at an antique store downtown? *If I didn't imagine the gift tag, does that mean I wasn't seeing things when I saw that light beneath the water, out there by myself today? Was it only my reflection?*

Upstairs in the blue room, I slide my recliner away from the bay window and push it flush against the door. Even if I sleepwalk, this will keep me from leaving the bedroom. And, I tell myself, it'll ensure I wake up if the door is forced open during the night. Almost as if I'm expecting to be able to sleep.

Hours later, I still can't rest. When I take out my phone and dial the number, it goes straight to voicemail. I lower my voice, speaking softly so as not to wake the girls.

"Hi, Dawson. It's Felicity Wheeler. Would you call me when you have a chance? Just wanted to catch up."

CHAPTER TWENTY

Now

As promised, Friday is the day my mother brings home a Frazier fir. I jump up to help her carry it up the steps, but when I'm holding the prickly, sap-sticky branches at one end, with her grasping the trunk, it's plain I'm not much use.

She scoots the couches in the living room around to make room for it in the corner by the window, and screws it into a tree stand while Tess and Frankie chase each other with tree branches that have fallen off. Frankie pauses to whisper to Tess, and I know she's asking her where their father is. I know I promised I'd make certain he would be here.

When my mother goes to the basement and returns with a cardboard box full of ornaments, I spend a few minutes looking through them. Some of them I made by hand, in school. My mother adjusts the tree in the stand and then trims a few stray branches until it's even. This is the first Christmas I've been here without my father. When this was Glen's job, it was punctuated with growled swear words and hisses of impatience. Now, to my surprise, it's almost a tranquil scene, and missteps or corrections are made with gentle laughs, extra sets of hands appearing to help. Next, they plug together several strands of lights, wrap them around the tree starting at the bottom, looping over and around all the way to the top. But when my mother plugs the cord into the wall, the lights pop and all the strings short and go out.

"The hardware store should have them," she says. "You wouldn't mind running up there, would you?"

"Not at all." I cross the room to the hallway, take my purse from the hook by the front door, and then turn back to give Frankie a hug. I stop short of making a promise to return with her father in tow. Better not make a promise I might not be able to keep. But when Tess gives me a meaningful glance, I give her a quick, certain nod.

"I'll try," I whisper.

"Thanks."

I pull on my sweater and head to the car. The green sweater I'm so fond of has seen more wear this last week than in the entire year I've owned it. It's not meant for everyday wear, either; I notice the delicate knit on the sleeves has started to unravel over one of my forearms. I haven't taken Tess up on her offer of Holly's clothing. This time, as I walk across the yard, the chickens don't pay me much mind, pecking for bugs in the soil. Though I wouldn't say I'm fond of them, there's something almost familial about their disinterested bustle. I wonder if they miss the rooster.

The sun peeks through a patchwork of clouds as I drive over the bridge and into town. In an age of chain stores and disappearing independent businesses, Pemberton's Hardware is a curiosity: a family-owned hardware-and-whatever-else shop. Two streets up from the Cotton Blossom diner, it's a long, narrow building, cluttered with rows of tools, paint, miscellany, in no discernible order. I walk inside, expecting Christmas tree lights to be somewhere obvious, considering the time of year. Yet, the front of the store is just a display of power tools, a kerosene grill, a stack of boxes of light bulbs. Glancing at the product category labels hanging at the top of each aisle of the store, I choose the one marked DECOR and begin to look for the lights. Walking past cans of paint, displays of every size of bolt and nut and screw, I walk swiftly down the aisle and turn the corner to try the next one.

"Oh—look out."

At a shuffle of steps, I pause. Trying to catch my bearings, I find myself face to face with an armful of two-by-four beams, stacked high enough to block the stranger's face.

"Excuse me." I move back, at the same time the stranger sidesteps, the mumbled apologies only distracting me. When I lift one hand up to shield my face, my forearm jostles against the stacked wooden beams, which clatter to the floor in a protracted crash that echoes throughout the store, one glancing off my foot.

"Are you all right?"

"Yes. That was my fault." My face burns as I bend to try to help collect them.

"Not at all. Are you sure you're—oh my God, is that you?"

My heart jolts in the same breath that I look down to see my hands next to his. Without moving, I lift my eyes to see James Finley, half certain he is an apparition. His deep brown eyes are bright with alarm, not twelve inches of space between us.

"Lissie?"

When I see the same shock and fear reflected on his own face, I know, with a sinking feeling, that this is real. "But—what are you doing here?" Even in surprise, his voice is smooth and warm as coffee. My answer is a half-voiced gasp of surprise.

"Everyone all right back there?" A friendly shout from the direction of the cash register stuns both of us.

"Yes." I snap to, standing quickly, brushing my hands on my jeans, then turning away. "Everyone is all right."

"Felicity, wait."

"You could hurt someone with those." Fingers trembling, I point weakly in the direction of the lumber he's still collecting, though my eyes rest on his. Silent shock slows my thoughts, just as it did that night, when I saw him at his window. My stomach flips with nerves and my heart races, and I feel as though buried fragments of rock stir and turn beneath my skin. "You ought to be more careful walking around blind corners."

I leave James collecting the two-by-fours as I hurry down the length of the aisle. I touch each item I pass, scanning for Christmas lights, my mind reeling with surprise. It was only a matter of time until I ran into James Finley, right? I ought to have guessed that he might live nearby. My thoughts are scattered, and, keen to get to Silas's house and get him in shape to see his children, I approach the checkout counter.

"Hi—excuse me." My hands rest on the counter by the cash register. "Where would I find Christmas tree lights?"

"Lissie Wheeler!" The man behind the counter breaks into a wide, though crooked smile. Charlie Pemberton has the same gray eyes and ready smile as his father, who used to be a constant presence here. "Haven't seen you in years. I guess ladybugs always do fly home." He's seated behind the checkout counter with a couple other men, one of whom I've never seen before. The other, though, looks familiar: his name is Barrett, or Garrett. He played football for the high school up the street.

"Jared," he offers, giving me a look as though I was staring at him for a different reason.

"Charlie, where would I find—"

"Almost didn't recognize you," Jared says. "You look good."

"Thanks," I answer quickly. "Charlie, where would I find Christmas tree lights?"

"They're over that way—" he begins to answer, but Jared leans one elbow on the counter, talking over him.

"So, whose was it?" He pauses for a beat, while I stare back in confusion. The sound of his voice calls up a recollection of a teasing singsong: *Bedbug, bedbug, fly away home.* I realize he must have been there, that game, that terrible night. "Oh, right. The immaculate conception. I forgot."

Charlie gently hushes him. By the cash register sits a stack of boxes of nails. I imagine how they'd sprinkle across the floor if I threw one of those boxes right at Jared's smiling mouth. He inches back, withdrawing from the counter, and Charlie is suddenly scooting the boxes out of my reach. Maybe I'm staring at the nails more obviously than I thought.

"Flawless customer service." Crossing my arms tightly, I address Charlie as if I've heard nothing. The old rhyme replays on a maddening loop in my mind: *Your house is on fire, your children are gone.*

"He... doesn't work here," Charlie answers sheepishly.

"Well, that makes all the difference." Biting my tongue, I sweep my hair back and into a ponytail. "Obviously, you would never hire a creep like this, whose life peaked when he was the meanest kid at recess." Charlie's eyebrows jump up in shock, a stack of wrinkles gathering on his forehead.

"Jeez." Jared exhales a breath that sounds like a punctured tire. "I was just—"

"It's all right. Boys will be boys." My deadpan answer is near a whisper, in a sharp contrast to their confident joking. "I should probably calm down—isn't that what you were going to say?"

"Damn," Jared whispers, though that mean smile still curves his lips. "Hope that chip on your shoulder keeps you warm at night."

"Plenty."

Chin tucked down, eyes on the floor, I turn toward the exit. It's likely enough Silas has a string of lights he'd be willing to lend us. That awful rhyme trips across my thoughts again, as if I can still hear those voices: *Bedbug, bedbug, fly away home.* After three quick steps, I have to pause, surprised by what feels like a sudden inability to breathe, one hand resting at the base of my throat.

Behind me at the checkout counter, the conversation redirects to Charlie's next customer.

"Hey, Finley, did you find everything you needed?"

With a hand on the doorknob, I wait, eyes on the floor.

"Yes. Thanks." James's voice is unmistakable. "Charlie, this is your father's store, right?"

"Yeah. Why'd you ask?"

"Does he know that you let your jobless friends hang out here all day, harassing customers?" I keep my hand on the door, turning my chin just enough that I can see him over my shoulder. Maybe it's the light, but he seems a faded impression of the dazzling young man my memory has no doubt embellished; his hair is shorter, those winsome eyes tamed behind a set of wire-framed glasses.

"Oh, I know her," Jared explains. "We're friends. That's—"

"I know who she is." There is a warning note, a tension I don't remember ever hearing in his voice before. "And you're not her friend."

"Oh, but you are?" With white knuckles on the doorknob, I turn to face them. When my eyes meet his, I could swear my heart shuffles inside my chest, forgets what it's doing and stumbles over its own rhythm, an infuriating reminder that I have never been able to rely on the signals it sends me. "Throw your jacket over a puddle for somebody else, James Finley."

CHAPTER TWENTY-ONE

Now

Outside, the breeze is refreshingly chilly. The parking lot is empty, save for one or two cars I assume belong to the men inside. Behind me, a sign outside a nearby store clatters to the ground, knocked over by a sudden wind. I don't remember leaving the car unlocked, but the door is just barely ajar, the cab light on. I slouch into the seat, leaving the door open, swallowing big breaths of cold air that leave me lightheaded.

I turn the key in the ignition. The car coughs, misfires, the whole thing jolting. The engine runs, but it sounds like it's full of rocks, making the same dreadful noise it did last week. I take the key out, then try it again. This time I think it sounds even worse.

"Thanks a lot, you absolute piece of—" My fists hit the wheel, hard enough the horn sounds, and I shout back at it with some of the language I've been trying to hold back around my nieces. Out of breath, close to tears, I prop my heels on the ridge of the open doorway, leaning over my knees.

Cursing the vehicle, I step out and take out my phone, calling for a tow truck to Mr. Potter's repair shop, the only one I know of in this area. I'm on hold for a few moments, and wander to sit down at a bench on the sidewalk. A flock of starlings settles nearby, pecking and shuffling about disinterestedly.

"All right, ma'am," the man answers. "Should be just about an hour."

"An hour?" I repeat. "For a tow truck?" I tilt my chin back and sigh, my glance catching clouds of a deeper gray that are spreading their way across the sky. A gust of wind rattles a nearby signpost.

"My closest tow driver is an hour away," he says. "I'm sorry, but we can't just get things done on a whim out here."

"I understand. Thanks for your help."

The line goes silent. A steady rain picks up like a chilly shawl settling over my shoulders, sending the starlings to seek cover in the branches of a nearby sycamore. I was certain that I had locked the car before I walked into the store.

Someone coughs nearby and my shoulders lock with tension. It's then I see James, standing on the front step of the hardware store, one arm holding the two-by-fours he's purchased. He takes a step forward then looks pointedly at the distance between us, raises his eyes to mine as he takes another step, as if asking for permission. I recall the day I first saw him at practice: the coach yelling, *This is football, not chess*. But his combination of precision and daring seems tailor-made for this moment. He approaches to stand next to the bench.

"Hi, Felicity."

Before I've had a chance to respond, he places a small shopping bag on the bench at my side. Through the translucent plastic, I see a package of Christmas tree lights. I have to lift my chin to look at him: he's taller than I remembered. Maybe I'm the one of us made smaller, worn down by the years that have passed.

I open my mouth to speak, but find no words. Thirteen years have given me time enough to play out this meeting in dozens of variations. To craft plenty of eloquently damning conversation starters, should I ever see James Finley again. It's plain now that none of those thought exercises has prepared me for this, for the undiluted confusion that blossoms inside my ribs when I look at him.

"Thank you, but…" I shake my head.

"Is something the matter with your car?"

"No. Not at all."

"Okay." He speaks softly, taking a step away. "I get it—I'll go. But I couldn't just stand there and say nothing."

Pretty funny, I'd like to say. *Isn't that what you do best?*

But I don't say it, instead watching silently as he walks back into the parking lot, takes his time unlocking his car. After placing the wood in the trunk, he turns back one final time, with a faint smile that makes him look, for a moment, younger than he is.

"You probably think that's pretty funny, coming from me."

"James, wait." As if waking up, I stand from the bench, picking up the shopping bag. "Thank you," I say pointedly, indicating the tree lights. "I didn't mean to talk to you like that."

"It's all right, Felicity."

"No, it isn't. I'm sorry." My behavior would have been defensive, bordering on unpleasant, if he'd been a stranger. But what is the appropriate way to speak to the person your heart broke for in a dozen different ways, who's not even properly to blame for it?

"I heard about Holly. I'm so sorry."

"You did?" A different curiosity grabs me. How much does he know about my sister? "So, you still live around here?"

"I wouldn't say *still*," he answers, and I get the sense he's condensing some detail here. "I moved back about a year ago. You?"

"I'm only here temporarily. Caring for my nieces, until we get things a bit more settled." He answers with a slow nod, as if it's just as plain that I am also omitting a good deal of detail. "Also, I might have misspoken when I said my car is fine."

"I heard." Had I really thought, only a few moments ago, that he was less handsome now than he once was? The quickly changing light sweeps over his features and the wind's playing with his hair.

"They spent all afternoon decorating their Christmas tree. My mother just sent me out to get lights, and to—" I stop short of talking about Silas. "Anyway, it's going to take an hour for a tow truck. Looks like this errand is turning out to be a failure on pretty much all counts."

"I'll drive you to your mother's house, if you like." As if to prove he means it, James crosses to the other side of the car and opens the passenger-side door, offering a polite smile. "You could have said you needed help."

To you? No, I couldn't have. I'll never do that again in my life.

But then, inexplicably, my feet are walking closer. I'm smiling an uneasy smile back at him, sitting down in his car, with only this unplaceable curiosity to blame.

"Thanks. I hope you're not ruining any plans for me."

"Not at all," he answers. "I'm meeting someone for drinks in an hour, but—"

"Oh, James, you'll be late. I don't want to inconvenience you." For some reason, I feel guilty just hearing these words. "I'll wait for the tow truck."

"Really, it's no problem," he says. "It's just Redford, anyway—he won't mind. You remember him? He's back in town for the holidays."

"Of course. I ran into him at the gas station." I pause, deciding not to tell James that today's car trouble is a repeat of what brought me to the gas station last week. "He seems to be doing well."

"Yes, he always is." James laughs kindly. "Wonderful job, great apartment. Despite being the only one of our friends who never took anything seriously, it turns out he's always known what he was doing."

"That's nice to hear."

He shifts gears and backs out of the parking space, then onto the street. Watching the unlucky rental car grow smaller in the rearview, I grasp for something to say.

"So, they sent you out to pick up Christmas lights, and what else?"

"Oh—nothing."

He nods. "I thought for some reason you said there was something else."

"Holly's ex." My hand flutters open, curls into a loose fist. "I was going to swing by and pick him up, so he could help with the tree. Only—I think I'd rather not. Not right now." James continues to listen, resting a hand on the steering wheel, giving a neutral nod of his chin. "I did tell Tess I would try to bring him," I murmur, arguing aloud with myself. "But I've already been out longer than I meant to. And…" Finally, I cut myself off, not wanting to admit that I'm reluctant to see him alone.

"Silas McDaniel, right?" The look that crosses his face makes it plain this doesn't surprise him. What else might he know about my sister's life?

"Yes. You know him?"

"No. I saw him get thrown out of a restaurant once, at eleven in the morning."

As he brakes at a red light, I pause, the shock of seeing him washing over me once again. Pushing that current away, down into my memories, I turn back to the present.

"How long did you say you'd been back?"

"Ah." Looking up through the windshield, he seems for a moment to be studying the traffic light intently, waits until it turns green, and resumes driving. "It was a year in August."

"Why?"

"Why?" he echoes with a gentle laugh. "I wouldn't know where to start."

At the beginning, my heart insists. *Start where we ended, and tell me all of it.* I'm nearly bold enough to say it, but not quite.

"I didn't really plan to move back here, if that's what you mean," he adds. I want to ask him why, but again, hold back, worried I might already know the answer. "Sometimes—I don't know—one piece of the puzzle changes, and it just seems like a good time to leave."

"Yes." I've employed the same sort of intentional vagueness with enough regularity to recognize the tactic when I see it. "Sometimes, it does."

"What do you do now?" he asks. Pursing my lips, I turn to face out the window.

"Sorry—that was a bit blunt."

"It's fine," I answer. "I'm a nurse. After I left St. Ben's, I moved to Chicago, waited tables. Finished high school online." I didn't move right away, but he doesn't need to hear the details. "I live in Saint Thomas now, in the Virgin Islands."

It's plain that neither of us is ready to talk. Thirteen years after the fact, maybe we never would have been. Maybe we still don't have to. But if he's been living here for over a year, he must know more about this town than I do. "Did you ever talk to Holly?"

James shakes his head. "Only when I happened to go to Cotton Blossom."

"How often was it? Did she—" My hands clasp tightly in my lap, and there's a sharp hitch in my voice. "Did she seem happy?"

"I didn't see her often." James turns onto the street that leads out of town, toward the water. When he speaks, his voice is low and gentle, his words carefully chosen. "Holly was always buoyant—she was Holly. But she wasn't the same person—not exactly." A momentary look passes between us. *But neither are you,* I'd like to say. *Or me, for that matter.*

"So, you're saying she didn't seem happy."

"No—only that I can't say. The handful of times I saw her at the diner, she seemed, maybe, different."

"I wouldn't know," I answer bitterly, the more disappointed at how unable I am to hide how I feel.

"Sorry to hear that. You two were so close." He draws in a breath, pauses, then eyes me carefully. Rain begins to fall, tapping against the windshield. "It's no help, but considering what happened, I doubt Holly would ever have been glad to see me. For all I know, if she looked unhappy when I saw her, it was just because the jerk she went to school with happened to be sitting in her diner."

"That's not it." I bite my lip until I can control my voice again. "Holly never really spoke to me again, after what happened. If you think she would have felt protective of me, you're wrong. She didn't care." I barely stop myself from adding: *She didn't care any more than you did.*

Finally, the wind brings what it's been promising, a sudden sky-cracking downpour of rain. With the vehicles ahead of us slowing down, he taps the brakes, bringing the car almost to a stop.

"I'm so sorry, Felicity."

"For what?" Turning to him with a blank expression, it takes me a moment to catch up, and when I do, I hold both hands out, as if I could push it away. "Oh, no. We are absolutely not talking about that." My hand lands on the door handle, a reflexive grasp at escape, until I remember we're in a moving vehicle. "I should have waited."

Without turning to face me, he raises an eyebrow and nods.

"James! I meant, back at the hardware store. Waited for the tow truck. You should—"

"Up to you," he nods. "Do you want me to turn around?"

"Would you, please?"

We're coming up to the bridge that crosses the canal, beyond which the buildings will thin out, the trees grow taller, leaving us, I can only imagine, that much closer to the wilderness, alone with all our ghosts. As James slows down, looking for somewhere to turn the car around, I hear a loud bell nearby, as cars ahead of us slow to a halt.

"What's that?"

He draws an irate sigh. "Drawbridge." James turns his chin to look out the rearview. Cars behind us, lined up already. No shoulder, the road narrow. "I think we're stuck for a minute," he says.

I give a resolute nod and watch furiously as the little drawbridge raises, a boat passing on the water that seems to be moving at an impossibly slow pace. I shake my head, firmly clearing my throat, and we sit in silence for what seems like ages. People talk about denial like it's objectively bad, but sometimes it's a survival tactic. This polite distance between us is fragile, and were it to break, I know we couldn't cross back into pleasantries.

"You're right, of course." Speaking calmly, he nonetheless pauses between words, lips pursed to the side, tossing fretful glances my way. "I shouldn't have brought it up. It was a long time ago. When you're a kid, it feels like a relationship ending badly is the worst thing that could ever happen. Everything seems so high-stakes."

"But now it doesn't."

"No, not really," he agrees. "It's almost like, even when I'm in a relationship that has every reason to be ideal, it just…"

Leaning against the headrest, I turn my cheek so that I'm facing him. "Even when you can't find a reason to leave, it's like you still can't find a reason to stay."

"You, too?"

"Yeah. A man proposed to me last year, actually."

"Oh?" James looks at my left hand.

"Yes," I answer, aiming to change the subject. "I panicked. Left the country, in fact."

He almost smiles, then appears to remember. The rain falls so thick around the car it feels as if the outside world is gone, that it's only the two of us here.

"I don't want to dwell on it," he says. "But it's hard not to wonder."

"Then don't." I watch the boat pass by, the water churning under the falling rain.

"That's for the best," he agrees. But what's simple isn't always easy. Only another moment passes before he opens his mouth again. "I was so in love with you." He says this so softly it almost knocks the breath out of me, the pain of it spurring me to anger.

"You shouldn't even be allowed to say that word." His eyebrows raise, turning to me with a look of shock, this infuriating innocence of his. "If you loved me, you were awfully quick to think the worst of me."

"It was clear enough what happened."

"Fine, but admit to me you never loved me." I straighten my shoulders and attempt a calming breath.

He won't admit it, though, fixing me with a troubling stare that keeps us at a stalemate. When I hear a car horn honking behind us, I see the bridge is open, the road clear ahead of us, and he turns back to the windshield. I'm picturing my tidy little apartment, my cup of tea every morning, closing my eyes and imagining beach glass. As he drives further out of town, the pine trees grow taller, closer together, and I stare out the passenger-side window, focused on the indifferent rain as it falls.

"What do you mean," he says, "when you say I was quick to believe the worst about you?"

"That I'd lied to you," I answer, still facing the window. "That I was an easy—backwoods—slut like everybody said." Shadows of myself, like unwelcome listeners, gather around me as I speak, and I remember looking up at him from the canoe, his shadow in the window. "Your mom looked at me like I was a bug, and told me to leave, and you just watched me go."

"I thought I knew you," he says, thoughts apparently wandering away. "It was so unlike you."

"You were absolutely determined to believe what everybody else said, rather than me."

"That's not fair. I stood there in front of everyone we knew asking you to talk to me, and you just—"

"And I begged you to talk to me," I insist, the pitch of my voice growing dangerously soft and unpredictable. "Alone. Not in front of everyone else."

"As if anybody needed proof you'd been with someone else?"

"But I didn't want to talk to *anybody*," I answer. "It was like you wanted me to stand trial. I wanted to tell you, but I didn't know how."

"Tell me what?"

I had promised myself this wouldn't happen. That I had learned this lesson the hard way, once, and once was enough.

"Stop the car, James." I make my voice cool and even, holding a hand up to admit defeat. "I'd rather walk in the rain than sit here and listen to you tell me you loved me, when—" Curling a threatening grip around the handle of the door, I bite down on my tongue and turn to the window; his eyes steal in my direction, then flicker away.

"Felicity, what is it?"

"When you think I would have so much as laid a hand on anyone else willingly."

CHAPTER TWENTY-TWO

Now

James hits the brakes hard, pulling to the side of the road, and I'm not sure whether I'm gasping for breath or if it's the seatbelt catching against my chest.

"What did you just say?" As the car slows to a halt, wheels protesting on the wet grass and gravel at the roadside, I take my hand from the door, reaching to cover my face instead.

"What happened?" He can't help it, but the effect of him finally asking me this, finally asking and listening, melts my anger, knocks out any defenses I had against this sadness. But those words mean something different now than they would have thirteen years ago.

"That isn't important now, is it?" I brush a stray hair away from my forehead. "I only wanted you to know that it wasn't what you thought."

"Jesus Christ, Felicity, not important?" He's talking through his hands, his voice breathy and low. "How can you say that?" He shifts the car into park, exhales softly, then throws on the turn signal as an afterthought, even though we're already parked at the side of the road.

Could I have been any more thoughtless, to fail even to consider how our past hurt him as well? It's like seeing a bandage pulled back, finding hurt worse than you expected beneath. "It's possible that I'm so used to thinking about it, it didn't occur to me to say it more gently."

"That's all right." But he's staring out at the rain-blurred trees with something I can only describe as numbness, a bewilderment in his eyes I can't bear to sit with, as if he's trying to measure an ocean with a yardstick. "What happened?"

I pause to breathe, shaking my head. "The specifics aren't important. I was raped. There was alcohol involved."

James nods slowly, looking over at me through those dark lashes. "Who was it?"

"An acquaintance."

"And you didn't tell anyone, because—"

"Because I couldn't." I almost say, *You just have to believe me,* before I realize that he doesn't have to believe me, that I don't need anyone to take my word for it to be true. "So, that's it, James. That's what I wanted to tell you that night."

He wrings his hands, then crosses his arms, giving the appearance of wanting to do something very much, but not knowing what, or how. His hand rests finally on the back of my seat, as if he'd touch me but doesn't want to draw too near. I raise my arm, a muscle memory I didn't know I'd held onto, guarding the soft space between my collar bones and my jaw. My throat burns and, once again, I have to fight to take a breath. Almost as if there's an arm across my throat, not enough to make me fear for my life, but enough to remind me of my lesser size. I remember it now. More clearly than I have for years. The struggling to breathe. James's jaw tightens, eyes darting between me and the distance beyond the window.

"It wasn't your fault."

"Why do you say that?"

"Because I'm looking at you, and I can see you blaming yourself. And... I don't want to pretend I could make any of this better, okay? But it wasn't your fault."

"You can't possibly know that." Anger sharpens, stretching me thin, as if I'm carrying knives in my pockets, seconds from cutting through whatever fabric is holding me together. For the third time, I say out loud the words I'm beginning to fear aren't true. "It doesn't matter now, James."

"It matters to me." James has always been like this, so naively confident that the world will bend to his sense of right and wrong. "I never thought something like that could happen to someone I knew."

"Don't tell me you're that naive."

"I mean, I didn't think it could happen to someone I—" He stops suddenly, rests his chin in his hand, and looks out the window, shaking his head. "I did love you." Turned to the window, I wait for an overwhelming sadness to fade, but it doesn't.

"Was it somebody I know?"

Unable to look directly at him, I shake my head as if to say, *No.*

"I wish you would tell me."

"Please," I cut in, voice sharp again, "just give me a moment." I know better than to dwell on these dead-end memories, but my body remembers. Those solid forearms, their weight on my clavicles, which felt like matchsticks. I let my eyes close, rest my forehead on one hand against the window, waiting for my heartbeat to slow to a manageable pace. My other hand squeezes into a fist, closing on thin air, looking for something concrete to touch.

And suddenly, his hand is holding mine. For a single breath, I let myself feel the warmth of his touch, my smaller hand inside his. Then, opening my eyes, I nod my head, as if to tell him I've got it, and pull my hand free.

"Why'd you leave?"

"What do you mean? Why did I leave school?"

"And at some point, not long after, you moved away."

"Yes. Well, you know." Though I don't say it, my memory turns up images like a tide. I could see how much it hurt him to look at me that day. And I knew it would only be immeasurably worse if he knew the truth. I let my answer trail off, making it plain enough that I don't want to explain any further. *Because that's what girls like me do for boys like you. When you need us to, we disappear.* "Are you okay to keep driving? It's just that my nieces are waiting for me, and I don't want to be gone all afternoon."

"Right. Of course."

I tilt my chin back and watch the waning daylight through the trees, the water on either side of the road a brazen, reflected amber. It's tiresome, to speak of these things aloud. Somehow both traumatizing and tedious. My gaze ticks left, and I find myself studying his rather numb expression on the sly. And, amid the tangle and annoyance of loose ends, feelings long ago hurt, there's something different. I'm glad he knows.

"What are you thinking about?"

"Nothing." His response is sullen and too ready.

"Then you won't mind if I change the subject." Resting my weight on my other shoulder, I turn in the passenger seat to face him, knees crossed. Pretending I'm not watching him is taking more effort than I want to give. "Why did you really move back? I mean, how have things gone for you?"

He lifts one shoulder in a shrug. "Not bad." Outside the car, the forest is closer, thicker, the ground on either side giving way to mud and water. "Undergrad's kind of a blur—I had a double major, so, you know, not a lot of free time." He speaks as though he's reciting from memory, but gestures nervously with his right hand, as though offering an explanation for a series of missteps. "Moved to California for grad school, then—back here." I'm watching James as he speaks, the careful part in his hair, the gentle set of his mouth as he chooses each next sentence, the steady but constant motion of his hands.

"You're not married."

"No."

"You know, I can't help but wonder why." This is an overstep, but one I allow myself, figuring he'll forgive me, given the circumstances.

"What do you mean?"

"Come on, James. I don't think there was anyone at St. Ben's who wasn't at least a little in love with you."

"No, they weren't." He laughs softly in protest, a hand lifting to his face in embarrassment. "Most of those people didn't know me."

But I did. The thought twists in my chest. I'm speechless, faced with this bittersweet truth, something so hard-won but now worth so little: *I knew you.*

"It's not for lack of trying. I just—I don't know. Not to overshare, but..."

"Please," I murmur. "We're past that, I think."

"Well, meeting someone was never the hard part. It's just that I don't want to be the guy who pretends to want something real, only to fail miserably when people need me to show up."

"Hm."

"What had happened was, I went to a wedding with my girlfriend—we'd been together a few years—and the bride threw the bouquet right at her." He laughs, shaking his head. "As in, I could tell they'd talked about it. And she gave me a look—all of a sudden, everything fit together. Why she never seemed quite happy. When I found a house for sale in Brightwater, I made an offer. I was here a month later."

The road narrows and he drives over the tiny bridge that leads to my mother's house.

"Maybe you saved yourself some trouble, leaving me when you did. I'm not good at the real thing. I can't do that."

"I didn't leave you."

"What would you call it?"

"You were the one who walked away," I remind him. "You were the one who watched me leave that night, and wouldn't talk to me." He exhales a sharp sigh, shaking his head again.

"Change the subject again?" I offer. "Man, we're bad at this, aren't we?"

"I'm a little surprised you're in nursing," he says. "You always said you wanted to teach."

Back in that fairy tale we dreamed up in the swamp, we were supposed to be married with three children by now. "I didn't have any idea what I was talking about back then."

"Is that so?" This seems to pique his interest, and I can't tell whether he's teasing me or actually asking.

Already, we're passing over the bridge. Even from here I can see the house, see right in all the windows.

"Thank you for driving me." Unclasping the seatbelt, I shoulder my purse and pull my coat tighter.

"Will I see you again?"

"Oh, James, I——" I have to avoid his gaze, my eyes falling to his hand, resting on the console between our seats. "It isn't that I don't want to, but this isn't easy for me. You understand that, right?"

"Yes," he answers. "Of course."

"Thank you." I cannot help but feel that, between the two of us, I have more to lose. I am the one of us who had to piece myself back together, who knows firsthand how fragile a seemingly solid foundation can be. The door opens under my hand and I swing one foot to the ground. "Take care, James."

"You, too."

I'm crossing the driveway, trying to collect myself in preparation for seeing my family again, when James catches up to me.

"Hey, wait."

"What is it?"

"You forgot these." He's holding the bag of Christmas tree lights.

"Thank you." For some reason, I stand here without even moving to take them, waiting for him to say something more. James twists his heel in the dirt, looking up at me through lowered eyelashes, and it's plain that the forgotten shopping bag was not the first reason he came after me.

"I'm sorry, Felicity."

I look uneasily toward him without meeting his eye.

"For not listening when you needed me to." James speaks haltingly, as if second-guessing each word. "Even before what you told me today, I've always wished I could change how I acted then." Every few moments, he looks up at me, anxiously guessing at my response, then back to his shoes.

"So, um." I nod toward the two-by-fours in the trunk of his car. "What are you building?"

"A bookshelf." He laughs with relief. "I have been living here over a year, and I'm still unpacking my books."

"Take it from someone who knows." I nod wisely. "It's easier not to acquire more than you can take with you."

"Is that so?"

"Yes," I answer, not hesitating a bit. "Unless you're ready to leave your belongings behind when it's time to go."

"But what if you don't plan to leave? Is it always when—not if?"

"So far." I fold my arms against the chill. James studies me for a long moment, then draws close enough to place the shopping bag in my hand.

"Maybe, before you leave, you would let me take you out to dinner. If you're still here next Saturday."

"Maybe." Heartbeat skipping, I find my curiosity overpowering my better judgment.

"Can I pick you up at seven?"

"Yes." His mouth instantly curls into a soft smile.

"I'll see you then."

"James?" I stuff my hands into my pockets, I want so much to clasp my fingers around his. "I'm sorry, too."

"No." He shakes his head, illuminated with a certainty that I hardly recognize on him. "You don't have anything to be sorry for."

And he doesn't know it, but I do. I'm still holding back part of the truth here, and I don't have any intention to change that. I didn't tell him when it happened because the boy who hurt me was his best friend. But even now, despite the cost of my silence, I would choose to keep that secret again, even though it meant losing everything.

CHAPTER TWENTY-THREE

Now

I hurry inside, anxiety and a dozen apologies on the tip of my tongue.

"Sorry," I say, clattering in the door. "I'm so sorry. The stupid rental car…" I throw my purse onto the hook and peer around the doorway to the living room.

"No problem, Felicity." Silas sits across the couch, feet propped on the armrest. "We were wondering what took you so long, though."

"Where—" There's the decorated tree, the box of ornaments. Silas is alone in the room. "Where is everyone?"

"I heard about poor Elvis." He shifts his weight, leaning on his elbow, relaxed as could be. "Otherwise I would have met you at the door."

A rush of cold seems to fall heavily around me, along with the uncomfortable combination of wanting to run to a dozen places at once, while feeling unable to move.

"Where are the girls and my mother?"

"They're out back." Silas nods in the direction of the back door. His eyes look clearer, and I realize there is no smell of liquor wafting from his direction. "Go and see them if you don't believe me."

"I meant to stop by and pick you up." He holds my uneasy gaze, lets me stammer a near apology before he speaks.

"Did you, though?" he snorts. "Come on—I know you don't want me here."

"That isn't true." I walk into the room, fighting a growing sense to turn and run. "Silas, there was something I meant to ask you the other day."

"Oh, yeah?"

"Would you mind—" Something about his overly relaxed posture prevents any polite communication. "Sitting up? It's just—"

"Yes, I would mind."

"Holly had plans that night." I lean forward over my knees, the air between us warm with anger. "Who was she going to talk to? What did you really argue about?"

"What?" Silas pulls himself upright, work boots landing with a thud on the floor. His mouth hangs just slightly open, eyes suddenly soft. "What do you mean, she had plans? With—with who?"

"Why, I—" For a moment, I'd been absolutely certain that it was him. "A friend of hers told me. She didn't know who."

Silas covers his face, his hulking shoulders curling forward. "Felicity, I've ruined things before. I've made plenty of bad choices, most of them for the same reason." He's speaking at a rapid mumble.

"What reason?"

"Getting drunk," he answers plainly. "Did I upset her that night, make her want to talk to someone else? What if I'd kept it together, and she'd come home with me instead?" If I had found it uncomfortable to watch him crying, this bleak self-reproach is painful to hear.

"I can't answer that." Does he mean it, though? His expression has none of the immediate, surface-level emotion it did before, when he was intoxicated. "But, to be honest, I have had similar thoughts. Wondered how I might have changed things, how I could have been a better sister."

"Have you? You certainly had Holly fooled." The look he levels at me is frightful, twisted with bare dislike. "Maybe we both let Holly down, but I can tell you that losing you meant more to her than losing her marriage did."

It had never occurred to me to think that Silas envied me, in any regard. And yet, there's a ring of truth about his words, leaving me counting up all of the voicemails from Holly, over the years away, that I never returned.

Without another word, I hurry outside to find my mother in the yard, Tess and Frankie helping her collect eggs from the chickens' coop.

"Is everything okay?" I ask.

"I was going to ask you the same thing," my mother answers. "Took you long enough. Whose car was that?"

"There was a problem with the rental car." I hesitate. "It was James Finley. I ran into him at the store. He drove me back."

Her eyes sharpen for a moment, before I redirect. "I have the lights."

"Let's go back inside," Frankie says, tugging on my coat pocket. "I want to tell Dad about your pictures from Saint Thomas."

Back in the living room, the girls and my mother fill up the space with warmth. Tess opens the lights and, moving nimbly as a shadow, begins to hang them, calling for her sister's help to stand on the other side of the tree. They hand the cord back and forth, laughing softly.

"Have you eaten, Felicity?" my mother asks. "There's soup in the kitchen."

"That would be nice. Thank you." I'm glad for an excuse to take a moment alone, but when I walk through the hall and into the kitchen, the smell of my mother's vegetable soup reminds me that I haven't eaten in hours. After serving myself a bowl of soup, I place it to cool on the counter, then take a few minutes to tidy up. I don't hear Silas walk into the room until he's two feet to my right, pouring a glass of iced tea from the pitcher in the refrigerator.

"Oh, you scared me!"

"Sorry." He takes a sip and leans against the refrigerator door, something unnerving in his glance.

"You didn't have plans to meet with Holly, later that night?"

"If I told her I'd be there, I would have been there."

What if he was?

What if he doesn't remember, or claims not to?

"It's just that so much about it seems off." It's impossible to eat with him standing here, so I start washing the dishes in the sink, wondering if he's waiting to say something, or perhaps for me to speak. "You know, Rob Dawson met me at the airport the day I got back. He doesn't seem to think anything's amiss. But…" Just as I begin to wonder how much I'm comfortable sharing with him, something surges forward in his expression, and I recognize the darkness in his eyes that, I suppose, has been there all along.

"Why would you be talking to Dawson?" He looks at me incredulously.

"Well, because he's— " I pause, rest my hands on the rim of the sink. "How's that any of your concern? Is he a friend of yours?"

"I am not friends with that prick." His voice is low, his consonants sharp. "And I'm shocked you'd consider him a friend, for that matter."

"What on earth do you mean?"

Silas gives me a troubled look, then shrugs it off. "He always looked at Holly wrong."

As little as I trust Silas, I also know what it feels like for Rob Dawson to look at you the wrong way. "How so?"

"He looked at her like he didn't know or care that she was somebody's wife," he answers. "My wife."

"He shouldn't have been investigating what happened to her," I murmur, almost speaking to myself. "No way to be objective there."

"Yeah, well, he could never turn down a chance to try to make me look bad."

"And what did Holly think of Dawson?"

"Holly liked everyone. But Dawson was one person she would have sent straight to hell, if she could have done it herself." His features twist into a scowl. "Sometimes I wonder if they ever—"

"You wonder what, exactly?" I have a pretty good idea of what he's about to say, and it must show in how I answer, because he shuts down entirely, face smooth, showing a degree of control he didn't have when intoxicated.

"Forget it." Silas crosses the room, then, standing right at my side, too close to me, tosses the last half of his iced tea into the sink. As ice cubes rattle over my fingers, I whirl around to face him, my eyes snapping to his.

"I think it's time for you to go home, Silas."

"Don't tell me I can't be around my children."

"Quit it. You're—" I gasp, checking myself before the words are out. I don't want to admit to him that he scares me.

"You look like your sister sometimes." He scowls, leaning too close to me, and I press my back against the counter, almost into the soapy water in the sink. "But not when you're angry. She was always sweet."

"You don't need to tell me she was the prettier one." I lift up a hand to push him back, but he seems to recall himself, and moves a step away from me, bitter eyes lingering on mine.

"Holly wasn't just pretty. She had what people call inner beauty." My chin starts to tremble as he speaks, and I bite down on my tongue. "You move like you always think someone's about to hit you. Like, if anyone so much as touched you, you'd shatter." He reaches up, flicks a finger at my arm in a gesture that could almost be playful.

"Don't touch me." When I push his hand away, his fist is cold under my own. "I don't trust you, Silas. I don't want you around the girls without my supervision. That's final."

Silas holds my gaze for what feels like years.

"You'll change your mind about that."

"I would hope so. But I need you to behave in a more responsible way for that to happen." Something in my voice aims to calm him, and I realize I'm bordering on frightened. "I'm not saying you can't visit them, but you absolutely can't show up when I'm not here, and not when you're—"

"I'm sober," he snaps.

"That's not good enough. I don't make excuses for bad behavior just because you happen to love the people you harmed." I reel my temper in, recognizing the outline of this particular anger, one that isn't about Silas.

"Go to hell."

"I hope your day gets better," I mutter, talking to his back as he leaves the room. Forgetting my food altogether, I follow him into the living room, see him put on a cheery face as he tells the girls goodbye, then walks out the door.

"Doesn't the Christmas tree look nice, Aunt Lissie?" Frankie climbs onto the sofa and tilts her head, so I sit next to her, while Tess stretches out in the armchair.

"It's wonderful." They've dimmed the overhead light to let the tree sparkle.

"Yes," she agrees, with a precious, solemn nod. "I'm sleepy."

"Would you like to take a bath and put on your pajamas?" She answers with a nod and a yawn. "Why don't you go and pick out your nightclothes? I'll be right up to start your bath." Frankie walks up the stairs, humming softly as she goes. "Mom, can I help you with anything?"

"No, thanks. I'm going to put away the leftovers," she answers. With a pang of hunger, I remember that I forgot to eat, then notice Tess's eyes on me in the low light.

"I'm sorry I was gone so long."

"It's okay."

"The car made that noise again. I'm going to switch it for a different rental."

She nods, scratching at a hangnail. "Why were you so upset when you came in?"

"I wasn't," I answer. "Just in a hurry to get back, probably. Hey, did you have enough to eat?" She doesn't answer, her catlike eyes watching me in the dark, giving me an impression almost that they somehow widen to let in more information, words unsaid. "I'll get you another bowl of soup. Or maybe you'd rather have something else?"

"No—I'm okay." She stretches, rising to her feet, turns to walk toward the stairs. "I'm going to change into my PJs too."

"I'll be right there." I hurry into the kitchen, where I nearly collide with my mother. "Oh—sorry. I just—"

"You didn't eat anything? It's that vegetable soup that used to be your favorite." I realize she must have made it for me.

"I was going to," I answer. "Is my bowl still out? I got distracted. If I can leave it out until they're done getting changed, I'll eat then."

Climbing the stairs, I reflect that it's not difficult to see how an entire evening could disappear like this without a moment to eat, always another task at hand. While Frankie's bath is running, I check my phone, then step into the hallway to listen to a voice-mail. It's from Mr. Potter, from just an hour ago. He must have called when he was closing up for the day. My heart sinks at the familiar, half-amused lilt in his voice. He's checked the rental car over, for the second time. Not a thing the matter with it. A soft chuckle follows, as though it's a kindness in the face of my obvious mistake. His voice on the recording is kind but maddening, and the question he asks will echo in my ears for the remainder of the night: *Are you sure you're not hearing things?* I make myself a note to call the rental company in the morning to request a different vehicle. Even if Mr. Potter is right, I know I won't be able to look at the car again without wondering if I'm losing my mind.

CHAPTER TWENTY-FOUR
Before

That night, when I saw the headlights, I hoped they'd pass on by. When the truck slowed to a crawl, matching my lopsided pace, I knew I was being followed.

Finally, the truck stopped behind me, though I kept walking. *I should be afraid, right?* Then I realized that I must already have been afraid, heart racing, my head buzzing with adrenaline. My arms and legs trembled, my chest tight and burning with adrenaline. Over the idling engine, I heard footsteps land on the ground, then circle around the truck to catch up with me.

"Hey, do you need help? Can I call someone for you?"

I tightened my crossed arms, half turned my face to speak. I had intended to say, *I'm fine* or, *Leave me be* or, *Get the hell away from me*, but I couldn't decide which it was, and some jumbled mess of syllables spilled out.

"Jesus Christ. I didn't know it was you."

Hearing steps draw closer, I threw an arm out to the side, a gesture that wanted to say, *Don't touch me*, but instead sent me off-balance to land on my elbows in the roadside gravel.

"Felicity, it's me, Dawson. Come on." He offered me a hand and put a steadying arm around my shoulders as I stood up. I could feel his eyes on me, heard his breath rush as he gasped. *So I scraped my knee*, I thought. *Big deal*. Dawson had to lift me up for me to get into the pickup, its tires splattered with mud. He closed the door behind me and reappeared in the driver's seat moments later. I fidgeted in the seat, looked down at my legs, feeling that the cheerleading skirt left an awful lot of skin exposed. Dawson reached to pick up a jacket from the floorboard.

"You're freezing." He handed the jacket to me, tossed it over my lap. "What are you doing out here?" He took a backpack from behind the driver's seat, handed me an unopened bottle of water. "Do you want to tell me what's going on?"

I opened the water and took a hesitant sip. "Okay," he said, clearly nervous. "You don't want to talk, that's okay—I'm going to call your sister, all right?"

"Don't." I took the phone from him, one arm reaching across, the other struggling to keep me upright, afraid I'd fall right over across the seat. I pulled the phone back and wrapped my arms around my body, throwing a suspicious stare his way. "You can't tell her you saw me. She'd be furious, if she knew I…"

"Knew you what?"

"Forget it." I could hear the alcohol in my voice, words blurring together as I tried to answer him.

There had to be something I didn't know about that night. Cody had been there with Holly and Page. I needed to know what he had seen. So, earlier that day, I had asked Cody to meet me after practice. When I saw his car I waved and smiled, hurrying over to meet him. It had been a crisp, sunny afternoon, a reminder of the cooler days ahead of us. After a quick greeting, I cut right to it: I need your help. I need to talk to you about what happened on Labor Day weekend. He answered with an understated frown, eyes downcast. It was obvious how badly it had hurt him to lose Page. There was no doubt that he loved her, that he felt responsible for what had happened.

"Felicity, you don't drink. What the hell?" I could hear Dawson's voice, but he sounded miles away.

*

"I know it's hard," I breathed. "I'm really sorry. Are you doing okay?"

He nodded his head, but raised one shoulder in a half-hearted shrug.

"Are you?"

"I think so. But I'm not sure about my sister." I paused. "I need you to tell me exactly what happened. All of it. Even if you think it will upset me."

"I don't know," he sighed. "It's just that I had to go through it with the police several times. It's——"

"I'm sorry, Cody." I touched his wrist, then drew back, wary of making my point unclear. "Please—I'm really worried about Holly."

"Okay. Do you mind if we drive while we talk? It's a bit of a nervous habit," he added. "I like to keep moving when something is bothering me." I nodded, feeling entirely on his side. It sounded exactly like something I might have said myself.

Cody had driven outside of town, past fields of fading, rustling summer crops. As he drove, he began to speak, telling me about that night. The three of them were sitting on the metal beam, a couple of yards above the water, playing truth or dare. Holly asked Page: Truth or dare. Page chose the latter. Holly dared her to jump into the water. "She couldn't swim," he said, blinking hard. "We both tried to help her out. When we couldn't, she went looking for you and James to help."

While we waited at a stop sign, he produced a bottle of whiskey from beneath the seat, offered it to me. I shook my head, surprised, but he insisted: "You're nervous, and it's making me nervous." I tried a small sip, wincing at its sharp flavor. Cody parked the car near a long-deserted gas station and turned to me frankly. "I've told you everything I remember. What exactly is it that you wanted to know?"

"I guess I don't know. I just wish I understood." I was afraid to ask him the question that rested at the pit of my stomach, but I think he knew it: Was it true, what people were saying about Holly?

*

"Holly didn't do anything wrong." With erratic motions, I sat up, then slumped over, face in my hands, sitting up to look at Dawson frantically. "It isn't fair."

"What isn't fair?" he asked. I realized maybe Dawson hadn't heard the rumors that were whispered at my school. "Is Holly okay?"

"No!" I wailed. "And she won't tell me why."

"Should I drive you home?"

"No." If anything, I preferred the numbing anonymity of walking in the dark, hoping the forest or the road would somehow swallow me down. Dawson looked out the windshield as if the night outside offered him any direction.

"Where's your boyfriend?" He took note of the jacket I wore, one eyebrow ticking suddenly upward. "James Finley, right?" Everything around me began to spin, so I had to close my eyes.

Cody sipped the whiskey as easily as if it were water. He handed the bottle back to me, laughed gently when I refused.

"Truth or dare, Lissie?"

"No," I said, redirecting. "I need to know exactly what she said."

"And your turn's next," he answered.

"Fine. Dare." He handed me the bottle and I resolutely took a drink, coughing as it stung my throat.

"Your turn."

"Why did Page jump, if she couldn't swim?"

"It was so dark, Felicity." He looked so terribly sad that I almost wanted to hug him. "I feel like you're asking questions you don't want answers to."

"I know Holly would never hurt her." My voice bordered on pleading.

"Maybe it was the Reverie Girls." He leaned closer. "You know those stories. The lonely ghosts, out in the fairground, on the swamp. Leading people off their paths, pulling them down."

"I don't believe in ghosts, Cody."

"I know—me neither. But even the air that night felt off, like the place already knew something was going to go wrong. It was only waiting for the right opportunity."

He was right. I didn't want to say it, but I had felt it, too. And how else could I explain that voice that I heard calling my name, but James didn't? I imagined those lukewarm arms around my torso. Was that deadweight, a dying girl trying to cling to me, or was it something else, something that pulled me down with intentional force?

"My turn," he said. "Choose truth or dare."

I didn't like the way he looked at me, so I chose truth.

"You're a virgin, aren't you?"

"Felicity, wake up. Please." For all his officious manner and big-brother attitude, Dawson was only nineteen. His hand wavered in the air as if he was afraid to touch me, then patted the back of my hand. "Do you need to go to the hospital?"

"No! I'm awake."

"Okay," he said, withdrawing his arm, checking the road over his shoulder as he prepared to start driving. "Okay. I'm going to call your parents' house—"

"No—please." My hand fluttered about uselessly, searching for the handle of the door. "You don't understand. You can't tell anyone you've seen me." Embarrassed, I turned in my seat to glare at him. I was afraid I'd start to cry, then realized with some removal that I already was crying.

"Felicity, help me out here. What do I do?"

"Jesus, Dawson, what are you looking at?" He didn't flinch. If my anger was intended to scare him, that was long since done.

"I have to ask."

"No, you don't." The words rose from my throat, intended to tell him again to back off, but as I cowered against the door, squeezing myself into as little a space as possible, I saw that the answer may have been apparent regardless. And though I closed my eyes and covered my ears, that answer blazed across my mind, like so many tiny fires I couldn't put out.

I had opened my eyes to see skin. I wondered distantly when I had gotten into the back seat of the car. I spoke, though oddly, the precise words escape me—stop, or no, or something similar. Cody shifted, one forearm pressed across my collarbones, and I was so afraid they'd snap that I almost didn't notice I couldn't breathe.

The next thing I remembered was Cody sitting in the seat next to me, checking his reflection in the rearview mirror. He lifted one hand to brush his hair into place, then turned to look at me: "Hey, ladybug, you okay?"

"Am I supposed to be okay?" I made an attempt to straighten my clothes, then drew my knees up to my chin, covering my face.

"Oh, my God, Felicity." His contented gaze slipped into boyish dismay, eyes searching my face for some answer I didn't have. "You said you wanted to."

"I would never."

"But you said—" Looking very hurt, he reached to touch my shoulder, and I jerked backward, away, knocking the back of my head against the doorframe.

"Lissie, I'm confused," he said. "You gave me no sign you didn't want to."

"That isn't what I remember." My hand rose to my throat again, and when he moved to touch my knee I swatted at his hand.

I reached for my jacket—no, James's jacket—on the floor, and when my hand brushed the whiskey bottle, I grabbed that as well and took a drink. "Hey." He raised an eyebrow, gave a regretful smile. "Leave some for me, okay?"

"I told you to stop."

"No, you didn't." His response was so earnest, his eyes bright with regret, that I thought at first that I had misremembered.

"I need to go home."

"Why did you keep asking me about that night, Felicity?"

"Because I want to know why Holly's acting different."

He paused to give me a meaningful glance. "You wouldn't be here if you didn't believe Holly had done something terrible, would you? She was angry with Page, and she wanted to prove that she was braver than everyone else."

"That's not true."

"You know it is. How do you know I haven't been holding some of the truth back?" he asked. "To keep her from getting in any more trouble?" He opened the car door and moved into the driver's seat, caught my gaze in the rearview. "If anyone had reason to believe she had pushed Page in—more than rumors, I mean—her life would be over."

Crying loudly, I began to cover my ears against his words. Cody drove back to his house, near our school. He slowed to a halt in the drive and gave me a heartbroken stare. As we sat in silence, I understood the agreement I'd made: this didn't happen.

When I opened the car door, the ground rushed up to meet me. I was half a mile down the road before I realized I'd scraped the skin off my knees, that my palms were raw and bleeding, smarting in the breeze. I thought of the Reverie Girls and waited for that ghostly voice to call to me again, told myself if it did I'd jump right into that water like Page had. Surely, anybody would do anything to get away from feeling this way, no matter what the cost. I was halfway home, pulling James's jacket around my shoulders against the chilly night, when Dawson recognized me and picked me up.

I realized I wasn't breathing properly, all gasps and shakes, and when Dawson began to speak again I threw myself against him and sobbed out loud, holding onto his shoulders as if I were drowning. "I don't know why she jumped, but it wasn't my sister's fault. It was—"

"What?"

"The Reverie Girls," I whispered, wide-eyed, pulling back to look at him. "There was something else in the water with us. Something that wanted us to stay there." He blinked in shock, then nodded along, and I was certain he believed I'd lost my mind. "Don't tell anybody about this, please, Dawson." *Please* crossed my lips again and again, turning into an incoherent mumble.

Finally, he rested an arm around my back. "I won't," he said. "It's okay. I won't."

CHAPTER TWENTY-FIVE

Now

Brightwater's historic district is a few blocks of elegant old buildings, painted in varying pastels, huddled around the canal. Aside
from a couple of art galleries, I find it the same as I left it: the
post office, housed in a converted Victorian house; the brick-lined
sidewalk; the streetlights decked with holiday wreaths. Yet, as I
walk to the new café next door to the antique store, I avoid the
gaze of people who walk past me, anxious to steer clear of any
unnecessary conversation.

Inside the café, I find Dawson already waiting for me, seated at
a table near a window. I expected he'd be punctual. He's a flurry
of helpful gestures: waving me over to his table, offering to take
my jacket, then pulling out a chair.

"Were you able to find parking?" Where my coat was unbut-
toned, a speckle of raindrops leaves dark spots on my gray blouse,
a detail I don't think he misses.

"Yes, just up the block." The new rental car, a graphite-colored
sedan, was more of a nuisance to parallel-park than I had expected,
but I could also blame it on lack of practice.

"Have a seat."

I nod another thanks and sit.

"Thanks for meeting me, Dawson."

"Are you all right?" he asks. "You sounded upset on the phone."

"I'm quite all right." I realize after I've spoken that I answered too quickly. "I wanted to talk with you a little more about my sister."

"Oh." He curls a hand around his coffee cup with something like disappointment.

"I saw the news. An accident?" My hand rests on the blue-checkered tablecloth between us, fingers tightening together, as if I might squeeze answers from the air itself. "Really?"

"You must have been expecting that," he answers.

When a server arrives to take our orders, I ask for a cup of green tea with lemon, while Dawson orders a refill on his coffee and a sandwich.

"Nothing to eat?"

"I had a big breakfast." I can't bring myself to eat, not while I'm thinking about the details of my sister's death, which seems to be almost always these last few days.

"Is there something on your mind?"

"Well, yes." I choose my words carefully. "You're still on Holly's case?"

"I was, but the investigation is closed now, of course," he answers. "Why?"

"You were sweet on her for years," I answer. "It must have been hard on you."

"That was long ago," he answers, a bit too quickly. "Yes, at times. Thank you."

"Were you friends with her?"

"No," he answers. "No, she didn't want much to do with me. I assumed it was because Silas was jealous, but it doesn't matter now, and I never held it against her."

"Silas does seem—well—I don't know. Do you know what I mean?"

"I don't want to say anything against him." But as he speaks, his eyes cut to the side, his mouth screws into a frown.

"You don't look so sure."

"She chose him, and I understand that." He glares at the tablecloth, smoothing a wrinkle in the fabric with one finger. "But every time Silas got into trouble, I thought of her. He doesn't respect himself enough to clean up his act, let alone anybody else. Your sister deserved better."

"She did." For a moment, I imagine Holly with Dawson, remembering the quietly devoted way he used to look at her, when she wasn't paying attention. It's hard not to see him now as the man Holly should have married.

"Anyway, it's not hard to imagine Holly looking at Silas and thinking the girls need a reliable guardian around. I guess that's why she brought you into this."

"Maybe that's it." I don't want to admit to him that there's more, that something about Silas's laugh frightens me. "I've been thinking, and—" I pause, noting that he looks awfully worried to hear this. "Holly did come home, after the party. Her purse was in the closet."

"A handbag being potentially in one location—the diner—and then, later, at another—that isn't necessarily indicative of her movements. You understand this, right?"

"I do, but I don't think she planned to leave the house and not come back."

He purses his lips, eyes heavy with sorrow. "Felicity, she may not have. Maybe she went out for a walk, or took the canoe out, just intending to get some fresh air."

"In the storm?"

"Your sister was a free spirit."

The server comes back to place my tea in front of me, then, moments later, returns with Dawson's lunch. I thank him, then wait quietly until he's walked away. "I know she was. But something feels really wrong to me."

"I don't want you to feel that way." He sets into his food with such an indifferent appetite that I have to look away. "What can I do to help you, Felicity?"

"There's something else. Sorry—" I send a wincing glance at his plate. "Somebody killed my mother's rooster."

"You saw this?" Dawson gives his sandwich a regretful glance and pushes the plate away.

"I found him in the middle of the driveway, but—"

"The driveway?" he echoes. "Could it have been hit by a car?" I reach into my purse to show him the gift tag, now faded almost beyond recognition.

"See? These are my initials. It was around the rooster's neck." He studies the paper scrap in my hand, lets out a patient sigh, then returns to his food.

"And I found her bracelet at the antique shop. Whoever killed her must have left it there."

"Okay," he breathes, rubbing his temples. "I cannot explain a scrap of paper to you. But it seems it might be easy to mistake it for something it's not." Sighing, I pick up the lemon slice, which slips in my fingers, splashing a few drops of tea on my hand. "But I can tell you, with some certainty, that a murderer, who is presumably trying not to be caught, would not ditch a piece of evidence in a public place. Do you see what I mean?"

"But how did it get there?" My tea is cooling, and I've let it steep for too long so that it's bitter and lukewarm. "Dawson, I'm trying to tell you that I feel scared."

"You have no reason to be afraid—I promise." He rests his hand on mine, and I'm surprised to find the gesture comforting, his palm pleasantly warm. "Is there any chance someone else could have taken the bracelet from your mother's house and sold it for a few dollars? Before you answer that," he says, lifting a hand to hold back my imminent response, "you should know that Tess, your—your niece? She used to frequent that shop with Holly."

"Are you accusing my niece of stealing her deceased mother's jewelry and pawning it for cash?" I take a breath and remind myself that Dawson is my friend, and that, if nothing else, he has always had good intentions.

"Think about your sister, Felicity—really think. Guilt can change you. A recollection of doing the wrong thing, or, on the other hand…" he stammers, then lifts his eyes to look at me. "Not doing enough to help—that can weigh on a person."

"Oh, Dawson." I look down at his hand on mine, not so much touching it as sheltering it. "I barely remember that night."

"Really?" His eyes meet mine, and he speaks so softly that I feel a sudden twist of sadness in my chest.

"Really. I've left it in the past, and you should do the same."

"What I meant to say is that Holly may not have had to look far for a reason to act recklessly. And I'm not talking about the Reverie Girls. Ghosts don't hurt people." I tug my hand back, then pick up the lemon wedge from my tea and twist it in my fingers. "Maybe I don't have anything you would call proof, but I know something isn't right."

"I should be going. I have a meeting in half an hour." He glances down as if embarrassed.

"Okay. I'm just going to finish my tea, and then I'll be on my way. I don't like to leave my nieces with my mother for too long."

"You're grieving, Felicity. You're taking care of a lot of people here. Please remember to look after yourself, too."

"I'm trying."

"I can see that you are." He pauses. "But I would have liked to see you eat something."

Beneath his rather official demeanor, I recognize the pulse of concern in his eyes, worry lending his features an almost tender look.

"Holly wouldn't have wanted you to stay, not if it was more than you could manage," he says, making his way toward the door.

"I can manage."

And you don't know what Holly wanted, I want to shout. *You never have.*

CHAPTER TWENTY-SIX

Now

Since our first day here, Frankie has requested visits to see my mother where she works at the school. One morning, too tired to invent another excuse, I finally agree.

"Really?" Tess chirps, curled on the sofa across the room. I didn't realize she was listening. Too late to backtrack, I dress and brush my hair and, feeling very much like we're going to a funeral, make the drive into town. A back road cuts through the pine forest and to the employee parking lot at the edge of the campus, so that I don't see the familiar rooftops until, through the clearing trees, the school is right in front of me.

Shifting the car into park, I focus a hostile gaze on the familiar landscape. The stone walls of the chapel and, next to it, the main hall, sit at the boundary of the courtyard. To our other side, there are office buildings, sports fields. Only once my feet land on the pavement do I realize: this is almost precisely where my mother picked me up, after the game, the last time I was here.

"The parking lot is nearly empty. Where is everyone?"

"It's Christmas break," Tess answers, getting out of the car. "Obviously." *That's just as well*, I think. I'd rather not run into anyone, or see students in the familiar uniform.

"Then why is Grandma working?"

"All the stuff she doesn't do when she has to cook all day." Tess leans back into the car to unclasp Frankie's seatbelt. "Deep-cleaning, prep work, things like that."

The girls bound ahead of me. For them, I see, this is fun: visiting Grandma at work in this grand old building, all its hallways and nooks inviting exploration, the statues in the corners watching over it all. If I didn't know my way, I could follow them, but I do know my way. Even now.

They race each other down the main hallway, Tess slowing her pace to let Frankie keep up.

"Not too far ahead, okay?" I call. "Don't lose me back here."

They don't listen, skipping ahead to find my mother. Frankie and Tess cut through the atrium, which echoes with their whispers. I follow them to the doors into the back hallway. The set of doors clatters behind them and I hurry to keep up. Drawing near the cafeteria, I hear their happily chattering voices, then my mother's deeper, rougher voice, joking back with them.

For a few minutes, I listen through the doors to the hum of their voices, then begin to wander. Walking through the dining hall, and then into the atrium, I'm crossing my arms, holding onto myself as if not to lose where I am in this moment. I remember the uniforms and the sound of the bell. After everything changed, I felt so out of place that the grandiosity of the building felt imposing, rather than beautiful. Now, though, I do find myself admiring it. These towering rooms, the ceilings so high. Fine carpets on the lustrous wood floors. Even the potted plants and vases of cut flowers were always in impeccable shape. There's a Christmas tree in the main entryway, fragrant and tall, so flawless it looks artificial. The whole place seems to whisper with promise, of young people who have never had to wonder whether they'll go on to do important, interesting things. I wonder if other students' parents ever warned off bad behavior by saying, *You don't want to end up like that Wheeler girl, do you? Not the pretty one, that's Holly. The quiet one.* While my sister got to stay in school, with all of the people I had counted as friends. I turn swiftly back and head for the cafeteria, ready to leave.

"Hey, girls?" I knock on the door, then push it open and peer inside. But it's just my mother. "Where are they?"

"They went outside to play on the soccer field."

"Thanks. Oh, Mom, I'm going out on Saturday night, just for a couple hours."

"You are?" Plainly shocked, she questions me as if she thinks she's misheard.

"I can stay in, if you like."

"No, no. You've been looking after everyone else—you should take some time for yourself. Who are you going to see?"

"I, um—"

"You said you didn't have any friends here," she smiles. "But maybe you do."

"It's James."

"You can't be serious, Felicity." When I hesitate, she speaks more quickly. "Out of all the people in the world, you turn up here and decide to let James Finley take you out for dinner? Do you not remember what happened?"

"Tell me what happened, then, Mom."

"Well—I know that you were pregnant, and he—"

"It wasn't him."

"It's flat-out cruel," she mutters, her voice distorted with the threat of tears, "that you continue to lie to me about that. You and James were always together. It was obvious."

"Has it ever occurred to you that you might not know everything?" Lacing my arms across my chest, I turn toward the door. "You're so in thrall of your own feelings that you never bother to look beyond them."

"I do know that you were desperately unhappy, and that the boy you loved never even stopped by to check on you." My mother takes a step back from my anger, her eyes softening. Even now, I hate that she's right. "Maybe I don't know everything, Felicity. Is there any chance you'd tell me now?"

"No. There isn't, Mom." Before she can throw her *why* at me, or whip up another evil concoction of her own guilt and regret and whatever else, I continue. "My mistakes are on my conscience, whatever they may be. But nobody is ever going to put me in a position of having to defend what I know to be true. Not again."

There is a strangeness to her expression, as she regards me now. A change in the shape of her brow, in the sharp set of her lips. I wonder if she's doubting herself, for what must be the first time, when it comes to either of her daughters.

"He's picking me up at seven on Saturday," I add quietly, "and I won't be out for long."

"Very well." Even after she answers, I stare, daring her to say another word about it. "I'll be home a little after five, Felicity."

"Okay, Mom. I'll see you then."

I take a shortcut outside through a back door. The sun's not quite shining, but it's a bright, hazy day nonetheless. I walk through the courtyard, past the fountain in the center, and the statue of St. Benedict outside the chapel. I can hear their voices, and follow them to the soccer field. Tess and Frankie have found a tossed-away soccer ball somewhere, and are kicking and chasing it, tearing blithely across the grass. Tess is fast, and, watching her blonde hair ripple out behind her, I note that she's beautiful. There's a smoothness in how she moves, the set of her shoulders almost regal. She spins on her heel and kicks the ball gently to Frankie, who picks it up in her hands and runs the other way.

"Aunt Lissie!" Frankie shrieks, laughing. She hurls the ball at me full force and, no time to jump out of its way, I catch it and kick it back. Frankie picks the ball up in her arms, then takes off running again before throwing it in Tess's direction.

"You're supposed to kick it," Tess laughs, demonstrating as she gives it a solid kick towards me. Her eyebrows lift, as if in surprise, and she turns an expectant smile my way. *No*, I think, *not my way.* Someone's behind me.

"Oh, hi, Cody. I didn't expect to see you here." The soccer ball bounces off my knee; startled, I laugh before sending it back in her direction.

"What's up, Felicity?"

"We're visiting my mom at work."

"Oh, these are your sister's children?"

"Yes. How about you?"

"Same as you," he answers. "Visiting my old man at work. He's trying to talk me into a job here. I told him *no way.* I've been back from Manhattan for eight days and I already can't wait to get back." He watches the girls playing, then turns to me with a contemplative smile. "Do you like kids?"

"I do." I hold up a hand to block the sun from my eyes, smiling back. "I am a pediatric nurse, after all." It is so strange now, the awareness of his body near mine still not a pleasant one. As if Cody weren't perfectly predictable. He never did anything he wasn't certain he could get away with.

"How are they doing?" In the shifting light, his expression is hard to read.

"I don't know, to be honest. I'm trying my best, but they don't know me. And—well, never mind."

"What is it?" Teenaged Cody never used to do this, to look at people as if their thoughts mattered to him. Or, maybe, he just didn't look at me that way. I lower my voice and take a few steps back from the soccer field.

"Sometimes I think of those girls, of everything they're going through, and all I can think is, why the hell did Holly want me here? Why did she think I was equipped to fix any of this for them?"

"Don't be so hard on yourself—*ow*." Stepping so that we stand in shadow at the side of the bleachers, Cody walks into one of the metal beams, bumping his head, then turns to me, laughing softly at himself. "You're Felicity Wheeler."

"Was."

"No." Cody shakes his head, giving me a daring half-smile. "You talk like what happened was your fault, but I was there, too. Remember?"

Don't I? At this, I suddenly want to scream, my hands knotting into fists in my pockets. When Frankie kicks the ball toward me, I miss it. Cody stops it under his toe deftly and I remember he used to play on the soccer team.

"Felicity, can I say something to you?" Inside my sleeves, the hairs on my arms stand on end. "It's important."

To whom? I wonder, my attention wandering as I kneel to take the ball from under his foot with both hands.

"Would you listen, if I apologized?"

"What?" The ball slips from my hands as I stand up too quickly, head nearly colliding with the metal beam. Only, Cody reaches toward me to stop the impact, his hand pinched between my head and the steel above it.

"Sorry." He draws his hand back, then turns pointedly aside, as if to allow me some privacy in my shock.

"What did you say?" I give the ball a weak kick in Tess's direction, my nervous gaze ticking between Cody and the girls out on the field.

"An apology isn't enough," he murmurs. "And I know that. But I do want you to know that I feel awful about what happened between us. I've put a lot of thought and effort into being a better person. I don't want anything from you—that's all I wanted to say."

It takes a minute to calm myself. Breathing in, slowly, then out, slowly. The look on his face is genuine—I think. I don't have to forgive him to accept that he's sorry.

"You don't need to say anything. I'll go." Hesitant, he takes another step away from me, into the sunlight. "It is always nice to see you—I do mean that."

"I appreciate it, Cody. That couldn't have been easy to say." Out on the field, Tess and Frankie are still playing, though I see Tess glancing our way every few moments. "They said Holly's death was an accident. But I don't think it was."

"Really?" Cody turns to face me, angling his shoulders my way. "You've got to do something." He's as he always has been: radiating absolute confidence. Confidence that a person can just speak something and make it into fact, into action. The world hasn't exactly proven him wrong.

"I will," I answer. "I've learned more than the cops seem to know, just by looking at what's there in broad daylight."

"You think it would help if I talked to someone?" he asks. "One of my father's old friends is a judge. I'm sure he could ask someone to look more closely at what happened to Holly."

"I don't know."

"Look," he says, his voice softening again. "I promised myself I would never hurt anybody else that way again. That if I had a chance, I'd help you, if I ever could."

"Yes, I suppose that might help." I give a shaky sigh. "I just keep feeling I'm letting her down, Cody. It feels awful. I can't sleep—I can barely eat."

"Holly would have wanted you to feel some peace about all of this. Even if it meant leaving. She would forgive you."

"I would love to leave," I admit. "But I can't."

I turn out toward the soccer field, where Tess and Frankie have ceased their game and are sitting in the grass, talking together. "I should get them home."

"Okay, Felicity." Cody turns back, angles his shoulders toward me. "Do you have plans on Saturday evening?"

"I—"

"Nothing special," he offers. "Thought you might want to come out for a drink, get a change of scenery. As friends."

"I can't on Saturday, Cody. But maybe another time."

"I'll see you later, then." He lowers his chin in a respectful nod, eyes lingering on mine. I see Tess lift a hand and wave as he walks away.

"Ready to go?" I ask. They shrug and nod their heads. "Tess, how do you know him?"

"Oh, um." She flashes a smile, still breathing hard from running. "Everyone knows everyone here, Aunt Lissie. Maybe you forgot what it's like." She flashes a rare grin and I'm charmed right into agreeing with her. It's a small town, maybe even a friendly one, at times. Maybe I had forgotten what it's like.

CHAPTER TWENTY-SEVEN
Before

After I dropped out of school, Holly was my only focus. The hours of her day, the schedule we used to share, had not changed. Not one bit of her daily routine was different, and it seemed to me, through a haze of confusion, that I had absorbed all of the shock for her, of what had happened to Page, of the terrifying rumors that followed. I watched her longingly as my double, hopeful that I could experience some normalcy vicariously. But we were no longer one whole, and with an equal and opposite reaction, Holly pulled away from me. One afternoon when she came home from school, she looked up and saw me watching from the bay window, and turned around to walk toward the dock instead of coming inside.

But I was desperate for Holly to speak to me. I no longer even cared to talk over what had happened the night Page had died. Our bond was more important—I would have done anything for her to ask me how I was doing, or to answer when I asked her the same.

I walked outside after her without bothering with shoes or a jacket, despite the damp chill of the autumn afternoon. My bare feet were silent on the grass. Holly sat at the edge of the dock, feet dangling over the water, unaware of my presence.

"Hey." When I spoke, her shoulders tensed. I knew she would have to at least walk past me in order to walk away from me. "Sorry to corner you out here. I just wanted to say hi."

In response, without turning around, she lifted one hand and fluttered her fingertips, as she might have waved hello to an acquaintance in passing. The distance of the gesture dissolved my cool.

"Holly, you haven't talked to me in weeks."

"What do you want?"

"I miss you. Things are different now, and—"

"Yeah." With a cold breath of laughter, Holly turned over her shoulder to eye my slightly rounded belly. "No shit."

"You're shutting me out."

"Well, you obviously haven't been sharing with me, either."

I walked to the end of the dock and dropped to sit on my knees in front of her. "Holly, I know you didn't do anything wrong that night. If Page jumped in the water, it was her own fault." Her eyes widened with an unspoken warning. "I was there that night—I remember. There was something else in the water. Something scary."

"Only little children are scared of ghosts." Holly sneered this at me, but I took note that she didn't say whether she believed in ghosts or not. At the sound of tires on the gravel drive behind us, she leapt up and turned toward the house. I had to shuffle out of her way, nearly slipping over the edge.

"Are you expecting someone?" I asked. "Holly, meet me here again after dinner. I want to talk, without Mom or Dad overhearing."

Without looking back, Holly strode off toward the house, leaving me alone, staring into the water. I didn't recognize the car in the driveway, and I almost didn't recognize Holly's friend Silas, wearing a white button-up shirt in place of his usual t-shirt with cutoff sleeves. Sensing that something was off, I had followed, but when I walked into the kitchen, only my mother and Holly were there, seated quietly at the table.

"What's going on?"

They both lifted a finger to hush me, and I overheard voices from the living room. While my mother, Holly and I sat in the kitchen pretending not to eavesdrop, Silas asked Glen for his permission to marry Holly.

Once Silas had left, without receiving any real answer, Glen's footsteps sounded down the hallway. He had such a way of walking, as if he had never in his life tried to move furtively. And the way he stood in the doorway of the kitchen, at ease in his anger.

"Which one of you is going to tell me what's going on?" His gaze swiveled between me and Holly, as if he hadn't noticed we never talked these days, as if he thought we shared some secret just to spite him.

"I don't know what you mean, Dad." Holly didn't look very happy, I thought, for someone who had just been proposed to.

"You know exactly what it means when a boy shows up with a question like that."

He didn't have to hit anyone to be a menace, his anger blunt but unpredictable. He took one step toward Holly, pointing at her as his mouth opened to speak, and then—I was certain that I was hallucinating—my mother was on her feet, standing calmly between them.

"Don't say a word," my mother said, her calm voice yielding not a single inch. "Try me, Glen. I dare you." Glen looked at her a moment longer, then mumbled something indiscernible and left the room. My mother kissed Holly's forehead and ruffled her hair. Like a magic trick she'd been hiding the whole time, that she chose not to reveal until just this moment, she had been ready to dare Glen for Holly's sake but not for mine. We heard those loud footsteps up the stairs, down the hallway, and, minutes later, tromping out the front door. The clap of a car door closing, the engine as it drove away.

After an excruciatingly quiet dinner, I crept outside, sitting in my jacket at the edge of the dock. I waited for hours, hoping for Holly to meet me, and for Glen to come back. I fell asleep waiting, and woke up near midnight with freezing cold hands. Accepting that neither of them was coming, I went back inside and crawled into bed.

CHAPTER TWENTY-EIGHT
Now

Saturday's sunset is flawless, fading into a fragrant, crisp evening. I walk outside to wait for James on the porch at ten to seven, hoping to prevent any chance greeting between him and my mother. Stars peek through the haze overhead, and the beautiful night strikes me with a sense of foreboding. When I see headlights, I walk out to meet James in the driveway, hopeful that seeing him will dispel my nervousness. But he's guarded, and I can't make out his expression in the near dark. As he drives into Brightwater, we exchange overly pleasant, brief questions and answers, each too eager to lighten the atmosphere. Anxious to fill the silence, all I can manage is an unspoken list of the things I can't talk to him about: how I argued with my mother. How I'm afraid that sleeplessness is making me look older. How I'm scared every time I do drift off, because I don't want to wake up knee-deep in the lake again.

By the time James parks downtown, the quiet between us feels resigned. We walk a few paces apart, past one, then two closed restaurants. But Cotton Blossom, which is always open, is only a few blocks up. James pauses outside the door, studying me with some concern. "Are you sure this place is okay with you?"

"Yes, it is. But I'm going to ask a favor."

"What's that?"

"Sometimes, it feels like people around here look at me and see nothing but sad stories. What if we'd never met, and we could just—I don't know, talk? Could we?"

"Yes." And then, finally, James smiles, reaching to hold the door open for me. "Well, it's really nice to meet you."

The diner where my sister used to work is so crowded that I barely recognize it as the same place I ate lunch just last week. There's garland and strings of twinkling lights along the walls, and it's so packed that I reach for James's hand as we move through the crowd, half afraid I'll lose sight of him.

After he orders drinks at the bar, we slip through the room and he finds a quiet booth under a hanging stained-glass lampshade. When he takes my coat, his hands brush my shoulders; his smile as I sit in the bench is all warmth.

And, as we promised, I talk with him almost as I might with a stranger, or a new friend, drawing out the things we don't know about each other, rather than stumbling over old mistakes. I learn that James Finley is a high school teacher, art history and photography. When his last relationship ended, he agreed to let his ex keep their dogs, a pair of corgis, but could not give up the cat, now his sole roommate in a restored Victorian row house.

"And what about you?" he asks. "How long have you lived in Saint Thomas?"

"Only a year, but I love it. It's as if I've finally found a place that feels—" Not like home, I think. Not peaceful—it's a thriving city. Where nobody knows anything more about me than I want them to. "It's just right. Almost like I could buy myself a bookshelf, fill it with books."

"Really?" He grins.

"Yes," I answer. "I'd have to buy one—I wouldn't know how to build my own."

"Roommates? Pets?"

"It's only me," I tell him. "That's how I like things, I guess."

"Have you always felt that way?" he asks, as if he doesn't know the answer.

"No," I answer, "but I think we learn the truth about ourselves as we grow up."

Three, we had promised each other. Two girls and a boy, or two boys and a girl.

"I don't always love being alone," I admit. "But it seems to be more within my range than any of the alternatives."

"So, then, what is it like," he asks, "being with two children around the clock?"

"Oh, they're lovely." My face breaks into an easy smile. "Frankie is five. She's adorable, and she has this gentle, loving personality that just shines." *Like her mother.* "Tess is twelve years old. She's sharp, and she doesn't say much, but for every word she says, you can tell there's an ocean of thought behind it. She—concerns me, a little."

"How so?"

Because Tess knows something about the night her mother died, and she isn't telling anybody. Because I know what it does to you, to hide a secret so dark, and I can hardly eat for fear she's going through something similar. A procession of images ticks across my mind: the purse; the bracelet; the rooster. Silas, showing up on a whim, nobody the wiser without Elvis to broadcast his arrival.

"I shouldn't stay out very late."

"We can leave whenever you're ready." He studies me closely, and I feel the illusion between us flickering. We could pretend to be two strangers, but we both know otherwise. "What is it? Do you need to leave now?"

"I don't believe Holly died by accident. But nobody in this town wants to listen to what I think about anything, much less the police."

"That's not true," he says. "I'm listening."

"Tess says that she was asleep all that night, but I think she saw Holly leave the house with somebody. And things have happened that have made me concerned for her safety."

James watches me, and I can't help but feel he's sizing me up, that I've said too much. "Please be careful."

"I am," I answer. "I never planned to come back here, certainly not to stay. But I can't leave before I know that the girls are safe."

"Of course." I sense a quiet pulse of disappointment from across the table. "You have a life there."

"It's so hard not to wonder how things might have happened." My hand stretches across the table, rests dangerously close to his.

"Who's to say where we'd be now, if things had been different? Would we be sitting here, strangers, over ten years of lost time between us?" I let my fingers trace over the back of his hand.

"I don't think either of us can blame ourselves for what happened. Maybe that's all we can ask for." James doesn't answer my questions, but I know what he's thinking: that only makes it harder to accept the way things ended. I know it because I'm thinking the same thing.

"It must be getting late."

"Probably," he says. "Maybe you'd let me buy you one more drink?"

"I think so, yes." I stand up and smooth my dress with my hands. "I'm going to the restroom. Back in a minute."

I walk past the bar to get to the corridor that leads to the restrooms, the low lights and smell of old cigarette smoke giving almost an impression of stepping back in time. The pine garland that lines the corridor is intended as a holiday decoration, but it gives me the sudden sense of having stepped through a doorway and into a forest. As I'm walking back out into the corridor, my reflection catches my eye in the mirror above the sink, and I'm briefly frightened, having mistaken myself for Holly. I push the door closed firmly behind me as if I could lock any ghosts away within, and walk back toward the seating area, looking for James.

There is a jovial shout from across the crowded room: "Hey, ladybug!" There's no telling if it's directed at me. Still, near where the corridor opens into the barroom, I pause and take a step backward into the shadows. I tell myself firmly that it isn't because I'm scared, but only that I'd rather avoid the bother of running into another old acquaintance. Yet, over the noise of the crowd, all the laughter and voices, this one stands out.

With broad, confident steps Cody crosses the room, and people seem to step out of his way without even meaning to.

"Hey, Felicity. I didn't think you'd be here." His smile is broad and warm, one hand clasping mine in greeting.

"Hi, Cody." It's impossible not to return his smile.

"Didn't you say you couldn't come out tonight?"

"I did not say that, exactly." I remove his hand from mine with a scolding smile. "I said I couldn't meet *you* on Saturday night."

"Okay, I get it." Cody's smile is sheepish, giving me a sudden impression of a kid caught at their parents' liquor cabinet. Just as I intend to make an excuse and step away, he leans on the doorframe next to me, a curious gleam in his eye. "You look nice."

"Thanks." His statement hangs in the air, and I sense there's more to it. "What is it?"

"You look different. But I can't tell how, exactly." Cody seems to be taking stock of my appearance. Feeling a bit silly, I realize it's true that I did put in more effort than usual. At Tess's insistence, I even wore one of Holly's dresses, black jersey with a snug waist and a knee-length skirt that drapes at every move, as if it's begging me to dance.

"All right, all right." Forcing a laugh, I step as if to walk away from him. "It was nice to see you, Cody."

"You look like Holly."

"What did you say?"

"I didn't mean to say that out loud. Sorry, Felicity." He murmurs the words as if by accident, as if he's thinking aloud, lost in memory, then turns back to me. "Correct me if I'm wrong, but this doesn't look like a dress you would buy for yourself."

"I'm sure I don't know what you mean." As my pulse picks up, I blink, looking at Cody with some confusion.

"You're right—what do I know?" His hand brushes my shoulder, then skims my waist. "Only, you know, it looks more like something your sister would wear." His smile is so polite, as if he's arguing a point of no importance to either of us, this hand that gestures around my torso like it might be a welcome sign.

"I—" Dozens of words seem to freeze in my mouth, and I find I can't inhale.

"Hey, look." Cody nudges me and glances upward, eyeing the holiday decor. "Mistletoe! Hm?"

"Don't touch me." Standing as tall as I can, I realize the words sound wrong: all the anger in my mind has come out fearful, a whisper, and suddenly this wrong feeling is in my limbs, too. "Cody, you ruined my life."

"I—" His surprise fades into a sullen frown. "I did apologize."

"It wasn't only that. You—" *I don't know why, but it feels so hard to breathe.* "What you said afterward. That you would have told people that Holly hurt Page on purpose, if I—"

"If you what? Told people that you cheated on your boyfriend?" His laugh is so gentle, as if, even now, he doesn't understand.

"That's not what happened." The words burn in my throat.

"What, exactly, do you remember?" Cody gives me a playful smile, a gentle squeeze on my upper arm. "Come on—you were more than a little drunk."

"I—" I wiggle my arm, inching away until he releases his hand. My voice falls to a whisper. "I remember." As much as I wish I didn't. As if a gear has shifted, my heartbeat strikes a manic pace, and even to look at Cody makes me dizzy with dread, vivid and heavy as the very day it happened.

"And—Felicity, you weren't there, that night. How can you say that I haven't been holding back some of the truth all this time, to protect you and your sister both?"

"Well, she doesn't need protecting now, does she?" I inch backward, my shoulder blades bumping against the wall. "And I do not accept your apology."

"I can't make you accept it." Instead of backing off, though, he steps closer. "You blame other people for that night, because the truth hurts you. Your sister was human."

"Give me some space here, okay?" I try to deliver these words as if I'm half amused, but I can hear the edge in my voice, and suddenly I'm holding an arm up across my chest, as if to claim some air I can breathe on my own, and, once again, he pretends not to hear my words.

"Oh, is that a dare?" He laughs, as if my discomfort is invisible. I stumble backward and the heel of my boot clatters against the wall again. When he opens his mouth to speak, I'm already recoiling. But something else catches Cody's attention. He turns his chin, looking toward the bar, then smiles and waves.

"Hey, Fin! Look who I found."

I see James wave at us, then he catches my eye, tilts his head.

Then, all of a sudden, I can hear James's voice drawing closer amid the chaos of the crowd, the music, as he encounters Cody.

"Hi, Cody. Yeah, good, how are you?"

"Fine, man." Cody claps a hand against my shoulder and I grit my teeth. "Did you know who's here? It's like seeing a ghost, right?"

"Yeah, I did, in fact," James answers. His voice drops a note as he turns to speak to me. "I was just looking for you, Felicity. What's wrong?" Everything around me seems so loud, so close, that when I feel a hand on mine, I jolt away, realizing only afterward it's James's hand, not Cody's.

"Oh, is this a date, then?" Cody raises his eyebrow. "You should know—ladybugs, they'll break your heart. Or don't you know that already?"

"Is that true?" James's polite smile fades as he fixes Cody with a contemplative stare. Something sparks behind his eyes, and he takes one measured step so that he's in between me and Cody.

"You've really got to love the holidays in this town, you know," Cody says. "Everyone comes back. It's like a family reunion." As if I'm here for the holidays.

"Something wrong, Finley?" Cody asks. James's arm slips around my back, fingertips curling around my waist. "Whatever," Cody continues. "I can see I'm intruding here. I'll be at the bar if you two want to join me."

"Not now, Cody." He stares for a moment, then turns back to me. Finally, still chuckling to himself, Cody walks back toward the crowded bar. I inch out of James's arm and he looks down at me with a resigned sadness.

"Felicity, I think we need to talk."

"I can't." Distantly, I recognize a rush of shame, of being so tired of lying that it makes me suck my breath in, a sudden, sharp gasp. And then I can't slow the dizzying pace my lungs set, clapping both hands over my mouth in a pointless effort to steady myself.

"Tell me what happened."

"I'd prefer not to." How foolish I was, to hope that I could pretend to talk with him as if I were anyone but who I am. "I'm fine."

"That's not true." James touches my chin so that I lift my face to look at him, the other resting between my shoulder blades, which feel as brittle as glass. "What did he say to you?"

"I don't know." I can hardly recall a word Cody spoke to me—nothing, really, other than the knowing brush of his hand along my waist. He asked what I remembered, and then it was all I could see. My eyes are burning, and I'm clenching my teeth so hard it hurts. James's eyebrows draw closer together and I see his gaze jolt across the room, then back to me. He wraps both arms around me, and I let my eyes close, pressing my face into his chest, finding an unexpected calm there. As if he senses my relief, he holds me tighter.

"I want to leave."

"Maybe a walk, then. We'll find some fresh air, get out of the noise."

"Yes, please." I nod my chin emphatically. "Would you get my coat? I left it at the table."

"Of course." James squeezes my shoulders, then releases. "Wait right here for just a second, then we'll go." He turns away and walks back toward our table, past the crowded bar. I let myself slouch against the wall, all my tension wilting into a quiet sense of defeat.

The next thing I see, he's swinging a fist into Cody's jaw.

CHAPTER TWENTY-NINE

Now

The crowd around them ripples backward. Cody drops his glass, which breaks against the floor.

"What the hell, Finley?"

"Is there something you need to tell me?" James holds Cody in place by one shoulder, and Cody glances toward me, then the opposite wall, unable or unwilling to look James in the eye. My heart beats in a frantic, dizzying patter.

"I have no idea what you mean."

"Hey, remind me: how long have we known each other?"

"I don't know, asshole—what is this about?" Cody's still half smiling when James shoves him backward with both hands.

"First grade," James says. "We've been friends since first grade. I will give you one more chance to tell me the truth."

As he lifts one hand tenderly to his jaw, Cody's eyes flicker my way, expressionless, then back to James. "I don't know what you're talking about."

"The one good thing, the one real thing I ever had. What did you do to her?"

I find myself sent straight back into that terrible memory, a crowd hungry for scandal, uninvited eyes flickering in my direction. It's too much. I can't stay. Forcing my way through the crowd, I skirt the room, keeping close to the wall.

"Please," Cody laughs. "She couldn't keep her hands off of me."

Walking with my head lowered, I'm nearly at the door. At the sound of a muffled impact, I turn back just in time to see Cody tripping sideways, catching himself on a chair. And James, dragging him back to his feet so he can look him in the face to speak to him.

"I don't believe you, Redford."

Disbelief washes over me, trickling from my eyes. Cody lifts one hand and James bats it away, holding his arm aside.

"She's not worth all this, Fin."

"You're the one who's not worth all this." James pulls his fist back, but then abruptly drops his hands, looking at his friend as if he's never seen him before. "I thought I knew you." He turns away, shaking his head.

"You're a fool, and you always were." Cody draws himself upright and throws a sudden punch that catches James square on the face. His voice drops low and sharp. "Nobody would make such a fuss over something they've already had."

The bartender is shouting at Cody to leave, and he answers with a cold stare, pushing a bar stool to the floor as he walks out. The room is silent, everyone apparently holding a collective breath.

As the door swings shut behind him, I see one or two people clap James's shoulder.

"He's had that coming for a long time. Guy doesn't know when to shut his mouth."

"Someone get the man a drink."

I'm blinking, frozen here at the edge of the corridor, watching from the shadows. James turns my way and I see blood on his face, promptly forget everything else, and run to his side.

"Oh, my God, James." Before I know it, I'm placing both my hands on his cheeks, tilting his chin back, tracing a finger over the bridge of his nose. "I don't think it's broken, but—excuse me." I turn to make eye contact with the bartender. "Could I have a glass of water and a napkin, please?"

"I'm okay."

I hold a napkin to his nose, blinking furiously as the blood soaks through it. His words echo in my ears: *The one good thing, the one real thing I ever had.* My hand is still on his face when James turns, pressing his cheek into my palm, and suddenly it's all I can do not to throw my arms around him, all I can do to hold back the words *me, too.* Kneeling to the floor, I pick up his glasses, the frame slightly bent, and return them to him.

"How about that walk?"

"Are you sure you're all right?"

"Yes," he answers, his eyes warm and patient, though he still holds a hand at his nose. "Let's get out of here."

I quickly collect my purse and help James put on his coat, although he doesn't need help. The quiet and cool of the night air is a relief, though it leaves no cover of noise, all the things we haven't said.

"So—"

"Yeah," I murmur, nodding my head as we walk. Damp leaves and pine needles litter the ground from the recent rain, and now, close to eleven, the narrow streets are quiet, the shopfronts dimly lit or empty. James is walking with his hand still at his nose, and I wince, seeing it hasn't stopped bleeding.

I unwrap my scarf and hand it to him. He shakes his head, and I turn to face him, placing a gentle hand on his shoulder. He pauses, the toes of our shoes brushing, and I fold my scarf at the corner and use it to dab at his nose.

"I would have always taken your word over his."

I look into his eyes for a moment before we continue walking.

"What are you not telling me?"

"Cody believes that Holly is to blame for Page's death. He felt he was protecting her by not sharing more about what happened that night."

"So, you were protecting her, too." When James speaks again, his voice is lower, sharp with understanding.

"I would do it again."

"Don't say that."

"I'm sorry, James, but it's true. Whatever Holly did that night, I know that she didn't have it in her heart to cause Page any real harm. Besides, even if I had told anyone about Cody, who would have believed me?"

Shadows swarm my thoughts as I speak. That blithe, friendly tone Cody used when he asked me: *What exactly do you remember?* Even Holly didn't believe me.

James turns so that we're face to face, and I slow to a stop on the sidewalk. "I would have."

"We can't—" *We can't know that for sure*, is what I'm about to say. And maybe those words are true. But a memory of James crops up to interrupt my thoughts, an image of him at eighteen, sad-eyed, wondering aloud what to say, how to help. He is so different now, in some way that I can't measure. "I don't even know where I'm going," I sigh. "I just needed fresh air."

"My house is pretty close."

"Your car is parked near the diner."

"I'll walk back and move it later."

"Are you sure you're all right?"

"Of course." He throws a mischievous look my way. "It was worth it."

We walk down a side street, lined with maple trees that blanket the ground with leaves like faded stars. We pass a shopfront up a small hill from the sidewalk, and I follow him up a flight of stairs to a row house with a single chair on the front porch.

James has always been precise. Even now, holding my scarf to his nose, he unlocks the door of his house, places his coat neatly on the hook. He reaches a hand to take mine as well, but I hang it up myself. I follow him through a study that opens into a living room and kitchen, see a rather rotund tortoiseshell cat lift her chin to look at us from the back of the sofa. James stops in front of a side table, thumbing through a stack of records. The cat lifts her chin at me curiously and I step near to pet her. He chooses one, slides it out of the sleeve, and puts it on the record player. The needle scratches as it lands, then music starts.

"What are you doing?" I point to the armchair. "Sit down." He does, and I help myself to the kitchen, find a clean cloth and some ice in the freezer. I sit on the arm of the chair, take his chin in my hand, holding the ice against his nose while I clean blood from his face. When our eyes meet, I catch my breath, notice that I'm smiling.

"How does it feel?" I pull the cloth back, see that the bleeding has slowed.

"Better," he says.

"What were you thinking?"

"Felicity, if I can be honest, I wasn't thinking."

"You shouldn't have done it."

"I'm not so sure about that."

"It was impulsive." Though I give him my best scolding glare, my eyes are watering again. "And foolish."

"You've always been the practical one here," he answers. "You know that."

"I had to be." My voice breaks. Without asking, I slide into the armchair next to him, circle my arms around his chest.

"Okay. I know." The humor in his tone fades, and I can feel the solidity of his arms wrapping around me, as if he's catching all the anxiety in my chest against his own. James pulls me close, presses his face against my hair.

"You were my girl," he murmurs. "I should have protected you."

"That's the drinks talking."

"No, it isn't. And anyway, that hit to the face cleared my head," he counters, laughing.

I lift my forehead from his chest and look at him, so close our noses are almost touching.

"Oh, I like this song." I recognize the music coming from the record player. "You always had good taste." James shrugs and his smile is somehow both irreverent and guileless.

"I know what I like." He shifts in the chair and stands up, and I reach for his hand without thinking, trying to keep him close. Instead, he takes both my hands and pulls me up next to him, asking me to dance without speaking a word.

"You're a romantic, James." I let my fingers twine into his, drape my other arm over his shoulder.

"You were, too," he answers, drawing me closer. "Do you remember that?"

"We've been here before," I answer, leaning my head on his chest. "We know how this ends."

"Yeah?" He rests his chin on the top of my head. "Maybe we don't."

CHAPTER THIRTY
Now

As the song plays, I let my eyes close, let everything and everyone else fall away from my mind. My hand moves from his shoulder, resting around his neck, tousling his hair. I look up to him sadly, then turn my cheek to the side.

For so many years, I'd let myself think of James only as a source of pain. To feel his hands on mine, to hear his voice speaking about possibility, it throws this familiar sense of loss into a different light. For the first time since I can remember, I can't bring myself to be content with losing. The music shifts, and I remember in a rush the way James used to hold me, exactly as he is now. How I used to reach for him, my fingertips on his cheek. And the gentle flash in his eyes, the way he used to smile, just before he kissed me. I see that it hasn't changed a bit. I reach up to touch his face, let my lips brush his.

Back then, James and I had never even discussed anything beyond kissing, not in any detail. Not beyond promising that our first time would be with each other. Then, after Cody, any embrace was only a place to hide, one of so many places I looked for quiet or safety. He pulls me closer against him and I rise to stand on the tips of my toes, twining my arms around his shoulders.

The song ends and we fall back into the armchair. His hands tangle in my hair, and I'm suddenly desperately curious to feel every inch of his shoulders, my hands trailing along his arms as we kiss. When I find my fingertips playing at the buttons of his shirt, I draw back to look into his eyes. When we were young, we told ourselves *no*, more times than I could count. Back then I thought we had all the time in the world.

He lifts me to my feet, and I follow him to his bedroom, discarding my boots one at a time in the hallway. There's no hint of awkwardness between us, no uncertainty, almost as if we've never been apart. And when he holds me, when I feel his skin under my hands, it's like I've been underwater all these years and never even knew it and now I'm breathing, seeing in color, finally. And that's the word that lingers on my mind, when I rest next to him, my hand curled around his waist. *Finally*.

Nestling my toes into the bed sheets, I stretch, reaching my arms up as high as I can. He traces an admiring hand down my back. "I've been sleeping in an armchair, you know."

"Who's making you sleep in a chair? That should be a crime." He leans over to kiss my shoulder blades. "You're beautiful, Felicity." I'm trying to decide how to return the compliment, my eyes lingering on his shoulders, his chest, his lips. He nudges me with a grin, and I realize I've been caught out staring at him.

From across the room, a tinny-sounding chime rings: my phone, from inside the pocket of my dress, strewn across the doorway of the bedroom.

"Maybe I should check that."

"Up to you."

Feeling a pang of sadness, without knowing why, I lean back my chin, and he kisses my temple. My heart patters and I feel the tension creep back into my shoulders. It's been a long time since I let anything into my life that had the capability to hurt me. James blinks, studying the ceiling as if it's miles away, then turns a nervous gaze toward me, as if he's waiting for me to speak. My heart twists and I wrap my arms around him, pulling him closer.

I'd like to promise him things. Just as I did before. I ought to know better than to tempt disaster. The world put things in the middle of us we couldn't begin to stand up to.

"I'm not good at things like this, James." I cannot help but feel there's something uneasy in me, some terribly heavy thing, equally impossible to carry as it is to put down. James leans closer, placing a soft kiss on my temple, another on my cheekbone.

"Felicity, whatever happens after this, it's okay."

As I'm trying to find the right answer, I hear my phone chime again. Two messages in a row this late at night, it's a safe bet something's wrong. I stand up and walk across the room to take my phone out of the pocket of my dress. There are two messages, both from my mother.

The first one reads: *Is that you on the stairs?*

I don't pause to let myself think, scrolling straight to her next message.

Felicity, you're 30 years old. You don't have to sneak in when you come home late.

"James, will you drive me home?" Clutching my dress against my bare chest, I tap the phone screen to call my mother.

"Of course." He answers without hesitation, a note of doubt in his tone. "Did I say something wrong?"

Just as I begin to reassure him, my mother answers the phone. "Hi, Felicity."

"Mom, what's going on?"

"Why are you calling?" I can hear the tired warmth in my mother's voice. "You could just walk down the hallway, you know."

"What do you mean?" I ask. When my mother answers me, she sounds amused.

"You know this house creaks every time you take a step. You don't need to sneak in—you're not a kid anymore."

Suddenly, I'm freezing all over, feel the squeeze of my heart beginning to race. *I shouldn't be here. I should have gone straight home.* I look at James, my eyes widening, and gesture to the door as I step into the dress and fumble for the buttons.

"Where are the girls?"

"They're with me," she answers. "We watched a movie in my room and they fell asleep right here on the bed. Wait. Felicity, are you—"

"Lock your door."

"What?"

"Get the girls and hide in the closet. Make as little noise as possible." Someone's in the house. And here I am, pacing circles in James Finley's bedroom on the other side of town, looking for my shoes.

"Felicity, what's going on?"

"No noise," I repeat. "Don't say a word. I'm not at home."

CHAPTER THIRTY-ONE

Now

When I hang up, James is already getting dressed.

"What happened?"

"There's someone in the house."

He buttons his jeans, then picks up his shirt.

"She heard someone come in, then walk up the stairs, go into the blue room—that's where I sleep, with the children." My hands shake as I feel for my boots. "They're all in her room. They can't—" I bend down to put on my right boot, get it on the wrong foot, then tug it off. "The thing is, they'd have to walk past that room to leave the house. I—" A rush of anxiety weakens my already wobbly knees, forces me to sit on the edge of his dresser. As I'm struggling with my boots, James crosses the room, shirt still on his arm, and pulls me against him, my cheek against his bare chest. "We'll go right away. Come on." As I lift my head to look at him, he pulls his shirt on, then helps me to my feet.

Though it isn't more than a mile back to where his car is parked, every moment seems to stretch into a long, uncomfortable pause.

"Why doesn't she lock the door?" I whisper, the words hissing against my fingers as I clutch both hands to my face. "She never locks the door."

"I'm sure that will change after tonight." He reaches to squeeze my hand, then releases it. The panic in my chest has taken the place of whatever spell had been cast between us, and I realize now that, distant memories aside, James and I are strangers.

"I'm so sorry for this."

"Don't be." He answers without hesitation, though I can't discern whether his rather solemn expression is one of worry or more impersonal. "The car's right here." He unlocks the passenger door first, and I sit down gratefully.

The drive seems to take years. I'm staring out the window as if I could find something useful there, and James keeps saying gentle things, as if he thinks I need support, or soothing, or something to steady my nerves. I wouldn't even know if I did. I'm all senses, as if the night outside could answer my questions, that darkness that has called my name before seeming to laugh at me now. All I can picture is that big house, so far away from everything, sound muffled by the trees and the water around it.

I hear the end of a sentence and jerk my head to look at him. "What?"

"Have you felt safe there until now?"

"I haven't felt safe in years." My voice comes out low, almost sharp, and his gaze flickers my way with surprise. "I lock doors everywhere I go, James. And windows. I can't sleep if there's one hairpin out of place. I don't make friends, not really. I—" When I realize I'm gasping, I crack the window and breathe in the cold, damp air. I'm not the person James used to know. I'm too brittle to trust anyone, more likely than not to snap and frown at any stranger unlucky enough to offer me help or a kind word. His touch on my wrist eases, holding more lightly, then letting go, and somehow this soothes me. "I haven't felt at ease there, these last few days, but that doesn't mean anything, coming from me."

"What would make you say that?"

The footprints in the driveway. The way I fall asleep in the chair, then wake up knee-deep in the lake, barefoot and wearing my nightgown. The voice I hear, that I've always heard. But there's more.

"Tess knows something." This is one thing I am certain of. "I've been a girl with secrets. I know how it looks. She knows something about where Holly was that night. She could be in danger."

As we pass over the bridge, I open the window and stare out into the night. The fog is dense, but not impenetrable. If anyone came to my mother's house, they would have had to pass this way. Maybe they're still there. James whispers curses at the narrow bridge as the car approaches it.

"They should have this thing better marked," he says. "How many times has someone driven off into the creek?"

"It hasn't happened yet," I answer. "There's the streetlight, after all. And the only people who come out here know the road pretty well."

From the driveway, I can see the windows of the blue room, dark now. I realize the immensity, the thickness, of the dark around us. How it stretches out in every direction. I realize that a car isn't the only way to get here. Someone could have come by foot, snuck in or out. Just as easily by boat. Or hidden somewhere.

Once we're in the driveway, I'm cracking the door open before the car even stops.

"Mom?" I can hear the shrill edge in my shout, rattling the silence. I turn toward the shadowed staircase, imagine Tess and Frankie hiding in a closet in the dark. I'm a nurse. I'm familiar with injuries. I don't have the luxury of living in an imagined world where harm doesn't come to children. But the thought of any harm coming to these children, I find, is so much worse than I could have imagined. I lose my balance momentarily, grabbing onto James's hand with a desperate grip.

"Felicity, we're in here." When I hear my mother's voice, I swivel on one heel, only James's arm keeping me on my feet. She's sitting in the living room in her bathrobe. Blinking, I let go of James's hand and rush forward. Tess sits at my mother's side, holding Frankie on her lap, a blanket tucked over them. It's only once my arms are around them, that I'm certain they're real, that I find I can inhale again.

"I'm sorry," I whisper, feeling Tess squirm in my embrace. "I'm so sorry. Are you okay?"

"Yeah," she answers, a defensive edge in her voice. "We're fine, seriously. Your hair's a mess, though." I pull back, note the fear in her eyes, then embrace them again, pressing a kiss to Frankie's temple. Tess would answer that she was fine even if it weren't true. "Who's that?"

"His name is James," I answer.

My mother sighs sharply, and I answer her with a look that's sharper still. "Not now, Mom. We have actual concerns, here. Has anything else happened?"

"I heard the footsteps again," she answers. "After we got off the phone. Down the hall, back toward the blue room. A few times. Whoever it was, they knew we were in there."

"How do you know? Did you hear a voice?"

My mother has never willingly admitted to being frightened, but her eyes skirt away from mine, her gaze lingering on the wall. "They knocked at the door."

"What?"

"Not really like a knock," she says, hands folded tightly on her lap. "Like you would if you were tapping your fingers on a counter." She places a hand on the coffee table, drumming her fingertips along its surface in a triplet of taps.

"They knew you were in there." *And they wanted you to know it.*

"And I heard them walk back down the stairs, and out the door."

"Did you hear a car?" I stand up quickly and turn to the window, the dress swirling around my knees.

"No."

"They're still here." Hands squeezing my temples, I'm halfway back across the room, pacing toward the other doorway. "In the house, or out there. I don't know, but we can't stay."

"I'm not going anywhere." My mother wraps her arm over Tess's shoulders. Before I can argue with her, James is standing in front of me.

"If you like, I'll check the house. You can sit here with them."

"But you won't know where to look."

"I've been here before." He squeezes my hand in his and I look into his eyes, just long enough to take a breath, to feel the floor beneath my feet.

"Okay." As I take my seat by Tess on the sofa, I can't help but feel we ought to be running to the car, leaving as quickly as we can—anywhere but here. Frankie's eyes are heavy with sleep, Tess's wide as an owl's.

"I'm so sorry I wasn't here."

"This isn't your fault, girl," my mother answers, clucking gently. "You didn't sneak into your own house and scare everyone half to death. But whoever it was, they're gone now."

"We don't know that."

She hisses at me softly, her eyes darting toward the children.

"I don't think it would be a kindness to pretend that there is nothing to be scared of." She stares me down until I turn away, only because I don't want to lose my temper right now. "They already know that isn't true. And I still think we should leave."

"I don't want to leave." Tess wraps her arms around her little sister, resting her chin on top of her blonde head. "That's the only thing that could make this worse."

"I know, but—"

"Felicity?" James's footsteps are loud on the stairs, as if in a hurry, and then he's in the doorway, one hand braced on the frame. "Come upstairs."

Following him up the shadowed staircase, out of sight of my family, I cling to his hand. At the landing, he turns to face me.

"Is everything okay?"

James hesitates. Whatever he's about to say is going to change this: not only this home I've returned to, but this space between the two of us. He draws a breath to speak, his eyes bright with distress.

"Stop." I stand on my toes to wrap my arms around his shoulders, desperate for one last moment to pretend. As we kiss, his hands press along the length of my back, pulling me so close to him that I know there's no pretending, because I can tell that he is scared for me.

"You asked me if everything is okay." He lowers his chin so that our foreheads touch. "You know the answer to that. There's nobody else in the house. But there is something you need to see."

I walk with him down the hallway, open the door and walk again into the room that still feels like my childhood bedroom. For a moment, it feels like stepping back in time.

"Look—your picture's still on the wall." He laces an arm around my back.

"Is that the recliner you sleep in, the one that you told me about?" I begin to step into the room, but his arm hugs me closer, signaling to wait.

"Yes, but why?"

James doesn't answer me. The recliner's in place, only one of the bedside lights on, the room half shadowed. It's then I see it. My old cheer uniform, taken from its place on the shelf, draped across the chair.

"Oh." My breath seems to chill in my lungs. It's cut into ribbons, deep slashes through the fabric, laid out on the chair as if staged. I imagine the footsteps that my mother described, pacing from one end of the hall to the other, tapping at their door. "Oh, James, this is so—mean." A dozen other words are more fitting, but before anything else, I feel hurt. I walk quickly to the armchair as though toward an old friend who has suffered some insult.

"Felicity, don't touch it."

"You asked if I felt safe here." In the draft off the bay window, stronger than usual, I feel even more forlorn. "This is the only place I almost did." The spot where I sleep, or fail to sleep, and where I watch over my sister's children. Where, on occasion, I twist the chair around to face out the window. I lay a hand on the arm of the chair and draw back with a gasp. Before I register the red on my hands as blood, James is pulling me away.

"Didn't you hear me?" He turns my hand over as he speaks, pressing his fingertip over the scratch on my palm. "There's glass everywhere."

It's only then that I notice the window is broken, my one safe place to rest now within full grasp of the night outside. And whoever broke the window took the time to collect every last shard of glass, and place them all on the recliner. The entire scene gives me an overwhelming sense of dislike, almost as much as fear. Whoever did this wants me gone. Silas's words trip across my mind, unbidden: *Like if anyone so much as touched you, you'd shatter.*

"Please, talk to your family again." James traces a stray wisp of hair from my brow, his fingers smudged with red from the cut on my hand. "You can't stay here."

"I need to check outside." I move to stand at the bay window, the yellow bedside light shining behind me. I wonder if anybody is out there, if they are looking in at me right now. James begins to protest again, and I answer him with a somber stare. "You can come, too, and walk around the yard with me. But I'm afraid they're not going to agree to go anywhere, and I can't leave them." He gives a slow blink, then removes his glasses, folding the wire arms one side over the other. With an uncertain look of agreement, he follows me back down the stairs. Taking the flashlight from its place at the table in the hallway, I look into the living room to find my mother where I left her.

"I'll be outside for a bit. Just going to take a quick look."

"All right." She rises to her feet, looking perfectly regal in her dressing gown and slippers. As she comes near me, I first think she wants to argue again about whether it's safe to stay.

"I know you don't want to leave," I begin. "I know you don't want to alarm them." But she looks past me, directing her glare at James instead.

"I certainly never expected to see him again."

"Ignore that. Come here." Reaching for his hand, I pull him toward the doorway, but my mother steps along with us.

"Do you know what this girl went through, to protect you from the consequences of your own actions? And you never so much as called her."

"Mom, stop." One of my hands rises to warn my mother back, the other across James's chest, as if I could shield him from her misdirected anger.

"No. I won't," she says, pausing to look closely at his face. "And what happened to his nose?"

"I'm fine," he murmurs quickly.

"I wasn't asking you," she snaps. "He needs to hear this, Felicity. You can't go on protecting people forever." James gives me a sorry, knowing look, then lowers his gaze.

"Mom!" It's been a long time since I saw this protective impulse in my mother, even longer since she looked ready to protect me from anything. Holding her arm, I walk her back from James a few steps. My whisper is a show of manners only; I know James can hear us. "What I told you back then was the truth. I am not going to say it again."

"Really?" My mother turns that glare at me now, as if I'm telling her one plus one is three. "Jumping in to defend his honor, after all this time?"

"Well—yes, I suppose I am." Cheeks pricking, I turn back to James. He's standing where I left him, politely watching the wall as if he can't hear us, though I make out just the hint of a smile at the corner of his mouth. "Mom, I'll be back in a few minutes."

The flashlight sweeps the shadows of the yard. I walk with deliberate steps, pushing into the brambles and the damp grasses at the edge of the water. At each step, I want even more to shout out loud: *Come and get me*, or, *I know you're here*. And then, standing at the edge of the dock, James just a step behind me, I realize it's a game. The tap on my mother's door. The rooster, now dead, who would otherwise have announced any visitor. And here I am, combing the dark with a paltry flashlight, only the maddening silence answering.

"They've gone." I turn back to James. "I'm not sure why I know it, but they're not coming back. Not right now, anyway."

With a sigh, I walk back onto dry ground, pulling him behind me, my hand tight on his.

"I don't like to leave you here."

Still holding his hand, I walk him back to his car. "I need to get the children back to bed, and I need to be here in case they wake up. And—"

"What is it?"

"I can't ask you to do this."

"What do you mean?"

"You don't have to say it." I squeeze his hands once more, then step back. "Tell me it was nice to see me, or say that you're concerned. But I don't want you to feel that you have a stake in this."

"What if I did?" James opens the door of his car, then turns back to me with a measured, questioning look. "Would you want my help?"

"I don't know what I'm dealing with right now." Answering him honestly may be hurtful, but I am so tired of the sensation of telling half-truths that I do it anyway. "James, I don't really trust my own mother's judgment here, or the police, to be honest. I don't even know what I'd ask of you if I did."

"Cleaning the glass off your chair so you don't cut your hands." He appears to have been ready with this response. "Sitting outside the door so you can try to rest."

"No need. Truthfully, I can't sleep lately." I'm trying to make James laugh, but his mouth quirks into a concerned frown. "When I do, I usually wind up sleepwalking. I'm not much fun to be around."

"You're trying to scare me off, aren't you?"

"Yes," I admit, glad it's getting across. "And you should pay attention."

James pulls me into a fierce hug. He presses a kiss to my temple, then rests his chin on my head. I linger in his arms only a moment before stepping back.

"Can I call you?"

"You can." I can't bring myself to say it, but I can't promise that I'll answer if he does. "Goodnight."

I hurry back across the yard, aiming to make it inside before the taillights disappear to leave me alone in the dark.

CHAPTER THIRTY-TWO
Now

I'm sitting on my bed, staring up at Holly. She's standing in between me and the dresser, glaring back at me as if she's a distorted version of my own reflection. When she stomps her foot, I hear a splash, and look down to see water, dark as night, lapping around her ankles, around my own, here in the room we've grown up in.

"That's my sweater," she says. "You can't wear my clothes." The hardwood floor feels damp under my bare feet, but for some reason I'm unbothered by it.

"Sorry." I tug it off, wearing only a camisole beneath, and toss it lightly to land on her bed.

"You're so thin." The sound of her voice is sweet and clean as a flute, but I see shadows in her gaze: blame, or judgment. "How are you so thin, even now?" My heart rises as Holly sighs and finally takes those few steps across the gulf that has grown between our sides of the room. She sits at the foot of my bed. Her hair is wet, too, and the skin around her eyes looks gray.

"I know that something bad happened to you." She scoots a bit closer, then places a blanket over my bare shoulders. I've waited so long to hear these words, turning with relief to face her.

But my feet are so cold. The water is deeper, and in the shadows beneath the opposite bed, I think I see a hand reach up, then dip back down.

"You can tell me what happened, Lissie."

This isn't how it happened. But this alternate version of things is so much better than that. Ignoring the rising water, I lean into Holly's embrace. Her shoulders are chilly, yielding under my hands, and I squeeze my arms tighter, desperate to gather her against me.

There's mud under my knees and a mist of rain on my face. Rain-damp soil yields under my fingers, loose and crumbling.

I wake with a start, and see the cotton of my pajamas is soaked through from sitting on the ground. The sky is gray and yellow, streaked with orange in the east. I reach down, the tips of my fingers raw. *Why here?* I wonder, shaking my head to dispel the sleepiness. There's a strange smell, something under my hands. And feathers.

It's Elvis. The flowered sheet, dark with mold, rests tangled at my knees. *No need for an alarm when you've got him around.*

Fighting down a kicking queasiness in my stomach, I run to the porch, finding I left the side door wide open in sleep. I check each room for intruders, as I do every time I walk into the house. Upstairs, the blue room is quiet, filled with the comforting sounds of children breathing in sleep. The walls are solid, the floors dry—except for where I have tracked mud in. I go into the bathroom, close the door, and start the shower, running the water as hot as it will go.

Several days have passed since the break-in, but I have to consult the calendar to find that it's December 18. James did call me, the day after it happened, though I didn't answer. He sends messages, every day or so, to ask how I'm doing. Answering him honestly is out of the question, and I respond, often a day or two later, with a one- or two-word response, just enough to tell myself that I'm not ignoring him. Because I rarely sleep a solid night, the days run together, and it feels as though three or four very long days have passed since that night, though it has been more like ten. After nearly two weeks here, of this same air, the same view, I need to leave, even if only for a few minutes. All I want is to drive the car out to the highway, drive fast, let myself pretend I can turn my back and leave all of this behind me. And then I'll come back.

But first, I turn on the lights on the Christmas tree, start a pot of coffee for my mother when she wakes up. I make a breakfast tray for the girls, with fruit and yogurt and cups of granola, then prepare a plate for my mother as well. Before I walk out the door, I leave a note on the tray: *Going out for a drive. Back before lunch.*

I walk out the side door and circle the long way around the yard, instead of walking directly to the car. Passing over the narrow bridge feels almost dangerous after so many days of rain, the embankment beneath it steep and muddy. But, once I've put a few miles in, the spell begins to break. For a few stolen hours, I drive on the open highway. I stop at a coffee shop, though I find the smell of coffee turns my stomach, and I order tea instead. The nausea is hard to shake, and I blame that dreadful dream, those horrible memories combined with the shock of finding myself digging up a dead rooster. Before nine, I turn back, hoping that getting back home and seeing Tess and Frankie will help me feel better. From a distance, home is less daunting, and I wonder whether the change of scenery has lifted my mood, or if it's just an illusion.

At first, when the car begins to shake, I think it's the pavement, cracked and worn from too many years without repair. But then the car jolts, the engine growling. The familiar set of sounds that sent me to the same repair shop twice before, diagnosed as absolutely nothing. Except that happened in a different car.

Pulling to the side of the road, I turn to face the faded crops in a wide field. Aside from a little shock of despair, I don't feel anything. I find I have to bite back a wave of uneven laughter, a cold, mean sound that shakes out of my chest. Why did I think I could do a thing like go for a drive on a pretty morning, enjoy an hour or two of solitude? And, realizing what I've done, my breath stops. I'm stranded out here, and my family is at the house, without me. Again.

What was I thinking? This is a different car. I know I'm not putting the wrong kind of gasoline in it. This car hasn't been anywhere near the first rental car, the one that kept doing this exact same thing, that the mechanic told me was imaginary, that the tow driver thought was an excuse to get a new car. My hands feel awfully cold as I reach into my purse and get out my phone, my fingernails still chipped and gray from digging in the yard. All the time I've been back, there was only one person who believed me without hesitation. It rings just once before he answers.

"Hey," James says. "How are you?" A car flies by, just yards away, and I feel a gust of wind off the highway. "Are you there?"

"I'm here."

"Felicity?"

"James, I need to talk to someone. No—" I take a breath, guilt adding to the sick feeling in my stomach. "Not someone. I need to talk to you. I'm sorry I haven't called."

"I told you, it's okay."

"No, it's not. That's not what I want—dodging your messages. I just—"

"What is it?"

"I'm not sure how to say it." *I might be losing my mind, or I might be scared with good reason, and I'm terrified that both are true, and how am I going to be any good to anyone if that's the case?* Before I can try to form an answer, a car slows down and pulls up behind mine. A man steps out of the car, someone I don't recognize, and my body responds with a torrent of fear I didn't know was in me, my feet moving me away before I even realize what he's saying.

"You need any help, ma'am?"

"No." My voice is sharp, unfriendly. "Just stopped to make a call. Thank you for asking."

When the stranger hesitates, my hand closes tighter around my phone.

"Felicity, what's going on?" James asks. The stranger hesitates, as if waiting for me to change my mind, then returns to his vehicle, gets back on the road.

"The car, James. Again. The same thing."

"But it's—"

"A different car. I know. Look, could you just talk to me while I figure out what the hell to do here?"

"And leave you by yourself? Absolutely not," he answers. "Tell me where you are."

"At the side of route 11, about ten miles outside of town."

"I'll be there in ten," he answers. "Wait in the car. And lock the doors, would you?"

"Yes."

When I see James's car pull up behind mine, I open the door and walk to meet him, trying to make a show of looking stable, certain, anything but how I really feel.

"Hi, James." I know I look like hell, jittery and restless, half sick to my stomach with nerves.

"Morning."

"I don't know what to do." To make this admission hurts, and I can't quite bring myself to look him in the eye. And so I'm almost surprised when he pulls me into a firm embrace, the stubble on his jawline against my temple.

"Come sit down." I follow him to his car, which is dry and warm. "Do you want me to look at the car?"

"No. Please, let's just go."

He lowers his chin in a careful nod, holding me in a gaze that invites me to speak, to draw near. I don't, keeping my face smooth, once again fearful that all the sharp edges I've concealed might shock, even hurt him.

"Do you want to call the rental company so they can deal with the car?"

"Not right now." I say this as if I don't have the time, but the truth is I'm overwhelmed.

"Tow truck?"

"No."

"You sure?"

"I can't!" I snap. "I'm sorry. I don't even know where to start, what to think. I don't know how to manage a stranded rental car on top of—" I stop talking, otherwise I know I'm going to burst into tears. With a wash of guilt, I realize yet again that the first thing I wish for when I close my eyes is to leave. Get on a plane and go back to my sun-washed apartment, where it rarely rains, where I never have to drive, where nobody depends on me.

"I just wish I could take them somewhere I know they'd be safe. Even for long enough that I could get one single night's rest. So I could figure out what to do here. I feel like Holly needs me to do something, and—"

"Take them to my family's lake house," he suggests casually.

"Isn't it far away?"

"It's a couple hours by car," he answers, "then a short hike in—it's difficult to get to. But," he adds, "by boat, not that far. It's on the other side of the lake."

I pause, and a second goes by before I realize I haven't instinctively refused the idea.

"You can see or hear anyone coming ages before they get close to the house," he says. "Phone reception's good. Felicity, it's safe. And—quiet. You all could relax there."

A solid night's sleep sounds better than I want to admit, as reluctant as I am to accept a favor.

"You need to do things on your own," he says, eyes on the road, his voice low and comforting. "I respect that. If you want me to handle this for you, just say so. I'll put the keys in your hand right now, lend you a car to drive out there. I'll call your rental company to deal with the other car. Let me help you with this," he says. "Please—it's the least I can do."

"Okay, but—"

"Yes?"

"You said you'd give me the key. Maybe—maybe you could come, too." I pause, trying to sound brave, remembering that I make a point of not needing help from anybody. "Only because, you know, I've never been there before, and I'd rather not be alone with the children, in case anything happens."

"Of course."

Though I can't bring myself to talk, I lean back in the passenger seat, turn my chin so I'm facing him as he drives.

"I shouldn't have left them by themselves," I mumble. "I should have stayed at the house. I just needed a change of scenery."

"Felicity, I don't think it's them you need to be worried about," he says. "At least, not only them."

When we arrive and I let him inside, the girls are in the kitchen with my mother. I frown when I find the back door unlocked. My mother smiles when she sees James.

"Every time Felicity leaves the house alone, she comes back with you." When her gaze lands on me, her smile vanishes. "What happened?"

"We shouldn't stay here." Hearing myself say it out loud, I realize I've been holding these words back since my first day here. "I don't feel safe, and I'm afraid none of us is." I lean closer to my mother, lowering my voice to speak to her. "If you could just agree with me on this, I know they'll listen to you." Despite all her mournful hints that she'd like to improve things between us, I fully expect my mother to do what I've come to expect of her: when I'm desperate enough to ask for her help on faith, she'll dig her heels in.

"Why? What's changed?"

"You remember the trouble I had with the rental car?"

"They replaced it, right?" my mother says.

"Yeah," I answer. "And then, just now, it happened again. Mom, I know I don't have any proof, but I just…"

She shakes her head, clasping my hands in hers. "You can't keep waiting for proof. Don't you see?"

"What do you mean?"

"You know something's wrong." The light from the window catches her eyes, as if they gleam with meaning. "Don't put yourself on trial, when you already know the truth."

She's taking me seriously. I bite the inside of my cheek to stop myself from crying.

"You need to get them out of here. But Felicity, I can't go. This is my home. If it gets bad enough I have to leave, I'll walk out, but until then…"

"Mom, please."

She shakes her head with a firm scowl, turning back to the fireplace.

"You were there?" She looks at James. "You heard this?"

"I didn't need to."

"James's folks have a lake house, a couple hours away. There's room for me and the girls to stay a few days. At least until I decide what we need to do next—we'll be back by Christmas, I promise."

I halfway worry she'll say something embarrassing, but instead she looks right at him and says: "Thank you."

"I don't want to." Tess delivers these words flatly, a blank deadpan, and my mother gives me a pointed look. "I'm not going. We're not going."

"Tess, please?" I whisper. "Things aren't normal right now. I have to know you're safe." I want to tell her that I can't sleep, that I can't sit still, unless I have eyes on her, or someone I trust does. That I want so badly to sleep. That I'm so tired I don't know who I am anymore.

"No."

"But I want to," Frankie whines, grabbing Tess's wrist. "I want to see the water and make snow angels in the sand. Tess, please."

"With him?" she asks, looking to James. "You like her, don't you?" she says, teasing both of us. But he's entirely unperturbed, smiling back warmly and quietly so that he doesn't really need to answer her.

"Fine," Tess says. "Then we can go. But I don't like it."

"We'll leave in ten minutes," I say, not wanting to waste any time before she changes her mind.

"I'll tell Silas you're going," my mother volunteers. "Just so he's aware."

"No." I give her a brief, gentle hug. "Don't worry about it. I'll call him." Over her shoulder, I catch James's confused glance, and answer with an almost imperceptible nod. He knows I'll do no such thing.

"Would you help them out to the car, please?" I ask him. "I'll be right out."

Once they're out the door, I address my mother once again, standing directly in front of her so that she can't brush me off.

"You shouldn't stay."

"You don't need me there." She gives a resigned half-smile, then walks to the sink and begins washing dishes. I follow her, standing with my back to the counter. "You were right, Felicity. I ought to have put more trust in you, all along."

"Don't let that push you into making the wrong choice now."

"I failed you, somehow, somewhere along the way. I have this terrible feeling that there was something I didn't protect you from, and maybe I'll never know what it is, but I'm so sorry."

"Thank you, Mom." I reach to hold her hand, warm water and dish soap around my fingers. "Everything is okay now. With me, at least."

"Is that the truth?"

She knows when I'm lying. She always does. I remember James telling me, *It wasn't your fault*. That I ought to tell her what happened. All my mother sees is that something's wrong, and she's blaming herself. Maybe she's felt this way for years, and now I'm walking out with all this sadness unresolved between us. A rush of sadness rises up in me, so sharp I have to let go of her hand. I wave a brief, warm goodbye from the doorway, as if I'm not afraid that it will be the last time I see her.

CHAPTER THIRTY-THREE
Now

It feels like a long drive to pick up James's other car, a rugged SUV which he explains is necessary to drive off-road to get there. I don't know whether it's nerves, or my stomach, or what, but I'm feeling ill, a bit clammy, then too cold, my stomach uneasy. I cross my arms and fold my knees up, and if I could, I'd sleep. I can't, though, just watching the terrain change as we get closer to the other side of the lake. James stops for groceries at a little roadside market, along with some takeout for the girls' dinner. I recite, as I normally do, the list of things that keep me grounded: stretches before bed. Sea glass. A walk after dinner. Green tea with a slice of lemon. I hear the turn signal click on and the road becomes gravelly.

"Are you feeling okay?"

"More or less."

"You don't get carsick," he says, studying me with a hint of concern. "Do you? You never mentioned it."

"It's just stress." My answer snaps out more sharply than I'd intended, and I reach out to rest my hand on his over the gear shift. "Sorry. I really am fine."

He turns momentarily to me with a half-smile. Through my haze of fatigue, it occurs to me, with an almost scientific precision, that in all the places I've traveled, all the years we've been apart,

I have yet to meet someone with eyes that could compare to his, deep and complex as molasses.

I open the window, pulling my jacket close, as dirt flies and the smell of fresh water fills the air. After parking at the top of the trail, we hike another quarter-mile or so through the woods, before the house comes into view.

"Wow," Tess whispers. "Tight."

"We're here."

The curtains are drawn for winter, but the house charms me immediately, with wide porches that wrap around the second and third floors.

I'm silent, the girls chattering, as we walk inside. He unlocks the door and apologizes for the cold. "I'll turn the heat on right away." I walk into an entryway that opens into a high-ceilinged family room, windows looking out over the beach. He turns around a corner, opens a doorway into a bedroom, and sets his duffel by the closet. "There's a set of adjoining bedrooms downstairs, if you'd like to take a look."

"Thanks—I'll unpack." I pick up the girls' suitcases, one after the other, take a step toward the staircase, then reach back, an afterthought, and pick up my own bag as well. James takes notice, almost as if he's surprised.

"Oh—right. Let me help you." He takes the bags from my shoulders and carries them down the stairs behind me, opens a door on the right side of the hallway. It's dark, and when he reaches across my shoulders to flip the light switch, I'm suddenly looking right at the button just below the collar of his shirt. When the overhead light blinks on, I'm still looking at him.

"I'll take those." But I don't, not right away. My hands drift to his shoulders, trace down the lengths of his arms, resting on his hands. Hearing footsteps on the stairs, I blink, take the suitcases, and cross the room to place them at the foot of the bed.

"This is lovely."

"The adjoining bedroom is through that doorway, and the bathroom is across the hall."

"Thank you." The room is decorated in shades of white and blue, the carpet under my feet a plush navy. I can't help slipping my shoes off to feel the carpet under my feet, which James seems to find funny, stifling a gentle laugh, his face turned to one side. When Frankie and Tess appear in the doorway, he offers to find something to cook for dinner, then returns upstairs.

"Is this our room?" Tess asks, her face somber.

"Yes, if you want," I answer. "I know there's just the one bed, but I'm sure it's big enough for you both." Frankie tugs on my hand, so I lift her into my arms, and she leans her head against mine. I realize it's late for her, past nine.

"And what's over here?" Tess checks each of the doors: a closet, a glass door that opens onto a patio over the lake, then the one to the adjoining bedroom. "Oh—can we use both of these rooms?"

"Yes."

"Frankie, we can each have our own bed. Okay? Like hotel rooms," she says. "And you can just knock on this door if you want to come in."

"Are you sure?"

Frankie, usually attached to her bedtime routine, seems sleepy enough not to mind the change. While Tess goes into the opposite room to unpack, I'm helping her undress and get ready for bed. I tuck her in and rest on top of the blankets next to her once the lights are off, and just when I think she's asleep, I hear her voice.

"Aunt Lissie, why were you scared? Why did we leave Grandma's?"

"I was afraid we weren't safe there, but Grandma didn't want to come with us. She will be okay. We'll call to check on her tomorrow."

"Are we safe here?"

"Yes." I can answer this, at least, with full certainty. "And you're always, always safe when I'm around."

"Okay," she answers with a relieved, gentle sigh, as if that's the end of the matter. In minutes, she's asleep, and I sneak across to check on Tess. To my surprise, she's in bed, too, staring at the ceiling, arms crossed over her chest.

"Tess, thanks for coming with me."

"Yeah, well, not like you gave us a choice." She answers me with some diffidence, the kind that hopes I'll look closer.

"You understand there's a reason for that, right?"

Her eyes wander away.

"Tess, were you awake that night, when your mother came back home?"

Her eyelids close, open, then flutter down again.

"Were you awake when she left again?"

I can hear Tess's voice echoing, that day that she yelled at me: *That's what Mom said, too. How long is it going to take for you to go off into the swamp and never come back?*

"I want you to be happy," I say, dropping my voice low and soft, "and I want you to do all the stuff you want to do. But for that to happen, I first need to be certain that you're safe. If you know anything, I need you to tell me."

"I understand." Her voice sounds close to mechanical. "If I did, I would. The police said it was an accident, you know? If there's anything worse than my mom dying, it would be if they're wrong."

She was awake. I don't know what she saw, but I'm sure that she's covering for someone—for some reason.

"Do you want me to sleep in here with you?"

"No," she answers, though something in her voice is kinder. "I haven't had much alone time lately."

"No," I answer. "None of us has."

"Where will you sleep?"

"Probably in Frankie's room. I think there's another guest room somewhere—I'm not sure."

"Imagine having a second house where you can lose track of a bedroom here or there," she grins, something mischievous in her laugh.

"I'm sure James knows it by heart," I answer, laughing. "Goodnight, Tess."

"Goodnight."

I sit with her a few minutes longer, until I'm certain she's genuinely asleep, one hand resting on her shoulder.

When I walk back upstairs, it's nearly ten. There's a fire going in the stone fireplace, curtains open over the lake to show the moon, a soft half-circle hung in the velvet sky. The master bedroom is on the second floor, which I assume is where James will sleep. Suddenly, I'm lightheaded, bracing my arms on the sofa for balance. A thought sinks into my mind like a stone in water, ripples circling out. I can't keep blaming this feeling on jet lag, and it's more than a stress reaction. I've felt this before, the sudden spells of lightheadedness, the low-key nausea, always waiting in the background.

James walks into the room and sits on the couch behind me. "You okay?"

"I think so," I answer. "Thank you for bringing us here."

"Sure thing." When he chooses a seat on the large sofa facing the fireplace, I sit on the opposite corner, arms crossed over my knees. "Anything to drink? There's wine, and I think brandy in the cupboard."

"No, thank you. Oh, maybe a cup of—" I remember I've left my tea at the house, a small realization that, combined with all the rest, sends my resolve toppling.

"What can I get you? Oh—" James turns to speak to me, takes a single glance at my face, his features softening in recognition.

"I forgot to pack my green tea." I tell myself I'm not crying, but my lips tremble as I speak, and I keep hearing a strange noise, then I realize it's coming from my own throat, these little sobbing breaths that threaten an earthquake. "I'm sorry—this is so embarrassing."

"Not in the least." He places a soft kiss on my cheek, then draws me close against his chest, one broad hand smoothing the hair from my forehead. His hands smooth over my shoulders, fingertips squeezing gently along the tension in the muscles there. I let my chin drop back, leaning so that my forehead rests against his cheek. "Holding it in doesn't help." It's not that I'm not listening to him, but when I feel his lips move against my temple, I bite down on my own. "If you need to cry, it's—"

"No," I interrupt, gently. "I can't, James. You don't understand."

"So—tell me." He circles both arms around my shoulders, holding my hands in his. I can't tell him, though, what I don't understand myself. If I let emotion get the better of me now, how am I supposed to get back up and keep going? "There's an end to this, you know," he says. "It won't always be like this."

"Not if I can't find out what happened to my sister."

"You cannot go chasing after what happened to her. I'm afraid that—" He catches himself, and, as I turn back just enough to see his face, it's plainly true. The line of his brow is tense, eyes trained on mine. It's the same expression he wore that night so long ago, when he dragged me out of the water. As if we're at a seance, I feel the air around us shift with meaning. James and I share a tense gaze, and I can almost feel the ghosts of the past taking their seats around us.

"It's impossible not to wonder," he says, his thoughts apparently following my own. "Page must have been aware she couldn't swim."

"Even if Holly dared her, she never meant for her to get hurt."

"I know." His hug tightens around me. "I didn't mean that."

"Besides—if you'd been there…" He begins to interrupt me, but I squeeze his hand to stop him. "We weren't alone in the water. It was as if something else was there, trying to keep all of us down. And that voice I heard."

"Yes," he says. "That voice calling you. It—"

"You didn't hear it," I remind him. "That place is beyond explaining. I'm not saying the ghost stories are true, but it seems like the kind of place terrible, unbelievable accidents are more likely to happen. Nobody—nothing human—is to blame for any of it."

James lowers his eyes, a terrible sadness in his expression, giving me a sense almost that there's something he's not saying here.

"I'm sorry. I hope I didn't upset you."

"Upset? No." James's arms wrap around my back and he pulls me into a kiss. "Scared, maybe. That you'll get lost in this, get yourself hurt. When maybe there's something for us on the other side of it."

"You don't know how much I've missed you."

"Really?" he whispers. The tenderness in his voice calls tears to my eyes again. "You don't give me that impression."

"So much that I've spent all these years avoiding anything that reminded me of you, or of home." I trace the crest of his cheek with my fingertips, turn his face toward mine. "I'm not trying to scare you off here, but I promised myself I would never go through that again."

"What—falling in love?"

"Love is just what people call the way they feel right before they get hurt." I scoot back to sit on my knees, watching him with an unyielding frown.

"What if you're wrong about that?" James asks, an uncertain smile turning up the corner of his mouth. "I missed you, but I guess that's obvious. You know, I used to look out the window at my parents' house, thinking of that night. You were so pale, and I could see the moon in your hair as you left. It felt like you were fading away."

"That's one of those things I try not to think about."

"I would do anything to promise you that nothing will hurt you again. To see you happy."

"Do you mean it?" I ask. He offers his hands, and I reach across the space between us to hold on.

"I mean it."

I lean forward into his embrace, wrap my arms tightly around his shoulders. "Being here with you, it's almost like we could be anywhere."

"I wish we were. Anywhere."

"Where would you want to be?" We take turns listing places we've visited: the mountains in Canada, a village in the Scottish countryside. My sunny apartment in Saint Thomas, with the window that gives a view of the crystal-blue sea.

"More than anything, I think I'd want to be right here with you," he says. "We'd come down on holidays. Have a quiet New Year's Day together, here."

"I'd wear your sweater over my pajamas."

"We'd sit together and talk and drink tea all day."

"Cook dinner together and drink wine."

We both pause. It feels dangerous, that this daydream is both so close and so impossible. It's almost a spell that we don't want to break by speaking, and, in holding the silence, soon fall asleep in the firelight. I wake an hour later, gently turning around to face him as he sleeps. I think I could look at his face for years and never want to look away. My stomach turns again, either nausea or nerves, or maybe it's just happiness. And, as much as I don't want to wake him, I can't resist leaning forward to place a gentle kiss on his mouth. Slowly, he opens his eyes.

"That's a nice way to wake up."

I answer him with another kiss, then rest my chin on his shoulder, feel his heartbeat quicken under my own.

"What are you thinking about?"

"How you look when you're sleeping." I laugh softly and move close to him. "I wondered, you know. More than once."

"And? Is it everything you dreamed of?" he laughs.

"Pretty much."

James stretches and yawns. "No surprises here, Lissie," he says, his tone soft but serious.

And could I say the same? I've doubted most things and people in my life, James among them, but I realize now that never, not once, did I doubt the truth of my own feelings for him.

"Okay: sit up. It's late." Happily, I wrap my arms around his chest and pull him up with me. "I'm rather excited to sleep in a real bed."

"Past your bedtime?"

"No," I answer, pulling him to his feet, resting my head against his chest. "Past our bedtime."

CHAPTER THIRTY-FOUR
Now

Three days pass, quiet hours punctuated with walks in the woods, cups of hot cocoa on the deck, assembling puzzles by the fireplace. Each morning, I wake early, the room pleasantly cool, the down blankets heavy and soft, well before dawn. James sleeps like a prince, his features so relaxed, chin just tilted upward. I can't help but feel he's made of something entirely different from me, brighter and less twisted, but it's a difference that beckons me closer, all of our pauses and movements perfect complements. I tiptoe downstairs in the dark, crawl into bed beside Frankie to be there when she wakes.

But on the fourth day, the weather changes. A damp snow blows in over the bay, making its way over us in the morning. Snow is a rare event here, and I hope it will make the girls happy, but Tess is restless and pacing, like how I remember Silas looking when he needed something to drink. I make them grilled cheese and soup for lunch, and when I walk past the table to refill Frankie's glass of water, she looks up at me and says, "Thank you, Mom."

I don't make anything of it. I would never try to take Holly's place. But Tess pushes her plate away, slouching into her chair.

"Is that one of Mom's shirts, too?"

"No," I answer, keeping a neutral tone. "No, this is one of my own."

"Well, I don't like it," she snaps. "You shouldn't try to be like her." She pushes her chair away from the table so quickly it almost tips over, then runs across the room and outside onto the deck.

"Is she angry with me?" Frankie looks up from her soup with large eyes.

"No, she isn't." I drop into the chair next to hers, my plate untouched. "She's sad. It isn't your fault." My eyes track across the room, watch her pacing in the snow. I walk across the open living room to the coat closet by the door, and find her jacket, then turn to go outside.

While Frankie is finishing her lunch, I follow Tess outside onto the deck. She's so slight, her blonde hair damp with the snow, frame thin under her sweatshirt and pink camouflage pants.

"I brought your coat."

"Me?" she asks, as if there were someone else here.

"Yes, you."

"I want to go home."

"I know."

"And yet, here we are," she snarls.

"You understand why we're here?"

She huffs another sigh and her voice breaks into a whine, a voice that children use when they're begging for things to be different. "This is so stupid."

"I wish it were, Tess."

"Whatever."

"I know." I can hear how irritating I must sound to her. "Tess, when we talked the other night—I have to ask you again. Are you quite sure you weren't awake?"

"I'm sure." She doesn't turn to look at me, but her hands tighten on the railing, sweeping damp snow down between her fingers. "And stop asking me. It's bad enough my mother's dead. Why are you so determined to make it worse?"

For a moment, my insecurity gets the better of me, and I'm speechless.

"These bad things only started happening once you were around!" Tess yells. "If you would just leave, I bet they'd stop."

I hear the door slide closed as James slips outside. Tess is so upset she doesn't notice, and continues talking. "You made me one promise. Do you even remember that?"

"I promised to keep you safe."

"You promised not to make me do anything against my wishes. I don't know you. I don't want to be here. I want to go home."

I bite the inside of my cheek to stop myself from crying. Tess is right: I've made too many mistakes here to hope for anything to turn out right.

"I'm sorry, Tess."

"I'm not a baby. I don't know why everybody talks to me like I'm a baby."

I take a seat on the bench and sweep my hair behind my ears.

"I'm sorry I made a promise I couldn't entirely keep. But I'm afraid we're not safe at my mother's house."

"You can't even say that for sure." She dashes a handful of snow from the railing with her bare fingers. "That's why you left to begin with—you're crazy. I wish you'd stayed away."

The worst part is that she's right. We can't stay here forever, and I don't have a plan, or anything like one. I'm meant to provide her with security, with certainty, and with just a few words, she's knocked me right over. I know she can see me floundering. Staring out at the water, I see James, walking around from the other side of the deck. He sits a few feet away from me. When she sees him, she seems to tame a little, pacing in an uneasy line, the soles of her shoes tapping on the deck.

"I want to go home," she demands. "Today."

"Tess, I think Felicity just wants to know you're safe," he says softly.

"Don't talk to me." She whirls to face him. "You're not my dad. Even my dad's not my dad. I don't know why nobody will tell me the truth."

"Wait." Arms crossed against the cold, I get to my feet, try to approach her. "Tess, what did you say?"

Tess shakes her head as she walks back inside.

James wraps an arm around my waist and we stand looking out at the lake. "She's in so much pain. You're doing a lot for her just by being here. Somehow, she knows that."

"I hope you're right."

"Felicity, how much does she know?" He gives me an uncertain look, almost as if he's hurt. "You can tell me."

I turn to look at him, eyes wide with fear. "I'm not sure what you mean."

He acknowledges this with a careful nod, silence settling around us. *Even my dad's not my dad.* She's covering for someone.

Downstairs, the door to her room is closed, and I don't knock. I remember being that age, needing space, being crowded by people who could never understand even if they wanted to, but I sit in the hallway outside her door for two solid hours, listening to her breathe. When I need to stretch my legs, I walk back up the stairs, reheat her lunch, and return to her door, giving it a soft tap.

"I brought you some food."

"I'm not hungry."

"You're right to be angry. With me, with everything. But I need you to talk to me."

"I want to go home."

"Not until I know how to make it safe."

I wait for a few minutes of silence, then head back up the stairs. As I approach the landing, the open dining room and living room on the first floor, I hear Frankie's little voice, talking softly to James. She's sitting on the floor, playing with a jigsaw puzzle, looks up with a hopeful smile when I come into the room.

"Frankie has asked about going for a trail walk before dinner," James says.

"That sounds nice," I answer. While Frankie goes to find her shoes, Tess walks quietly up the stairs and sits down across from me.

"I'd like to go, too," she answers. She makes no mention of her outburst earlier, and I see she's pleading in her silent way for it to be okay, and it's forgotten.

"Of course."

While I'm bending down to tie the laces of my boots, I feel suddenly faint, lightheaded, and sink down to sit on the floor. I blink, huddling for a moment over my shoes. I can't continue to pretend this is just nerves, or jet lag, when I've had three weeks to adjust to a single hour's time difference. I have a suspicion that this set of symptoms is not *just* anything. I'm not brave enough to form the words, even in my mind.

We hike out in the damp snow, down the hill, admiring the snow-dusted tree branches. The temperature hovers a few degrees above freezing, and I know it will melt soon. Tess is quiet, but seems more even-tempered than before. The fresh air clears my mind, and after a mile or so downhill I'm almost glad to be here. Maybe James is right: maybe there is an end to this, something worth waiting for on the other side of this bad dream. The trail passes through a campground, which has a small market, and we decide to stop for a snack before heading back. Bottles of water, pieces of candy, a loaf of bread to eat with dinner. When we've made our purchase and headed outside, I ask James to wait.

"Wait here, okay? I'm going to go back inside and use the restroom before we head home."

"Sure."

Back inside the store, I walk quickly down the aisles, scanning the small selection of toiletries and over-the-counter medicines. I make a selection, return to the counter, and stand with my back to the window while I pay, then hurry back to them.

The trek back to the house is longer, and colder, than the walk down, afternoon passing toward evening. The sun has warmed the forest, but as the sun wanes, the chill descends quickly. We go slowly and take frequent breaks, and I'm blaming it on Frankie, but I'm short of breath, and there's a dull combination of dread and anticipation humming in my stomach.

"You all walk so slowly," Tess laughs.

"We're sightseeing," I answer.

"Mind if I go up ahead? I'll meet you at the house."

"Sure." I wave and smile. Surprising me, she darts forward and gives me a quick hug, her face pressed against my chest, then hurries up ahead on the trail. I am so pleased she's feeling better that I don't scold her for going out of sight. She can't be more than a few steps ahead.

My mind buzzes with unanswered questions, and, as we near the lake house, I'm more than a little winded. James unlocks the door and we walk back inside, brushing our shoes on the doormat. Frankie runs in and leaves her coat on the floor, walks to the window to look out at the lake.

"Wait." I linger at the doorway.

"What is it?"

"Something's wrong." He raises an eyebrow. "The door was locked. Tess would have taken her shoes off. It's—it's quiet in here." Before he can answer, I run down the stairs and find her bedroom empty, then start calling her name. I'm back up the stairs and outside before he catches up, running down to the waterfront, where there's a little dock.

"There was a boat here," I say, the reality of it sinking in. "Wasn't there?" He doesn't need to answer me. I know it. "How far is it to the other side of the lake?"

"In this weather?" he asks. "Hard to say. But in good conditions, maybe two or three hours."

We're on the road inside half an hour. I'm trying not to think about Tess out on that lake, in freezing rain, her thin shoulders under her insufficient coat. I take out my phone to call Dawson, then reconsider, remembering the dark, unpredictable look that came over Silas when he talked about Rob Dawson. Dawson, who'd always been sweet on Holly.

"I need to talk to Silas."

"You think he'd tell you the truth?"

I don't say it out loud, but I'm afraid he'd do worse than that.

While James drives, I call my mother first, who tells me Tess isn't there. Her syllables are short. Next, I call Silas. For some reason, it doesn't surprise me when he doesn't answer.

It's nearly seven when James parks outside my mother's house, which looks like a different house with its roof covered in snow. "What can I do for you?"

"Keep your eye out," I say. "Just—look around, okay? And call me if you see anything. She hasn't gone far. She's right here—" My voice almost breaks. "I don't know how I know it, but I do."

"I will." Without a moment's hesitation, he leans forward and wraps me in a hug. "If you need anything else, just say it."

"You mean that?" I draw back from his hug, trying to fit everything I'd like to ask him into this dwindling moment.

"With all my heart," he answers. "For whatever that's worth."

"More than you know, James."

I lean in to kiss him goodbye, then get out of the car. Opening the back door, I help Frankie with her seatbelt, then collect our bags and head toward the house before he has a chance to ask what I mean.

CHAPTER THIRTY-FIVE
Now

As I bring Frankie inside, I'm imagining, in my mother's voice, all the things she'll say to me. Worst of all, in my mind I see Holly, looking at me with disappointment. I imagine what she'd probably think about me: that I have no idea what I'm doing.

But in the kitchen, a fire is burning, and my mother turns to greet me with a warm hug.

"I'll get some dinner together. Lissie, you must be hungry," she says, pausing. "You look awfully pale."

"I am hungry." Suddenly, I feel I'm about to cry, even though the sight of her usually sends all my defenses up. "How have I managed to mess this up so badly?"

"It's only been a few hours," she says. "Felicity, Tess is a sharp girl. I suspect she just wanted to leave, and so she left."

"But she's not here," I answer. As I speak, my mother's moving around the kitchen—I think she's putting food together, but I can hardly pay attention. "Where would she go?"

"We're going to find her." She turns from the counter and hands me a sandwich with sliced turkey and cheese. "Felicity, this isn't something you did. You know this isn't a new behavior for her, running off for a few days. She knows how to look out for herself—more than someone her age should."

"This feels different."

"Why?"

"I don't know."

I struggle to eat a few bites, then take my phone from my purse. It's not getting any reception, so I use the landline. I call 911, and the operator connects me to the police station locally.

"Dawson? It's Felicity. Tess is missing. I need your help."

"Slow down," he says. "Are you sure? You know, she's run away before. This may not be any cause for concern."

"Something feels wrong," I insist.

"Could she be with Silas?"

"He's not answering his phone." My stomach twists.

"All right," he says. "Listen, don't make too much of it." As if I needed reminding that he thinks I'm hysterical. "Come in first thing tomorrow if she hasn't turned up. I bet you when you wake up, she'll be asleep in her bed."

"Okay," I answer, miserable. "Thanks, Dawson. Goodnight."

As I hang up the phone, my mother turns to me again.

"Bet you anything she's with Silas," my mother says. "He doesn't have a landline, and his mobile doesn't get reception at his house."

I shiver, thinking of the last time I was there alone with him. The premonition that crawled up my spine. But it seems the most likely place Tess might have gone.

"All right, then. If that's what you think, I'm going over there to look for her." Despite the pit in my stomach, I can't finish my food. "You need to have eyes on Frankie, the whole time. I need her to stay in the same room with you. Try to keep her away from the doors—it's just, I don't know..." We're talking in lowered voices, while Frankie sits at the kitchen table.

"I know how to keep her safe in my own house," my mother says, clearly hurt.

"Thanks." I answer her politely. I always do. "If I don't come back, I guess, call the police. Don't bother calling Dawson—I'm afraid he's tired of hearing about us by now."

"If you don't come back?" She sighs. "Why are you so nervous around Silas? You're so suspicious of people."

"You're the one who accused me of killing your rooster."

"That was different, Felicity, I—"

"You're right," I answer. "If I had a better sense of when to trust people and when not to, my life would be a lot easier."

"What are you talking about?"

"Nothing. I'm going to go to Silas's house and see if she's there. If she's not, maybe he'll help us look for her. Is it okay if I use your car?"

"Of course."

CHAPTER THIRTY-SIX

Now

I park outside Silas's little house and walk up to the door. The mist is so heavy in the air it almost sticks to my eyelashes.

"Silas? I need you to come to the door. It's important."

Nothing. I knock hard at the door, wait a few moments.

"If you're awake, answer the door now. Please."

There's no answer, and, sighing with impatience, I reach to try the doorknob. It's not even latched shut all the way, falling open in my hand.

I draw in a sharp breath. The room is dark. I step inside, lighting up my phone screen to see. "Silas?" I call again, my voice a bit softer. "Tess?"

I walk through the darkened room, feel a breath behind me, and whirl, gasping, on my heel. It's the air from a heating vent, the nearby curtain swaying in its breeze. Trembling, I reach around until I find a light, and click to turn it on. I'm expecting to see empty bottles, but there are none, and it smells fresh, looks clean. Could they be hidden somewhere in this house? I make myself quiet, listen for any breath or movement, and creep through the living room into the bedroom.

The bed is empty. My eyes dart between the space beneath the bed and the closet in the corner of the room. I lower myself to my knees to look under the bed, shining the tinny blue light from my phone screen. Nothing. As I'm standing to check the closet, I see motion in the light coming through the blinds. Someone's in the yard. I drop to the floor and listen. Footsteps. Louder. Then, without a knock, the door opens.

Mind spinning, I try to think of any way I could talk Silas out of a rage, when he finds I'm sneaking around his house. I think of the size of his muscles, of the angry look in his eyes when he talks about Holly being gone. Finally, I'm eyeing the window, and wondering how fast I can get out, when I hear footsteps in the kitchen, and then down the tiny corridor. The closet door squeaks as I try to step behind it. Rising to my feet too quickly, I'm smacked with a wave of dizziness, and cross my arms tightly around my ribs. *Like if anyone so much as touched me, I'd shatter.*

"Miss?" The stranger standing in the doorway approaches me, and I stumble backward against the closet door. "I saw you come in. The man who lives here isn't home."

Half sobbing with nerves, I'm unable to answer.

"Are you here looking for Silas?"

"Yes." Disappointment rushes around me, materializing into a pins-and-needles sensation that clings to my neck and chest. "Have you seen him? Was there a child with him?"

"Are you talking about his daughter? Tess, right?"

"Yes." My chest heaves, and I can't swallow around the lump in my throat. The man takes a look at me and steps back, hands up.

"Would you be more comfortable if we talked outside?" With a hasty nod, I follow him out, one hand trailing the wall for balance.

"Are you okay?"

"I'll live."

In the daylight, I can see he's older than he looks, with a few days' worth of stubble. "I live next door," he says. "Silas was at home this morning, but…"

"I need to speak with him," I answer. "His daughter is missing. I was really hoping she'd be here with him."

The man's face droops a bit. "It's an awful shame," he says. "Silas was picked up for drunk driving earlier today. He's at the police station, probably until they let him out tomorrow."

"Well, if—if…" I sigh and brush my hair away from my face. "If Tess isn't with Silas, then I don't know where she could be."

"Wish I could help," he answers. "My wife and I will keep our eyes open."

"Thank you." I give him my phone number, just in case he really does want to help, and sit down in the car. As I drive away, a gentle mix of rain and snow begins to fall, wet and heavy, making the roads slick. The flakes begin to melt as soon as they hit the car, leaving a line of slush at the bottom of the windshield. It's not cold enough to freeze, but there's slush and mud coating everything. I think of Holly, alone in the water, in the cold. And for a moment, I think of that ghostly voice, singing my name, wonder if it's speaking to her as well, and I hope she isn't alone.

CHAPTER THIRTY-SEVEN

Now

At first, I mean to drive back to my mother's house, but then, finding excuses to avoid a difficult conversation, I begin driving the small roads, the low roads close to the water, looking for Tess, or for anything out of the ordinary. Wherever there's a dock, I get out and walk on foot, calling her name when I hear any movement. I forget entirely about sleep or food or anything else. Once, I check the clock on the car dash, and it's past three in the morning. I think of going home, then I remember what I said to my mother on the doorstep, and I'm still afraid to hear her answer, so I decide it can't hurt to keep looking. Besides, if Tess goes back there, my mother will call me.

It's a long, quiet night, and, finally, when I see traces of gray in the east, I head toward the police station. It's closer into town here, and when my phone picks up a signal, I anxiously check for messages. But there's only one, from James, asking how I'm doing. I write back: *We haven't found her*. A moment later, I send another: *Miss you*.

This time yesterday, I was asleep next to him, the room around us pleasantly chilly, the down blanket heavy and warm. Everything seemed possible. I've spent more nights this past month in chairs and, tonight, a car, than I have in beds. My limbs ache, either for comfort or for his closeness—I couldn't even name the difference right now. I'm almost nodding off when I remember where I am. Dawn is breaking, the sky still clouded over, but tinted pink where the sun is rising. I startle when I hear a rap at the window of the car, but then see that it's just Rob Dawson.

"Morning." I open the door, rubbing my eyes.

"Felicity? What are you doing?"

"You said to come here first thing if I hadn't found her." My voice is raspy with sleep "I've been out looking all night."

Dawson nods, waves toward the door. "Come in. Let's talk."

I follow Dawson inside. He brings me to his desk, and I sit down across from him, where he looks at me expectantly.

"You know that Tess has a history of running away, don't you?"

"Yes."

"Okay," he sighs. "Felicity, you have to tell me what I don't know."

"What?"

"Something's not right," he repeats. "What are you not telling me?"

"But Dawson, I have told you everything."

"Here's what I've got," he says. "When I called to inform you of your sister's death, you said you were expecting her call. You knew something was wrong. You get back here and you're all over the place. Wherever you go, there's trouble. A dead rooster. A bar fight. You're claiming the local mechanic doesn't know what he's doing. And then, you insist on taking these girls out of town. These girls you just got custody of, when you know full well there's a relative also interested in custody."

"But I had to."

"Why?"

"I'm scared," I stammer. "I need your help."

"There are rumors that Tess isn't Silas's biological child. What do you know about that?"

"She's said it herself," I answer. "If those rumors are true, it seems important now to find out who her biological father is."

"But you don't have any idea, of course." Dawson leans a bit closer to me. "I cannot help you if you're going to lie to me."

"If I didn't need your help, I wouldn't be here!"

"Tell me something else," he says. "About that night I picked you up. You were walking home crying. It was barely a week after Page Winslow's death. You were wearing James Finley's jacket. Felicity, let's talk about that night."

"Okay."

"Do you remember me driving you home?"

"I…"

"Would you tell me," he says, "if you did?"

"What do you mean?"

"I'll tell you what I remember, since I'm the one of us who was in my right mind that night." I wince and nod my head. "I picked you up, halfway home from your school. You were a wreck, Felicity—clothes a mess, bloody knees, falling-down drunk. It's a miracle you'd made it that far unharmed. You looked like a crime scene."

Maybe because I was, I want to shout. *But you're not asking about* that, *are you?* I curl my hands tightly around my knees and eye him resentfully.

"What happened that night?"

"Did you ask me then?" I realize I wouldn't remember if he had. I barely remember that part of the night at all. An inkling of suspicion clicks into place and I huddle into my chair.

"I did," he says, lowering his eyes. "But you weren't really able to answer me, beyond babbling about ghosts. And then, not two months later, you disappeared. Until Holly dies, leaving those girls in your care."

"What exactly are you trying to say?"

"That I think you may know who Tess's father is, and maybe who her real mother is, too."

"I don't have to listen to this." When I push my chair back and stand up, it screeches on the tile floor.

"You're right," he says. "But if Tess doesn't turn up, and soon, I'm going to come to you looking for answers. And I know you have some."

"So, are you going to help me look for her?" I ask, holding back tears. "Or not?"

"I'll send out an alert," he says. "Do me a favor: go and get some sleep. You look like you need it."

On my way back to the door, I pass a small cell. This is no jail, but I wonder if it's what people call a holding cell. A drunk tank. And, from the corner of my eye, I see a familiar figure, slumped half asleep on the corner bench.

"Silas?" I pause, just barely looking over my shoulder.

"Hey, Felicity." He jumps to his feet, a couple days' worth of stubble darkening his jaw. "What are you doing here?"

"Tess is missing." My face crumples. "I can't find her. I was hoping she was with you."

"Dawson!" he shouts, beating a fist against the wall. "Let me out already."

Dawson appears in the doorway, eyes rolling. "I see you haven't slept it off yet, have you?"

"This is bullshit and you know it," he's shouting. "Who told you to pull me over? You know this is bullshit. If you didn't, you'd breathalyze me."

"I saw what I saw," Dawson answers. "You'll have your chance to dispute it in front of a judge."

"You know that's not what this is about," he yells, then turns to me, lowering his voice. "What happened to Tess?"

My eyes water and pour over. "I took her and Frankie to stay at James's vacation house. I was so scared, staying at my mother's. It didn't feel safe. And it was fine—for a few days. She took off yesterday afternoon."

"Why wasn't it safe?"

"You already know that, don't you?" I step closer, closing both hands on the bars between us. "You're locked up, anyway, so you may as well answer me. It was you, wasn't it?"

"The hell are you talking about?" The anger in his voice is muddled with confusion.

"You snuck in that night." I lower my voice to a whisper. In my periphery, Dawson stands at the open doorway, waiting for me to be on my way, but he's far enough back I don't think he can hear. "You broke the window, left my chair covered in glass."

"Why didn't you tell me someone broke in?"

Figuring he knows the answer, I meet his stare coldly.

"You know in your heart I didn't do it," he hisses. "If you think I would do anything to threaten my own family, then tell Dawson, right now."

But I don't trust Dawson's judgment either, and it seems plain enough these two have enough animosity to keep them occupied without my help.

"Go on." Silas lifts his chin and calls in Dawson's direction. "Hey, jackass, come over here."

"Leave me alone." Raising my voice almost to a shout, I step away and move toward the exit. As I leave, I catch Dawson's eye, his stare unyielding, inscrutable.

It's only as I'm driving back, eyes bleary with sleepiness in the early morning haze, that I remember something else. Cody Redford, promising me he could get another set of eyes on Holly's case. That his father had friends who were influential, who could help. That he said he'd promised himself he'd help me, if he ever had an opportunity to do so.

And then there's the way he smiles at me. The confoundingly naive belief that I ought to just forgive him, even if I could do such a thing. But what about Tess?

As I cross the little bridge and pull into the drive, the mud slows the tires, and the familiar house rises before me. A sob rising in my throat, I take shallow breaths through my nose against the nausea that makes me want to curl into a ball right here in the driver's seat. But I don't. Make my hand pick up the phone again. Dial Cody's number, then cancel the call, shaking my head. It's too early, and what if he doesn't answer? I decide to send a message instead, choosing the medium that won't betray the shaking in my voice, the sleeplessness in my eyes.

I spend several minutes typing, deleting, and finally send a message to Cody's number: *I need your help. Please call.*

When I open the door, it takes two tries to stand up. I blink away an image of myself falling and scraping my knees. It's only mud beneath my feet, though, and I'm wearing blue jeans, and I'm thirty goddamn years old. People live with ghosts like this, though, and I suppose I can as well.

I walk inside numbly, and though I'm not sure what I'm expecting to find, it certainly isn't my mother, waiting at the door, pulling me into her arms. I try to tell her I'm too tired, too scared to talk, but it seems I can't even find the words for that.

"You've got to rest, Lissie." She takes me by the arm up the stairs, puts a glass of water by the bedside table. She lays the blanket over me, and it's only then I realize I'm in Tess's bed in the blue room, and remember again that she isn't here. She tugs my boots off and places them at the foot of the bed. "Tess needs you healthy, and Frankie. We all do."

CHAPTER THIRTY-EIGHT
Now

When I wake, bright yellow sunlight streams in at the bay window. For a moment, when I open my eyes, it's as if time has come unstuck, and I'm here in my old bed, in my old room, all my things on the shelf, and I don't know whether I need to get ready for school, or where Holly is, or where my mother is. And then, oddly, I wonder why James isn't next to me. And I sit up, finally, and remember.

It's much later than it should be. My limbs are so heavy, and my mouth is dry. I pick up my purse from where I dropped it on the dresser, now sitting alongside a cooling plate of pancakes and a cup of coffee. I reach into the purse for my phone and, suddenly remembering, find the pregnancy test.

As I'm walking into the hallway, I shout down the stairs: "Mom? Anything?"

"Nothing." She's at the foot of the steps.

"Why didn't you wake me?"

Without waiting for her answer, I walk down the hallway and, before I'm awake enough to change my mind, use the pregnancy test. It promises results in three minutes or less, and I sit it on the windowsill while I take a quick shower. Standing under the hot water, I count the hours that have passed. Still under twenty-four—less than a full day she's been gone.

I step out of the shower and grab a towel, press it over my hair, then pat my skin dry. And I reach for the pregnancy test. I double-check the instructions on the box. It's an unmistakable positive. Two lines.

My heart leaps. Before the fear surges in. Before the disbelief. Before any of that, I'm holding the test in my hand and feeling a surge of gladness, of hopefulness. A promise that there's something beyond this disaster I'm in. And I want all of it: a baby. James's baby. A home. And then fear sinks in. I'm scared of this, of staying. I have no idea what *home* could possibly look like. I run down the hallway and reach for my phone, call him immediately.

"Hello?"

"It's me."

"Hey," he says. "How are you?"

"I'm all right. Can you come over?"

"Sure. You're at your mother's house?"

"Yes."

"Have they found her?"

"No," I answer. "Just come over. I need you here."

I eat a few quick bites of breakfast, leaving the coffee alone, and pull a brush through my hair, which is tangling into curls as it dries. Downstairs, my mother is fixing lunch for Frankie. She greets me with a hug, and I let her sit on my lap while she eats her food. Her expression seems so placid that I almost wonder at her calm, then recall that Tess has run away before, that, to her, this isn't necessarily new.

I head outside into the yard, my boots and jacket still damp from last night. With melting snow and mud clinging to my boots, I pace, waiting for James. When the phone rings, I reach to answer it without a thought.

"Hello?"

"Hey, ladybug." Despite all the rest, the sound of Cody's familiar voice gives me a faint relief. "It's me. Are you all right?"

"Cody, a couple weeks ago, you said you'd help me, if you ever had a chance. I need someone's help."

"Take a breath, okay? Whatever it is, we'll fix this."

I see James's car come up the drive and wave to him. He parks and gets out of the car.

"You said you could talk to your father, that you could have someone take another look at Holly's case. Get someone on it besides Dawson—I don't know if I can trust him, Cody."

He's talking again, and I can picture the knowing way he nods his chin. "You sound stressed, Felicity."

"Can you help me?"

"Yes, but this would be easier if we could talk in person," he says. "Can you come meet me?"

"Well, I—"

"I just need to get a read on what's happening. So I know who to talk to."

"Okay." As James walks up to me, I reach out in a motion that's both asking him to wait and asking him not to leave, grasping his hand but holding him at arm's length.

"So, maybe in an hour?" Cody asks. "Meet me at St. Ben's, by the main entrance?"

"Why?"

"I'm at my father's house, by campus. It's easier."

"All right," I answer. "I'll meet you there."

"Just us, right?" he laughs. "Not looking to get punched in the face again."

"Okay." I'm hurrying through the rest of the call now, my eyes fixed on James's. "See you then." I end the call and put the phone in my purse, run my hands over my arms as if to brush invisible hands away.

I throw my arms around James.

"I missed you." His embrace lifts me off my feet, my toes just touching the damp ground beneath us, and I lean my face into his neck.

"You're cold," he says, holding me close against him, then sweeping a tentative hand across my still-damp curls.

"I'm fine."

As he studies my face, I see concern creep over his features. "We'll find her, Felicity. She can't have gone far."

"We can go inside in a minute. I just wanted to…" When our hands brush, he pulls me closer, and I let my forehead rest against his chest. Eyes trained downward, I imagine the small space between us crowded, picture my midsection heavy and rounded. I press his hands to my body and imagine him feeling the baby's kicks. I lift my eyes to his, smiling.

"James?"

"Who was on the phone?"

"Oh. Right." I wiggle loose from his hug, plant my feet on the ground. "I guess I should catch you up. I went by Silas's house last night, looking for Tess."

"I gather she wasn't there," he says. "How is he doing?"

"He wasn't there, either. He's in jail. Drunk driving, again. So," I continue, before I get off track again. "I was out all night, looking for her. I saw Dawson this morning, but he doesn't seem to understand how serious this is." His eyes widen and he draws back in surprise. "Just as I was coming home, I remembered, Cody Redford had offered to help. Said he could get his father's friends to investigate. So, I—"

"Cody Redford?"

"Yes." My voice dwindles, and I cross my arms tightly across my midsection. "I slept for a few hours, and when I woke up—"

"I'm sorry. Hang on. Redford—seriously? Is that who you were talking to just now?"

"James," I whisper, surprise creeping into my nervous chatter. "I need his help with this."

"And what, you couldn't ask him on the phone?"

"I did."

"Then why do you need to see him?"

"What—are you accusing me of something here?"

"I'm worried about you." But he speaks coldly, and his brow is a hard line.

"Well, what would you recommend that I do?"

"Not see him," he answers, as if it's simple. "Stop jumping in and putting yourself in harm's way—"

"Harm's way? Please," I sigh, a bitter taste in my mouth. "I'm the last person who will ever defend Cody Redford's character, but he isn't dangerous. At his worst, he's predictable. And people listen to him, James—in a way they don't listen to me. And you're asking me not to go, because—why?" He frowns and refuses to look at me.

"For once, Felicity, out of all the times I've asked you to be careful, listen to me. This is the only thing I'm asking of you."

"Then ask me for something else. Anything else." My fingers brush his elbow, then curl around his hand. "Don't you understand? I need to know what really happened to Holly, especially now with Tess missing—what else am I supposed to do, here?"

"For one? Try to spare a single thought for your own safety. You're in this deeper than you know, and I'm concerned about your frame of mind. And—"

"Slow down, James. Where is this coming from?" I thought James was the one person I could trust to take me seriously, but the look on his face says otherwise.

"And for another, stop saying that you're fine, when I can look in your eyes and see damn well you're not. How am I supposed to trust that you're telling me everything here, and that this isn't all going to backfire on me—again?"

"Oh." I feel a careful breath leave my lungs and take a resigned step away from him.

"That isn't it," he says, squeezing his forehead, tugging a nervous hand across his hair. "I didn't mean it like that. But Felicity, please. Just listen to me, on this one thing."

If I were the person he needed, I would see this for what it is. A moment where I need to move closer, not away, to reassure him of all those things I wanted to promise him. But his words chill the space between us. Once or twice I open my mouth to ask him a question: *Why would you say that? Why would you think that?* Until I realize he has every reason, because, after all, those things were true before.

"I'm so sorry—that came out wrong." He reaches toward me, but I cross my arms and turn slightly away.

"I'm not sure it did, James." Only a few nights ago, he had turned that gorgeous, sleepy smile at me and said: *No surprises here.* I should have known I couldn't return the promise.

"This was a mistake. All of this." My hand shakes as I wave at James's car. "Please—I need you to leave. Now." That isn't what I mean to tell him, of course. What I want is for him to move closer to me as I'm backing away, to reach across this space and tell me that he trusts me. "You don't care enough for Tess to understand that I'd do anything for her."

"I know that," he says, pleading, "but Felicity, just don't go to talk to Redford all by yourself."

"We were wrong, to jump into this as if we could pick up where we left off, only without any of the hard parts. I told you already: I can't ask you to do this."

"But—"

"And I need you to consider what you're asking of me right now."

In the silence that follows, I hear a creak, a wooden, shuffling noise, and glance up to see the curtains in one of the bedrooms rustling. My mother. She must have been upstairs for some reason. I pause to wonder what she may have overheard. She always keeps a window open to let in the air. "Tess said nothing bad started happening to them until I was here. That she thought it would stop if I left. Maybe she's right."

"What are you saying?"

"That this isn't real," I answer, speaking to myself more than to him. "This was a mistake." Once again, I've sold myself a hoax, another ghost story. The shattered pieces inside my chest have pulled like magnets toward him, regardless what wreckage that could mean for the two of us.

"You would really leave, before you've seen your own daughter home safely?" He speaks in an impersonal, chilly tone that makes me want to drop down and cry. "You're not who I thought you were."

"My own—oh, James, no." His assumption shocks me, until I consider how obvious it must have seemed.

"But you were pregnant—what happened to the baby?"

I exhale with the sound of someone who's just caught something too heavy to hold onto, then promptly wander off-topic. "I never meant that I would leave before I found her." My gaze wanders out toward the pine trees bordering the water, the mist that lingers between the branches. "I'd do anything to make sure Tess is safe. Because she is my sister's child."

"So, you weren't telling the truth? You weren't pregnant?"

"There's nothing I want more than to leave here." My admission lands with an impact, a wince flashing across his eyes. "But I'm not leaving until she's back home."

"Felicity, you haven't answered me."

"I miscarried." A tear slips over my cheeks, falling to land on my clasped hands. Why it still carries a sense of guilt, of admitting something I failed to do properly, I couldn't explain if I wanted to.

"Why didn't you tell me?"

"I'm telling you now. What more do you want?" My voice twists inside my throat, words I can't bear to speak stinging like so many wasps.

"I want to not feel like you're going to keep secrets from me, for a start." James removes his glasses, holding them in his hand with resignation. Can't he see what it costs me, to tell him these things? "How was this ever supposed to work, if you can't talk to me?"

I know the answer, but it's tangled up with all the rest of the things I can't find the strength to say. *How was this ever supposed to work, if you're going to put me on the spot when I need your trust?*

"I should never have come back here. Everyone I've tried to help would have been better off without me. This place has never had anything good for me, ever since…"

"Since what?"

"Since that night. Since that voice called me. That was when everything changed."

"Felicity, that wasn't a ghost. That wasn't the… the Reverie Girls, or whatever you've told yourself."

"What are you talking about?"

"That was your sister."

"No." I'm shaking my head, but it feels like the ground is rocking below me instead. "That's not true. Stop it."

"She called for you. I heard it."

"That isn't true," I repeat, tearful. "If it were, you would have told me then."

"I didn't tell you because I knew that you knew it." He sounds so disappointed that I have to look away from him. "I thought you'd come to it when you were ready. But you clung to that ghost story, so hard I knew you needed to believe it, somehow. It seemed like it helped you make sense of—of what happened. So I didn't see any reason to tell you."

"But it didn't sound like her."

"Sound carries differently over water. It was muffled. Besides, maybe that's only in your memory."

"James, no."

"I'm sorry," he says, as if he's surprised by how badly this hurts me. "Come here, please. I'm sorry." He tries to hug me, but I whirl away, brushing his hands off.

"How could you not tell me? How could you—"

"No, Felicity." He looks sad, so sad that it's catching, throwing me off guard. "You knew this. I'm certain of it." James waits for me to speak, but I can't acknowledge him, standing with my toes pointed toward the water, wishing I could run away from him this very minute, knowing somehow that the swamp's shadows and vines are the only place I'll ever feel truly at home.

"Was there something you wanted to talk about?"

He won't believe me.

I recognize the thorny barbs of fear around me, blocking my thoughts, my words. I remember begging him to speak to me and how he turned away. The cold look in his eyes that said everything he refused to: *Ladybugs will break your heart if you let them. And let me tell you, they know money when they see it.*

"Why'd you call?"

"I—" His impatience collides with my hesitation, and I'm shocked further into silence. *Tell him*, I'm thinking, *or you've learned nothing in all this time.* The other half of my mind whispers, *He won't believe you. You know what he'll say.*

"I'm so sorry." My voice comes out cold and gentle, even the energy of anger leaving me. "I tried. I really did."

"You still can—don't you see?" James moves close to me, reaching to place his hands on my arms, and I throw my elbows up, covering my head with my arms, trying to block out any noise or light. Arms dropping to his sides, he draws back, chin hanging down. "Should I bother asking why?"

Because, one way or another, this is what always happens when men like you fall for women like me. If you ask me to choose you over the loneliness that keeps me safe, I will vanish into the fog, every last time.

"Goodbye, James."

He looks at me a moment longer, then answers with a sharp nod and walks away.

I walk further into the shadows and stand on the porch. For a moment, I'm half hoping that he won't leave. That he stays, holds onto this harder, whatever it is, since I don't have the courage to meet in the middle. But, when I see the red of the taillights reflecting on the slick mud in the drive, I'm relieved. Being alone hasn't let me down yet.

Sitting in my favorite rocker on the front porch, I take a moment to compose myself before going back inside.

He wasn't wrong.

Somewhere, I knew it. That my sister called for my help, that I didn't answer, caught up in James's eyes. And ever since, I've known that maybe, perhaps, if I'd run to her when she called me, maybe we could have saved Page. But the fact of it hurts so much, even now, that the other story feels more true. Because if I can't blame the ghosts, I have to look at the tragedy of Page's death head-on, accept that whatever horrible things people said might have a chance of being true. And despite what people have always said, it's easier to believe a ghost story than to believe my sister could have done something to hurt Page. I've given too much for that version of things to be true.

CHAPTER THIRTY-NINE
Before

Glen's leaving, for good, sent my mother into a long, quiet mood, one I had never seen the likes of, and had no idea how to manage. For long hours, she would go silently about the housework, as if she was unable to be still.

That evening, I had tried to distract her, or to draw her out. Helping to clear the dinner table, a fourth place setting left unused, I chattered nervously, as if throwing coins into a well: *Mom, I've been thinking about baby names. Mom, I heard I could finish my high school diploma online. Mom, will we use the pink room for a nursery?* Finally, she turned to me, and though she seemed too exhausted to speak, her eyes were sharp with frustration, with the bare annoyance of having to listen to a sound one doesn't want to hear. "You know, you could still change your mind," she said, in a tone that let me know she very much wished I might.

So I left her to the dishes. Back in the blue room, I pulled on a sweater over my tank top, because the house was always drafty. I was sitting cross-legged on the bed, watching out the window where the new chickens were pecking lazily around the yard, when Holly came in, returning late from a study group.

"That's my sweater."

"What?" No longer expecting her to speak a word to me, I was too surprised to listen.

"I said, that's my sweater." Holly stood at the foot of my bed, the dresser behind her, so that she looked at me from where my reflection might have been. "You can't wear my clothes."

"Sorry." I pulled the sweater off, tugged it gently over my head, then tossed it lightly to land on her bed. She appeared to take this as an insult, picking it up with a huff and turning to place it in the dresser.

"You're so thin." The pitch of her voice was clean and sharp, somehow accusatory. "How are you so thin, even now?"

"I don't know."

"You look unwell." She was right, though I didn't want to admit it. The pregnancy seemed to be draining my body, leaving me always half afraid I was becoming translucent and gray.

"Do you think it's my fault Dad left?"

"I don't know." As if I had caught her interest, she turned, eyes landing on mine. "Is it?"

"He wouldn't have been so upset about Silas proposing to you if I weren't already pregnant." I was hurt that she made me spell this out. She must have known it. "And if he weren't so upset about Silas, Mom wouldn't have told him to be quiet. That was the last straw for him."

"Maybe you're right." She was still wearing her school clothes. "Either way, I don't think he's coming back."

"No." I wanted to ask her about school. I wanted to ask her if she had seen James and Cody and the rest of our friends, and whether anyone missed me, or talked about me at all. My heart rose as Holly sighed, crossing the room to sit at the foot of my bed. I looked at the modest gold ring on her left hand.

"So—are you going to tell me?"

"Tell you what?"

"Whose baby it is?"

I paused, felt the tension in between my shoulders as I laid there in bed. Holly was engaged to Silas now. Maybe the feelings she used to have for Cody didn't matter anymore.

"If I told you, I'd need you to promise not to tell anyone, no matter what, ever."

"Sure." Eyes lit with curiosity, she leaned closer to me.

"Cody Redford's."

Holly took a sharp breath in through her nose, and I felt right away that what I'd said was somehow wrong.

"You're lying to me." She rose to her feet, stepping back as though I might be contagious with something.

"No, I'm not, Holly."

Her face twisted with regret, or jealousy—either way something unbearable that it stung me to look at. "You're a liar."

"No."

Her anger was bigger than it should have been, and I realized her happy engagement was more complicated than it looked. That I'd been stupid to think it wasn't. "You're horrible, for saying something like that. Cody would never even look sideways at you. You were just my stupid baby sister, always tagging along."

And why had she said *you were*? When had I stopped being her sister? Shocked at her outburst, I'd picked up a pillow, held it over my face as I wept. She fell silent, and her chilly hand rested on my shoulder. "I'm sorry, but you shouldn't lie about things like that, Lissie. You ought to know better."

Only a month earlier, I'd believed I was standing on solid ground. Given time, I knew I could have found a way to live with the changes in my life. But if Holly, my cheerleader, my courage, could look me in the eyes and tell me she didn't believe me, I had no further reason to stay. That night, I walked to the bus station outside of town. Paying with cash, I bought a ticket for the most distant destination I could afford. I found work as a waitress, spending sleepless nights in the bus station for a week until I had saved enough tips to rent a tiny room. It was close to Christmas when I woke up to cramps and blood, took a bus to the hospital to find it was too late to do anything. A nurse told me the baby's heart had probably stopped beating days ago. Struggling as I was to feed myself in those days, my first thought was one of relief, which in turn filled me with bitter self-reproach. What kind of mother could I have hoped to make, if my heart's first answer to miscarriage was a kind of gratitude? Not long after, I took a job as a nurse's aide. Caring for strangers proved to come naturally to me, for which I was thankful.

After several months had passed, Holly and I caught up by phone, building a too-polite relationship that was surface level and pleasant enough, exchanging updates, as if I ever had any. I didn't work too hard to fix what I knew was broken, what had already bested me once. I didn't need to, because I wasn't going home.

CHAPTER FORTY
Now

I walk inside, passing through the living room, where my mother is seated next to Frankie, busy with a coloring book, crayons scattered across her lap.

"Aunt Lissie," she coos. I bend down and place a light kiss on her nose.

"Hi, baby."

"I'm coloring you a picture," she says. "And I made one for Tess. For Christmas."

"You're so thoughtful." I pause to study her, my thoughts quickly wandering away. I don't know how anybody could look at Frankie and fail to smile.

"Felicity, come in the kitchen."

"I'll be back to take a look at your picture," I whisper, patting Frankie's hair. "You're working so hard. It's beautiful." My mother rises to her feet and I follow her down the hallway.

The fire is still burning in the kitchen, and I sit on the hearth to dry my hair in its warmth.

"What's wrong?" My mother sits in the chair nearest the fire.

"Nothing."

"Felicity, I don't mean to be nosy, but—"

"When I say nothing's wrong, Mom, it doesn't always mean nothing's wrong. It means I don't—or can't—"

"Think I don't know that?" She smiles sadly back at me, and I ease my voice a little. "Sorry for pushing. I guess when I ask you anyway, it means I wish you did, or could, talk to me."

Silently, I shake my head. It doesn't matter now. I've tried. I can't. "I think I know how to find Tess. I'm going to talk to someone." I wind a lock of hair around my finger, then twist it free.

"To Cody Redford, right?" my mother adds. "I'm sorry, by the way. I didn't mean to eavesdrop."

I remember, now, the upstairs window closing as James and I spoke outside.

"I was upstairs to fold the laundry. I didn't realize I'd left the window open, or that—"

"What is it?"

"Well, it sounds like you think Cody Redford may be able to help you with finding Tess."

"Yes."

"That's the boy who was in your grade, right? The principal's son?"

"Yes."

"And why doesn't James want you to talk to him?"

I sigh and roll my eyes, inadvertently pitched back into our argument. "He doesn't want me to go by myself to meet him. Only, that's—"

"Felicity." My mother cranes her neck to look into my eyes. "Tell me." My voice breaks, and I realize how heavy it feels to stand, how heavy it has felt for all these years, to carry this secret.

"Mom, it was horrible." I let myself sink onto the chair next to her, arms around her shoulders. I'm not sure whether I'm crying with relief or with sorrow.

"And you were telling me the truth, the whole time. It wasn't James's child."

I shiver and draw in a calming breath. "He's so friendly, still—in his disgusting way. He still doesn't understand what he did, how it affected me." She holds me in a lingering hug that hurts me as much as it soothes.

"And now you think he can help you find Tess?"

"Yes. He'll know who to ask. Nobody else will listen."

"Felicity, I don't think you should go, either. Not because I think you're in danger, but because it'll upset you."

"I have to." Pressing my hands to my eyes, I let out a long sigh. "Mom, if you won't let me borrow your car, I'll walk. I mean it. But there is no time to waste."

"The keys are still by the door."

"Thank you." I walk softly out of the kitchen, then through the living room, place a kiss on Frankie's head and tell her I'll be back soon.

CHAPTER FORTY-ONE
Now

Outside the school building, the wind is warmer than it ought to be, signaling that foul weather is coming. It's making my hair curl and leaving a film on my skin. Cody has left the side door of the courtyard open, and I walk in, keeping my jacket on. It's chilly indoors. And quiet, with the unlit Christmas tree standing shadowed in the opposite corner, and for a moment I share this space with it, thumbing through memories of this place. Not all of them are bad.

"Felicity?" Cody looks out the door of the main office. I have a strange feeling when I look at him, even now. He's wearing a sweater and jeans, casual, the leather of his shoes soft and matte. "I wasn't sure you'd come." He has his hands in his pockets, and the look of regret on his face is almost boyish. "I'm so sorry. Before anything else, can I apologize for the other night?"

"That's not really why I called."

"Oh, it isn't? Well—" He sounds surprised, taken aback, then continues in a polite tone. "I feel like I need to. I'm so sorry for how I acted—I don't remember the details, but I was so much drunker than I had any business being."

"Well, that's true." It's not untrue, but it's not the thing I think he needs to apologize for most.

"I'm a bad drunk." He looks so regretful that I begin to believe he truly is. "I've gotten myself into trouble more than once."

"You've hurt people more than once," I interrupt, correcting him. "I think we're past apologies."

"I know an apology's not enough." He's right. Reluctantly, I meet his eyes. They're soft, as if he's asking me for something.

"Tess is missing," I interrupt. "She ran away, almost an entire day ago."

As he speaks, he holds out an arm to take my coat, hangs it on the hook by the office door. It's so effortless I almost don't notice it.

"If it's any consolation," and he says this as if he takes it for granted that it is, "I'm making this a turning point for me. I promise. Do you mind if we walk? Nerves, I guess," he shrugs. I follow him down the hallway, past the Christmas tree again.

"So, you seemed pretty shaken up on the phone." He eyes me with something that's tender but almost hungry, as if he wants a little too much to help. *Damnit*, I think *I'm not here to assuage your guilt.* "You weren't totally clear. Can you tell me everything that's happened as far as your sister and Tess?"

"Shaken up?" That's one word for it, I think. "Whoever killed my sister has been following me. Killed my mother's rooster. Ripped up my old cheer outfit. Someone's been tampering with my car. And—" I grab his hand to make sure he's listening. "Whoever it is—Tess saw them. And now she's gone, and I can't find her."

"I wish you'd told me." His tone shifts into genteel surprise. Unpleasant things have always seemed foreign to Cody. "What else do you know about the night she died?"

"I know Holly went home—she left her purse there. I know Tess saw her leave—with somebody. And Cody, don't tell anyone this, but I'm fairly certain Silas isn't her father."

"Ah." I follow him up the stairwell, and we linger in front of the large window that overlooks the front lawn.

"I know people think Tess is my daughter, but she isn't."

"People think that?" His eyes flicker to meet mine, then back to the windowpanes. Of course, I realize, he had no idea what I went through after that night. I never told him. But, though I couldn't say why, he seems unsurprised. I follow him up the stairs to the second floor, the motion sensor lights flickering on as we move down the corridor.

"Anyway, I found Holly's charm bracelet, at the antique store. The shop owner didn't know how it got there. And nobody believes me—except James. I thought he did, but..."

"Oh, Felicity, no." When he sees my eyes are watering, his mouth flattens into a frown, eyes ticking my way with something like concern. "What happened?"

"Me. I ruin things."

"No." He's shaking his head, as if he knows what he's talking about. "He didn't deserve to break your heart once, let alone twice. Fin has good intentions, but they never make it into reality, do they? You know that about him."

"Maybe."

"That's why he wasn't cut out for football. Whatever talent, whatever plans he might have, disappear as soon as the pressure's on. He freezes."

He didn't freeze when he found out you'd lied to him.

"I'm fine." I sniff and make a resolute attempt to hold my chin up. Tears roll unbidden from my eyes and I swat them away, determined to hold it in. Cody pats my shoulder, but I shrug slightly, not wanting him to come too close.

"Sorry. I don't know what's wrong with me."

"Some things aren't meant to be." He offers this as if it should be a comfort. "It hurts when your heart gets it wrong—I know, really. Don't beat yourself up." Suddenly I'm aware of his arm on me, remember where I am, and draw back, clearing my throat.

"I'm afraid that Tess running away has something to do with whatever really happened to Holly. You said you could help. That your father knew people who could get them to reopen the case." Cody gives me a sorrowful, sidelong look, and we turn the corner of the hallway, walk down the opposite staircase to the other side of the ground floor. It's dimly lit in the stairwell, and he reaches just ahead of my shoulder to push the door open.

"So, what I can do is, ask my dad to ask a couple of people. But he's out of town now, until Monday. And I'm on my way out of town first thing tomorrow."

"You what?"

"Well, not first thing in the morning," he admits. "I'll see my dad over the holiday. I can't ask him on Christmas, you get that, but I'll bring it up as soon as there's a suitable time."

"So you can't do anything." I pause and look back toward the main entryway. We've walked a nearly complete circle. "Whoever killed my sister knows that Tess saw them. She isn't safe. I need to fix this somehow."

"This place will kill you if you let it," he sighs. I look unhappily up at him, and his eyes land suddenly on mine, blue like a clear sky. "You're worried out of your mind. You're afraid you're not doing any good here, because you know it's true. That's one thing I can help with."

"How?"

"Airfare to Saint Thomas," he says. "Tonight. I'll call you a cab right this minute, if you want. Cash for any expenses until you get home. Some for after that, to get settled back in. And you have my word I'll help your family find Tess."

I should feel ashamed, and I do, but for a second, my heart leaps with joy.

"You said it to me yourself—those girls don't really know you. Why are you torturing yourself for this?" He waits just long enough for me to search for an answer, but not to find one. "So what if you're not cut out for parenting? You've always known that—haven't you?"

"Yes." It's such a weight off, such a relief to talk with someone who doesn't ask me to be more than the broken person I know I am. If only James could have seen it so clearly.

"I just want to smooth things out for you. Don't I owe you that?"

We're circling back toward the office, the atrium near the main doors again, and I let my feet shuffle to a halt, turn to look at him hesitantly.

"You know, I was pregnant. Back then. After—"

"Were you?"

"I had a miscarriage at seventeen weeks."

"Felicity, that's dreadful." Cody's expression registers confusion, and he appears almost shaken. Has his existence really been so shielded from consequence, that this should seem beyond imagining?

"I'd do anything if I could change it." But, as we're walking to the door, he tilts his head, looks at me, and says softly, "You're so like your sister."

"What do you mean?"

He gives me a sad, soft smile. "You're a lot tougher than people give you credit for."

"Thank you."

Cody takes his phone out of his pocket. Pulls up a travel app. I watch him enter today's date for departure, select the destination. "The next available itinerary has you flying out at midnight. Layover in Atlanta. This time tomorrow, you'd be home." His hand hovers over the purchase button. "I could have a taxi pick you up in half an hour," he says. "Or, maybe you'd rather leave in the morning? But I'm certain you can make the custody arrangements from wherever you need to be."

Custody arrangements. If I leave now, I'm a liar.

"I can't, Cody. Thank you—so much." Like a mirage, the desperate hope of returning to Saint Thomas vanishes. "I made Tess a promise."

"Yeah," he says, downcast. "I understand. Please take care of yourself."

"And if it does turn out that you get a chance to talk to your father about Holly, I'd appreciate it. You have my number—you can keep me updated."

"I will, Felicity." He looks regretful, maybe more than I've ever seen on him. "I'm sorry."

"You're sorry?"

"For all of it." I find, with surprise, that I feel sorry for him as well. For the first time yet, he appears to understand the weight of what he's saying.

"Goodbye, Cody."

CHAPTER FORTY-TWO

Now

My footsteps echo on the sidewalk, and the big wooden door swings shut behind me. My heart's absolutely racing, though I don't know exactly why; adrenaline, maybe. The temptation of walking away from here, of going back home. I walk down the sidewalk through the gardens, lingering for a moment. It's sad, a little, to really say goodbye to this place. I never had a chance to do that before. It's colder than it was when I got here, the wind blowing in capricious gusts.

As I approach the pine grove that conceals the sidewalk to the parking lot, I hesitate, hearing a rustle in the trees.

All this time I've been putting together pieces that held no significance. Damaged everything in my wake because of it. Maybe this is just a strange, friendly, small town. I shake my head and walk into the tree cover, making a beeline for the other side. But there's a voice in the back of my mind whispering, *Anyone could have followed you here*. But I'm so tired of being afraid. Instead of stopping to look behind me, I continue forward, disturbing a blackbird in the branches above.

My eyes are on its iridescent, blue-black wings when a heavy impact on the side of my head drops me to my knees. My field of vision crowds with stars, the noise reverberating through my skull. Time seems to slow, until I catch my fall on my outstretched palms, the sting of it snapping me back into my senses.

I need to yell for help—maybe Cody is close enough that he could hear me, but my mind is so foggy. It stings, but the sharp sensation wakes me, and I manage not to fall on my face. I scramble forward, and in the blurred periphery I'm aware of a figure wearing a mask of some kind. I dart sideways, off the walkway, and into the cover of the thicket, dashing into the forest as fast as I can manage.

By the time I'm something close to awake, by the time the need to blink every second subsides, I'm running through the pine-needle-covered forest bed, shoving through thicket and shrubbery. The figure behind me is drawing nearer, moving much faster than I am. Branches tear at my clothes and there's a dull ache in the back of my skull, warning me that once I stop moving it's going to hurt worse. I slipped as it hit me; I realize that this was meant to be a worse injury than it is. There are footsteps behind me. I'm ahead, but not by much.

I drop cowering to my knees, arms curled around my head. Though I'm afraid the sheer noise of my heartbeat will give me away, the footsteps move in the other direction. East, in about a half mile, the ground sinks lower, giving way to marshy ground and swampland. Toward the west, the school property borders the road to town. Turning in the direction of the road, I take in a shaky breath, then launch to my feet and move as fast as I can.

I don't care whether I'm headed for land or water, but pray to get quickly out of the woods. Staggering through one more ditch, I don't recognize the sensation of asphalt under my feet until I'm already hearing squealing brakes. I can sense the weight of the vehicle growing closer, blink dumbly in the headlights like a madwoman. The car's come to a stop when I stagger backward, half a sob sounding from my hoarse throat. I look wildly back into the woods, then toward the car.

"What in the hell are you doing out here?" a voice shouts, feet hitting the ground. "Shit, Felicity, what happened?"

The trees in front of me blur and dance, and I blink hard but can't focus. I hold a hand in front of my face, watch an uncountable blur of fingers wavering in and out of focus, then see the bright red on my shaking palms.

I hear footsteps in the brush again, a few yards back. Suddenly, here on the road, a set of arms grabs me. Before I can kick or scream, I'm pulled up from the ground, toward the idling vehicle. I struggle, weakly, bracing my hands on the side of the car door. When I turn over my shoulder to see Silas, a bolt of fear clears my confusion.

"Let me go." With a jolt, I throw an elbow back, catching him on the ribs, and slip away.

"How the hell did you get out here?"

"Get away from me." My foot slips in the damp roadside grass and I brace an arm on the hood of the car, trying to get my footing.

"What—are you bleeding? Jesus." When Silas takes a step toward me, I lurch backward, landing on my knees in the grass. I look up gasping, shoulders tensed for impact. Silas touches a hand to his chin, points to me, then back toward the trees, shaking his head.

"You still think I'm the one you need to be afraid of here?" Taking advantage of his hesitation, I get to my feet, ready to run. But he doesn't follow me. He stands there in his confusion, eyes wide with something that almost resembles concern.

Suddenly, I feel my mind focus, all the fogginess dissipating. I decide to take my chances with Silas—as if I had a choice. Letting myself finally drop into the seat, I press my hands to my eyes as he climbs into the driver's side and shuts the door. Silas takes what appears to be a towel from the floorboard and hands it to me. I press it to my head, hair damp with rainwater and blood, then wrap it over the scrapes on my palms.

"What are you doing out here?"

"Driving to my house," he snaps. "That okay with you?"

As he drives, Silas turns up the heat in the car, throwing a half-angry, half-worried look my way as often as he can while driving safely. I hold the flannel to my head again, then examine it, blotted with red. Suddenly, I realize the fabric in my hands is a shirt.

"I'm sorry about your shirt."

"My shirt?" He coughs out a laugh.

"Yeah."

"You just presumably got chased through the woods by someone—or something—that hit you hard enough you ran out in front of a car, and you're sorry about my shirt. Oh." When he sees I'm losing it, he tries to backtrack. "I'm sorry. That was clear, you were just—being polite."

"I feel like I'm the one who should be asking you what the hell's going on." I crack the window to get some air, regardless of the cold.

"Care to elaborate?"

"I needed to talk to you." My anger wakes me up a little. "I went by the police station today, trying to get help finding Tess. Heard you screaming your drunk head off about God knows what. Cursing Rob Dawson again." I brush my knees off, palms smarting. "I can't believe I was going to you for help finding Tess!"

"Fine thing to tell a guy who just pulled your bleeding ass out of the road," he snorts. "And, for your information, I was sober as a saint. Dawson pulled me over because he's a rat who's always had it out for me."

"And I'm supposed to—what? Just trust you?"

"Yeah? Well, you're no charmer," he responds. "And I'm telling the truth. I swear. On—on Holly's grave."

"Keep her name out of your mouth!"

"You think I'm lying? I mean it. Swear it on Holly's death and her life."

"Where's Tess?" My voice rises sharply, as if volume alone were enough to compel him—if I could only be loud enough. "Don't tell me you don't know. You hid her, or you sent her somewhere, or you—you—"

With a gentle exhale, something like the sound of a dry branch snapping, he slouches, staring out at the road. "Has anybody told you they're sorry, Felicity?"

"What the hell do you mean?"

His silence absorbs my panic. "Has anybody told you they're sorry, that you came back here to deal with one tragedy, and got thrown into an absolute mess with no right answers, no good outcomes?"

Once again, I'm too surprised to answer.

"Do you think I don't know that nobody in this town takes you seriously, if you've made one mistake in your life?" He speaks with no hurry. "Well, I'm sorry."

He's driving fast, I guess to the police or to the hospital, I don't know which and I don't have the presence of mind to have a preference. "Why did Dawson pull you over? What happened?"

"He's always had a crush on Holly," Silas says. "Years ago, I'm pretty sure he and Holly spent a night together." As he's driving, Silas turns to me, and I see a combination of dread and uncertainty on his face.

"And you think that's why he locked you up?"

"I saw Dawson. I saw him, from the road, and I could swear he was putting gas in a car. But when I slowed down and looked, it wasn't his car. He jumped back from it when he saw me. Whatever was in that gas can, it wasn't gas, and—"

"Silas, what kind of car was it?"

"I went to the station next chance I got and told him I'd seen it," he grumbles. "I don't know what he's up to, and you can call it my imagination if you insist, but I know I saw something shady. And I bet you anything that's why he pulled me over. Just to show me he can make trouble for me."

"What kind of car was it?"

"It was a gray Jetta." He huffs a sigh. "Why? You don't believe me? Think I'm just jealous of Dawson because he had a thing for Holly? I can put that in the past," he says. "But I don't have to like the guy. That doesn't mean I'm inventing stories about him."

"Silas, it was my car."

CHAPTER FORTY-THREE
Now

He hits the brakes, swearing, and takes an abrupt turn, heading in the other direction.

"How do you know?"

All my suspicions aligning, I tell him about the rental car misfiring. And the one after that. I'm brushing twigs from my hair, ignoring the myriad little scrapes and bumps. The only one worth complaining about is the lump on the side of my head, and that one could be plenty worse. Silas is swearing a blue streak as we drive.

"Why would he do that?" I whisper. I'd been half hoping, still, that I was somehow imagining it.

"I don't know," Silas says, "but we're sure as hell going to his house and asking him."

"Silas! No!" I'm pointing and gesturing back toward the woods.

"What?"

"If you saw him messing with my car, it isn't safe. He's a cop—he's armed. That was probably him, back there."

"Shit." He shakes his head, his mouth pursing. "Your place, then?"

"Yes, please."

We fall silent, him squinting out of the windshield, swearing evenly at the defrost. I'm looking over at him uncertainly. From the road, I see the house is still standing, as ever. Lights in the windows. I can see the twinkling glow of the Christmas tree. Even from here.

My thoughts are racing, but they're moving so fast I can't put anything together.

"Stop the car," I say, leaning close to the windshield as Silas pulls up to the bridge.

"What is it?" He slows down to a halt. I open the door and get out, pacing in the rain. The weather's picked up now, and it's not a downpour, but the rain is falling steadily, and the cloud cover is so thick it looks like midnight. I pace across the bridge, only a couple car lengths, then back to the other side. After a few moments, I pull the flannel shirt around my shoulders. Silas opens the driver's side door and stands, leaning against the car in the rain, his eyes following me cautiously.

"This is the only way to our yard by car," I say, trying to think. "It's too bright."

I brace against the side rail with my arms, wishing I could push it down. Stalk back to its other edge, pulling up the reflectors that show you where to drive. Beneath the bridge, the stream rushes, threatening its own banks. I bend down and find a rock, a broken piece of asphalt, and hurl it up at the streetlight. Silas curses and jumps back from me. It misses by at least a yard, sailing away to land in the water with a dull splash.

"What the hell are you doing? Take it easy," he says.

"I don't want anyone to be able to see out here," I cry. "This whole yard is on display. Inviting anybody right in. I'm tired of it." I bend down to pick up a rock but find myself crying, out loud, folded over my knees. "I want her back. I miss her. Why didn't she talk to me—why didn't she ask me what happened that day?" I sob, staring up at Silas as if he could have any idea what I'm talking about. "But I didn't tell her, and she never asked."

Silas clears his throat and reaches a hand down to help me up.

"Listen," he says, twisting the toe of his massive boot in the mud. "I wasn't totally honest with you, that day when you came by the house."

"What do you mean?" I look toward the house, wondering how loud I'd have to shout for my mother to come running.

"When I said I didn't know what broke your trust in people," he answers, stuffing his hands into his pockets, glancing nervously at me and then away. "Holly told me once about why you left town. What little she had put together, anyway. I'm sorry I gave you a hard time." I cross my arms, a defensive gesture, and look at him wordlessly. "Honestly, I think being with Holly brought out whatever good was in me. Since I lost her, it's like I can't think straight. Everybody looks like an enemy."

I'm too proud to tell him I feel the same way, and wait until he continues.

"Holly adored you. She'd be furious with me for being such an ass to you."

"She was wrong about me," I sniff.

"Agree to disagree," he says. "Holly liked 'most everyone. She was different from you in that way. But when she was sure about somebody, she was usually right. And she was sure about you."

"She saw the good in people." Holly and I were a team in that way, my cynicism grounding us, her optimism keeping us moving, keeping us brave. Maybe I can try to do some of both. Silas clears his throat and holds out a hand again. Grabbing hold, I rise to my feet and hurl another rock at the light post. It soars off into the dark, not even close to hitting.

"You're not gonna hit it like that." Silas walks off to the side of the road, almost to the streambed, and returns with a couple of larger rocks, slick with mud.

"Try this one." He puts it in my palm. "Throw it sidelong, so it spins a little."

I do, and this time, it hits, the light crackling into nothing, leaving us alone in the dark on the bridge. The darkness is thick, and the windows of my mother's house glimmer through the fog like distant reflections.

"Nobody's getting across this bridge in that kind of dark," he says. "Not unless they know the road better than you do. You okay, Wheeler?"

"Yeah," I answer, brushing the hair from my eyes. "I'm sorry."

"You already said that," he answers.

"I'm sorry for not trusting you," I answer. "You were right. I'm not all the way well. I've pushed everyone away, and I don't have a lot of friends right now." It's dark as anything, but I know the path well enough, walking up to the house in the sparse light that shines from the downstairs windows.

"As long as you're looking out for my girls, you can call me a friend."

I slow down as I climb the steps to the porch, trying to wipe the mud from my face before I walk inside.

"I was looking for you," I tell him. "When I found out you were in jail. Tess said something weird."

"What's that?"

"Sorry to ask you this, but is there any chance you're not her father, biologically?"

I tense a little as I speak. If he's got a jealous bone in his body, this is when I'll see it. But Silas turns to me with clear eyes, nodding his head.

"Holly came to see me one day. She told me she'd gotten herself in trouble, and she was afraid of what her father would do when he found out." He glances up at me as he speaks, and I realize Holly must have told him how my parents reacted to my own pregnancy. "I didn't want her to feel like I was rescuing her, or anything. I just asked her if she wanted me to marry her."

"You loved her so much." I'm trying not to start crying again, but he gently nods his head, as if to say he's been telling me this all along. "So—do you know who…?"

"I have my ideas," he says, his brow darkening for a moment, "but she wanted it in the past, so I left it alone. I was there when Tess was born. She's my daughter, in every way that matters."

"You're stronger than you think, Silas." I consider my words carefully, trying not to let on that they're the same ones I wish were true of me. "There's good in you. You don't need Holly to be here for that to be true."

"You really think so, or is that your concussion talking?"

"I'd know if I had a concussion."

Silas pauses, rests his chin in his broad hand. "Same to you, then. Thanks, Felicity."

"You're welcome." I stand up, reach to the door. "Come in. Frankie will be glad to see you."

CHAPTER FORTY-FOUR
Now

As we walk in the door, a rush of relief warms me. I hurry down the back hallway into the kitchen, where I find the familiar warm yellow light and a fire in the fireplace.

"What took you so long?" My mother barely turns from the sink, washing dishes. Silas lingers in the shadowed doorway.

"Aunt Lissie," Frankie bleats, holding her arms up, walking to me. I pick her up, taking care to turn my head away from her, though I squeeze her tightly.

"Lissie, is that mud on your face?" my mother asks, coming closer.

"Some of it." I drop into a chair, facing the light. Stare up at my mom as she watches me, leans closer. She doesn't ask me anything, just turns back to the sink and gets a washcloth, starts patting my face clean. "Frankie, darling," she murmurs, never taking her eyes off me. "Your daddy's here. Go and say hi to him, okay?"

"Hey, princess." Silas drops to his knees on the floor and squeezes his daughter tight. For the first time, I'm embarrassed to notice, I can see so clearly that he loves them, fully and entirely. That he's ill, and that maybe he could get better.

"Everything's fine. Your car is fine. But I'll have to go get it later." She nods, and I see plain as day that she's waiting me out, that she knows I need to say whatever's coming next. "Someone chased after me when I was walking back to the car. I went through the woods and got to the road. Silas picked me up." I sniff, chest heaving. She clicks her tongue and turns my chin down, parting my hair to look at the cut.

"How's it feel?"

"Not that bad." Elbows on my knees, I lean forward. When my mother touches my hands, I find I'm pulling them away from my eyes to look up at her. "I'm sorry I was mean to you. I hope you can see why I didn't try harder to tell you the truth."

"Oh, Felicity." She's neither alarmed nor angry. Just folding me into her arms, not even too tight, as though she knows it would distress me more. "I could tell that something was wrong, and I didn't want to accept that I couldn't just work out what it was."

In the background, I see Silas walk with Frankie into the living room, offering treats and a movie, promising her that everything will be okay.

"I wish I could fix it," she says. "I wish you could have told me and your father that something was wrong."

"If I couldn't tell you, I certainly couldn't tell him."

I wait for her to refuse me again, to insist that I never gave Glen a fair chance. Instead, she nods her head. "You're right. Something like this would have been way out of his wheelhouse."

I remember it now, the night after I left, how I cried in bed, telling myself that it was my fault. I woke up with only a cauterized anger for him. When Glen left, my mother and my sister and I should have been a team. The ones who were still there. "What I did was worse," I whisper. "Leaving you and Holly behind."

"You were taking care of yourself, when nobody else could," she says, her voice even and calm. "If there was anything to forgive, I'd forgive you, without reservation." I'd forgotten the kind of magic a mother has, to absorb and forgive like this. "You should have never had to go through all this. There's no good side to it."

"It's okay."

"It's not. You're okay, but what happened to you is not."

She dries my eyes, hands me the towel to hold against my head, and returns to the dishes, just like that. "I never thought that boy was anything more than an overprivileged brat."

"He's not," I answer. "We want for there to be an answer to things, but sometimes there isn't one. I think he understands enough to know it's not something an apology can repair."

"I'm not so sure," she answers, drying a plate, placing it in the wooden drying rack.

"Mom, there's something else I want to tell you."

"What is it?"

"Hey, Felicity." Silas is shouting from the living room. "There's lights, noises outside. Someone's on the bridge."

He comes down the hallway, Frankie curled up in one massive arm, and hovers at the doorway, as if asking permission. I nod, and he steps in and hands Frankie over to my mom. "I heard a car. You wait here."

"Absolutely not." I head after him.

"You have time to put on a coat," my mother says, reaching in one fluid motion to take a coat from the closet and throw it my way. Holly's coat, again. Rainproof, flannel lining. I see the sadness cross Silas's face again. I'm not sure whether it's that I don't want him to go out alone or I don't trust him, but I'm following him either way.

Walking down the front steps into the rain, the night is dark. I can see headlights cutting across the bridge at an awkward diagonal. Looks like someone nearly went off the road, narrowly missed going into the creek.

"You think they're conscious?"

"Who the hell would even—"

A sharp beam from a flashlight swings across the yard, and Silas and I both sink into the shadows. It looks as though, in the dark, someone drove their car into the side rail of the bridge rather than onto it. Silas dims his flashlight as we stand behind the tree. I hear shuffling noises, my eyes following them to see a man's figure in the dark. The dark blue of a uniform. Rob Dawson.

"Who's there?" Dawson calls. "Felicity? Mrs. Wheeler? I could use a hand here."

Seeing him puts fear in my heart, and the leaping of my heart brings on another wave of nausea. Silas takes a step forward, but I stay back, lingering in the shadow of the oak tree.

"Hey, Dawson," he yells. "What are you doing here?"

"Silas? The hell?" he spits. "I'm here for work. Why are you here?"

"My family lives here," he answers. As the flashlight beam passes over the yard again, Dawson's eyes fall on me.

"Felicity, is that you? What happened?"

"As if you don't know." A childlike wave of hurt mingles with my anger, and I'm surprised to find myself trying not to cry.

"What are you talking about?" Dawson takes a step toward me and Silas pushes him back with a sound that I can only describe as a growl.

Dawson's flashlight flickers back toward me. "Felicity, over here. Step away from him. Are you hurt?" The light dwells on my face and I blink, unable to see. The big-brother expression he always wears when he's looking at me now conjures only fear. "Silas, get away from her."

"Think you're clever?" Silas picks him up by the collar of his jacket, looking for all the world like he could bite his face right off. "If I hadn't been in the right place at the right time, she'd already be dead. No wonder you locked me up."

"What are you talking about?" Dawson wheezes. Silas pulls back a fist, tightens his jaw. "You think I don't know you had something to do with Holly going missing? What are you doing out here now, looking for Felicity alone?"

"You were the last one to see Holly at the party!" Dawson cries, shoulders thrashing until Silas lets him fall to the ground with a thud. Dawson gets to his feet, panting, straightening his coat. "You're the one who ruined your marriage."

I admit, though I can see their tempers are high, that was a personal blow. Silas finally hits him square on the mouth.

"Take it easy, Silas," I say. "He deserved that one. But no more. At least for now."

"Felicity, are you all right?" he asks, pointing the flashlight at me.

"Right in my eyes? Come on." My head throbs. "Yes, Dawson, I'm fine, no thanks to you."

"You don't look so good. Let's sit on the porch, get you out of the rain, at least."

Dawson's holding a hand over his mouth as Silas pulls him by the shoulder. Silas and Dawson both move to offer me a chair, but I'm more comfortable standing, leaning against a post, letting the mist cool my clammy forehead. They sit in the rocking chairs on the front porch, dusty and slick with rain. I stare at Dawson in the dark, touch a hand to the cut on the back of my head, shivering.

"Why'd you do it?" I ask.

"What do you mean, exactly?"

"Don't bother lying," I answer. "I know it was you, out in the woods by the school."

"Felicity, what are you—"

"I saw you screwing with her car," Silas growls. Dawson starts to stand up and Silas levels an index finger at his chest, pushing him back into the chair. "What have you got to say about that?"

At this mention, Dawson sighs, rubbing his eyes.

"Okay, I—"

"Talk, dumbass." Silas towers over him.

"He's getting to it, Silas," I murmur. I wait, and, finally, Dawson begins to speak. Next to Silas in his anger, Dawson's composure takes on a smug quality. Almost as if he's not even hiding anything here. I begin to sense what Silas finds so infuriating about him.

"I have no idea what happened to your sister," Dawson answers. "I swear. And your car, it—" Silas moves to hit him again and I reach out to stop his arm. "It was meant to scare you. It was meant to be an inconvenience. So you would decide to leave town."

"What did you do?"

"It's an old prank," he says. "Put some lacquer thinner in the gas tank. It throws the engine off, but usually runs through the tank before you can get it to a shop."

"You always talked about looking out for me, about how you were worried for me." My words are uneven and ragged around an unexpected lump in my throat. "You're the last person I ever expected to do something so cruel. The mechanic laughed at me. Everyone thought I was losing my mind, and I wondered, too, honestly."

"Look, everyone knows it's... not easy for you. And I didn't want to say anything, but I heard about the trouble you've been having, and I thought, if you had a reason to—"

"What trouble?"

"I heard you were sleepwalking. Having trouble, you know, keeping things straight."

I narrow my eyes at him. "Where did you hear that?"

"Redford," he shrugs. "He was the first one who was worried about you. Thought it might be hard, considering what happened in the past."

"Let me just get this straight," Silas repeats. "Someone put you up to this—messing with a woman's car? Someone who was driving around with kids—my kids?"

Dawson begins to mumble. "Cody Redford seemed to think it would be easy to get you to leave town."

"Seems like he's really set on making himself feel like the good guy," I mutter. "In any case, he was wrong."

"Yeah, he was. You're a real pain sometimes." Dawson says these words with something close to admiration, but I flinch, and Silas hits him in the stomach. They're a perfect match, these small-town rivals, both infuriating in their own distinct way, each suspecting the other of hurting Holly.

"That's my wife's sister, you dirtbag," Silas yells. I could intervene, but I don't. Dawson splutters an apology.

"But what about my cheer uniform? And the break-in?"

"Absolutely not," he says. "I would not do that. I figured maybe you'd done it yourself."

"Tell me the real reason you locked Silas up."

"I thought he was a danger to you. I'm still not certain he isn't."

I don't know why, but I believe him. Maybe he's not smart enough to lie convincingly. In any case, even now I can't picture him strangling a rooster.

"Remind me to punch you before you decide to open your mouth again," Silas grumbles.

"Both of you, calm down," I insist. "Dawson, for the record, subterfuge is not your thing. You don't have the personality for that. Silas, please, just stop hitting him for five minutes."

Overwhelmed, I step away from both of them for space, fresh air, I'm not sure. I make it down the front steps and into the yard before a spell of lightheadedness stops me in my tracks, trying not to throw up on my boots.

Moments later, I hear their footsteps behind me.

"What is it?"

"You all right, Felicity?"

They're both offering me a hand. Holding both arms out to demand space, I follow them back up to the rocker, where Dawson pulls a chair near me and they sit in uneasy silence, as if it isn't obvious they're waiting for me to say something. "I'm going to be fine," I answer. "It's not contagious, if you know what I mean."

"Well, well, I didn't know," Silas mumbles.

"Is this a congratulations sort of moment, or—"

I guess my expression must have given me away, because they both stop short.

"Well, where is he? I'll go find the guy, if that's what you want," Silas says. "Why isn't he here? You shouldn't be alone."

"Yeah, I'll go find him," Dawson says. "Unless, I mean, if that's not what you want—"

"Of course it is," Silas says.

"There's nothing wrong with choosing to raise a kid on your own," Dawson snaps. I'm staring out over the yard, silent, tears streaming down my cheeks.

"Shut up," Silas hisses, jabbing Dawson with an elbow, nodding in my direction.

"Sorry." Their whispers sound in unison. For the first time, they don't seem at odds with each other.

"Wheeler, if you need anything," Silas says, "you know where to find me." Dawson clears his throat awkwardly before adding in a quiet voice: "Same goes for me."

"As if she'd trust you," Silas says.

"None of this matters." I press my heels to the boards of the porch, tilting the rocker back and forth. "Tess is still out there somewhere. Dawson, why'd you come out here, if it wasn't to try to kill me?"

"Well, that was the thing," he says. "I got a phone call, at the station. Someone said Tess is nearby."

CHAPTER FORTY-FIVE
Now

We move inside to dry off, Silas watching Dawson like a hawk the entire time. I fill him in on what happened outside the school, while he shakes his head in disbelief.

"What did they say about Tess?" I remind him that she's been gone for nearly a full day. That she disappeared on the boat from James's lake house.

"Yeah, someone called, and said—"

"Who? Tell me."

"I'm trying," he says. "They said I'd find her at the fairground."

There aren't that many places to really hide out there, and I wouldn't doubt that Tess knows all of them. I start to speak, but Dawson cuts me off. "Well, if you'd listen, I went out there obviously right away. I walked all the way up the dock and back. But there was nobody there."

"No," I murmur, talking through my hands. "No, Dawson, that's not it."

"What, you know where they meant?"

"Yes," I answer. There's a lump in my throat now, but it's not from my uneasy stomach. "I do know." I remember that water, so murky and deceptive on a beautiful day, with those hidden deep spots where the mud could swallow your whole oar if you dropped it. "There's a handful of places she could be."

"Can you tell me how to get there?"

"In this weather? With the water this high? It would take you hours, and—" I begin to speak, but change my mind and get up, start walking to the door.

"You can't go by yourself," Dawson says.

"Then you're coming with me."

"Are you out of your mind?" Silas asks. "Five minutes ago, you thought he was trying to kill you."

I shake my head again, pulling my wet rain boots back on. "Silas, you stay here with Frankie and my mother. Just in case." He starts to grumble but I silence him with a stare. "Frankie's scared. You want to do something for your daughters? Be here with her while I go get her sister."

"And what good is it going to do for her if I let you go out there by yourself and you get hurt?" he asks. "Or worse?"

"You have to stay with them," I answer. "Besides, if Tess is out there—you don't know it the way I do. It will be faster if I go."

I pull on Holly's coat and nod to Dawson. "You ready?"

Dawson follows me out into the yard. "So, where are we going?"

The canoe wobbles as we step in, then rights itself. The vessel moves silently through the water; the chilly rain that falls around us absorbs any small noise, giving me the impression almost that we're not really here. Dawson sits holding the flashlight across from me, while I paddle near the water's edge. In the rain, the water higher than usual, it's a bit more difficult to find my usual landmarks. More than once, we nearly tip over, the bottom of the canoe dragging along a root or a tree branch I didn't see just under the water. But, even in the dark, I find I know the way. Only after a few minutes in silence do I notice that Dawson is sending occasional nervous, guilty glances toward me.

"What is it?"

He looks down at his hands.

"What?" My hands tighten on the oar.

"I'm sorry, Felicity."

"It's foolish, I guess," I answer, glaring. "But even after all this time, I thought you were my friend."

"I was trying to do the right thing. Trying to help you. I thought it would be better for you to leave town, even if that meant getting scared a little."

"The right thing would have been listening to me."

"I know you don't want to hear about this, but I really cared about Holly."

My breath stills, my hand tightening on the oar. "How did Holly feel about that?"

"After she got engaged to Silas, she didn't want anything to do with me. I never knew why," he says, with a more poignant expression than I'm used to seeing on him. "One day we were friends—the next day she wouldn't even look at me. But that's in the past. My point is, I always felt guilty for not telling her about that night I drove you home. And when you showed up again, all these years later, hell-bent on putting yourself in danger wherever you could find it—I wanted you to be safe. I couldn't help but think she would have wanted you safe."

"How about letting me worry about my safety," I mutter. But I pause, sitting quietly in the almost-dark, thumbing over what he said about Holly.

We continue a little ways, the fog thick around us, the trees and foliage growing more dense as we turn up the creek that leads toward the fairground. The dark is deep and layered, and something about it draws me into its folds, searching through the variegated shadows for something familiar.

"So, tell me," he says. "What happened that night I found you walking home by yourself?"

"Oh." An owl cries, closer than I expected, and we both flinch. "There was a boy, and too much to drink. You probably don't even need to use your imagination." He nods, and I think he's embarrassed.

"Sorry, Felicity."

"I know you were expecting some sort of missing puzzle piece." When I pull the hood of my coat up against the rain, I sense Dawson glancing away from me, and I know he's thinking of that night again. "But memories like that are a dead end. It's better forgotten." Over his shoulder, I see the trees thinning, the skeletal structure of the fairground's old swing ride coming into sight.

"Up here, near the boardwalk, there's a place we used to tie up the boats. You used to be able to walk from there." I point to show him where I intend to go. "I think you still can, but you have to be careful. And if you follow the boardwalk about halfway around, near the edge of the lake, there's a spot where you can jump onto the old Ferris wheel and walk across it. If Tess is here, that's where she is."

"It was Redford," Dawson says suddenly.

"What do you mean?"

He looks at me for a moment and, understanding him, I nod frankly.

"How'd you guess?"

"You weren't the only one who—well, it was long ago, of course. Anyway, I figured you already knew for some reason. Whoa." Before he can finish his thought, I'm steering the canoe to the dock that connects to the boardwalk. "God, it gets creepier every time I see this place."

I move to stand, bracing my arms on the dock, but Dawson stops me.

"Why don't you let me go ahead? You said you think Tess is up that way—toward the Ferris wheel?" He waves his flashlight, looks ahead into the night. Vine-laden tree branches and Spanish moss obscure the view, but the shape of it is just barely visible up ahead. "I'd rather you wait here. I'll go and find her, then come back to you."

"Are you sure?"

"You looked ready to faint when I found you outside with Silas. It's just—places like this are awfully prone to accidents."

Without waiting, Dawson turns his back to me and walks away. It would be easy to dismiss his all-too-predictable concern, if I didn't know there's an all-too-real reason for these rushes of lightheadedness.

"Dawson, what was it you were saying about Cody?" I call after him, but I'm reluctant to raise my voice more than a little. The only sound is his footsteps, growing softer with distance.

A noise from down the boardwalk startles me: a muffled thud and a splash. I realize Dawson's left me sitting in the dark, that I told him to take the flashlight. I can almost make out the familiar forms of the fairground, the old swings, the dance hall in the distance. I steady myself with one arm, climb up out of the canoe. The wooden planks are familiar under my feet, seeming to whisper in greeting, and, although they're slick and a little unsteady, my feet feel sure.

It only occurs to me as I'm walking that this place has always tricked me with its deceptive feeling of safety, of being the sort of magic spot where nothing could go wrong. Page wasn't safe here. Tess surely isn't. And now I'm here, walking down a boardwalk that sighs under my weight, looking for Dawson. Dawson, who showed up to my mother's house, claiming that he received a phone call informing him that Tess was out here. Dawson, who always looked at Holly the wrong way, if Silas is to be believed. With a chill, I recall Silas saying that Holly would have sent Dawson straight to hell, if she could have done it herself. And why did he look at me so strangely this morning, when he insisted I might know who Tess's father was?

Dawson never told me who called, or described that call.

I've only come a few yards down the boardwalk when I have to duck under a curtain of moss that hangs from a gnarled oak. I'm moving slowly, checking before I step forward, half expecting the wood to collapse beneath my steps. A weight catches under my foot and I sail forward, grasping the moss with my fingertips as if it could support me. I land on my elbows, my palms scanning the wooden planks for something, anything to grab, when I hear what I could swear is a gasp or a sigh behind me. Some kind of breath. I hold my own breath, inch forward silently on my elbows, and reach out an arm to prod the dark form where I've just tripped.

It doesn't move.

It's warm.

My heart lurches, struck with a fear I can't even put into words. I can't think her name. I can't bear it. But as I reach out, find a shoulder, a solid weight, I realize this isn't Tess. It's Dawson.

"Dawson, get up," I whisper. "What happened?" He could have slipped or fallen anywhere—knowing Dawson, he might not have taken the care I would with this boardwalk. I should have gone ahead. I should have gone with him. "Wake up," I hiss, my hands reluctantly scanning his body for an injury, double-checking that he's breathing. I hold his chin and turn his face, trying to see him, and then draw back with a gasp. My hands come back slick, damp, and suddenly I'm aware of the smell of blood, almost masked by the familiar, incense-heavy smell of the swamp.

Dawson breathes, but he isn't moving. I can't get him back to the boat—he's far too heavy—and while I'm reluctant to leave him on his own, I have a feeling telling me Tess is near. I swallow a curse, wishing I'd come here alone instead. I reach desperately forward, sweeping an arm along his leg. I'm looking for a gun, but it still feels indecent—until, finally, I feel what I think is a holster under my fingertips. My stomach churns.

The holster is empty.

I take my phone out and check the reception: one bar. It's worth trying, so I dial 911, then wait, my hands shaking, rainwater on the screen. I remember from before, I can call emergency services without a phone plan, but—the call won't go through. Not without a tower to take the call. With a hand up to hold the water out of my eyes, I pace back up the boardwalk, looking to see if I can find a spot where there are fewer trees, to let more signal through. At the sound of branches creaking, I stop moving.

"Tess, are you here? Can you hear me?"

But it's not Tess who appears from the trees, walking up the narrow trail toward me. It's Cody.

CHAPTER FORTY-SIX
Now

"Cody?" I blink once, then again. "What are you doing here?"

"Hey, Felicity. I was out for a walk," he answers, "before the weather got bad."

"But it's been raining all afternoon." And, I notice, his clothes are almost completely dry. I can name that strange feeling now, that flicker of warning that crossed my mind when I saw him earlier this afternoon. That was fear.

"The police got a phone call that Tess was here, somewhere. So—I brought Dawson out here—"

"Did you?" There's something mournful in his stare. "Why did you do that? You could have just stayed at the house." The rain falls loudly around us, a pattering, indifferent downpour. Fighting confusion, I begin again to explain.

"Someone called the police station, and said that Tess was here. And now Dawson's…"

He already knows all of this. My eyes dart behind him and I can almost imagine a flicker of gold, drawing me away.

"Oh, Felicity." He tilts his head. "I gave you every chance to leave—I outright asked you to leave town. You know I'm not really in the habit of asking for things, right?"

"Y-yes." Don't I know it—better than most. I see Dawson's flashlight in his back pocket.

"But for you? I begged you to leave."

"Cody, stop it." I inch side to side, looking for a path around him or away from him, and he follows every tiny move I make.

"And do you know why?"

"No."

"Because I didn't want to hurt you, Felicity," he answers, seemingly offended that I don't understand him. "I still don't."

He swings the flashlight. This time he doesn't miss.

CHAPTER FORTY-SEVEN

Now

The first thing I notice is the ringing in my ears, the faint whistle that sometimes accompanies radio static. After this, the sharp pain in my head. It sends all my senses looking for distraction: my hands scrambling on damp wood, eyes blinking through this stinging rainwater. Only, the rainwater is warm, and sticky.

Then I remember.

When I manage to get my bearings, it's evident I'm still on the same stretch of the boardwalk. Curling my knees inward, I try to sit up, leaning my weight on one elbow. Cody sits at my side, elbows resting on his knees, hands tented in front of his face. His eyes are gently closed, as if he's deep in thought.

"Goddamnit. This wasn't meant to happen." He speaks softly, a disappointed whisper that slips through his fingers. "I did everything I could to try to make you leave."

"To make me leave? What do you mean?" I lift a hand to the side of my head, then, wincing, draw it away. "Wait. Was it you, in the house that night? Did you kill the rooster?"

"He didn't suffer."

A scream of shock freezes in my throat, dissolving into a paralyzing chill.

"All of it—all that effort—was only to get you to leave town. Because I didn't want this to happen."

"You know where Tess is, don't you?" To my surprise, the words come readily, though the effort of speaking leaves me dizzy with pain, head throbbing. "Cody, why? Why do you know that?"

"Because I brought her here." With an almost genteel annoyance, he leans his chin slightly to look at me. "She's perfectly safe, of course."

"Why would you—"

"Because I saw her getting closer to you—beginning to trust you. She was going to tell you."

"Tell me what?" I stammer. "When did you see me with Tess?"

"Are you really going to make me spell this out?" Cody shifts one hand to his forehead, turning a quietly furious gaze on me.

What was it that I wanted Tess to tell me? *Tess was supposed to tell me who.* Trying to think around the racing of my heart and the throbbing in my temple, I bite my lip with effort. *I had begged Tess to tell me who she saw. That's it. Who she saw Holly leaving with.*

"You couldn't have!" Panic gets me on my feet, pushing up from the planks with splinters in my palms, clinging to the railing as I pull myself up. Before I can take one step, Cody is standing in front of me. He places a hand on my shoulder, an almost affectionate reminder that I couldn't fight him off if I tried. "Why?" Tears of shock run freely down my face.

"Well, you never asked, but…" Cody hesitates, something diffident in his tone, as if he wants to confide something, but fears being scorned. "Holly and I were…"

"What? Since when?" I glance down and see Dawson's gun in his coat pocket.

"Don't you think I thought of that?" he murmurs smoothly, following my eye. "Holly and I—that went on for a while, actually." His tone turns musing, hand still resting on my shoulder. Wendy had said something about Holly the day I picked up the girls from her house, something that, at the time, had struck me as rude. *Holly had things she couldn't explain sometimes, nice things.*

"High school. It was off and on. After she left Silas, it was more on. We never told anybody."

"High school?" My knees begin to tremble. That was back when Silas offered to marry Holly. "Tess—is yours? How?"

"She had always liked me," he offers, as if the fact that this is true should absolve him of anything. "It was probably a month after Page died, Holly came over to talk to me about you. She was worried about you, and she thought I'd know if something had happened between you and Fin. I almost thought her coming to talk about you was a pretense."

"So what did you tell her?"

"I told her I thought it was Rob Dawson," he says, almost laughing. "He has no idea why she never talked to him again." I never expected to feel sorry for Dawson. Unimaginative, dependable Dawson, who'd only ever loved one woman.

"Where is my niece?" The effort of shouting makes my head whirl again. When I slip, he catches me, the one hand tightening on my arm, the other on my waist, and lowers me to the ground.

"As I said, you don't need to worry about her safety."

"But why Holly?" I weep, slapping weakly at his legs. "Tell me."

He drops to his knees, eye level with me, and the sadness in his face is gone, replaced with an emotionless stare. "Don't play coy, Felicity."

In a single, swift motion, he hauls me to my feet, half carrying, half dragging me along the boardwalk, out over the deeper water.

"Please, Cody, you have to tell me." My fingers grasp for his hands, for anything to hold, as if I could remind him that he's human. "I need to know why she died."

He stops walking, turns me so that I'm looking out over the railing, his hands tightly gripping my upper arms. I'm haunted with a sudden vision of Holly as she appeared in my nightmare, that first night back here. She had tried to pull me out here, looking between me and the swamp as if to say, *You, there. You, there*. Is this what she wanted, for Cody Redford to throw me in after her?

Or did she want to show me something? To our left, the Ferris wheel is in view, the water darker than night beneath and around it. A pulse of recognition surges through me. Holly and I took these very same steps, rushing to try to find Page in the water, not knowing that it was too late.

"This wasn't supposed to happen to you." He speaks in a low whisper, and I can feel his breath against my ear. "Felicity, you've never been a troublemaker. You were the quiet sister. The one I didn't have to worry about."

"Why would you worry about Holly?" Cody doesn't answer me. A sudden vision sends me deep into memory, my tears beginning to dry. I remember the night Page died, how I climbed onto the scaffolding. A single glance between Holly and me was enough to send me jumping into the water after Page. Holly and I never needed words to communicate—until something changed. Until I kept a terrible secret for Cody, in exchange for him keeping one for Holly. One so heavy that I convinced myself of a ghost story, dreaming for years about the Reverie Girls, rather than what I knew to be the truth.

"Cody, answer me. What did Holly know about you?"

"You're in no position to make demands." He says this as if I need any reminding, trapped between his body and the thin railing that separates me from the water.

"How come you weren't trying to help get Page out of the water?"

"Be quiet, would you?"

"What did you do, the whole time Holly ran to find me, before we came back?"

"None of this matters, Felicity." Tension builds in his voice, his hands closing tighter on my arms.

"You said it was truth or dare. That Holly dared Page to jump. That she was a little too convincing."

He pushes me forward against the rail, my arms flailing for a grasp. It's a fear worse than death, because it's a familiar one. The old Ferris wheel rests on its side like a spool, as if the vines covering its form are the only thing keeping it from rising up and spinning away.

"What if it wasn't Holly who dared her?" I turn my chin, almost able to see him. "That isn't it, though. From what I remember, you always preferred truth. Why would you hurt Page, Cody?" What was it that Dawson had tried to tell me, before that owl spooked him and the subject changed? Right after he correctly guessed Cody's name. *You know, you weren't the only one who...*

I don't need to wonder. "It sounds like Page was going to tell the truth about you. That's something you've never been able to accept, isn't it?"

"Be *quiet*."

"How did you convince Holly to stay quiet for so long?"

"I told her it happened by accident," he says, "which is the truth. And I told her nobody would believe her over me, which, I think, was also the truth."

Holly had been so cold to me, so distant. Maybe what I didn't see was that she was terrified that Cody would spread lies that could send her to jail.

"And Holly was going to tell the truth about you, too. But—why now?" The understanding settles between us just as I feel his fingers twist into my skin, twisting just like the recollection of Holly's frantic, despairing phone call to me. Cody can't stand to admit the truth of what he did to me. "What happened between us—what word did you use to describe it? Misunderstanding, right?" This distortion of the truth, one so familiar to me, is enough to make me clench my teeth. There was no misunderstanding about it. But

I try to make my question soft, the same tone I might use to ask a patient: *Now, how did you get hurt?* "I know you didn't mean any harm, Cody. How did she find out?"

"She was the one who brought it up. She was always talking about you." Cody sighs, something regretful, almost sensitive, in his voice. "I may have let on, accidentally, that we hooked up—once. She was furious. Jealous, I guess."

Holly, who had kept quiet about Page's death for so long, had finally realized what Cody had done to me as well. *What if I do know what happened?* Holly had asked me. *If I can fix it, will you come home?* And she wasn't going to keep either of those secrets any longer.

Holly must have pieced it together, Cody's admission to her only confirming what she had dismissed as lies from me years ago. Or perhaps it came to her in one terrifying moment of clarity, as it does now to me. Combing over old fragments of memory, Holly surmised that what Cody did to me was no misunderstanding. That Page's death was no accident, but a means to silence her. She must have met him that night to demand that he admit the truth. And Tess saw Cody leaving with Holly that night. What does that spell for her?

I whirl around to face him, grab onto the collar of his coat. "How could you?"

Before the shock subsides, I hit him as hard as I can, both my fists pale in the dark, and then shove backward against his shoulders. When his grip loosens, I'm already running, without stopping to wonder where I might find safety.

But I don't make it far. Cody's faster than I expected, fast as his mean sense of humor. He's stronger than me, on a good day. Now I'm dizzy, nauseous, reeling with the pain in the side of my head. Blood drips into my right eye every few moments, salty and burning. When I lift a hand to wipe it off, I stumble. Looking up, I see him standing over me.

"It's like I said." He bends down to lift me up, one arm wrapping around me so tightly that my toes brush against the ground. "You're tougher than people know. You should give yourself credit for that."

"Where is Tess?" I throw weak punches at his face and chest.

"She'll be fine, all right? Would I harm my own child?" he asks, as if I've offended him.

"Like you did to Page? And my sister?"

"I did not!" He gives me a shake, like a child with a broken toy. "I keep trying to tell you this. I would never hurt anybody. Your sister, and Page? They—they fell in the water, and they couldn't get back out."

"Where is she?" My voice rises again, sharp as my splitting headache.

"I can't listen to this anymore." Cody brushes the hair from his forehead, drawing a deep, slow breath. Grasping me with both arms now, he takes a step nearer to the railing. "I'm sorry. Really, I am—I hope you know that."

He throws me against the railing, and the aging wood splinters and groans, tearing into my skin, something popping in my arm. Before I can move or cry out, he's holding me over the edge of the railing, the upper half of my body over the open water, arms pinned to my sides.

"No." Twisting back, I struggle to free my arms, desperate to cling to something: to him, to the railing, to thin air. Dread rises in my throat as I feel the water looking expectantly up at me. "Please, no."

The surface of the water is so dark, shifting beneath the falling rain as though something stirs in sleep there, turning over, beginning to wake.

"No—I can't. Anything else but that." I glance down at the gun in his pocket, raise my eyes to his. He shakes his head.

"You weren't shot, Felicity. You came out looking for your niece, and you were sleep-deprived, and emotional, and delusional. Slipped somewhere, hit your head. Things like this happen out here."

"I'm pregnant."

"Okay, that's the second time you've used that line today." Cody patiently detaches my clawed hand from his arm, taking another small step forward so that I'm leaning backward over the railing.

"It's not a line. It's true." I reach for a fistful of hair, then for his sleeve. He tosses his chin, slapping my hand away.

"That's enough." His hands close tightly on my shoulders, the cold glint of resignation in his eyes sending a pulse of fear through my body.

"What would you be, Cody, if you were sitting in a room alone?" I ask. "With no one to listen to your jokes, distract you from the truth about yourself?"

"I don't know." I can feel his posture sag a little as he answers, hear a withering sadness in his tone.

"Well, I do."

With one solid shove, he sends me toppling over the railing. As I fall, I catch the faintest glimpse of Cody's face, perfectly expressionless as he pushes me over the edge.

Beneath the surface, I lose any concept of up or down. All I can think of is how to get out.

But only one of my arms is working properly, and the cold water sends a searing pain through my nose and mouth. When I feel silt and tangled roots beneath my hands, I push off with both feet. It feels like it takes years to break the surface, and then I instantly slip under again, my limbs flailing uselessly. As Cody stands above me at the edge of the boardwalk, he's as calm as he can be, as if he's consoled himself: all he has to do now is wait.

I slip beneath the water again, spit out a mouthful. "Help me up, Cody." I fight for purchase and get an elbow up onto the boardwalk, but I'm too weak to pull the rest of my weight up, my other arm pulsing with pain.

With the toe of his shoe, he nudges my fingertips away from the edge. When my hand slips off the planks, I try to keep hold of the supporting beam, but there's water in my ears and my vision blurs, head throbbing. I tilt my chin back to keep my nose above the water.

He kneels and pries my hand from the beam. *Just keep a grip*, I tell myself. *It's simple. Just hold on*.

But I can't do it. My hands fail. I'm gasping one more time for help. I let go and slip into the water. As I'm falling, I remember it, the sound of that voice calling my name, bell-like, urgent. Even now, I can remember it so clearly, it's as though I'm back there. Again, I am summoned by a ghostly voice, distorted by mist, or trees, or whatever boundary separates death from life.

CHAPTER FORTY-EIGHT
Now

The same things have always befallen Holly and me, one way or another. This truth comes back to me, from a great distance—or maybe I'm the one washing up against it.

I open my eyes in the dark, blink against the grit and slime of the muck. I reach down to my foot, lodged in a root, and pull on my ankle, trying to free it. I feel weeds, grasses, possibly fish, brushing my arms and my face. Under the water, my hair catches on a branch. I open my eyes in the water and suddenly I'm no longer frightened, no longer terrified by the cold and the dark. But it isn't dark: there's a glow here, a light, if I could only reach down far enough to get to it. I can feel rocks under my hands, a fingernail catching on a buried root. And then, finally, I see it: light. Warmth. A lack of fear washes around me, a sense of relief that I've never tasted, but always longed for. I'm home. And Holly is here, too, I can sense it. I'm at home with Holly and I'll never leave again. Here, with the rest of them. They're not killers. They never pulled anyone down into the water, not against their will. Just girls forgotten, silenced, deaths we were too happy to call accidents and blame them on ghost stories.

"I'm so sorry," I weep. "If only either of us had dared to talk to the other—I could have told you that I understand. That I understand why you didn't try to ask me what was wrong. I love you, Holly." Her green eyes are warm and soft, and her arms wrap around me.

"I'm so sorry I wasn't there for you, Lissie."

"If I had listened when you needed me to, we wouldn't be here." The outline of my hand wavers, threatening to blur into the silt around it. "I was hurt, and I let it make me cruel. All these years we could have been close, like we used to. You were my best friend."

"We never stopped being best friends," she answers. "I loved you, and you loved me, and that's forever."

"We've given so much to get each other back," I whisper. "I'm never losing you again."

"You can't stay."

"Why not? I've already lost everything else."

"But you haven't," she answers, her voice so soft and kind I sob just to hear it. "You have been so brave, and you have done so well. And you need to keep going."

Around her, the tea-colored water glows amber and warm, and if I didn't know better, I'd think it could be a sunrise. But there's a pale form that watches me from behind Holly's shoulder, darts forward to swirl around my chest, as if embracing me, then away just as fast. My entire body pulses with a sweet, almost forgotten grief, and I recognize her, the child I never had.

"It's—" I feel as if I'll choke on my tears, they come on so fast. But they're not salt or warm; they're cold, gritty. Something is wrong.

"She's with me," Holly whispers, her eyes growing wide with urgency. "She's not alone. And you have to leave here. Tess needs you—and she's not the only one."

"I don't want to leave you."

"Lissie, it isn't time. One day," she promises. "But not this one. Now *go*."

And then, just as quickly as she appeared, Holly is gone, and I'm alone. I open my eyes to a thick darkness, then, finally, kick hard against the mud beneath my feet and find the surface.

I feel in the dark for something solid, reach for the ground, find my way to shallow water. I know Cody's watching from where he stands on the boardwalk, though I can't risk trying to get a look and see where he is. The rain's helpful now, disturbing the surface of the water. I open my eyes in the murk and I can see the beam of his flashlight not far off, pull my legs up under me. I slide behind a tree, tuck myself into its roots, and finally, barely, let the tip of my nose come above the surface.

It breaks every impulse I have not to surface with gasping breaths. It's so difficult I'm holding onto the cypress root, holding myself down. I exhale a single, long breath, then let myself draw one in, forcing myself not to hyperventilate. My limbs are burning, and I'm afraid when it's time to move I won't be able to. I alternate taking breaths with trying to get a glimpse of Cody where he stands at the edge of the boardwalk.

But then something interrupts my vigil. The voice, again. Not Cody. Someone else, calling, not too far away. But it isn't the Reverie Girls. It's not otherworldly at all. It's Tess, calling out my name, calling for help.

CHAPTER FORTY-NINE

Now

Tess is here. Where would Cody hide her? When he found me, his clothes were dry. The old dance hall. I can't see it, but even so, I could find it in the dark.

"Help! Can anyone hear me?"

Several yards off on the boardwalk, Cody sighs with annoyance and shakes his head, then turns on his heel and walks away. When he's out of sight, I let myself rise to the surface, head and shoulders above the muddy water, taking big, grateful gulps of air that burn in my lungs.

Crawling onto the marshy ground, I balance the weight of my shoulders with one arm, the other dragging uselessly. Panting for air, I wipe silt and algae from my eyes, still dizzy. Covered with mud, I can't make out the shape of my arms against the ground and grasses beneath me.

I follow him at a distance, first moving through the marsh, then onto the damp grasses that mark the edge of the dry ground. Hanging back in the dark, I trip on a cypress knee, like crooked fingers reaching up from the tree's submerged roots. I know he's heard it. I inch backward into the curtain of vines that hangs over the Ferris wheel. For a moment, Cody looks in my direction, then seems to relent, assigning the noise to an animal or a falling branch.

When he's a good distance away I drag myself onto the boardwalk. I don't need to remind myself now to walk silently, to move with the rain. I keep back until Cody reaches the dance hall, disappears through the door. Then, out of sight, I pick up pace. I can still hear Tess's voice shouting for help. The once-blue building stands like a ghost in the night, its entire structure leaning at a slight angle. I creep closer, right up to the front steps of the building. There's a precarious lean to the porch, and as I climb the stairs I grab for the banister, then have to stifle a cry of pain.

"Hey, Tess." I can hear his voice, falsely friendly. "What's all the noise for? I thought I asked you to keep it down."

"I want to leave. Why are we out here?" At the sound of her voice, my eyes water as though it's been years, not one day, since I've seen her. *I'd never harm my own child*, he'd said. Just like he said he hadn't harmed Page or Holly.

Inside, the wide-open hall reaches to the ceiling, a balcony overlooking the dance floor from the second story. It must have been lovely, when it was different—lit up, and full of music, on a beautiful autumn night. But that was years ago; now, it's cavernous, dark, vines creeping from the corners across the tiled floor.

"What are you doing up here?" Cody asks, speaking to Tess. "I told you to stay on the ground level, remember?" Hearing his footsteps on the staircase, I step inside, keeping to the shadows. Only Cody's flashlight breaks the darkness. My shoulders curl in, tense, as I watch. Cody sets the flashlight on the floor and greets Tess.

She doesn't look to be hurt, but I can see that she's afraid, that her confidence is searching for footing here, that it's flickering, and I feel a desperate need to protect it. "You said to meet you out here. I want to go home now."

"I really need you to stay calm here," Cody answers. As I take a step toward the staircase something skitters over my foot, a shadow about the right size to be a mouse or a large spider. The shadow disappears behind a larger, hulking shape, which at first appears to crouch and sigh, but, upon closer inspection, is the age-warped and dusty old piano, calling to mind ghosts of old dance parties.

Going up the staircase, I move slowly, hoping the sound of the rain on the roof will cover any small noise. The stairs sag as I move, and I use my uninjured hand to hold onto the carved banister, ducking as I rise to the level of the second floor. The stairs are littered with clods of soil and crumbled bits of plaster that press into my hands as I creep up on my hands and knees.

"You can go home, Tess. I would never keep you against your will." I see him leaning toward her, my body tense with desperation. "I'll walk you out. Come with me."

Crouching at the top stair, I settle down, let myself take a single, deep breath. Cody's back faces me. In this low light, everything looks black and white, the beam of the flashlight forming a little bar of light that reaches up the wall. I reach out an arm, wave in the dark, my hand fluttering like a wing. Tess's eyes dart my way. She gasps, then tries to cover it with a cough.

"I heard something," she says, acting frightened. "Over there." She nods away from me, off to the other side of the landing. Distracted, Cody turns to look. In a single fluid motion, I step up to the second floor and move across the landing.

"Tess," I whisper. "Turn off the light."

She picks up the flashlight and turns it off. In the last second before Cody turns around, I grab onto her hand and run down the darkened balcony. Adrenaline gives me a sudden energy, but it's more than that. It's energy I realize I've been holding in for years, that I've swallowed, playing safe, using it only when I've needed to move on. Now, I can wield it like a weapon or a tool.

I hear Cody's footsteps behind us, hear him collide with the edge of the balcony, swearing. The old wood sags and I can feel the impact even here, a few yards off, but it doesn't break. I pull

Tess behind me and step into the corner. I cling to her hand as I move, pull her body closer to mine, as if I could reassure her. I can hear her terrified breaths, Cody's footsteps near us in the dark. I make my voice as quiet as I can, lean close to her ear.

"I love you, okay? I'm on your side here." I let go of her hand and reach to take the flashlight from her. "Stay right here. Wait for me."

Without the flashlight, without even the ambient light of the outdoors, it's pitch-dark. I hold the flashlight tightly in my hands and press my back against the wall, inching toward him. *Help me*, I think again, apologizing to the old fairground for every time I've hated and feared it. I make no sound as I move. He's crashing through the dark in my direction. The injury in my shoulder, now that I stand still a moment, sends jolting waves of pain-fueled nausea all through my body. With a sigh, I sink down to the floor. *Only for a moment*, I promise myself. Only so I don't faint and fall over altogether.

"Felicity, you're smarter than this," he yells. I can hear him but I can't see him. "I didn't want this to be difficult for you. You know that." Steps again, then he's close, too close. I can feel the age of the building under my palms, plaster and soil, bits of the outside that have found their way in over decades of neglect.

I hold my breath and throw a pebble-sized bit of plaster. It sails past him and clinks to the floor on the ground level.

Cody pauses, then takes a hesitant step in that direction, as if he could look down into the dark.

I follow it with another, ninety degrees the other way.

"Where are you?" His breath catches, and he twists on his heel, looking into the shadows. "Is there someone else here?"

I know what it feels like, to hear whispers around you, moving through a space where you assumed you'd be safe. To know you're a target but not know when you'll get hurt again. An imposter in a world where you once felt like royalty. Now, blinking mud from my eyes, I send this at him like it's a curse, throwing pebbles into the dark around him until he's frightened and disoriented. All the while, I take tiny steps, inching closer to him until I can hear his breath. I tighten my hand on the flashlight. It's not a sure bet, but it's all I have.

I throw a stick, the rain muffling its sound, until it hits on the landing across from me. I can almost hear Cody flinch, hear the hiss of his breath and the jagged step as he whirls around, looking for an assailant. "Where are you?"

"Truth or dare, Cody."

I swing the flashlight and feel it connect with his head, a dull smack. When he hit me, he made it look so easy. It's not. My hands tremble, and the flashlight drops to the ground. I sink down to reach after it. Cody's hand lands on my shoulder and I struggle for balance, negotiating with the pain in my right arm, my fingertips brushing against the flashlight. I remember the feeling of his hands on my body, his elbow resting across my neck. And I recognize the sound, so close now, right in front of me in the dark. He's laughing at me. My hand closes on the flashlight, and I swing straight at his temple.

Finally, he loses his balance, hands trying to cover his head. But he grabs for me, his hand closing on my arm as I back away, and I yelp with pain, pushing him away savagely with my free arm. I hear the weight of his body hit the stairs with a sickening clap, one that seems drawn-out, a ghostly sort of wheeze or groan. I begin to back away, and I could blame it on an awareness of danger, of wanting to put more room between me and Cody Redford, enough to last the rest of my life. But the truth is, it sounds like something horrible, a determined howling, and I'm frightened in a way I didn't think I could be. It's only as I'm backing into the corner, wrapping an arm around Tess, that I realize the staircase has collapsed.

CHAPTER FIFTY

Now

"Aunt Lissie." Tess's voice trembles, devoid of her usual sass. She's right where I left her, sitting in the corner of the balcony on the floor. I throw one arm around her body, the other one sore and useless at my side. Tess is warm. Unhurt.

"Are you okay, Tess?"

"Yes."

My hands shake as I click the flashlight on. It's slick with blood, and my stomach turns. I take a long look at Tess, then point the light toward the stairs. Track around the rest of the balcony. There's no other staircase, no other way down.

Besides, Cody's down there. Alive, maybe, or dead. I'm not sure which frightens me more. I turn back to Tess to see tears running down her cheeks.

"I'm so sorry. Everything is going to be fine."

"It's not," she answers, her chin trembling. "What happened to you?" I realize I'm bleeding, covered in mud, that I must look like a monster. Tess covers her face with her hands. I huddle next to her and sink gratefully to the floor. "I'm so sorry," she weeps. "I was such an asshole."

"I'm the one that needs to be sorry." I can hear the rain tapping on the roof, and I know the water outside is higher than it ought to be. I wonder how much it would take to knock the rest of this balcony down. It's bad weather for this. It isn't all that cold, but it doesn't take terrible cold to get you hypothermic. Just time.

"*You're* sorry?" she repeats after me. "This is all my fault. I lied to you. I knew he was my real dad. He told me once, if I ever needed help, I could find him. You almost died." She's gulping big sobs down, and seems more childlike than I remember.

"You knew he was your biological father." My hands are so cold they sting, and I'd rub them together if my left arm hurt less. "Tell me what you saw."

"Mom came home from the party," Tess recounts. "She said she was going to sit on the front porch and talk with him. She was getting ready for bed—she had left her purse, her bracelet on the dresser. I was watching from the window when they walked to the boat. I just thought she'd come back." She sounds so young when she cries. "I thought it had to be an accident. Mom liked Cody. She said once that he was troubled, but that he wanted to do better."

"She did see the best in people."

"It made me so angry, that you saw something different. It made losing her even worse." She covers her mouth as she sobs. "I took her bracelet and ditched it at the antique store. I was hoping it would confuse you enough that you'd just drop it. I feel awful."

"Tess, none of this is your fault." I reach up with my good hand and squeeze her shoulder. "Just as I said before: none of these problems should be your problems."

"Am I an accomplice?" She turns to me with wide eyes, lips trembling. "My life is so messed up—I'll never be normal, or happy, or anything like that."

I let her cry, holding her against me with my right arm. "That's not true. You're young, and you have good people in your life, if you choose to let them support you. I know how it is to feel that way, Tess."

"You do?"

"Yes." My toes begin to prickle with cold, and, in a surge of faintness, I lean my head on my knees. "I'll tell you about it another time. Trust me on it, though. For now."

"Okay."

Holly wanted me in Tess's life. She wanted to know that I would be here if she couldn't be. All this time, she saw things more clearly than I had. To our right, the floor creaks, another crunching exhale of rotten beams and plaster.

Holly wanted me here for Tess. And what good will I have done, if I got us out of immediate danger only for us to fall to our deaths?

Tess turns to cast a leery stare toward the collapsed staircase. "Is he dead?"

"I don't know." I'd cross to the balcony, shine the light down, but for one thing, touching the flashlight makes me feel ill, and for another, I don't have much trust in the structural integrity of the building.

I think of Dawson, unconscious there on the boardwalk. Wonder if he'll wake up, go for help. If Silas will send anyone after us. Whether they could find us, even if he did. We sit silently huddled together, every minute crawling by. My mind blurs with pain and cold, and I think of the pregnancy test, still hidden in my purse back at the house, and my shoulders toss with sobs of shock. Drifting in and out, only one thought hangs in my mind: that Tess is safe. That someone, surely, will find her. Every few minutes, Tess murmurs something, squeezes my hand, and I nod and mumble back, but I can't keep my eyes open. The weight of being awake slowly comes untethered, a sense of relief and numbness lulling me to sleep.

"Wake up," Tess growls. Her wiry hand digs into my bicep, squeezing, and I can hear urgency in her voice. "You've got to stay awake. Come on."

"Ow," I wail, pulling my arm back.

"Oh God, I'm sorry—I didn't mean to really hurt you."

"It wasn't you."

She takes the flashlight and looks at my arm, then falls silent.

"Hello?" Tess smacks the flashlight against the wall as she raises her voice. "Anyone out there? Anybody?" She sighs, exhales a curse word. I don't have the energy to admonish her. "Wait," she whispers. "Did you hear that?"

I shake my head no, holding my temples against the dizziness that follows. Again, Tess beats the flashlight loudly against the wall behind us, then shines the beam over the railing, toward the doorway.

The noise and the light make my head throb and my consciousness fades again, and, finally, the dark and cold become a comfort, rather than a threat.

When I hear James's voice calling my name, I'm certain I'm dreaming: *Felicity! Shout if you can hear me.* The sound alone, echoing in the dance hall, sends my head spinning.

And when I open my eyes again, he's standing in the doorway, the yellow beam of a flashlight in his hand. His hair's stuck to his forehead with rain.

"Felicity! Tess, are you in here?"

"We're over here," Tess yells back. "Up here."

He crosses back to the doorway and shouts into the distance: "This way. I found them."

"Look out." My voice is a sandpapery whisper, and I lurch forward, catch myself on my hands, then draw one hand back up, wincing. "Tell him to be careful."

"Cody fell," Tess calls, pointing frantically at the remnants of the staircase. "He's over there—somewhere."

The beam of light circles the floor, then pauses. I hear James's footsteps move across the room. "Yeah," he says. "He's here."

I blink again, and I don't know whether my eyes stay closed or not, or for how long. When I open them, James is standing on the ground level, looking up toward us.

"I don't know what to do." Tess's voice quavers. "There's no way down. She's hurt." She begins to stand up and James lifts a hand.

"Stay where you are—I don't trust that floor." He scans the room, pushing hair from his brow with his forearm. There are more voices outside, people behind him in the doorway. He waves to the dusty piano standing in the corner. "Help me move this. On three." With a groaning of old wood and creaking, it moves. I hear a shuffling, discordant protest from the old keys.

"Piece of cake," he says. "You okay, Tess?" His face appears, his eyes level with our feet, and as his eyes find me in the shadows, I see the cheer in his voice is a front.

"I'm fine," she says, though her eyes begin to fill with tears.

"All right: what I need you to do is stand up—very carefully, walk to the railing—I'm holding it from this side, see?—and just climb over. I'll catch you."

She swings a leg over the railing, swivels around, and jumps down into his arms. He helps her to the floor, and I hear her cry, "Dad!" That means Silas is here. There's a murmur of voices from below that I can barely distinguish from the whispers in my mind.

"How'd you find us?" My head jolts with pain when I speak, my body numb and damp with the cold. His eyes are hollow with sleeplessness, and his hair looks as though he's spent all night in the rain.

"We can talk later. Come on." James holds an arm out and I shake my head. With a sigh, he continues, speaking quickly. "I went to your mother's house to talk to you. Silas was there. He told me you'd come out here." James looks away from me, the set of his mouth shifting just enough to let me know there's something he's not saying.

"James, I tried to tell you."

"You have to walk toward the railing. This is as close as I can get to you."

"Please believe me."

"Believe you?" He blinks in momentary shock, as if the question is absurd. "Of course I do." With one hand, he grips the edge of the balcony, the other reaching out toward me. "All of that can wait. Can you walk?"

With a hand against the wall behind me, I slowly rise to my feet. Between my wobbling knees and the slanted floor, I'm not sure which I have less faith in. The floor creaks and an involuntary cry slips past my lips, the sound of it alone enough to send me dizzy with pain.

"Now, this way."

I lift one foot to step forward, then change my mind, slouching back against the wall under a throbbing wave of pain in my head. A new fear steps forward from the crowd of phantoms in my mind, one that reminds me I'm in shock, that I have taken several falls. That, as a nurse, I know what this could mean. *Will I lose the baby?* Haven't I done what Holly told me to—and couldn't I stay there, in the amber light with her, where nothing can go wrong? "I can't. I'll fall."

"Felicity, I am not going to let you fall." His voice drops low and urgent. "But I need you to jump."

Eyes scanning the narrow floor of the balcony, the drop to the ground level below, I feel the pain in my arm, the aching in my head, my field of vision wavering as if it could collapse just as easily.

"Don't look down." James's voice calls me back, and I manage to keep standing. "Look at me, Lissie. Not down. Just one more step."

I inch onto the railing, trying to hold my weight steady with just one arm as I turn myself to face him. He holds my gaze and nods. I lean forward and let go, just as the balcony behind me creaks and sags at a precarious angle.

His arms close around me, and for a blessed moment, everything is still.

CHAPTER FIFTY-ONE
Now

I could have sworn that Holly was here while I slept. During the night, I was certain that I had lifted my head, half awake, to see her sitting at my feet with a wise, warm smile. I wake with a lingering nostalgia, an impossible desire to flip back to the page I just lost. The memory of the night before settles around me, and I remember that Holly is still gone. The air in the room has a warmth, as if she only just walked out the door. And I still cannot go with her.

My memory of the prior evening seems so distant that, at first, I'm fearful that was a dream as well. Then I catch sight of the bandages on my right arm, lift a clumsy touch to the stitches on the side of my head. The other arm won't move, held in place with a snug sling. Dreams and reality have been blurring too much for my taste, lately.

When I manage to stand up, everything hurts. Crossing to the window, I pull the knit blanket from the foot of the bed and wrap it around my shoulders. Out in the yard, as I look through the bay window, I can see Tess and Frankie playing in their jackets. I tap on the window, then open it.

"Morning," I shout. Frankie stops and looks up, waves at me with a smile.

"Morning, Aunt Lissie. You slept late."

"What day is it?"

"It's Christmas Eve."

With one working arm, getting dressed is an effort. I eventually manage a pair of leggings, and then untie the sling, slipping my arms into a flannel shirt, since I can't pull anything over my head. But fastening buttons is so painful my eyes water, any inkling of movement in my shoulder throwing a nauseating wave of pain down my arm. Clearing my throat, I walk to the door of the room and pull it open.

"Mom? Are you there?"

For a moment, I can't say why, I'm so afraid that she won't answer. Then her footsteps sound on the stairs, and in moments, she's standing in front of me.

"Morning."

"Hi." A rush of relief hits me, and I blink at my tears. "I need help with my buttons."

My mother fastens the buttons on my shirt, then helps me back into the sling. Before I have to ask, she steps to my other side and sweeps her fingers through my hair, fastens it into a ponytail.

"Thanks."

"I made coffee, if you'd like some."

"I think I'll have to pass, but thanks." The smell of coffee, even faintly from downstairs, sends waves of nausea through my stomach. "What happened last night, after they took me to the hospital?"

"Silas brought the girls here. He slept on the couch."

"And Rob Dawson?"

"In the hospital with a concussion. He'll be fine." She gives me a worried look. "There's a police detective downstairs. I've already told him everything, but he wants to run through a couple details with you. Are you up for it?"

"Sure." I follow her through the corridor and down the stairs. In the living room, she leads me to the most comfortable armchair.

"Felicity, this is the officer I told you about." She nods at the man sitting on the couch, then puts an ottoman under my feet.

"Ms. Wheeler, I'm Detective Wes Grant." He rises to his feet, leaning across the coffee table to shake my hand, then resumes his seat. Reddish hair and hazel eyes soften his somewhat official manner. "I only have a couple questions."

"About my sister?"

"Mr. Redford confessed early this morning." He speaks with the ease of someone who knows what he's talking about, the words rounded like an older brother's cadence that sets my nerves at ease a little.

"To what, exactly?"

"Your sister's murder. But there was something else, too. That's why I'm here." He folds his hands on his knees, his pause taking on meaning. "He made some allusions to the death of a girl named Page Winslow, and events that followed. Is that something you have information about?"

"It is."

"I'd like to talk with you about that—"

"Really?" For so many years, I've taken it for granted that nobody cared what I knew, what I had been through. "Gladly. Only, I don't think I can handle that, right at this moment."

"Of course," he says. "I'm going to leave my business card. Enjoy the holiday—and rest up. Everyone is glad you're all right."

"Thank you."

When Detective Grant has left, I make my way into the kitchen, where my mother is at the table with her knitting.

"So, I heard you saying to James that you planned to leave." She gets up and turns to the counter, then returns to the table and sits a plate of food in front of me: toast, eggs, a pear, sliced in half. "Will you be leaving, then?" She turns away quickly to the stove, and I'm suddenly aware of the tempting smell of butter in a skillet.

"I don't know, to be honest."

"Really?"

"Whatever happens, I'm not going to disappear again. And honestly, I'm not the person here who should keep custody of Holly's daughters."

"No? What do you mean?"

"They should live with their father, once he's ready."

"And you?" My mother's smile falters. "Where will you be?"

"Never more than a phone call away." Half done with my food, I realize I can't eat another bite. "This is delicious, but I'm afraid I have a bit of morning sickness." Her face softens into a smile.

"I'm happy for you." With this admission, words begin to tumble out, and I can sense how excited she is to talk to me. "Silas told us about your pregnancy."

"I gathered. How long did that take?"

"I don't think he intended to share your personal business. Yesterday evening, just after you left with Dawson, James knocked on the door. He said he needed to speak to you, if you were willing to see him. And Silas just said to him: *I think there's something you need to know.* You should have seen his face. Felicity, what's wrong?" I focus on her steady gaze, her solid elegance, until I find the words.

"What if something goes wrong again?"

She folds me into a warm hug. "You won't be alone. No matter what." I soak in her embrace, breathing in this bittersweet feeling of hope and sadness, until it's too much and I inch back.

"Thanks, Mom." I take a sip of water, then manage a few more bites of the eggs and toast. After placing the plate in the sink, I approach the screen door. "I'm going to sit on the porch for a bit."

"All right, Felicity. I'll be here."

It's warm for winter, though that's hardly unusual here. Though I took a shower last night, after returning from the hospital, before collapsing into bed, it feels like it will take days to wash all the mud off. Watching the sunlight in its patterns on the yard, the chickens walking their familiar paths, I hardly register the sound of another car in the drive, now that I'm not on edge, and so I'm surprised when my mother walks to the back porch and lets James out.

I move to stand up and he shakes his head. "Don't get up." He's clean-shaven, his hair combed, but his eyes jump from here to there, carefully studying everything but me, betraying his nerves.

"Hi, James." I want to hold his hand, but I can't read his expression. "I'm sorry I didn't tell you."

"You're sorry?" For a split second, he looks up from his shoes, his eyes meeting mine, eyes wide with regret. "I came here last night to ask you to forgive me."

"For what? Please, sit." I reach toward him, but stop short of touching. With a nervous glance, James sits next to me on the porch swing, setting down a paper shopping bag by his feet.

"For putting you in a corner when I should have listened to you. I was scared. It's no excuse," he says. "I was so afraid you'd put yourself in danger."

"Well, you weren't entirely wrong." A jolting shiver runs from my shoulders down to my toes, leaving me feeling cold. The sheer certainty I was dead. The depth of ice-cold terror when I knew that Tess was in danger. When I open my eyes, he's turned toward me, his eyes lowered.

"And the baby you lost. I didn't have any right to expect you to have told me about that. That's your life, and it's in the past, and you don't owe me any of it." The tenor of his voice is even, calm, but as he speaks, I feel his shoulders tense, as if he's bracing for a hit. "I understand completely if you don't want to see me again. But I want to apologize, if you're willing to hear it."

"It was a girl." Was it only last night that I dreamed I saw my sister under the water, that there was a warm, glowing spirit beside her? My hands feel cold, and so empty, that I move to place them under my knees.

"Oh—what am I thinking? Here." James slips out of his coat, wearing a fresh button-down shirt underneath, and reaches out to me, scooting closer to lay the coat over my shoulders.

"James." Abandoning caution, I wrap my right arm around him, pulling him close against me. "It wasn't only your fault. I was afraid to tell you the truth, because—" Pausing to catch a breath, I draw back to look into his eyes, my hand on his cheek. "Because I want this more than anything, and that terrifies me."

It terrifies me still, for the seemingly endless moment that I wait for him to answer me.

"I can't blame you if you don't feel the same," I whisper. "But I can't let you go without telling you." Then, finally, he's gathering me into his arms, holding me close against him as we kiss.

"Me, too," he answers. "I've wanted to hear you say that for so long."

"It isn't only me, you know."

His hand rests for a moment on my midsection. "I know."

"I need to be there for Tess and Frankie, too. That's not going to change."

"I wouldn't want it to." James places a kiss on my temple. "I want this—you—all of it. Oh, and I brought you a Christmas gift." He offers me the bag, and I open it to remove a heavy box neatly wrapped in brown paper. Inside is a beautiful glass teapot, a pound of dried tea, jasmine green.

"Thank you. You know how much this means to me. Oh—I have something for you, too." Smiling at his pleas to slow down, I walk back inside, up the stairs to the blue room, rummaging in the dresser until I've found what I wanted. Head rushing, I take my time going back down the stairs, then return to sit at his side with cheeks flushed.

"What is it?"

"I didn't have a chance to wrap it. Close your eyes." He does, and I put the book from the antique store in his hands. He flips the cover, running his fingertips over the soft, aged paper.

"*Doctor Zhivago*, as an anniversary gift?" We share a laugh, and I see his mischievous smile when his eyes land on Olga's inscription to Ed. "Well, we know they made it at least two years." His smile fades as he looks up to meet my gaze. "Felicity, will you stay?"

"Well, I will have to go back to Saint Thomas to settle things. Close out the lease on my apartment, pack my things." With a bittersweet smile, I snuggle closer to him. "It deserves a proper goodbye."

"Why not keep the apartment? We can go there for holidays."

"I'd like that." I can't contain my smile. "How about next week, then?"

"If you're inviting me to spend New Year's with you in the Caribbean, you should know I'm accepting," he says. "And if you think I'm going to let you carry anything heavier than your purse, you're in for a surprise."

Just like that, the ghosts around us fall silent. I've faulted us both for holding onto the past, but I failed to understand our particular kind of courage. For so long, we carried our histories, despite how they weighed us down, despite how their sharp edges hurt to carry. Nobody would bear that for anything less than a precious burden. And it occurs to me that I've been wrong about the two of us, until this very moment. That with people like us, hope can lie dormant, even underwater, even for years, until we are strong enough to meet it.

CHAPTER FIFTY-TWO
Fifteen months later

The following winter passes in shades of gray and green, brown and rust. Some might say they're muted, but no color here ever really is; the amber and dark and evergreen of the swampland in winter is just another one of its expressions, not a temporary reduction of vibrancy or wildness. Yet, when spring breaks, all tendrils and fragrant breezes, it's a welcome change, bringing warmer, longer days.

Our baby is a fretful one, with green eyes like a changeling, and James's dark hair. He will only nap when coaxed into it, held and rocked. But with the warmer days permitting, we spend an occasional weekend afternoon in a rowboat, the fresh air and soft motion lulling the child to sleep. James sits across from me, holding the oars, while the baby curls in my arms, wrapped in a muslin blanket the same shade of pale blue as my dress.

"Lissie, over there. Look."

I lift a finger to my lips. "He's nearly asleep."

He nods, then points instead. Just in the distance, almost obscured by a weeping willow, a blue heron bobs its head, craning its beautiful neck to preen its feathers. I look back to James and smile. The baby gives a yawn and, finally, closes his eyes, curled against my belly on a diagonal, just as he was when he was inside it, nestled at an angle the nurse described as *challenging*. Short-tempered with the discomfort of labor, I answered her that I'd always known my insides were tangled. The heron takes notice of our presence, flutters its wings as if in slow motion, and takes flight. I turn my eyes back to the trees that surround us, the rowboat nudging past a tangle of grasses, near the border of the lake. Out here, where we once whispered our plans for the future, named the children we would have. We wouldn't say it out loud, even if the child weren't finally sleeping. This way, The Reverie. That way, the placid, shallow waters that border the lake. James raises an eyebrow, and I shake my head no. I never go too close to it, these days, not that it doesn't call to me.

It wasn't an easy birth, though I imagine they never are. Yet, the experience was dark, in a way I couldn't share with James, afraid to dampen his joy. My mother told me that labor will send you through a strange passage, that you go right beneath your surface and middle layers to whatever's at your center. And what I found was that there's something dark in me, strange but familiar, and I know too well what promises wait beneath it. I've heard that some women don't lose it when they give birth, which, having been there, sounds almost mythological. I did. I wept for mercy with each contraction, wave upon wave until I felt submerged. And then, beneath it, I found the place I knew, the place that felt immediately like the home I had always missed, sweeping me into a current of mud and vines under my hands, of Holly, of honey-colored light that was brighter than morning, and, once again, I wanted to stay. Then, I felt James's hands on mine, pulling me back to where we were, and he said, "Keep your eyes on mine; you're nearly there."

So I wrenched my way back to the living world, away from Holly, reminding myself that she had been laid to rest, several months past. The memorial service was on a balmy November day, uncharacteristically sunny. The church was so crowded, nearly everyone in town was there—even Dawson, who shed a few tears when he thought nobody was looking. I approached to stand at his side, waited for him to gather himself, and then spoke: *Cody Redford told Holly a lie about you, and that's why she stopped speaking to you.* There was no easy way to say it, but Dawson deserved to know that it wasn't his fault. I had to walk away before he responded, unable to hold any more sadness that day. It was then I felt the baby kick for the first time. My eyes landed on James, where he stood a few yards away with my mother and the girls, and, as if sensing something momentous had happened, he smiled and walked over to embrace me. Questions left in the past, of what might have been, lie buried in almost everyone I know, never to be answered. How could James and I have been so lucky?

I thought we would name the baby Holly, but it was a boy. We chose a name that was new to us, never used in either of our families: Asher. James likes it because of its meaning: blessed. Fortunate. I like it because it makes me think of fire, dry warmth, a hopeful warning against the gloom and murk I grew up knowing: *Not this one. This child is not for you.* James's smile when the doctor announced it—*A baby boy!*—was pure joy, like I'd never seen on him before. And mine was, too, but maybe for a different reason. I know the world is unkind to everyone, but it's unkind to girls in a different way.

Every so often, I spare a thought for Cody Redford, sitting in a cell, with no one to lie to, nobody to mirror back his lies about what he really is. At the end of the day, there was no Cody Redford to mourn. There was no good in him that had been overwhelmed by circumstance, any more than there was any real evil. Just a vacuum of wanting and taking, and an occasional flourish of false guilt. I hadn't wanted that to be true about him. I see that denial now for what it was: just talking off the edge of a cliff, pleading with an empty space to answer me. There was never anything but my own echo. But I forgive myself that. For having wanted to see something decent in the father of the child I never had.

I was glad my child wasn't a girl. For me, I guess the danger you know is more frightening. Maybe that's the reason I don't get too close to the swamp, keeping my distance from the skeletal fairground in its depths. I moved in with James two months before the baby came, when Tess and Frankie moved back in with their father. Each morning I wake up in our home, to the sound of a child's cry, next to the only man I've ever loved, and every time it feels too good to be real.

But there's seldom a night, especially during the winter, when I don't look out the window across the lake and see a wisp of light beckoning, hear that familiar voice that has always known me by name. One day, I'll follow it. Hopefully not until I'm well into my old age. I know just who that wilderness belongs to, and that I belong to them just the same. Yet, for now, I think, they're content to wait for my return.

A LETTER FROM KELLY

Thank you so much for reading *The Woman in the Water*. If you would like to keep up to date with my future releases, you may sign up to my email list below. Your email will never be shared, and you can unsubscribe at any time.

www.bookouture.com/kelly-heard

Writing is usually a mode of escape for me, and my stories often take place in an imagined world that only parallels our own. This story, while overall not an exception, did send the characters to some places that felt surprisingly familiar. The topic of complex trauma is so familiar, to so many people, that I felt a real obligation to get this one right. I hope I have represented Felicity's experience with the nuance and respect it deserves.

Although this story does not reflect any of my own experiences, I'm fond of all of these characters (with a couple of exceptions), and that made it easy to identify with their individual struggles to integrate their past and present. In this way, the book does reflect some of my own convictions, particularly that we should listen to women when they tell us things we don't want to hear.

Connecting with readers is one of my favorite aspects of writing. If you would like to discuss this book or ask me any questions,

I would love to talk with you on Twitter, Facebook, Goodreads, or on my website.

—Kelly

@KHeardBooks

KellyHeardBooks

kellyheardbooks.com

ACKNOWLEDGMENTS

Pasha, thank you for your advice on stories like these. Believe it or not, I did take some of it to heart. Sorry for all the things I borrowed and then lost, or damaged, or never gave back.

Jane, I could never have written anything at all without you. You are the most perfect and dazzling Libra in the universe. "I wish I were a girl again, half savage and hardy, and free."

John, thank you for this wonderful life. I love you more every day.

I have always depended on connections with others to find my own potential. I would like to thank Erin Young and Katie MacDonald, without whom Hollins would have been a lot lonelier. Rachel Loncharich and Kate Lutes, without whom Rochester would have been a lot lonelier. My original girls, Maggie O'Toole, Devin Miller, and Heather Ireland. My former housemates, Erin, Elizabeth, and Charlie. Anna Deepa Nigro, my star consultant on all things witchcraft and parenting. And especially Laurel, the first friend who wrote stories with me: you are always in my thoughts.

Cara, I am eternally grateful to have worked on this story with you. I couldn't be prouder of the books we have created together.

Dr. Kelly Dorgan, I want to be like you when I grow up. Thank you for seeing me and my goals and speaking them back to me so clearly.

I'd like to thank everyone at Bookouture for their support and expertise. I am lucky to be part of such a talented and kind group of people.

Jenny Page, I don't know what I would do without you. When I am in the midst of writing a sloppy and scattered first (or second, or third) draft, knowing that you will one day have it in your hands is a massive relief.

Jon Appleton, thank you for your incredible eye for detail.

While my favorite album of 2020 was Phoebe Bridgers' *Punisher*, this book probably would not exist in its current form without Taylor Swift's *Folklore*, so I can't help but feel there is an acknowledgment in order there. Felicity crystallized in my mind when I heard the line "anywhere I want, just not home."

I owe a massive thanks to the book blogging community. Thank you for the tireless work you do to help connect readers with books.

CPSIA information can be obtained
at www.ICGtesting.com
Printed in the USA
LVHW110411200721
693166LV00003B/357